PRAISE FOR *SATISFIED WITH NOTHIN'*

"*Satisfied with Nothin'* is a record of the racial tensions of the American South and the personal struggles of African Americans to find a level playing field in a supposedly democratic society. . . . [R]esonates with righteous anger against those who would destroy the best in any man."

—Mary A. McCay, *Times-Picayune* (New Orleans)

"This novel of a black male experience is extremely emotional and insightful. . . . The brutal honesty of the characters' circumstances, emotions, and realistic experiences make this an exceptional literary piece that some readers will compare to Richard Wright's *Native Son*."

—Lillian Lewis, *Booklist*

"A candid portrayal of life in America from a Black male perspective, probing contemporary issues such as the exploitation of Black athletes and the problems of apathy and despair in the Black community."

—*Michigan Citizen*

"Hill's eloquence makes *Satisfied with Nothin'* look simple, but it is a complex piece of literature that probes deeply into some of America's most severe societal banes—racism, complacency, and despondency. The author takes a hard stance on issues and proffers solutions that demand a lot of sacrifice. . . . *Satisfied with Nothin'* is not just a well-authored novel. It is a call to a people for positive change."

—Kevin Omo Oni, *The Philadelphia Tribune*

"Both serious and humorous, invoking a broad spectrum of feelings as readers are compelled to either rejoice or cry as each chapter offers something special."

—Deborah Lewis, *Sacramento Observer*

ERNEST HILL

SATISFIED WITH NOTHIN'

A NOVEL

SIMON & SCHUSTER PAPERBACKS
New York London Toronto Sydney

To my parents, Mr. and Mrs. Charley Hill Jr.,
who taught me to never be satisfied.

Simon & Schuster Paperbacks
A Division of Simon & Schuster, Inc.
1230 Avenue of the Americas
New York, NY 10020

This Simon & Schuster trade paperback edition August 2008

SIMON & SCHUSTER PAPERBACKS and colophon are registered trademarks of Simon & Schuster, Inc.

For information about special discounts for bulk purchases, please contact Simon & Schuster Special Sales at 1-800-456-6798 or business@simonandschuster.com.

Designed by Karolina Harris

Manufactured in the United States of America

1   3   5   7   9   10   8   6   4   2

The Library of Congress has cataloged the hardcover edition as follows:

Hill, Ernest, date.
Satisfied with Nothin' : A novel / Ernest Hill.
p. cm.
1. Afro-American men—Louisiana—History—Fiction. I. Title.
PS3558.I3875S28   1996
813'.54—dc20   96-2970
CIP

ISBN: 0-684-82259-8
ISBN: 0-684-83405-7 (pbk)
ISBN-13: 978-1-4165-5698-5
ISBN-10:   1-4165-5698-2

ACKNOWLEDGMENTS

The completion of this project is due in part to the assistance of many people. Donald Northcross, a native Southerner and close friend dating back to our days as members of the Northeast Louisiana University football team, proved very helpful in perfecting the dialogue as well as the dialect of key characters in the novel. I thank him for his invaluable support, encouragement, and the numerous other ways that he has helped move this project forward.

Brenda Stevenson took time from her very demanding academic schedule to read several drafts of the manuscript and provided incisive advice concerning storyline development. Robert Harris Jr., Barbara Bair, and Kent Rasmussen also read versions of the manuscript and provided insightful editorial comments.

I would also like to thank Mr. Al Wilson for his support, and my parents and siblings for their unrelenting love, encouragement, and inspiration.

C H A P T E R 1

" J A M I E Ray, time to git up!" his mother yelled from the kitchen. "You gon' miss the bus if you don't git yo'self out that bed right this minute."

Jamie rolled over, pulled a pillow over his head, and pretended not to hear.

"Jamie Ray, don't let me have to come in there and git you up."

Jamie sat up, rubbed the sleep out of his eyes, and stared at the wall. It was seven o'clock Monday morning.

He was still only partly conscious, but his ninth grade teacher's words were already ringing in his ears: "When you go to the white folks' school next year, if any of them call you 'nigger,' you just hold your head up high, look them straight in the eye, and say, 'I'm black and I'm proud.'"

Jamie got up, stretched his arms above his head, and yawned loudly. Moving sluggishly, he went to the bathroom, washed up, and returned to his bedroom. He sat on the chair where he had laid his clothes and began to dress. Rising slowly, he pulled his pants over his slim muscular legs, blew all the air out of his lungs, and flopped down on the chair. For several minutes, he sat in total silence thinking about what the day held in store for him.

In the past, the first day of school had always been exciting and full of anticipation. But this morning was different. Instead of being excited, Jamie felt fear and doubt moving rapidly through his body. He dreaded being called "nigger" by white folks and he didn't know if he had the courage to stand up to them like his teacher had said. He didn't even know if he was smart enough to make it at the white school.

"Jamie Ray! Fo' Chrissakes! What in the world's takin' you so long in here this mornin'?" his mother asked, opening his bedroom door and looking inside. Jamie was sitting in the chair holding his socks in his hand and staring blankly into space.

"What you jus' sittin' there like you crazy fo'?" she asked, her voice filled with irritation. "You better c'mon in here and eat yo' breakfast 'fo it git cold. You gon' fool 'round and make me late fo' work. I ain't got time to waste this mornin'. Mrs. Thompson be out there befo' you know it. Make haste now," she said, turning and walking away.

Jamie finished dressing, walked into the small, cluttered kitchen, and took a seat at the table. He watched his mother take a pan of biscuits from the oven and place them on the table. Then, moving quickly, she crossed to the refrigerator, removed a carton of orange juice, and set it in front of him. That done, she took her seat, closed her eyes, bowed her head, and blessed the food.

"Lord, thank you fo' the food we 'bout to receive fo' the nourishment of our body in yo' son Jesus' name, Amen."

She paused.

"Jesus wept," Jamie mumbled softly.

She raised her eyes, poured herself a cup of coffee, and began to talk.

"Best way to git 'long with white folks is to never look 'em straight in the eye." She paused, sipped her coffee, then resumed. "Jus' pick out a spot on they fo'head and look at that if you jus' gotta look at 'em. But if you can, it's always best to look down at the ground, smile, and say 'yessuh' and 'nosuh' to the menfolks and 'yes ma'am' and 'no ma'am' to the women folk. Jus' stay in yo' place and don't act uppity, and you won't have no trouble with white folks."

She paused abruptly, removed her shoe, leaped from her chair, and swatted a roach crawling up the wall. Then she nonchalantly sat back down to her breakfast.

"When you git over yonder 'mongst them white folks, mind yo'self and act the way you been raised. I don't want 'em thankin' you ain't got no home trainin'. You understand me?"

"Yessum," Jamie responded, breaking off a small piece of bread and dipping it in the thick syrup he had poured on his plate.

"I 'spect thangs gon' be a lot tougher at the white school. Jus' do the best you can. Lawd'll make a way somehow."

"Yessum."

"You need some lunch money?" she asked.

"Yessum, I guess so."

She slid some coins next to his plate. Jamie counted them. She had given him a dollar and fifteen cents.

"Mama, lunch ain't but seventy-five cents."

"Well, might be a little mo' at the white school. Anyway, it's better to have it and not need it than to need it and not have it. Jus' brang me my change back if it's any. Lawd knows I ain't got money 'nough to waste."

"Yessum," Jamie said, putting the money in his pocket.

Mrs. Griffin glanced at the clock.

"Lawd, look at the time. Jamie, you better hurry up and go fo' you miss the bus."

Jamie ate the last bite of food on his plate. Then, rising quickly, he gathered his school supplies and headed for the door.

" 'Bye, Mama."

" 'Bye, baby, I'll see you later. You be good now."

"Yessum, I will."

"Now I might be a little late gittin' home this evenin'. Mrs. Thompson havin' a dinner party tonight so I gotta git everythang ready today 'fo I leave."

"Okay, Mama."

"Don't you brang nobody in my house while I'm gone."

"I won't."

Jamie opened the door and the fresh morning air hit him in the face. He walked out across the porch, down the steps and started out of the yard. Though it was only seven-thirty, the neighborhood was bustling with activity: grown-ups were leaving for work; the sanitation crew already was out collecting garbage; and the street was full of young folks en route to the bus stop.

He walked along the road at a brisk pace. It was late and there was a very real possibility that he would miss the bus. As Jamie turned the corner and broke his stride, he noticed the large concentration of people in front of Mrs. Betty's café—the designated bus stop.

"Bus ain't come yet," he mumbled to himself.

As he neared the large bay window in the front of the café, his eyes fell on the newspaper Mrs. Betty had stood upright in the window. Spread across the front page, in bold black letters, was the headline:

FIFTEEN YEARS AFTER BROWN DECISION
SCHOOLS INTEGRATE IN NORTH LOUISIANA

No sooner had he finished reading the headline than he felt a gentle tap on his shoulder. He turned to see his best friend Booger standing behind him.

"What's happenin', J.R.?" Booger asked, loudly.

"Man, I'm waitin' on you to tell me," Jamie responded.

Booger held out his right hand. Jamie slapped it and then gave him a soul shake.

"Runnin' kinda late this mornin', ain't you?"

"Yeah, man. I didn't wanna turn them sheets loose."

Booger smiled.

"Hey, I hear you. I felt the same way myself. You know me. I ain't never been in no hurry to go where I ain't wanted. And them white folks sho' don't want us at they school."

"Ain't that the truth."

Booger turned and looked about.

"Man, look how everybody standin' 'round like we doin' somethin' wrong. Far as I'm concerned, the black school was good 'nough fo' me."

"Me too," Jamie said, quickly. "But I guess that don't matter now. Like it or not, thangs 'round here done changed."

The bus pulled up and stopped.

"Well, I guess we fixin' to find out," Booger mumbled.

Jamie and Booger took their place in the short line of

students that formed in front of them. As those ahead of them piled onto the bus, Jamie glanced over at Mrs. Betty, who stood watching them from the doorway. She had a wide, prideful smile spread across her face. As the line inched forward, she yelled out:

"This is us day, chillun. Show 'em we's jus' as good as they is. Make us all proud."

Flanked by Booger, Jamie walked to the back of the bus, sat next to a window, and looked around.

"Booger."

"Yeah?"

"Check out how quiet everybody is."

"Man, I tol' you that 'while ago. Everybody actin' like we goin' to a funeral."

"We jus' might be."

As the bus pulled away, Jamie glanced back over his shoulder at Mrs. Betty. He knew that this was a big day for her and many other blacks in the little farm community. To them, this day was evidence that the doors to the white world had finally opened.

Jamie turned around. Booger had laid his arms and head on the seat in front of them and was well on his way to falling asleep. Nervous, Jamie sat quietly staring out the window, watching familiar landmarks pass and wondering what would happen when the bus pulled up to the white school.

The bus made several more stops, then rolled across the railroad tracks that separated the black and white communities. Instantly, the narrow, bumpy, dirt road was transformed into a smoothly paved, two-lane highway and the small, tin-roofed wood-framed shacks disappeared. The houses they passed grew larger and more luxurious as they moved farther from the black part of town. Many were huge brick homes and others were old plantation-style, whitewashed, wooden structures.

Jamie moved his face closer to the window. He had gazed at the white world many times, but each time it seemed more fascinating and mysterious than the time before. For years, he had wondered what precious secrets white folks kept guarded in their quaint, isolated communities.

The bus turned south onto main street. Within seconds, the small town of Pinesboro came into view. Outside his window, he saw the parish court house, post office, library, fire station, and bank. His eyes fell on the movie theater. How many times had he climbed the steps to the balcony while trying to imagine what the movie looked like from the white folks' section?

The driver slowed the bus, turned right, and accelerated. They were now on the west side of town, where most of the people who lived in Pinesboro worked. In the distance Jamie could see the early morning sun reflecting off the tin roof of the saw mill. To the east side was the garment factory and one of the town's three cotton gins.

Gradually the bus slowed until it was barely moving. Up ahead, Jamie could see a line of cars and several other buses. He nudged Booger.

"Wake up, man. We almost there."

Minutes later the bus pulled up to the main building of the school and stopped. Through the window, Jamie could see a huge marquee. "Welcome to Pinesboro High School" the sign read.

"Well," Booger said, sliding out into the aisle, "I guess this is it."

Suddenly Jamie's throat felt dry. He raised his hand to his mouth and began clearing his throat.

"You awright, man?" Booger asked.

"I guess so," Jamie said, his voice cracking slightly.

A surge of nervous energy passed through his body. He tried to stand, but couldn't. His stomach became knotted

15

and his heart began to pound. Small beads of sweat formed in the center of his brow. He took a deep breath, trying to gain his composure.

The bus driver turned around in his seat.

"Let's go, fellows. I ain't got all day."

"Yeah, J.R. What you waitin' on?"

"Nothin'," Jamie said rising slowly, "I'm right behind you."

Jamie followed Booger off the bus and into the building, entering a huge, open vestibule. It seemed to be the point at which all the rooms in the structure began or ended. To the right was a long narrow corridor leading to the classrooms, and straight ahead were several glass doors that led out of the building and onto a sidewalk. The students' route was marked with large signs and arrows. Eighth through twelfth grade went in one direction and elementary students went in another.

Jamie followed the others through the doors and outside. As he walked silently through the moderate-sized campus, following the sidewalk as it twisted and turned between buildings, he felt as though he were in a dream world. It was a beautiful school. The buildings sparkled with newness. Pine trees surrounded by flower beds had been strategically placed throughout the spacious campus and were set off by a plush green lawn that was so evenly cut it looked artificial. Sighing quietly to himself, Jamie had to admit that Pinesboro High was a virtual paradise compared to his old black school with its dilapidated buildings and small, barren campus.

The winding sidewalk finally ended in front of the gymnasium. There, Jamie stopped and gazed at the building.

"Booger."

"Hunh?"

"They gym's bigger than our whole school."

"Man! These white folks got it goin' on."

"Ain't they though?"

"I see why they fought to keep us out of here."

They looked at each other, then laughed loudly.

"C'mon, man. Let's go."

They went into the building, passed through the lobby, and entered the main auditorium. Jamie, Booger, and the other blacks sat on one side of the building while the white students sat on the other. Jamie looked around the room; it was so grand that he found it intimidating.

The floor was a college-sized parquet floor, with a huge black bear painted at center court. On the east end of the building was a huge score clock. Underneath it were several jerseys encased in glass and mounted on the wall. Hanging from the rafters were several championship banners. Jamie was trying to read them when he heard the sound of a man's voice.

"Let me have your attention, please."

Startled, Jamie lowered his eyes and looked. Standing behind the microphone was a pudgy, silver-haired white man.

"For those of you who don't know me," he drawled, "my name is Mr. Brian Watkins. I am the principal here at Pinesboro High."

Jamie stared at him. He didn't look particularly mean, but something about him gave the impression that he wasn't very friendly either. Jamie listened intently as Mr. Watkins issued a few cordial opening remarks and then began reading off class assignments. When he finally came to the tenth grade roster, Jamie sat up straight.

"Here we go, Booger," Jamie whispered, "this is our class."

"Man, I hope we in the same room."

"Yeah, me too."

Jamie listened attentively as a tenth grade teacher named Mrs. Diggs was introduced. A few moments later, Mr. Watkins called his name.

"Awright, Booger, keep yo' fingers crossed."

Jamie walked to the front of the gym and stood off from the small group of white students that had gathered behind the teacher. Then a smile spread across his face as he heard the principal call Dennis Mitchel. Booger rose, walked to the front of the gym, and stood next to Jamie.

"Come this way, class," Mrs. Diggs instructed, after the last name had been called.

They followed her out of the gym and to her classroom.

"Sit wherever you want to," she said sternly as they entered the room. "We'll try it like this for now. But, if I find out that you all don't know how to behave, I'll assign seats. I hope you all conduct yourselves like high school students and not like you're still in junior high."

The desks were arranged in six horizontal rows. Jamie took a seat in the center of the fifth row and Booger sat next to him. No one sat in the seats directly in front or behind them.

"For those of you who are new and aren't familiar with the way we do things here, I'm your homeroom teacher. Each morning after the first bell, you'll report here. If you're not here by the time the second bell sounds, you're late. If you're late, don't bother coming in. Go straight to the office and get a late slip. Do I make myself clear?"

"Yes ma'am," the entire class answered.

"Now, in the morning I'll take roll, and Mr. Watkins will make the morning announcements. After that, a bell will ring and you'll go to your first period class. Are there any questions?" There was silence.

"Good."

She took a stack of papers from her desk.

"Now, I'm going to hand out two forms. One is for background information on you and your family; the other is your class schedule. Take one of each and pass the rest back." She handed the papers to the person sitting in the first desk. "Make sure you put your name in the right-hand corner and fill them out as neatly as possible. When you're finished, turn the papers facedown on your desk and sit quietly."

Jamie stood and reached forward to take the papers from the girl seated two chairs ahead of him. His hand accidentally touched hers.

"Yuck!" she yelled, jerking her hand back and frantically wiping it on her shirt.

The whole class snickered. Embarrassed, Jamie took two forms and nervously handed the rest back to the boy sitting behind him. He hated how ashamed they had made him feel. It was as if he was something dirty and less than human. He looked to his right and his eyes met Booger's.

"I'm 'bout two seconds from clearing this room, homey," Booger whispered, his teeth clinched tight. "I ain't gon' sit here and take this."

"Don't worry 'bout 'em," Jamie said softly, "jus' don't start nothin'."

"Yeah man, I'm cool. But I got my limit."

Mrs. Diggs pounded her fist on her desk.

"All right, class, settle down. We have a lot to do today and we can't get it done with everybody talking."

When the lunch bell sounded Jamie was more than ready for a break. In the cafeteria he and Booger found a table together. As he ate, he noticed that just as they had done that morning, all the white students sat on one side of the room and the blacks on the other. All morning, he had wondered how many of his old teachers would be at the new school. But, as he sat staring at the teachers' table, he realized something that none of them had expected. Only two black teachers had been hired to work at Pinesboro High. The rest had been spread out over the parish or not hired at all. Seeing those two black teachers sitting among all those whites unnerved him. It was as if someone had abruptly yanked his security blanket away.

He had a strong desire to go outside and sit in the sunshine. He needed to clear his head before the bell sounded.

"Booger, you ready?"

"Yeah, let's git outta here."

As they made their way down the walk, two white boys walked over and leaned against one of the metal poles that supported the roof. Suddenly, they started sniffing the air.

As Jamie and Booger approached, the one closest to him pinched his nose and looked around at the other boy.

"Scott," he said loudly, "I smell a gar."

"A gar!" Scott replied, acting confused. "What kind of gar, Mark? Is it a ci-gar?"

Mark took his fingers from his nose, sniffed the air again, and looked at Scott.

"No! It's not a ci-gar."

"Is it vin-e-gar?"

"No! It's not vin-e-gar."

As Jamie and Booger walked past, Mark shouted, "I smell a nig-gar."

Booger stopped, turned, and faced Mark.

"Jus' ignore 'im, Booger," Jamie pleaded. "It ain't nothin' but a word." He grabbed Booger by the arm. "C'mon, let's go."

"Naw, man," Booger, pulled away. "You know me better than that."

As Booger stepped forward, students began to gather on both sides of the walk.

"Kick his butt, Booger!" someone shouted.

"Shut up, nigger!" someone yelled a reply.

"Make me, honky," came the response.

Booger spoke calmly. "You talkin' to us, white boy?"

Jamie's body stiffened. His mind raced as he tried to think of something to do before Booger had gone too far.

"Y'all the only niggers close enough to smell, ain't you?" Mark smirked.

There was silence.

"Whitey," Booger said, holding his thumb and the adjacent finger about an inch apart, "I'm 'bout this close to goin' upside yo' head."

"Yo' mama," Mark spouted defiantly.

Suddenly, Booger grabbed Mark's shirt collar, slammed him against the pole, and rammed his fist into his stomach. Then, with no hesitation, Booger drew back his clenched fist and leveled a vicious blow across the left side of Mark's face. Instantly, Mark plummeted to the ground.

"Git up, Mark," someone yelled from the crowd.

Dazed, Mark staggered to his feet, pulled a knife from his pocket, and clicked it open.

"I'm gonna kill you, nigger!"

He lunged forward.

"Look out, Booger!" someone yelled a warning.

Instinctively, Booger stepped to the side, grabbed Mark's wrist, and rammed his arm against one of the metal poles. Then, in one swift movement, Booger bent at the knees, retrieved the knife that had fallen to the ground, and stood. Instantly, Mr. Watkins rushed from the building, grabbed Booger from behind, and slammed him to the ground.

"Turn me loose!" Booger shouted angrily.

Mr. Watkins pushed Booger's head into the dirt.

"Git yo' nasty hands off me!" Booger screamed.

21

Mark spit toward Booger.

Suddenly, everyone was fighting. In the confusion, Jamie tried to get to Booger, but couldn't. He watched helplessly as Scott kicked Booger in the back of the head with the toe of his boot while Mr. Watkins held Booger down. Moving wildly, with teeth clenched, Jamie picked up a wooden soda crate and swung it with all his might. It struck an unsuspecting Scott on the side of the head. Scott's knees buckled and he fell unconscious. Jamie dropped the crate and looked in Booger's direction. Now both he and Mr. Watkins were pinned underneath a mass of struggling black and white bodies. As Jamie moved toward Booger, his eyes wandered back to Scott. He was still lying on the ground, but now, he was moving and blood was trickling down the side of his head.

Jamie mumbled a brief prayer.

"Lawd, I hope didn't nobody see that."

In the distance he could hear the frantic sound of a single screaming voice rising above the tumultuous noise: "Riot! Riot!"

Ten minutes later, a small battalion of policemen, armed in full riot gear, swarmed the campus and brought things under control.

"This is the ringleader," Mr. Watkins shouted, pointing to Booger. "He is a troublemaker if I have ever seen one."

"I ain't no troublemaker," Booger screamed, blood oozing from both the back of his neck and the corner of his mouth. "But I ain't scared of y'all neither," he said, gasping for breath.

"Shut up!" one of the cops yelled, twisting Booger's arm behind his back and handcuffing him.

"What you doin'?" Jamie screamed. "Y'all can't do that."

The policeman looked at Jamie angrily.

"Boy, you better shut your mouth before I cuff you."

"Cool out, J.R.," Booger advised. "They thank they bad."

Suddenly the policeman pushed Booger in his back.

"Move it, coon. You goin' to jail."

Jamie followed them outside and watched them put Booger in the police car. As they drove off, he left the campus, running toward town. When he made it to town, he cut into the alley behind Mr. McGill's restaurant and banged on the kitchen door.

"Who that bangin' on that do'?"

"Mrs. Irene, it's me."

A heavyset woman appeared at the back door.

"Jamie Ray Griffin! Why you ain't at school?"

"Mrs. Irene, there been a little trouble."

"What kind of trouble?"

"They done took Booger to the jailhouse."

"Lawd Jesus!" she said, removing her apron from her waist. "What that boy done now?" She grabbed her purse and hurried toward the door.

"There was a riot at the school."

"C'mon, baby. Make haste," she said, leading the way to the street. "You gotta tell me while we walk."

When they arrived at the police station, Mark's father, the school's principal, and the sheriff were sitting in the office talking.

"Where's my boy?" Mrs. Mitchel asked, as she entered the room.

"Are you Mrs. Mitchel?"

"Yessuh, I am."

"Ma'am, I'm Sheriff Dearborn. Your boy has been arrested."

"Arrested!"

"Yes, ma'am."

"Fo' what?"

"Assault with a deadly weapon."

Mr. Watkins stood and faced Mrs. Mitchel.

"And you can just consider him suspended from school for the rest of the year for bringing a knife on campus."

"Suh, to my knowledge, he don't even own no knife."

"He owns one awright," Mr. Watkins insisted. "He tried to cut me with it."

"Mrs. Irene, Booger ain't tried to cut nobody. He took that knife from that white boy," Jamie said, his voice trembling.

"Boy, are you calling me a lie?" Mr. Watkins asked in a threatening tone.

Jamie didn't answer. He stood motionless. He could feel his heart pulsating in his throat.

"Jamie Ray, go'n over yonder and sat down and keep yo' mouth shut," Mrs. Mitchel ordered.

Jamie slowly walked to the opposite side of the room.

Mrs. Mitchel turned her attention to the sheriff.

"Suh, he ain't no bad boy. I ain't never had no trouble with 'im. If you jus' let me take 'im home, I'll see to it that he behave from now on."

"Ma'am, that ain't up to me," the sheriff told her.

"Suh?"

"Whether or not he stays locked up depends on if either of these gentlemen wanna press charges."

Mrs. Mitchel looked at them pleadingly.

Mark's father spoke for the first time.

"I just want that boy to stay away from my son. It don't matter to me how it's done, as long as it's done."

"Suh, you won't have no mo' trouble with 'im," Booger's mother answered quickly. "I promise you that."

"Ma'am, we're decent folk," Mark's father continued, "and decent folks got a right to go to school without being afraid of getting attacked. Now, we ain't looking to cause you a lot of grief by sending your boy off to jail. We just trying to protect what's ours. You can understand that, can't you, ma'am?"

Mrs. Mitchel dropped her head and looked down at the floor.

"Yessuh," she said submissively, "I understand."

"Glen, I'm satisfied."

"Good enough."

The sheriff turned to Mr. Watkins.

"Well, what about you, Brian? You wanna press charges?"

Mr. Watkins sighed deeply.

"Well, I guess not. But I don't want him back at my school. That boy is more trouble than he's worth."

Mrs. Mitchel turned and faced Mr. Watkins.

"Suh, I promise you he won't cause no mo' trouble. Please, suh, if you can find it in yo' heart to give 'im one mo' chance, I'll be eternally grateful."

Mr. Watkins rubbed his chin thoughtfully.

"Well, it's against my better judgment. But you keep him at home for the next five school days. Then I want to see both of you in my office. If he agrees to behave himself, I may let him come back. But, I can't make you any promises."

"Thank you, suh," Mrs. Mitchel sighed, quickly turning her attention to the sheriff. "Can I take 'im home now, Sheriff?"

"Well Mrs. Mitchel, I wanna keep him overnight."

Suddenly her eyes grew wide.

"Overnight!"

"Yes, ma'am."

"But I thought you jus' said you wasn't gon' charge 'im with nothin'."

"I'm not."

"So, why can't he jus' c'mon home with me then?"

"Because my deputies had a little trouble with him

ERNEST HILL

when they brought him in. He was really disrespectful.
He gon' have to learn to respect the law and the officers of
the law. We'll let him out first thing in the morning.
Spending the night in jail will do him some good."

"Yessuh, he got to learn respect," she said, not wanting
to anger them. "Can I see 'im fo' I go?"

"Yes, ma'am. You can go'n back there now if you
wanna."

When Mrs. Mitchel and Jamie Ray walked up, Booger
was lying on the bed staring at the ceiling.

"Boy, it hurts my heart to see you caged up like some
kinda wild animal."

Booger sprang to his feet and rushed to the bars.

"Mama, I'm gon' need a lawyer."

"You ain't gon' need no such-a thang. They ain't chargin'
you with nothin'. But they gon' keep you locked up tonight
and you can't go back to school fo' five days."

Angered, Booger slammed his forearm against the bars.

"Mama, this ain't right." He spoke through clenched
teeth. "White boy pull a knife on me and I end up in jail.
We gotta fight 'em. We oughta brang charges against 'em."

"Hush yo' mouth, boy!" Mrs. Mitchel said, lowering her
voice to a whisper. "You gittin' off easy. When you was a
little boy, white folks 'round here cut ole man Jackson's
tongue clean out of his mouth fo' talkin' back to a white
man. That ain't been that long ago. Now, if they took a no-
tion, what you thank they could do to you fo' pullin' a
knife on a white man?" She paused. "Booger, you best
learn yo' place and learn it real fast. One of these days
them uppity ways of yourn gon' git you in mo' trouble
than you can git outta."

"Mama, times done changed. The law's on our side
now. We ain't got to bow and scrape no mo', and take
whatever white folks dish out."

26

"Son, I jus' talked to the law. And you best understand that the law, Mr. Watkins, and ole man Evanston is on real friendly terms."

"I shoulda knowed wasn't no use tryin' to talk to you," Booger mumbled, lying back on the bed.

"Boy, don't you mistake the fact that y'all is goin' to school with white folks fo' change. White folks 'round here don't care no mo' 'bout you today than they did yesterday. They don't want y'all in they school now no mo' than they ever did."

"Mama, I know that."

"Well, you better start actin' like it. 'Cause I'm gon' tell you somethin'. The law 'round here moves at its own gait and it takes care of its own. You best remember that 'fo you start talkin' 'bout how much thangs done changed and what you is and what you ain't got to take."

Booger walked back to the bars.

"Mama, maybe it ain't so much times done changed as it is the people. All I was tryin' to say is that black folks these days is tired of shufflin' and beggin' white folks to do what's right. Maybe we done decided to make 'em do it."

"Baby, I been livin' in Pinesboro fo' thirty-seven years, and if it's one thang I've learned, it's that colored folks don't make white folks do nothin'. Leastwise not 'round here."

Frustrated, Booger looked down at the floor.

"Mama, what I'm suppose to do 'bout school? If I miss a whole week, I'll be so far behind that I might not ever catch up."

"Don't you thank you shoulda thought about that 'fo you went and got yo'self in all kinda trouble?"

Booger didn't answer.

"Now's good a time as any fo' you to learn that when

you make yo' bed hard, you gotta lay in it. And you sho'
nuff made a hard bed when you pulled a knife on a white
boy."

"Mrs. Irene, me and Booger mostly got the same classes.
If you want me to, I can brang his homework to 'im."

"Problem solved," Mrs. Mitchel said. "Now, I'm gon' go
back to work. Booger, mind yo' manners and keep yo'
mouth shut and I 'spect the worst of this mess be over first
thang in the mornin'."

C H A P T E R **2**

THREE days after the riot, school resumed. Cautiously, Jamie stepped off the bus. He had expected things to be tense, but he was still startled to see a white policeman patrolling the bus stop and another sitting in a car across the street.

Puzzled, he started toward the school entrance, then slowed, seeing two officers standing next to the door. Maybe something else had already happened. As he approached the building, he stole a look at them, then quickly went inside and paused to collect himself. The anger and hatred he saw on their faces unnerved him. Timidly, he walked through the vestibule and made his way down the sidewalk among the ugly stares of white students and still more policemen. He was halfway through what to him felt like walking a gauntlet when someone shouted, "NIGGER GO HOME!"

Momentarily stunned, Jamie hesitated. The words forced him to think of Booger. He felt a nervous churning deep within his stomach as there flashed in his mind a picture of those angry white folks descending on him. Wordlessly, he moved on. As he walked, he told himself to be calm; try to look natural. But he didn't know what to do with his hands, they seemed so heavy and awkward. He decided to put them in his pocket, so that no one could see them trembling. For some odd reason, he felt guilty. He felt like an intruder. Although he knew he had done nothing wrong, he couldn't get it out of his mind that those cops were there to protect the righteous whites from black folks like him.

Jamie walked on. The veer in the sidewalk told him that he had made it to the black side of campus. Relieved, he paused, removed his hand from his pockets, and looked around. His eyes fell on the small enclave of black students huddled behind the math building. He moved next to them and listened.

"They want a fight, we'll fight 'em."

"Yeah, ain't nobody scared of white folks."

Jamie stood aloof, fighting against the fear that he felt sapping the strength from his wobbly legs. He looked across the walk and then back at the small battalion of frustrated blacks. Lawd, please don't let it be no mo' trouble, he secretly prayed.

When the bell sounded, he followed the sea of black students to the sidewalk, then hustled to homeroom. After homeroom, he went directly to his first period English class, took his seat and looked around. Just as he suspected, his white classmates were staring at him. They had seen him hit that boy with the crate, he thought. He decided not to do anything to attract any more attention to himself. He'd just lie low for the next couple of days until Booger came back.

After the tardy bell rang, Mrs. Gilbert rose from behind her desk and walked to the front of the class.

"Can anyone define the term 'functional illiterate'?"

There was silence.

"Now, I know somebody knows the meaning of the term."

Jamie slid down in his seat, dropped his head, and lowered his eyes. She was looking straight at him.

A black student raised his hand.

"What's your name?" Mrs. Gilbert asked.

"Bubba, ma'am."

"Okay, Bubba, stand up and define the term for the class."

Bubba stood nervously twiddling his thumbs and gazing up at the ceiling.

"Functional illiterate is somebody who always be goin' to a lotta functions, like churches, or parties and they don't be knowin' how to act, 'cause they ignorant of how you 'spose to act at them kind of functions."

The class erupted into thunderous laughter.

"All right, settle down."

Embarrassed, Jamie sat slumped in his seat, wishing he could somehow disappear. He felt a deep shame as he sat listening to the bone-wrenching laughter of the white students. To him, their laughter wasn't directed only at Bubba, but at him and every other black person in the room.

Jamie closed his eyes and tried to ignore the warm vapor-like sensation emanating from just beneath his shirt collar. Why did Bubba have to open his big mouth, Jamie wondered to himself. Nigguh knowed he didn't know what that word meant.

"Bubba, take your seat," he heard Mrs. Gilbert say.

He watched her hastily scribble something on a pad and abruptly turn to a well-dressed white boy sitting up front.

"Jerry, can you define the word for the class?"

"Yes, ma'am."

Jerry stood and faced the class.

"A functional illiterate is a person that can't read or write."

Mrs. Gilbert coaxed him.

"Well, Jerry, you're on the right track, but you need to carry your definition a little further. How does the word 'functional' affect the definition?"

"Oh!" Jerry exclaimed. "A person who is illiterate can't read or write. But a person who is a functional illiterate can read and write just enough to be able to function in society."

Mrs. Gilbert smiled approvingly.

"That's absolutely correct."

As Jerry took his seat, Jamie glanced at Bubba and secretly vowed never to open his mouth in class unless absolutely necessary.

Jamie's eyes followed Mrs. Gilbert as she moved to the center of the room.

"I am an English teacher, and this is an English class. I am here to save the world from functionally illiterate people. In this classroom, you will diagram sentences until you have mastered each component. You will tell me what each component is, what it modifies, and why. You will read literature and discuss what you have read in depth." She paused. "Note I said 'read.' I did not say 'call words.' You will also write a short essay every two weeks and read it to the class. Does everyone understand?"

"Yes ma'am."

"Good. Now, let's find out how much you already know."

Jamie sat with his eyes fixed on Mrs. Gilbert. She seemed more like a drill sergeant than a tenth grade English teacher. He watched her parade back and forth across the room. Her huge beehive hairdo, thick-lensed cat-eyed glasses, slightly haired upper lip, and wrinkled, pale white skin gave her a very intimidating presence.

He held his breath as she walked toward him.

Please God, don't let her ask me anythang, he prayed.

She stopped at the desk directly in front of him.

"What is an adverb?" she asked Judy Adams, the only black girl in the class.

"Who?" Judy asked, pointing to herself.

"Who?" Mrs. Gilbert said sarcastically. "Your feet don't fit a limb."

The white students laughed.

"What is an adverb?" Mrs. Gilbert asked a second time.

"I don't know," Judy mumbled softly.

Jamie's eyes shifted to the large clock on the wall. "Ring bell. Please ring. Please God don't let her ask me."

Mrs. Gilbert took Judy's name, scribbled it on her pad, and then walked back to the front of the class.

"Who can tell me what an adverb is?"

Jerry's hand flew up again.

"OK, Jerry," she said, softening her tone.

"An adverb is a word that modifies verbs and adjectives."

"It modifies verbs, adjectives, and what?" she asked.

Jerry slapped his forehead with the palm of his hand. "Adverbs!"

"Very good," Mrs. Gilbert said, reaching out and affectionately ruffling Jerry's hair with her hand. Turning to the class she said, "Be verbs, repeat after me. Am, are, is, was, were, be, being, been."

"Again!" she barked and the class promptly repeated the "Be" verbs a second time.

When the bell finally rang, Jamie leaped from his seat, grabbed his books, and hustled toward the door. When he was almost there, he heard Mrs. Gilbert's burly voice blurt out:

"I want to see Bubba and Judy at my desk."

Jamie hesitated and looked around; for a brief moment his eyes met Bubba's. Then, with no further thought, he bolted from the room.

A few hours later, during noon recess, Jamie spotted Bubba sitting out in the schoolyard. Thinking that he might be feeling awkward about what had happened earlier, he approached him cautiously.

"Mrs. Gilbert is a mean, ole white lady, ain't she?"

"Mean as they come," Bubba responded nonchalantly.

"What she want with y'all?" Jamie wanted to know.

"She said we need special 'tention," Bubba explained.

"Special attention?" Jamie exclaimed, frowning.

"She say her class too advanced fo' us."

"So what she gon' do 'bout it?"

"I don't know, man."

"She didn' tell you nothin'?"

Bubba removed an envelope from his English book.

"She give me this letter to take to mama."

Jamie took the envelope and examined it closely. He noticed that the back flap was tucked inside the envelope but not sealed. He carefully removed the folded piece of white paper from inside and began reading:

Dear Mrs. Slater,

I am recommending that your son be placed in our special education program. He is not at the level academically where he can successfully compete in our tenth grade curriculum. The pace in the special education program is more suited to

his needs. I would be more than happy to speak with you concerning this matter if you so desire.

Sincerely,

Mrs. Patricia Gilbert

"Bubba, did you read this?" Jamie asked.

"Naw, it wasn't fo' me to read."

"Nigguh, they puttin' you in the retarded class," Jamie
said, handing Bubba the letter.

"You lyin'," Bubba responded.

"If I'm lyin', I'm flyin'. Read it yo'self, if you don't believe me."

Bubba took the letter, turned his back, read it, and then,
as though not the least bit concerned, folded it and placed
it back inside his book.

"What you gon' do?" Jamie asked, obviously worried.

"I'm gon' tell mama I don't wanna go in no retarded
class. They can't make me go if I don't wanna. Ain't nobody retarded."

"But what if they try to make you?"

"I jus' won't go. I'll quit school first."

Jamie thought of Judy.

"Bubba, what they gon' do to Judy? They plannin' on
puttin' her in the retarded class too?"

"Naw, but I heard somebody say they gon' put her back
a grade."

"Can they do that?"

"I guess so. They did it."

"Can they jus' do that to anybody?"

"What you keep askin' me fo'? I done tol' you I don't
know."

When the bell sounded, Jamie hurried to the gymnasium for his P.E. class. Still disturbed by the earlier events

of the day, he dressed quickly and followed the rest of the class out to the track where Coach Terril clocked each of them at forty, one hundred, and two hundred twenty yards. After class, Coach Terril told Jamie to go in his office and wait for him. As Jamie sat waiting, he wondered what he had done wrong. He wondered if Coach Terril had been there when he had hit Scott with that soda crate three days earlier.

Coach Terril entered the office and sat behind his desk.

"What's your name, son?"

"Jamie Ray Griffin, suh."

Jamie's voice trembled as he spoke. He didn't look directly at Coach Terril. Instead, he kept his eyes lowered and fixed on the desk in front of him. He took a deep breath in an effort to relax. He hated himself for being so nervous in front of a white man.

"How old are you?"

"Sixteen."

"So that would make you a tenth grader." He paused. "You haven't failed, have you?"

"Nosuh. I'm in the tenth grade."

"Son, you ran some fast times out there. As a matter of fact, you ran the fastest forty of any kid that I've ever clocked. You ever participated in organized sports?"

"Yessuh."

"Which ones?"

"Basketball mostly," Jamie answered. "And some baseball."

"You've never played football?"

"Nosuh. We didn't have no football team at our school. I mean, 'fo we integrated. But I played a lotta touch football."

"You interested in going out for our team?"

"I don't know, suh."

"Well, Jamie, I'm the head coach and I'd like to see you come out."

Jamie didn't respond.

"Son, you have a lot of raw talent. With some coachin', you'd probably be a decent ball player. That is if you haven't picked up too many bad habits." He paused. "Do you smoke?"

"Nosuh."

"Drink?"

"Nosuh."

"Chase women?"

"Nosuh."

"You ever been in trouble with the law?"

"Nosuh."

"Would you have any problem playing with white ball players?"

"Nosuh."

"Well, I just might be able to make a ball player out of you." Coach Terril smiled. "You interested?"

"I don't know, suh. I mean I have to ask my mama."

Jamie could feel the nervous perspiration running down the side of his face. He wished he had the courage to tell him that he wasn't interested in playing so that he could leave.

"Why don't you talk to your father instead? I hear colored women have a tendency to be overprotective. Better yet, why don't you let me talk to him?"

"He dead, suh. He got killed on a oil rig down in south Louisiana."

"That's too bad. How long ago did it happen?"

"Little over six years."

"Well, why don't you talk to your mother tonight and we'll have a locker for you tomorrow."

The next day Jamie returned to school with his mother's

permission to play. During P.E., Coach Terril helped him pick out his equipment. Then they went back to his office. As Jamie sat in a chair next to his desk, Terril jotted some notes in a ledger.

"I'll get you a locker before school's out," he said. "Our equipment manager will put your gear in there for you."

"Yessuh."

"What position do you wanna play?"

"Well, when we play touch, I always play quarterback."

Coach Terril chuckled softly.

"You interested in any other position?"

"Running back?" Jamie answered, puzzled.

Coach Terril jotted that on the pad.

"Now, since this is a small school, all of our players usually play both ways. On defense we'll probably start you out on the corner."

"Yessuh."

"But we'll experiment until we find the best place for you."

"Yessuh."

Coach Terril looked down at the pad.

"Okay, now I need to get your height and weight."

Jamie walked over to the wall and stood with his back against the chart.

"Five feet eleven inches," Coach Terril said, quickly writing the information on the pad.

"Now, let's get your weight."

Jamie stepped on the scales.

"One hundred eighty pounds, give or take a pound for your gym clothes," he said smiling.

"Well, that's all for now, Jamie. We'll see you after school."

Jamie went to the locker room and got dressed. When the bell sounded, he hurried to the main campus for afternoon recess. He didn't tell Coach Terril, but his mother had agreed to let him play only on the condition that some of the other black guys were also going to play. When Jamie got back to campus, he saw his friend Larry.

"Hey, Larry," Jamie ran to catch up with him.

"What's up, man?"

"You made yo' mind up yet?"

"Bout what?"

"Goin' out fo' the football team?"

"Aw, that."

"Yeah, I got my stuff a little while ago."

"Hey, look like you on yo' own."

"What you talkin' bout?"

"Ain't none of the brothers gon' play ball fo' these white folks now."

"Why not?"

"You don't know what happened?"

"Naw. What?"

"All the white folks quit the band."

"So?"

"Nigguh, they quit cause the music teacher's black."

"Fo' real?"

"Yeah. Ain't that a trip?"

"It sho' is," Jamie said, wondering what he was going to do.

"Hey, they didn't hire but two of us in the first place. Then they gon' pitch a fit cause one black man put in charge of somethin'." He paused. "Man, guess what else they did?"

"What?"

"They say we can't wear they band uniforms."

"No joke?"

"I kid you not. Home, we gotta buy our own."

Jamie looked at him, stunned.

"Is that right?"

"You better believe it."

"Man."

Larry looked at him angrily.

"You still wanna know if I'm gon' play?"

"I guess not."

After Larry departed, Jamie sat under a pine tree by himself, thinking. He wondered what the guys would think of him if he played and what Coach Terril would think if he did not. After giving it some thought, he decided to play. He had already given his word to Coach Terril and he was afraid to lie to a white man.

When Jamie entered the locker room and began searching for his locker, an eerie silence fell over the room. As he walked, he was aware of the cold, unfriendly stares of his new teammates.

"You won't have no trouble finding your locker!" one of the boys yelled, pointing to the back of the room. Silently, Jamie walked to the rear. In the far back corner he saw a locker with a huge watermelon sitting on top. His name was scrawled across the face of the locker. The two lockers next to his were empty.

"That there's for your water break," one of them smirked.

The room erupted with laughter.

Jamie turned and saw that most of the players had gathered behind him. Near the front, one of them was posted in the doorway, watching. Jamie watched one of them cross the room and sit down in front of the locker next to him.

"The reason there ain't nobody living next to you, is we concerned about property value. You know what I mean?"

Anger swept through Jamie's body. He decided to ignore them. He turned and started dressing for practice.

"Why don't you sing us a song?"

"Yeah. Cut a step while you at it."

Jamie continued to ignore them. He removed his pants and underwear and took his jock from inside his locker.

"Look at the size of that pecker."

"That ain't no man. It's a gorilla."

"Hey boy, turn around here and let us see your tail."

Jamie felt a powerful surge of hot anger.

"Leave me alone."

Without warning, one of them grabbed him from behind, lifted him off the floor, and slammed him into the locker, exposing his naked rear end. Frantically, Jamie struggled to break free as the rest of them moved closer, yelling and screaming obscenities.

"Feel his hair and get lucky."

They took turns rubbing his head.

"Get the balm!"

"Yeah, I bet he'll dance then."

A player rushed to turn the shower on, while another slowly approached, carrying a container of balm. As Jamie struggled against those holding him down, someone spread balm over his genitals. Then they dragged him into the shower and held him under the rushing water. The force of the cold rivulets stung his naked skin. He flushed warm with anger. Why were they doing this? He hadn't bothered them. He struggled with all the force he could muster.

"What's wrong, nigger? Don't you like it?"

The water activated the balm and it became hotter and hotter. Jamie's eyes quickly reddened and filled with tears. The sharp, burning sensation around his genitals was almost unbearable.

In the distance, he heard a dissenting voice.

"Let him up."

Dumbfounded, Jamie saw a huge white guy moving forward, yelling:

"Get off him."

A single person responded to his demand.

"What's wrong, Big John?"

Another one joined him.

"Yeah, we just having a little fun with him."

For a brief moment, Big John stared at them coldly. He looked from one to the other, but didn't speak. Then he turned to Jamie.

"You all right, man?" he asked, softly.

"Yeah," Jamie mumbled, baffled.

He extended his right hand to Jamie.

"Let me help you up."

Jamie took his hand and pulled to his feet.

"Thanks."

"If you wipe that crap off with a dry towel it'll stop burning in a few minutes."

"Awright."

Jamie took a towel and carefully wiped the hot, greasy substance from his groin and returned to his locker. At that moment he felt degraded and angry.

"What's going on in here, men?" he heard Coach Terril ask.

No one answered.

Jamie saw that they were all looking at him. He stood wondering if he should tell. But before he spoke, Coach Terril addressed him directly.

"Son, is there a problem?"

Jamie avoided his eyes. He wanted to say yes, but something deep within stopped him. He tried to mask his anger.

"Nosuh. Everythang's fine."

Coach Terril looked about.

"Do you need to get taped?"

"Nosuh."

"Good," Coach said, turning to leave the room. "We'll take the field in twenty minutes."

Jamie sat down with his back to everyone. He was thinking about leaving when he felt someone sit on the bench next to him. It was the person who had helped him earlier.

"You sure you all right?"

"Yeah," Jamie mumbled. "I'm sho."

"My name's Johnny Williams."

"I'm Jamie Ray Griffin."

"I apologize for what happened a few minutes ago. It was mean and uncalled for."

Jamie looked at him with a confused stare. Who was this guy? Why was he going against his own for a black person he didn't even know?

"Thanks," he mumbled softly.

"What position do you play?" Johnny asked.

Jamie shrugged his shoulders.

"Cornerback, quarterback, tailback. I don't know yet."

There was an awkward silence.

"I saw you run in P.E. yesterday. You're pretty fast."

He paused, but Jamie didn't comment.

"I play tight end and outside linebacker."

"Really?"

"Yeah."

"That's good."

Johnny turned and pointed to the far corner of the room.

"My locker is around the corner. When you get ready, stop by. We can walk out together."

"OK," Jamie answered.

Later, as the two of them slowly walked toward the practice field, Jamie still wasn't sure why Johnny was being nice to him and that made him uncomfortable. They reached the field and Johnny handed him a ball.

"Let's see what kind of arm you got."

"Awright," Jamie mumbled.

He fanned out seven yards to Jamie's right.

"I'm gonna run a flag route, okay?"

43

"Hunh?" Jamie frowned.

"I'm gonna run downfield about fifteen yards and then I'm gonna angle toward the flag."

Jamie looked downfield. There was no flag in sight.

"What flag?"

"The corner of the end zone," Johnny explained.

The other players on the sideline were watching. Jamie knew they were evaluating him. He desperately wanted to win their acceptance. He wiped the nervous perspiration from his hands.

"Ready?" Johnny yelled.

"Yeah," Jamie answered.

Johnny sprinted down the field. Jamie drew his arm back and released the ball. As the tightly spiraling pass sailed through the air, silence fell over the field. Jamie had so timed his throw that the ball fell into Johnny's hands just as he had made his break to the flag.

Johnny jogged back and handed him the ball.

"Great pass! Man, you got a cannon of an arm."

A tall, lanky boy with stringy blond hair walked over and took the ball from Jamie's hands.

"I'm Sam Butler, the quarterback," he growled.

Baffled, Jamie saw another guy spread out to the right.

"That's Andy," Johnny told him. "He's one of our starting receivers."

"Aw, I see," Jamie responded. Now it was clear. They were turning this into a competition.

"Andy, give me a chair route, on one," Sam instructed.

"OK," Andy responded.

Johnny looked at Jamie's confused face.

"He's gonna run downfield, turn out, then sprint up."

Jamie watched Sam hold the ball out in front of him as though taking a snap from the center. Then he barked out a series of signals. "Down, set, hut." He dropped backed seven steps and hurled the pass down field. The pass wobbled and began losing velocity. Andy, his face tilted back, slowed to a jog, adjusted his route, and started back. The pass was short. He stopped, caught the ball, and threw it back to Sam.

Johnny took the ball from him, handed it to Jamie, and spread out to the right.

"Chair route."

Jamie nodded affirmatively.

He watched Johnny jog downfield ten yards and turn out. Just as he turned up the field, Jamie calmly released the ball and watched another perfectly spiraling pass sail over Johnny's left shoulder and land squarely in his outstretched hands. Both he and Sam stood awkwardly avoiding each other's eyes.

Suddenly someone yelled from the sidelines:

"Sam, his arm's stronger than yours."

"More accurate too," someone else added.

Sam looked at them angrily, his lips quivering.

"Any monkey can throw when there ain't no pressure. We'll see how good he is when he has to read defenses and remember the plays."

When practice began, Jamie quickly dazzled both the players and coaches with his speed and agility. When practice ended one of the players approached him.

"Man, you're all right," he said with a twisted smile. "I hope you ain't mad because of what happened in the locker room."

"Naw, I ain't mad. Let's let bygones be bygones."

It wasn't exactly an apology, but he was grateful that someone other than Johnny was speaking to him cordially. The locker room incident no longer mattered. He was being accepted.

A few days later prior to practice, Coach Terril entered the locker room and sat down next to Jamie.

"Son, we've decided to play you at tailback."

Jamie stared in disbelief.

"There is no doubt that you would do a good job for us at quarterback. But right now, you would be more help to the team carrying the ball."

"Yessuh."

Coach Terril smiled.

"Well, I'll see you out on the field."

Jamie nodded, but didn't speak.

For a long time, Jamie sat trying to understand Coach Terril's decision. He had outperformed Sam. How could he be more help to the team at tailback when the quarterback was the most important player on the field? Jamie never fully understood, but he quickly excelled at his position. Midway through the schedule, he was leading the district in rushing, scoring, and in all-purpose yards. His success on the field made him a local celebrity. On campus, both his teachers and his peers showered him with accolades. Off campus, local whites greeted him with kind words and friendly smiles. His popularity continued to grow with each passing game.

After the homecoming game, Jamie sat frantically dressing in front of his locker. The noisy dressing room was full of white men and boys who had come to visit with the players. Jamie's eyes went from face to face; he had seen a lot of them before. Every Friday night, many of the same people crowded into the locker room to congratulate, or console, their favorite players. Being pinned in among the sea of noisy whites always caused him to feel ill at ease. He had stood to leave when he heard someone call to him from across the room.

"Say Jamie, what you doing tomorrow?"

Jamie looked up. It was Johnny.

"Aw, nothin' special."

Johnny walked over and stood next to him.

"You wanna come over for supper?"

46

"Hunh?" Jamie asked, startled.

Johnny smiled.

"You wanna come to my house?"

Jamie chuckled nervously, but didn't answer.

"My old man is quite a Jamie Ray Griffin fan."

"He is!"

"Yeah, he talks about you all the time. So I figured he would get a kick out of having you over tomorrow evening, if you can make it."

"Awright."

"Good, my folks'll be happy to hear it." Johnny smiled and placed his hand on Jamie's shoulder.

"Can you make it around six-thirty?"

"Yeah," Jamie said softly. "No problem."

Six o'clock the following evening, Jamie crossed the railroad tracks into the white community, and paused under a large oak tree, thinking. When he got to Johnny's house, should he go to the front door or the back door? Johnny was all right, but he wasn't so sure about the rest of the white folks in his community. He didn't want to offend anyone by ignoring established racial customs. He walked on with nothing resolved in his mind. He didn't want to be late; he would decide when he got there. As he walked, he stared straight ahead, watching the wide, winding sidewalk rise and fall before him under the fading light of the setting September sun. As he followed the sidewalk, he lost himself in peaceful thought. One day he would live in a neighborhood with big houses and nice clean sidewalks that stretched into eternity.

Suddenly, the weariness he felt earlier returned.

"I guess that's the house," he mumbled to himself.

It was a large brick house perched just off the road amid a cluster of pecan trees. He slowly walked to the front door, nervously pressed his finger against the white button, and waited. A few seconds later, the door swung open. It was Johnny. Jamie was calmed by his warm smile and politeness.

"Hi, Jamie. How you doing?"

"Fine."

"You have any problems finding the house?"

"Naw."

"C'mon in, man."

Jamie entered slowly. This was the first time he had ever been a guest in a white person's house and he felt uncomfortable.

"Come this way."

Jamie followed him down a short hallway to the living room. Inside, a small child was playing in the middle of the floor.

"That's my baby brother, Tommy James."

Jamie looked at the small boy. He was five years old with light brown hair that fell over his baby blue eyes. His chubby, freckle-covered body rested on short, stubby legs that were slightly bowed.

"Have a seat, Jamie," Johnny said, pointing to the sofa. "I'm gonna tell my folks you're here."

As Jamie sat on the sofa, waiting for Johnny to return, he slowly dragged his feet over the plush gray carpet. Its softness was soothing to him. Out of the corner of his eye, he saw Tommy James cross next to him, stop, and gaze at his hand. Cautiously, the little boy reached over and rubbed the back of Jamie's hand with the tip of his finger.

"You're black!" he shouted.

Jamie shifted nervously and swallowed. His eyes were fixed on the small, white fingers touching him. The little boy was acting as if he was trying to see if the color would rub off.

"Guess what?"

"What?" Jamie played along.

"I know where black people come from."

Jamie was silent. He wished the little boy would leave, but he didn't dare tell him.

"They come from black cows."

Jamie listened, astonished.

"Know how I know?"

Jamie was curious, but he kept quiet, fearing that the boy's parents would walk in and hear them.

"My Aunt Lucy told me. Know what else?"

Now he felt even more ill at ease. Was this what Johnny's parents thought about black people? He listened as the little boy rattled on.

"Next year, I'm going to school. I'll be in the first grade."

Jamie looked away. If he ignored him, maybe he would leave.

"Aunt Lucy said she gon' make Mama send me to Jefferson Davis so I won't have to go to school with no niggers."

Jamie flinched. Jefferson Davis was the all-white private school. Maybe he was wrong to come here. Why was he subjecting himself to this? Even this little boy was making him feel less than human.

He decided to leave. But as he moved near the edge of the sofa, the little boy climbed up next to him. Jamie cringed. He held still as the little white hand rose and fell gently on the crown of his head.

"How come you don't have real hair?"

Jamie suddenly was ashamed of his kinky hair. He felt compelled to answer, but his tongue seemed thick and twisted.

Johnny appeared in the doorway.

"Tommy, stop it!"

Startled, the little boy jerked his hand away.

"What do you think you're doing?"

Tommy climbed down off the sofa without answering.

"Jamie, I apologize. I don't know what got into him."

"That's awright," Jamie said, not wanting to cause a scene. "He didn't mean no harm."

"Yeah, but he knows better."

There was silence.

"Man, come this way."

Jamie followed him out of the room and into the kitchen. Mrs. Williams stood at a counter preparing a bowl of potato salad. She was a slender, comely woman of about thirty-five, with a tanned-brown face and thick, shoulder-length hair.

Johnny introduced them.

"Jamie, this is my mother."

Jamie glanced at her and then quickly lowered his eyes.

"How you doin', Mrs. Williams?"

"Fine, thank you," she said, smiling warmly. "I'm so glad you could make it."

"Yes ma'am."

"Can I get you anything to drink?"

"No ma'am."

"Well, I'm going to get myself a glass of water."

Jamie watched her take a glass from a cabinet and walk over to the refrigerator. She slid back the panel and placed the glass inside. His eyes widened as she pressed a button, and first ice, then water fell into the glass.

"Jamie, I hope you like barbecue."

"Yes ma'am, I do."

"Good. That's what we're having."

Johnny interrupted her.

"Mom, I'm gonna take him out back to meet Dad."

"Okay, honey."

"C'mon, man."

Jamie followed Johnny out of the door and into the spacious backyard. Mr. Williams was standing next to a custom-made barbecue grill. He was tall and solidly built.

Jamie guessed he was in his early forties. His hair was graying around the edges and his skin was beginning to wrinkle.

"Dad, he's here."

Mr. Williams looked up, smiling.

"What you say, Jamie?"

"How you doin', Mr. Williams?"

"I'm fine. Please have a seat."

Jamie sat on a foldout aluminum chair next to the grill. He watched Mr. Williams take a pipe from his pocket, fill it with tobacco, light it, and take a series of short, quick puffs. Jamie looked around. The backyard was covered with large trees of different types. There also was a swimming pool surrounded by umbrella-covered tables and lawn chairs.

"I've wanted to meet you for some weeks now," Mr. Williams began.

"Yessuh," Jamie said.

"Dad, I've already told him how big a fan you are."

"Me and half the town."

Mr. Williams's enthusiasm made Jamie feel at ease; he sensed his admiration was genuine.

"Son, you're a helluva ball player. I mean, every time you touch the ball I get excited."

Jamie smiled, not knowing what to say.

"You make everything look so effortless. I guess you were just blessed with a lot of natural ability and instinct."

"Yessuh," Jamie agreed. "I guess so."

Mr. Williams looked at Johnny.

"Now you take my boy here. He's a pretty good player himself. But for a different reason. He's good because he's smart. He has good size and strength all right. But he's slow."

"Daddy, I'm not that slow."

Mr. Williams looked at Johnny strangely.

"Son, you know I love you dearly, but you couldn't run out of sight in two days if your life depended on it."

They all laughed.

"Seriously, Jamie," Mr. Williams began again, "Johnny catches passes because he reads defenses well, not because he can outrun anybody. The same thing's true on defense. He makes a lot of tackles because he's always in the right place at the right time. That comes from a knowledge of the game, not from natural ability."

Jamie said nothing. It really didn't matter to him why Johnny caught passes or made tackles, but he sensed that it mattered a great deal to Mr. Williams.

Mrs. Williams came out and looked at the grill.

"How are things coming out here?" she asked.

"The meat's done. We can eat whenever you're ready."

"Johnny, could you help me bring everything outside?"

"Yes ma'am."

"Want a hand, Johnny?" Jamie asked.

"Yeah, c'mon."

Jamie followed Johnny inside and helped him bring the food out. As he worked, he thought about Mr. Williams' comments. His words had puzzled him. Was he really implying that Johnny was smarter than him? He refused to give in to that thought. He must have misunderstood. After all, Mr. Williams had welcomed him into his home. He had spent the day preparing a wonderful meal for him. He wouldn't intentionally insult him.

They placed the food on a small table near the pool.

Jamie sat across from Johnny and Mrs. Williams placed a paper plate, knife, and fork before each of them. Then she sat next to Tommy James and across from her husband.

"Honey, the meat looks simply delicious."

"Well, let's just hope that it tastes as good as it looks. I may have cooked it a bit fast."

Mrs. Williams turned her attention to Jamie.

"Jamie, would you like chicken or ribs?"

Jamie hesitated.

"Oh, give him both," Mr. Williams responded. "He's still a growing boy."

She pushed both over to him. Jamie carefully took a drumstick, then a couple of ribs from the platter and placed them on his plate. Unsure of himself, he waited and watched. He didn't know if he should start eating, or if they were going to bless the food. He looked at the knife and fork. At home they always ate chicken with their hands, but he wasn't sure how white folks ate it. He would do what everyone else did. Mrs. Williams removed a napkin from the table and spread it across her lap. Then she lifted her eyes.

"Jamie."

"Ma'am."

"Is Henrietta your mother?"

"Yes ma'am."

"Doesn't she keep house for the Thompsons?"

"Yes, ma'am."

"Well, Mrs. Thompson is a dear friend of mine. She speaks of your mother like she's part of the family." Mrs. Williams smiled. "Sometimes I wish I could find a good woman like Henrietta to help me with things around here. Lord knows I could use some help."

Jamie didn't answer. He picked up a piece of chicken, bit it, and chewed slowly. He was ashamed of the fact that his mother cooked and cleaned for white folks. Listening to Mrs. Williams refer to his mother as a good, faithful servant angered him. He longed for the day when he could buy her a nice home like this one. Then white people would speak of her respectfully and with admiration.

"Jamie, how do you think the Gators will do against Dallas tomorrow?" Mr. Williams asked, changing the subject.

"Not too good, suh." Jamie forced a smile.

"Why's that?"

"No defense and no runnin' game."

"Well, I guess you're right," Mr. Williams agreed. "Who knows, maybe five or six years from now, you can solve half of that problem for them."

"Well, Mr. Williams, that'd be awright with me."

Mr. Williams smiled, pondering.

"Wouldn't it be something to play pro ball?"

"Yessuh," Jamie replied eagerly. "It sho' would."

"Well, you sure have the God-given talent." His voice became cheerful. "Don't you know the whole town would get a big kick out of that, especially if you were lucky enough to play right down there in New Orleans."

Suddenly Mrs. Williams entered the conversation.

"Well, Johnny's going to be an engineer. In spite of his size, he's more brains than brawn."

Again, there was silence.

Jamie sat baffled. Was she complimenting Johnny or making fun of him? He didn't know how to take her.

"What are your plans for the summer, Jamie?" Mr. Williams asked awkwardly.

"I don't really have anythang planned, suh."

"If you want to make a little pocket change, I can always use a good warehouse man down at the store."

"Thank you, suh. I'll keep that in mind."

After dinner, Mrs. Williams and Tommy went inside while the three men sat by the pool in the warm night air. Although Jamie enjoyed most of his visit, he was more than ready to go when Johnny offered to give him a ride home.

Mr. Williams walked them to the door.

"Jamie, thanks for coming over."

"Yessuh, thanks fo' havin' me."

"Aw, you're welcome in my house anytime."

Johnny drove the short distance to the tracks and stopped—fear kept most whites from crossing the tracks after dark. Jamie got out, walked around to the driver's side and paused.

"I had a good time, man."

Johnny smiled.

"Yeah, me too."

"Thanks fo' the ride."

"Aw, no problem. I'll see you later."

Early one morning the following week, Jamie left home walking toward Papa's little one-room café. He and Booger were supposed to have met after the game the night before, but Booger didn't show up. Jamie thought he might be at Papa's.

He opened the old screen door, stopped halfway, and looked inside. The place was already beginning to fill. Two guys were shooting pool and the long row of quarters lying on the edge of the table meant there was a host of people in line to play the winner. Several men were seated at the front counter and another group sat along the wall. But he didn't see Booger.

"Baby boy, c'mon in or shut that do'. You lettin' them ole flies in here," Papa said after Jamie had been standing there for a couple of seconds.

"Papa, you seen Booger?" he asked as he entered the room.

"If he'da been a snake, he'da bit ya," Papa said, pointing over in the corner behind the door.

Booger and Stanky were playing a game of dominoes. Jamie pulled up a chair and sat down next to the table where they were sitting.

"Hey, Papa, can I git the house special and the coldest soda water you got in that icebox?" Jamie asked as he watched the old, lean man scamper back into the little kitchen.

While he waited, Jamie examined the room. It was lit by a single bulb screwed into a naked socket in the ceiling. The walls were bare, but spotless. At the front of the room, a long wooden counter spanned from the far wall to the door leading into the kitchen. An old wood-burning heater sat in the middle of the oak wood floor; directly behind it was the dilapidated pool table. A jukebox was crammed in one corner and a pinball machine in the other.

Jamie sat wondering how many days he had spent in Papa's dingy little place. It was always filled with the young men from the neighborhood. None of them had gone to college, but they all thought they understood the ways of the world—especially topics like women, sex, drugs, sports, politics, and the most popular, white folks.

"Here you go, baby boy," Papa said, handing Jamie a fried bologna sandwich wrapped in wax paper.

"Where else you gon' git a sandwich like that except at Papa's Place?" Papa asked, glowing with pride.

"You know can't nobody make 'em like you," Jamie said as the old man hobbled off.

"Booger, what happened to you last night?" Jamie asked, turning his attention to the domino table.

"I had somethin' I had to take care of," Booger said, looking up at him.

Stanky slammed a domino down.

"Ten' to yo' business!"

Stunned, Booger looked at the table.

"That's ten, nigguh," Stanky smirked. "I don't care how many times you count it. You see it, write it down. You ain't gon' sat there and hol' no conversation and beat ole Stanky in no bones."

Jamie took a bite out of his sandwich to keep from laughing. He knew Booger didn't like for anybody to loud-talk him like that.

Suddenly the front door flew open.

"It's Mr. Hangman, y'all," the young, muscular man yelled as he entered the room.

Everyone stopped what they were doing and looked.

"Who on the table?" Hangman shouted.

"Me," Big Jack said forcefully.

Skinny was busy racking the balls.

"I'm shootin' 'im next."

Hangman reached in his pocket and pulled out two crumpled one-dollar bills.

"Skinny, I'll give you two dollars fo' yo' stick."

Skinny's eyes grew wide.

"Nigguh, you jus' bought yo'self a stick."

Hangman gave him the money, took the pool stick, and looked at Big Jack, yelling, "What you waitin' on?"

As Big Jack cued his stick, Jamie walked over to the table to watch. Big Jack broke, shot twice, then missed.

Hangman walked up to the table.

"Ole thang, I hate to skin you, but I need yo' hide!"

The place erupted in laughter.

Hangman ran the table, leaving only the eight ball. He gently stroked the cue ball, turned his back, and yelled, "Slow death'll kill a mule!"

The eight ball moved slowly across the table and fell into the corner pocket.

"Aw, Big Jack, that nigguh styled on you."

They all laughed.

Hangman looked at the quarter on the table and yelled, "Like the barber say, 'next!'"

The next player stepped forward. Hangman took the stick from Big Jack.

"Git on out the way. You don't play good nohow."

Papa walked to the edge of the counter and spoke to Jamie.

"Say, baby boy, you seen the paper today?"

Jamie walked over to him.

"Naw, Papa, I ain't seen it yet."

Papa handed him a paper.

"Yo' picture on the front of the sports page."

Jamie got the paper and moved next to the domino table and began reading the article. Stanky slapped his last domino on the table. Jamie looked up just as he yelled:

"Lay down dominoes. I can't make love standin' up."

"Nigguh, you dominoed?" Booger snapped.

"Yeah, git on yo' back. I can't count 'em like that."

Booger turned his dominoes over.

"That's too many," Stanky grinned. "Pencil broke."

Angered, Booger pushed away from the table.

Stanky challenged Jamie.

"You want some, Superstar?"

Jamie looked at Stanky. He was patting the seat of the chair Booger had just vacated. Jamie chuckled and looked back down at his paper.

"Naw, man, go 'head."

Stanky raised his voice.

"Aw, you too good to play with ole Stanky. What, Glen Terril don't 'low you to play with us common nigguhs no mo'?"

Jamie looked up again.

"Man, what you tryin' to say?"

"You the white man's boy. Got yo' name in the white man's paper. We see you ridin' 'round in the white man's car, and I even hear tell you eatin' at the white man's house."

Silence fell over the room.

Jamie pushed from the table, rose, and began walking away.

Stanky shouted a challenge.

"Nigguh, I'll beat you at anythang. White folks thank you so much. You ain't nothin'. Step outside with me. I bet you two dollars I can outrun you from here to the end of the road."

Booger put two dollars on the table.

"Go'n and school 'im, J.R. I got you covered."

Jamie shook his head.

"Naw, Booger, put yo' money in yo' pocket. I ain't got nothin' to prove."

Jamie knew he could outrun Stanky with no problem. But he also knew if he embarrassed him in front of everybody, he would have to fight him. And then he didn't want to feel like he was at odds with Stanky. It was like Stanky was trying to force him to defend white folks. Or even worse, he was calling him a traitor.

"Let's go," he said to Booger.

"Go where?" Booger asked.

"It don't matter, man, let's jus' walk."

They walked out of the building, down the steps, and out into the street. The sun already was rising up toward the center of the sky. It was going to be a hot day.

Jamie spoke first.

"Man, what you thank that was all about?"

Booger hunched his shoulders.

"Hey, jus' two cats that see white folks different."

"I didn't say nothin 'bout no white folks. I didn't even brang up white folks. He did."

"Naw, man, you brought 'em up."

"Booger, what you talkin' bout?"

"When you brought that paper to the table and started reading what the white man said 'bout you. That's when you brought 'em up. Cats like Stanky see the white man as the enemy. And they see you as the white man's friend. To them, that justa 'bout makes you the enemy too."

"Man, that don't make no sense."

"It makes sense and you know it do," Booger said sharply. "You thank cats like me and Stanky could go to them folks' house? You thank they gon' brang us home if they see us walkin' 'side the road? You thank they gon' put our picture in the paper, 'cept we done somethin' against the law? The white man gives you special treatment 'cause of what you do. But he hates people like me and Stanky 'cause of what we won't do. And if you wasn't such a good athlete, they'd hate you too. And you'd see them crackers the same way we see 'em."

When they reached the end of the street, Jamie said good-bye. He cut across the big open field that led to the back of his house. Walking slowly, his hands behind his back and his head down, he thought about what Booger had said.

Three weeks later, Booger's words flashed in his mind like a bolt of lightning: "The white man gives you special treatment 'cause of what you do." Jamie had failed two courses and was ineligible to play ball for six weeks. But Coach Terril spoke to his teachers and by the next day everything was fine. Both failing grades were changed to D's.

CHAPTER 3

T H E hot July sun beamed down on the old wood-framed house. Jamie Ray sat under the huge pecan tree next to the porch, begrudgingly shelling peas. He would rather be in summer school with Booger and the boys than at home shelling peas, and listening to a bunch of old ladies gossip.

He watched as his mother emptied a bushel basket of purple hulled peas onto the floor. She moved an old tin bucket from the corner of the screen-enclosed porch, turned it upside down, and gently sat on it. Shifting her feet so as to evenly distribute her weight on the bucket, she let out a big sigh.

"Jamie Ray eat these peas faster than I can shell 'em," Mrs. Griffin said, grabbing a handful of peas from the pile and placing them in the round mixing bowl sitting on her lap. "I mean, he eat mo' peas than anybody, and act like he ain't got time to shell nary-a-one. Let 'im tell it."

As she talked, she continued to heap peas in the bowl until she was satisfied with the amount. Jamie sat listening and wondering why she was talking about him as if he couldn't hear her.

"Henrietta, what got 'im so busy he ain't got time to help shell a few peas?" Mrs. Mitchel asked.

"Ball playin'," Mrs. Griffin responded. "Look like that boy play ball year 'round. He on the football team, the basketball team, and the track team. Look like no sooner than he through playin' one sport ain't long fo' he startin' another one. And if that ain't enough, when he do come home, he ain't in the house good fo' he done throwed them books down, grabbed a ball, and gone. I don't see 'im no mo' till it's time to eat or time to go to bed. Sometimes I thank that boy got ball playin' on the brain."

"Newspapers say he sho' nuff can play," Mrs. Jenkins said, sliding her thumb down the middle of the pod and letting the peas fall into the aluminum pie pan resting on her lap.

"I don't rightly know how good he is," Mrs. Griffin said matter-of-factly. "Course, I don't care too much fo' that ball playin. 'Specially that ole football. But let 'im tell it, he the best ball player ever been born 'round here. Now, he do have a right smart of them ole trumpets in the house," she said, sitting up straight with pride.

"You mean trophies, don't you, Henrietta?" Sister Willie Mae Jordan said with a loud laugh.

"Irene, I sho' wish that boy of yourn'd play ball so him and Jamie Ray could be close like they used to be. Booger like the brother the Lawd never blessed 'im with," Mrs. Griffin continued, ignoring Willie Mae's comment.

"Chil', you know them two is thick as thieves. They jus' as close today as they ever been," Mrs. Mitchel said.

"I guess you right. But Lawd knows I jus' hate to see Jamie Ray goin' off on them ball trips with all 'em white folks by hisself." She paused and looked up from her work. "You know he the only colored boy on the team."

"Is that right?"

"It sho' is."

"Lawd have mercy."

Mrs. Mitchel sighed compassionately.

"Henrietta, I understand yo' concerns. But Booger rather eat out the toilet than play ball fo' them white folks."

"Wonder why he that way?" Mrs. Griffin asked.

"Whenever I talk to 'im 'bout tryin' to git 'long with them folks, he jus' git mad and say white folks ain't worth the trouble. He jus' don't want no part of 'em."

"Sound like that boy full of the devil's hate," Sister Jordan said. "And the Lawd sho' don't like that."

"Ain't hate he full of," Mrs. Mitchel said in a protective voice. "He jus' mad, that's all."

"What he so mad 'bout?" Sister Jordan asked.

"He jus' don't like what's goin' on at the white school. He all the time talkin' 'bout how white folks ain't right."

"He knowed that 'fo he went over there," Sister Jordan said, digging her hands deep into the bowl, scooping up a handful of peas, and letting them fall back into place.

"Yeah, he knowed," Mrs. Mitchel agreed. "His problem is he jus' got a temper and don't know how to hol' it."

"He uppity. Jus' like that boy of mines," Mrs. Mary Jenkins interrupted. "And if he don't mend his ways, he ain't never gon' 'mount to nothin'. I tried to tell my boy that there ain't no such thang as justice fo' black folks in the white folks' world. I tol' 'im that the best thang fo' 'im to do was to mind his own business, and jus' do the best he can. But he jus' couldn't understand that. He carried on so much 'bout fightin' folks 'round here that I had to send 'im out to California to live with his aunt."

"Booger jus' like that," Mrs. Mitchel confessed. "He havin' mo' trouble since he went to the white school. Seems like he spend mo' time bein' mad than studyin'. His grades done dropped off and he keep gittin' expelled."

"Young folks these days jus' different, I guess," Mrs. Jenkins concluded.

Sister Jordan batted her eyes and made a hissing sound.

"I said it once and I'll say it a thousand times—they full of the devil's hate. They need to spend mo' time in church servin' the Lawd."

"Willie Mae, Booger full of hate awright, but not the kind you talkin' 'bout. He hate wrongdoin'. That boy's heart jus' too big. All he talk 'bout is how mad he gits every time they send somebody black to the office fo' stuff white folks started. Or when blacks git held back or put in the retarded class 'cause white teachers don't wanna teach 'em. Or when black chillun git expelled 'cause them white teachers and that white principal don't never believe what they say."

"I ain't exactly crazy 'bout white folks 'round here myself," Sister Jordan confessed. "But maybe them teachers and that principal is doin' the best they can. Might not be so much they prejudice as it is them chilluns is actin' up and ain't gittin' they lesson out."

"Maybe," Mrs. Jenkins said. "But maybe it's like Irene's boy say. White teachers ain't tryin' hard to teach 'em 'cause they don't thank they can learn nohow."

"Some of 'em can't learn," Mrs. Griffin said emphatically. "Shucks, weren't none of us too smart in the books. No matter how hard me and my brothers tried when we was comin' up, we jus' couldn't learn. After a while, Mama quit worrin' 'bout it and tol' us that God didn't intend fo' everybody to be book smart. She said he give different talents to different folks. Now, some folks got the gift of learnin'. But he didn't give it to everybody."

"That's sho' nuff the truth."

"Well, Henrietta, how yo' boy doin' in school?" Mrs. Mitchel asked.

"He ain't had no trouble with nobody," she answered proudly. "Matter of fact, most of the folks up to that school seem to like 'im."

"Well, that's good."

"His grades done fell off some since the school integrated. But, then, he don't study like he use to fo' he got interested in playin' ball. Now, every evenin' when he gits home from practice, he put them books down and don't pick 'em up no mo' till he leavin' the next mornin'. I'm still proud of 'im though," she said, changing her tone of voice. "I figure the white school's lot harder than the black school was. And right now, he ain't flunked no class."

"Well give thanks and praises 'cause that's sho' a blessin'," Sister Jordan said, loudly.

"I know that's the truth," Mrs. Griffin said, nodding her head in agreement. "Jamie Ray's coaches naturally look after 'im. Anytime it look like he havin' trouble in a class, one of 'em talk to his teacher and everythang always turn out fine."

"I can remember a time fo' integration, when us parents used to talk to our chillun's teachers," Mrs. Mitchel said.

"That's right."

"We sho' did."

Mrs. Mitchel placed her hands on the rim of the bowl and stared blankly ahead.

"We jus' don't git together at the white folks' school like we did at the black one."

"Well, Martha, how you 'spect us to?" Mrs. Griffin asked. "Ain't no PTA at the white school like it was fo' integration."

There was silence.

"Don't reckon white teachers is all that interested in what parents got to say nohow," Mrs. Mitchel added.

"Us colored parents anyway," Mrs. Jenkins added.

"Any parents," Mrs. Mitchel said again. "Don't seem to me they care what any of us got to say."

"Naw, Irene," Mrs. Jenkins disagreed. "White parents talk with them teachers all the time."

"How you figure that, Billie Mae?" Mrs. Mitchel asked.

"Cause they live in the same part of town—they go to the same church and most of 'em is either friends or kin to each other. So they don't need no PTA to keep track of they chilluns. Now, we ain't gon' git a chance to talk to 'em 'less we go to that school. And the only time most of us go up there is when they is havin' trouble with our chilluns."

"Chil'! You know that's the truth!" Mrs. Mitchel added. "They sho' ain't gon' ask us to come up to that school 'less there's a problem. And ain't none of us goin' up there 'less we invited."

"I ain't hardly goin' up there then," Sister Jordan said. "Lawd knows I don't feel comfortable 'round no lotta white folks."

"Who that comin' yonder?" Mrs. Jenkins asked, pointing to the two small figures walking across the large open field east of the porch.

The four women stopped what they were doing and stared at the two figures moving toward them. As they crossed the field and began walking down the old dirt road that ran in front of the house, Mrs. Mitchel leaned forward, narrowed her eyes, and frowned deeply.

"They heavyset one looks like Booger, but I can't make out the dark, skinny one."

"That's my sister Martha's boy, Eight Ball," Mrs. Griffin said.

"I didn't know Sister Harris had a boy that size," Mrs. Jenkins said.

"Lawd have mercy! Black as that child is, he out in that hot sun 'thout no hat on his head," Sister Jordan exclaimed.

Jamie Ray looked up. What he saw made him laugh out aloud. Eight Ball was wearing a white, short-sleeved shirt, black trousers, and red sneakers. From where he was sitting, all he could see was Eight Ball's huge snow white eyes, set off by his dark, glossy black skin.

"If that nigguh's little ole round head don't look jus' like a eight ball, I ain't never seen one," Jamie mumbled to himself.

"I wonder what they done got into now," Mrs. Mitchel said as the two of them came close enough for her to see that Booger's shirt was torn in several places.

"Booger! What happen to yo' clothes? I ain't got money fo' you to tear up yo' clothes like that. What you done got into?"

"Nothin', Mama," Booger snapped.

There was silence. He and Eight Ball walked alongside the porch and sat under the tree next to Jamie. Booger's mother's eyes followed him.

"Look like somethin' to me," Mrs. Mitchel said, her voice filled with anger. "Somebody best start explainin'."

"He got in a fight at school," Eight Ball said, avoiding Mrs. Mitchel's eyes.

"A fight!" Mrs. Mitchel shouted. "Booger! Sometimes I

thank you tryin' to worry me to death. What you fightin' 'bout now?"

"Same ole thang, Mama. I'm jus' standin' up fo' what's right. And while you gittin' mad, I might as well tell you they expelled me fo' three days."

"I don't thank you gon' rest till you done put me in my grave," Mrs. Mitchel said.

"Mama, this ain't got nothin' to do with you. See, you don't even know what happen and you done awready decided I'm wrong."

"Booger, I ain't gon' put up with much mo' sass from you."

"Irene, why don't you listen to what the boy got to say fo' you pass judgment?" Sister Jordan asked. "Go 'head and talk, honey. We listenin'."

"Ain't much to tell," Booger began. "This mornin', Mr. Watkins sent Stephanie Blackman home 'cause she had her hair braided and decorated with beads. I don't thank that's fair. They don't send them white girls home fo' the way they wear they hair. So, why they gon' send black folks home fo' the way we wear ours?"

"That's what you mad over!" Mrs. Mitchel said, shaking her head in disbelief. "That child ain't had nothin' to do but take her hair down and go'n 'bout her business. But no matter what she decided to do, it wasn't no concern of yourn. Booger, you can't go 'round fightin' other folks' battles. One of these days you gon' regret all the trouble you gittin' into."

"Mama, what you want me to do? Tuck my tail between my legs and run every time there's a little trouble?"

"Booger, it seem to me like it make a lot mo' sense fo' 'em to say yonder he go than here he lay. You keep on pushin' yo' luck with them folks if you wanna. I can tell you right now exactly what's gon' happen. One of these days, a group of 'em gon' git together and they gon' lay you out. Now you keep on startin' trouble with 'em and see if what I say ain't so."

"Mrs. Mitchel," Eight Ball interrupted. "Booger didn't start the fight, them white boys did. By the time we went out fo' recess, they had heard what happened. So they started beatin' on the trash cans with sticks and yellin' somethin' 'bout Africans. So after a while, Booger started yellin' somethin' back 'bout po' white trash. That's when one of 'em made a run fo' 'im. But fo' he got there, a group of 'em grabbed 'im and held 'em. And we grabbed Booger and he tore his shirt tryin' to git away from us."

"If that's all that happen, then what they expel Booger fo'?" she asked.

"'Cause I wouldn't back down from 'em. That's why," Booger said angrily. "The principal, the teacher on duty, none of 'em. They was confusin' that white boy holdin' 'im back like they was. All they was doin' was makin' 'im thank he bad. So I tol' 'em in front of everybody, to turn 'im loose, and let 'im hobo his way to me if he wanted to. I guaranteed 'im I'd pay his fare back. When I wouldn't take back what I said, they expelled me."

"Lawd Jesus!" Sister Jordan said, looking at Booger in disbelief. "These chilluns jus' full of the devil."

"Booger, y'all take them empty pea hulls out yonder and spread 'em across the road to keep that dust from kickin' up," Mrs. Mitchel said, continuing to shell peas and looking straight ahead as she spoke. "Y'all put some of 'em in them ruts. Fill 'em in the best you can. And Booger, on yo' way, you better pray and pray out where I can hear you and jus' maybe I won't half kill you when you git back."

C H A P T E R 4

O N E hot Sunday afternoon, Jamie and his mother walked into the little country church amid the singing of the choir and the thunderous sound of the church organ. He could tell from her excitement that she hoped this would be the day that he gave his life to Jesus. With little interest in sitting up front, Jamie stopped and turned in to the last row.

"Boy, what you wanna sat way back here with the devil fo'?" his mother asked.

"I don't know," he mumbled.

Dissatisfied, but unwilling to challenge his decision, she slowly made her way up front, taking her usual seat near the pulpit. Jamie leaned back on the hard, wooden bench. His roving eyes gazed at the small burgundy-robed choir, and then Reverend J. D. McCall, who sat with closed eyes, softly clapping his hand against his knee and swaying his head in time with the music. Jamie looked around the congregation, searching for familiar faces. He saw Aunt Martha and Mrs. Mitchel but, to his disappointment, neither Eight Ball nor Booger was there.

The music stopped. Rising slowly, Reverend McCall walked up and grasped the podium with both hands. Then, with slow, precise movements, the tall, dark, heavy-set man leaned forward, looked over the congregation, and in a very slow baritone voice said, "We livin' in some terrible times."

"Amen, Reverend." The collective response rose from the congregation, drifted up, and dissipated into the rafters.

"I stopped by Mount Zion this mornin' to tell you not to worry." He paused briefly, then began again. "Last night I had a little talk with Jesus and he tol' me to tell you every-thang gon' be awright."

Reverend McCall paused, stepped back from the podium, and pursed his lips. A deep, raspy voice called from the deacons' bench, "Take yo' time, Reverend. Take yo' time."

He looked to his right at the deaconesses' section.

"Jus' last week one of the sisters from the church come up and tol' me, 'Reverend, I don't thank I can make it.'"

"My Jesus," Sister Alberta's voice rang out from the back of the church.

"She said, 'Reverend, I believe my Jesus done left me.'" There was silence. Still facing the deaconesses, he spoke slowly and deliberately. "'I done lost my job and I don't know how I'm gon' pay my bills.'" Reverend McCall whirled to his left, now facing the deacons' bench. "'I don't know how I'm gon' school my chilluns.'" He looked back over his shoulder and spoke to the choir. "'I don't know how I gon' make it through one mo' day.'"

Reverend paused amid the shouts of "My Lawd."

"Well, church." He cocked his head to the side and looked up. "I'm sho' this mornin' that if my Jesus watches over the little bitty sparrow, he'll watch over you." He looked directly at the congregation. "Don't worry 'bout makin' it, Jesus'll make a way out of nothin'. He'll be yo' bread when you hungry. Yo' water when you thirsty. He'll be yo' rock in a weary land." Reverend McCall put his hands on his hips, looked over at the deacons, and bellowed, "Oh! I wish I had a prayin' church."

He turned back to the congregation.

"Don't worry 'bout losin' no job. Jesus gave you a job awready. He said go out into my vineyard and work and whatsoever I owe you, I'll pay. Ain't he awright?" Reverend asked in a loud shrill voice. "Ain't my Gawd awright?"

"Yessuh, he's awright," a man bore witness.

"Now, I have to tell you this mornin', you won't make no lotta money workin' fo' Jesus. You won't drive no big fancy car. You won't eat caviar fo' dinner. You won't live in no mansion. Folks gon' lie on you. You gon' lose yo' friends. You gon' find that this ole world ain't fair. You gon' be persecuted. Jus' like they persecuted my Jesus."

Reverend McCall took a white handkerchief out of his coat pocket and wiped the sweat from his forehead. "If you don't mind this mornin' and if you'll sat with me a little while longer, I'd like to tell the story of how they crucified my Jesus."

"Tell it, Reverend! Tell it!"

Reverend McCall began to sway back and forth, a smile etched across his face. "I know that many of you done heard the story," Reverend McCall began. "But every now and then I have to tell it again. Every now and then I like to search the record and review how they treated my Jesus."

"Take yo' time, Reverend," one of the deacons coached him.

"Well!" he said. "It was one Thursday evenin'. Ole Pilate made my Jesus stand trial. His only crime was that he had tried to do good. If you'll permit me, we'll jus' have Jesus' trial right here in Mount Zion this mornin'." Reverend McCall stopped, looked around the church, and in a loud voice said, "I call my first witness. Would you please take the stand and identify yo'self?"

"Preach, Reverend!"

"Tell it!"

Reverend McCall changed the intonation of his voice.

"I'm a baker by trade. I've lived here fifty long years. I had a good business till Jesus come along. One day he took all my customers to the riverside. He sat 'em down and took five loaves of bread and two fishes and he fed 'em all. He stole my customers and he ruined my business. Now I can't feed my family. I say he's guilty. Crucify 'im."

"Preach, Reverend! Preach!"

Now everybody in the little church sat on the edge of their seats, leaning forward. Some swaying, some waving their hands over their head, and others fanning themselves with church-issued cardboard fans. Reverend McCall walked to the edge of the pulpit, bent slightly at the knees, cupped his hand next to his eyes, and slowly searched the congregation.

"I call my next witness." He pointed to the corner of the room. "You over there. Please take the stand." He walked back to the podium. "Do you know this man Jesus?"

Again Reverend McCall changed his voice.

"Yessuh, I know 'im. You see, I'm a doctor by trade. And like the baker, I've lived here a long time. I had this patient fo' twelve long years. She had an incurable blood disease. Well one day, this man Jesus was out fo' a walk and my patient was on her way to see me. Suddenly she saw a crowd of people gatherin' 'round 'im. She got down on her knees and crawled through the crowd." Reverend McCall stretched his right hand out in front of his body. "And when she got close enough, she reached out, and touched the hem of his garment, and she was healed. This man Jesus took my patients and hurt my livelihood. I say he's guilty. Crucify 'im.

"Ain't Gawd awright."

Reverend McCall hurried to the other side of the pulpit and held up a single finger. "Now I call my key witness. You, over there with the white coat on, tell me, do you know Jesus?"

"Yessuh, I know 'im. He's the one that ruined my business. You see, I'm an ophthalmologist. I was workin' on a cure fo' blindness. I had a couple of blind patients here and I was makin' progress. Then here comes Jesus. He restored their sight and destroyed my reputation. Now no one'll come to me. They all turnin' to Jesus. The man that they say is the supreme ophthalmologist. The man that restored sight to the blind. I say he's guilty. Crucify 'im.

"Ain't Gawd awright."

The church erupted with a chorus of Amens and Hallelujahs.

"Well, this is the part of the story I like. Accordin' to Matthew, Mark, Luke, and John, the court found my Jesus guilty of goodness. His sentence was death by crucifixion. Look at my Jesus. He didn't git mad. He jus' sat there and didn't say a mumblin' word.

"Oh! I wish I had a prayin' church.

"We need to be mo' like Jesus. Sometimes we oughta learn how to sat there and not worry. We need to 'pend on his word. We need to trust that the least shall be first. Don't worry 'bout thangs in this world. We gon' have heaven. Look at my Jesus risin' from the dead. Look at my Jesus ascendin' up toward heaven. Look at my Jesus sittin' on the right side of my father's throne. Look at my Jesus writin' my name in the book of life—Reverend J. D. McCall, c'mon home my good and faithful servant."

Reverend McCall stood in the center of the pulpit, knees slightly bent, sweat pouring from his face, and a white handkerchief pressed against his left ear. His right hand was clenched tight, his eyes closed, and his head faced the floor. Each time he completed a sentence, he stomped the floor with his right foot. The words flowing from his lips now held a lyrical quality.

"Church, sometimes you need to close yo' eyes and meditate on Jesus. Can I git a witness?"

"Amen."

"Hallelujah."

"Every now and then, I steal away by myself. I close my eyes and thank about heaven. Church, look at ole McCall standin' at the pearly gates of glory. Look at me shakin' hands with St. Peter. Look at ole McCall in heaven's shoe department—pickin' out his golden slippers."

Reverend McCall ran out of the pulpit and stood in the center of the church. He placed the palms of his hands over his chest and began flapping his arms. Then, smiling, yelled:

"Them wings a little too small. St. Luke—if it ain't no trouble—I reckon I'm gon' need me a bigger pair. I 'spect I'm gon' fly 'round heaven all day long. Church, I won't worry 'bout gittin' tired and thirsty—thirst will be never mo'. I won't worry 'bout fallin' and hurtin' myself—pain will be never mo'. I won't shed no mo' tears over this ole unjus' world—tears will be never mo'."

Reverend McCall jumped up and down, waving both hands over his head.

"C'mon and join me in my father's house. He got plenty space. Fo' in my father's house there are many mansions and one is jus' fo' you. You don't need no money in my father's house. Everythang's paid fo'."

Suddenly Sister Willie Mae Jordan fell back in her seat and threw her arms out from her body. Flinging them wildly, she screamed, "Thank you, Jesus. Thank you, Jesus."

Several ushers rushed to the choir stand to restrain and fan her. Her tirade set off a chain reaction. A frail, elderly, woman leaped to her feet, shouting a series of unintelligible words. Another lady collapsed and fell into the aisle. Her arms began to twitch. Within seconds, her entire body came under convulsive attacks. An usher rushed to help her back into her seat. She stood fanning and encouraging her.

"Let 'im use you, child! Let 'im use you! Praise 'im the way you wanna. Hallelujah! Praise God! Let 'im use you, child! Let 'im use you!"

Then someone sitting in the back of the church belted out, "When I git to heaven, I ain't gon' cry no mo'."

The church picked up the refrain.

"When I git to heaven I ain't gon' cry no mo'."

Reverend McCall made his way back to the pulpit. He stood leaning on the lectern visibly exhausted.

"The doors of the church are open," he exclaimed gasping for breath.

"Don't wait till tomorrow. Tomorrow ain't promised to no one. You oughta git on board while the blood is runnin' warm in yo' veins. She's pullin' out now. 'Tis the old ship of Zion. Git on board! Git on board!"

Reverend McCall paused for a moment, collected himself, and launched into a song:

>'Tis the old ship of Zion
>'Tis the old ship of Zion
>'Tis the old ship of Zion
>Git on board, git on board.

"Git on board, church! Tomorrow might be too late," Reverend McCall interjected. He resumed the song, and the church joined in.

>It has landed many a thousand
>It has landed many a thousand
>It has landed many a thousand
>Git on board, git on board.
>
>It has landed my dear mother
>It has landed my dear father
>It has landed my dear sister
>It has landed my dear brother
>Git on board, git on board.
>
>There's no danger in the water
>There's no danger in the water
>There's no danger in the water
>Git on board, git on board.

Reverend McCall raised his hands; the choir stopped singing, and the music softened. He made one final plea. "Somebody oughta git on board this afternoon! Thangs in this world last a lifetime but heaven last fo'ever."

Reverend McCall backed away and collapsed into his seat. Jamie sat infuriated. He had watched his people praise and thank God for their poverty and their misery in this world. How could they actually believe that somehow they were better off and more righteous because they didn't have or want anything in this world? He had heard Reverend McCall preach a thousand times, but today, his sermon and the church's reaction caused him to feel more anxiety than usual. As the deacons took up the final collection, Jamie sat staring blankly ahead, with his mind whirling, until he heard a familiar voice say, "Lawd, Reverend McCall naturally preached today."

Jamie blinked and looked up. His mother and Sister Jordan were making their way toward the rear of the church.

"Jamie, Sister Jordan go'n give us a ride far as the quarters," his mother told him.

Jamie rose and followed the two chattering women out of the building. Outside, they strolled across the church lawn, climbed into the car and rode toward town. The church was located near the south side of Pinesboro's small black community. They lived two miles farther north. As the car rolled through the streets, Jamie sat quietly staring out of the back window. Soon the car stopped at a narrow intersection.

"Sister Jordan, you can let us off right here."

"Aw naw, Sister Griffin, I'll take you on 'round to yo' house."

"Chil', we can walk this little piece-a-ways. Ain't no sense in you goin' out yo' way."

"I don't mind, sugar."

She drove through the intersection and down their street. When their house came into view, she pulled the car off the road and drew to the shoulder. Jamie and his mother tumbled out.

"Sister Jordan, I sho' 'preciate the ride." Mrs. Griffin leaned and peered through the car window.

"Aw, child, don't mention it," she said, smiling. "You gon' make it back to church this evenin'?"

"Yeah, if it's the Lawd's will."

"You need a ride?"

"Naw, Reverend McCall gon' eat supper with us and I'll probably catch a ride with him."

"Okay then, I'll see you back at the church."

"Awright. You drive carefully now, hear."

Jamie and his mother moved to the side of the road and watched the car speed away. Mrs. Griffin smoothed out the seat of her dress with her hands and turned to Jamie.

"Jamie Ray."

"Ma'am."

"You feel like peelin' a few potatoes?"

"Yes ma'am."

"Well, make haste, baby, I gotta hurry up and fix supper."

It was late afternoon and the air, though still humid, was much cooler than earlier. A large cluster of white clouds had formed in the sky and now were positioned directly in front of the sun. Jamie removed his tie, unfastened his top shirt button, and followed his mother inside the house. She disappeared into the kitchen, and he went into his room, changed clothes, and sat on the end of his unmade bed.

He couldn't accept Reverend McCall's message—celebrate misery and poverty in this world and hope for something better in the next. He had been inside the white world and he had seen how they lived. Poverty might be good enough for the rest of his people, but it wasn't good enough for him.

Jamie heard his mother calling. He rose and walked into the small kitchen. Already the familiar smell of fried chicken filled the air.

"Baby, I'm gon' need them potatoes in a few minutes."

"Yes ma'am. How many?"

"Oh, jus' a few," she told him quickly. "I ain't gon' fry em. I'm gon' mash 'em."

Wordlessly, Jamie sat at the old rickety table peeling potatoes and watching his mother scamper around the small cluttered kitchen. She was always working. If not at home, then at Mrs. Thompson's. But she didn't have much to show for it. Jamie dropped a peeled potato in the bowl and started on another one. As he worked, his mind recalled his visit to Johnny's house. What nice things Johnny's parents had. Jamie paused and looked around the kitchen. He could never invite Johnny or anyone like him to his house. He would be too ashamed.

"Jamie Ray, that's enough." Her voice startled him.

She took the potatoes, dropped them in a pot of boiling water, and covered them with a lid.

"Anythang else you want me to do, mama?"

"Naw, baby. Soon as them potatoes git done, dinner'll be jus' 'bout ready."

Jamie rose, washed his hands over the kitchen sink, and went back into the livin' room. He sat on the sofa, locked his hands behind his head, leaned back, and closed his eyes. After a few minutes, a tiny voice in a remote part of his brain replayed Reverend McCall's words: "Don't worry 'bout thangs in this world, we gon' have heaven." Jamie opened his eyes. He could feel the anger rising from deep within him.

His mother entered the room.

"Jamie Ray, what's botherin' you?" she asked, wiping her flour-covered hands on her apron and sitting next to him.

"Nothin', Mama."

"Somethin' botherin' you," she insisted. "You been quiet ever since we left church."

"Mama, you wouldn't understand," he mumbled softly.

"Why don't you try me and see?"

Jamie rose, walked to the window and looked out. He wanted to tell her it was Reverend McCall's sermon, but he thought better of it. She would just get mad and think he was criticizing God, instead of Reverend McCall.

"Mama, you remember that time I went over to Johnny's house fo' dinner?"

"Yeah, I 'member that."

"Mama, you oughta see they house. They got a refrigerator in his kitchen that gives ice and water without openin' the door. They got wall-to-wall carpet, nice furniture, a swimmin' pool, and a big ole pretty yard." Jamie turned and faced her. "Mama, what we got?"

"We got our health," she answered him matter-of-factly. "And far as I'm concerned, that's jus' 'bout everythang."

"But, Mama," Jamie looked at her pleadingly. "Look at this house." His eyes, roving around the room, fell on the tiny sofa. "Ole couch covered with a bedspread so you can't see how raggedy it is." He walked over to the couch, bent and raised the spread. The legs were broken off and the frame of the sofa sat on four small wooden blocks.

"Jus' look at this," he exclaimed in disgust.

Quickly, he shifted his attention to the cheap linoleum beneath his feet. "Mama, look at this floor. This rug's so ole, you can't even tell what color it is." Jamie looked up at the ceiling. "Ole plyboard up there in the place of ceiling tile. Roof so leaky, when it rains we git mo' water inside than outside. I'm sick and tired of bein' po'. I'm tired of us never havin' anythang we want and always havin' to jus' git by."

His mother's voice became stern.

"Jamie Ray, I do the best I can."

"I know you do, Mama." He looked away, hesitated, and then spouted angrily: "I jus' don't see why it's wrong to want some of the nicer thangs in life. And I don't see why I have to wait till I git to heaven to git 'em."

"Jamie Ray," his mother sighed. "You goin' on and on 'bout what other folks got that you ain't got. The good book say thou shall not covet thou neighbor's possessions. And that's all you doin', honey. And that's as wrong as wrong can be."

Jamie walked over and kneeled in front of her.

"Mama, I ain't covetin' what belong to my neighbor. I'm desirin' my own."

"Baby, you act like we the po'est people in the world. Maybe we ain't got everythang we want, but we got everythang we need." She looked at him with loving eyes. "Honey, we don't need no lotta money and material things. Ain't you never heard Reverend McCall say 'it's easier fo' a camel to go through the eye of a needle than fo' a rich man to go to heaven'? Baby, salvation all that matters. Thangs in this ole world gon' pass by and by."

Jamie sighed and shook his head.

"What about the po' man, Mama?" he asked angrily. "How hard it gon' be fo' him to git to heaven? Seems to me they both gon' have a hard time of it. Make a man too rich, he'll lie, steal, and kill to hol' on to his money. Make a man too po' he'll lie, steal, and kill to eat and survive. Don't seem to me like neither one of 'em gotta worry 'bout spendin' no time in heaven."

"Jamie Ray, you gon' have to take that up with Jesus. He the one said that money is the root of all evil, not me."

Again, Jamie shook his head in disagreement.

"Not money, Mama. The love of money's the root of all evil. Why black folks always tryin' to use the Bible to show how evil money is? Why don't they never talk 'bout all the people in the Bible that was rich?" He paused, but his mother offered no answer to his question. "Mama, I've jus' 'bout decided that I don't want no part of religion. Leastwise, not the way y'all teachin' it."

"Boy, I ain't got time to sat 'round here and listen to that kind of crazy talk."

They were interrupted by someone outside.

"Sister Griffin, you home?"

She went to the window and peeped out. Reverend Mc-Call was in the front yard, walking toward the house.

"My Lawd, Reverend McCall awready here." She walked toward the door, mumbling, "I better git supper on the table so we can eat and git on back to the church." She paused and turned to Jamie. "Maybe the Reverend can talk some sense into you."

"No ma'am," Jamie rejected the idea. "I done had enough of Reverend McCall fo' one day."

She pushed the old screen door open.

"C'mon in and sat down, Reverend," she yelled. "Be careful on them ole steps. Don't fall and hurt yo'self. Supper'll be on the table in a few minutes."

Jamie sat alone with Reverend McCall while his mother disappeared into the kitchen. When she finished, the three of them took their places and prepared to eat. Reverend McCall, sitting at the head of the table, blessed the food, and then looked up.

"Sister Griffin!" he growled, his large black eyes moving back and forth over the table as he made inventory. "Sho' look like you outdid yo'self this evenin'." He paused. "I believe I'll try some of that fried chicken."

Mrs. Griffin, smiling warmly, placed the platter of chicken before Reverend McCall. Jamie watched him meticulously pick several choice pieces and then hand the platter back to her.

Again he looked over the table.

"Darlin', could you pass the peas?" He made his second choice.

Mrs. Griffin slid the peas to the head of the table. "Reverend, you want some potatoes and gravy?" she asked, politely.

"Well, Sister Griffin. I believe I will have a little taste of potatoes and a slice of that co'n bread if you don't mind."

For the next few minutes, Jamie contemptuously watched Reverend McCall empty his plate, refill it a second time, and empty it again. Then he reached down and loosened his belt buckle.

"Sister Griffin, if I could have a few mo' of them peas and another slice of co'n bread, I'm sho' I'll be able to brang that message tonight." He laughed loudly.

"Help yo' self, Reverend," she said, sliding him the peas. "We got a-plenty."

All was silent except the sound of chewing and the occasional clanging sound of silverware making contact with the bottom of a plate. Finally Reverend McCall swallowed the last mouthful of peas, leaned back in his chair, and placed his hands on his protruding stomach.

"Lovely meal, Sister. Lovely meal."

Mrs. Griffin smiled warmly.

"Can I git you anythang else, Reverend? A cup of coffee? A slice of sweet bread?"

Reverend McCall hesitated.

"No thank you, Sister Griffin. I couldn't eat another bite."

"You sho', now?"

"Yes ma'am." He nodded.

"Well, if you through eatin', why don't you go'n in the front and rest while I clean off the table."

"Awright, Sister Griffin, I believe I'll do jus' that."

"Good," she said, rising. "I'll be on in there directly."

Reverend McCall took the napkin from his lap and wiped the corners of his mouth. Then smiling widely, he pushed from the table and slowly rose to his feet.

"Ain't no doubt about it, Sister Griffin. You the best cook in Pinesboro."

His compliment caused her to smile.

"Well, thank you kindly, Reverend."

"Mama, I'm gon' go outside and see if I can't catch up with Booger," Jamie said, disgusted.

Mrs. Griffin turned and looked at him sharply.

"Make sho' you straighten that room up fo' you leave here. I know you didn't make that bed when you got up this mornin'."

"Yes ma'am."

Jamie rose, turned to walk away, then hesitated.

"Mama, you want me to help you with them dishes?"

"No thank you, baby. If you can jus' git that room cleaned up, that'll be a big help to me."

"Yes ma'am."

He walked out of the kitchen and disappeared into the dim, stuffy, bedroom. He opened the shades, raised the window, and glanced around. Other than the clothes lying on the floor and the unmade bed, the room was pretty much in order. As he busied himself making the bed, he thought of Reverend McCall. He hated the way he came and ate the food that his mother had to work so hard to buy. "He act like we rich or somethin'," Jamie mumbled. "Ain't enough he take mama's little money durin' church; he gotta come 'round here moochin' meals."

Jamie smoothed the wrinkles out of the spread, put the pillows in place, lay back on the bed, and closed his eyes. Soon the clattering of dishes in the other room ceased and he heard the soft bottoms of his mother's slippers sliding across the cheap linoleum. When she made it into the living room, Jamie heard Reverend McCall say, "Sister Griffin! 'Pears to me somethin' troublin' you this evenin'. Anythang I can help you with?"

"Well, Reverend, it's Jamie Ray."

Startled, Jamie leaped to his feet, moved to the doorway, and listened intently.

"What's wrong, sister? You can't make 'im mind?"

"Naw, Reverend, he ain't hardheaded. In fact, he's a good boy—and Gawd knows I'm thankful fo' that. But he's so worldly. He always tryin' to keep up with the Jones."

"What exactly do you mean, Sister Griffin?"

"Well, Reverend. In the place of lookin' fo' salvation, all he interested in is acquirin' worldly thangs. I know he means good. He thank we need that to be happy. But Reverend, it's like the good book say, 'what do it profit a man to gain the world and lose his soul?'"

"Aw, now I understand," Reverend McCall exclaimed. "Maybe it'd help if I had a word with 'im."

"Reverend, I sho' would be beholdin' to you if you would."

"I tell you what. As soon as this fabulous meal you served me settles, I'll do jus' that."

Jamie frowned. Reverend McCall was the last person he wanted to see. He had to leave before they came looking for him. He quickly looked over the room to make sure everything was in order. He picked the clothes up off the floor. Then, he quietly tiptoed through the house, eased the back door open, and stepped out onto the back porch. As he turned the corner, he paused to stare at Reverend McCall's shiny new Cadillac parked next to the house. He shook his head, mumbling softly, "Robbin' his own people in the name of the Lawd."

Jamie made his way out of the yard, crossed the street and walked over to what had been the black high school. When he got there, he discovered Mr. Shorty Gaines sitting under a tree on the old baseball field. Mr. Shorty was one of the oldest and wisest men in Pinesboro. He had seen or heard just about everything that had ever happened there, and he loved to talk about it.

"How you doin' today, Mr. Shorty?" Jamie asked, leaning against the tree that Mr. Shorty was sitting under.

"Aw, I'm doin'," he answered. "Sat down and take a load off yo' feet."

Neither one of them spoke or looked at the other. They both stared out at the open field that was overgrown with grass. The wooden bleachers surrounding the field were now dilapidated. The large screen behind home plate was full of holes and leaning forward. It looked as though it would crash to the ground at any minute.

"Mr. Shorty, I done got my mind set on playin' pro ball," Jamie began.

"Is that a fact?" Mr. Shorty answered without looking up.

"Yessuh. The way I figure it, I'm sho' to git a scholarship. After fo' years of college ball, I'll be on easy street. You know, when I make the pros and all."

Jamie smiled at the thought.

"The first thang I'm gon' do is buy Mama a big house. Then she can quit cleanin' white folks' houses. Might even hire one of them to clean hers. See how they like scrubbin' nigguhs' floors."

There was silence.

"I jus' don't see why she don't understand. She always tellin' me we ain't got it so bad and that I want too much. She always gittin' mad 'cause I wanna be somebody."

"You say yo' mama don't understand you, hunh?"

Jamie nodded his head.

"Everytime I try to explain thangs to her, she end up fussin'. Matter of fact, we jus' had a fallin' out a few minutes ago."

Jamie paused and looked at Mr. Shorty, who sat stone still, not showing the slightest reaction to his words.

"Sometimes teeth and tongue fall out and they close as any two thangs can be. But most of the time they git 'long 'cause tongue got sense 'nough to respect teeth."

Jamie looked at Mr. Shorty, confused.

87

"Boy, you thank yo' mama mean, don't you?"

"Naw, I jus' don't thank she understand me some-times."

"Might jus' be she understand you better than you thank she do. You ever tried to see thangs her way?"

Jamie didn't answer.

"Yo' mama don't mean no harm," Shorty continued. "She done lived 'round here a long time. And she done seen 'nough misery to know it don't do much good fo' a colored boy to sat 'round dreamin' 'bout a life he ain't likely to have."

Mr. Shorty paused, took a brown paper bag from his back pocket, and pushed the paper down until the neck of a wine bottle appeared. He removed the top and poured a small amount of the contents on the ground.

"Fo' the ancestors," he mumbled.

He lifted the bottle to his mouth, took a long swallow, and then let it slowly fall to his lap. He licked his bottom lip with the tip of his tongue, then looked up at Jamie.

"Boy, you ever heard of J.T. Pickman or Mookie Williams?"

Jamie squinted.

"Naw, I can't say that I have."

Mr. Shorty took another swallow from the bottle, swished the liquor around in his mouth, and spit it out.

"J.T. was a pitcher at the colored high school fo' inte-gration," Mr. Shorty began.

He lifted his eyes, looked at Jamie, then looked out at the pitcher's mound.

"That negro used to throw so hard, he'd wear out a brand new catcher's mitt in the run of a week." Mr. Shorty chuckled softly. "When you got to the field, you could tell fo' the game started if J.T. was pitchin'. If he was, you'd see that ole catcher huntin' round fo' somethin' to pad his mitt with. I mean, he'd be askin' folks fo' ole scrap cotton, rags, socks—anythang he could git his hands on."

Mr. Shorty lifted the bottle to his lips and took another drink.

"Do you know Coach Hobby couldn't hardly git his boys to catch Pickman. He had to brang the board of education—that's what he use to call that big ole paddle he used fo' disciplinary purposes—to the ball park to make Billy Ray Bates catch J.T.'s pitches fo' a whole game. Man, you could hear that Billy Ray cussing up a storm between innings. He'd be sayin' that nigguh jus' tryin' to bust my hand 'cause he know he can. Nigguh ain't gotta throw the ball that hard."

Mr. Shorty sat for a few seconds silently staring out over the old field, slowly shaking his head. Then he raised the bottle to his lips, drank, and began talking again.

"I 'member one day we was playin' a team from over yonder in Arkansas. They had a coach'd do anythang to win a ball game. Now they coach knowed he was outmanned. So guess what he done?"

"I don't know, Mr. Shorty. What?"

"He brung a busload of chilluns dressed in baseball suits with 'im. That's what. Them chilluns couldn't of been no mo' than twelve or thirteen years ole.

"Wasn't long fo' everybody in the ball park knowed what he was up to. When they came up to bat, he'd done tol' 'em to crowd the batter's box and to stick they head out where wasn't no mo' 'an a inch of that plate showin'. Man, that coach was some kind of a low down.

"Now, Herman Manning was pitchin' fo' us. Herman was a good ball player, but that boy was compassionate to a fault. He was so scared he was gon' hit one of them chillun that he walked the first three batters. Well, after he walked the third batter, Coach went out to the mound.

Herman was standin' there with tears in his eyes. They talked fo' a few minutes, then coach took the ball from 'im and beckoned fo' J.T. Boy, that J.T. ran to the mound and Coach slapped the ball in his glove, looked 'em dead in the eye, and said in a voice loud enough fo' us in the bleachers to hear, 'Straight down the middle, T.'

"Now, J.T. was 'bout six foot eight and two hundred and somethin' pounds. He was blacker than the bottom of a cast-iron skillet and he was mean.

"After Coach left the field, J.T. commenced to pawing the mound with his foot like he was some kinda crazy. Then he commenced to talkin' to hisself real loud so everybody could hear 'im. To the best of my recollection, he kept sayin' in a half-crazed voice, 'I'll kill a young nig-guh.'

"Curtis Jones hollered from the dugout, 'Stick it in his ear, T., stick it in his ear.'

"All of a sudden, J.T. kicked his left leg up over his head, reared back with the ball, and with one fluent mo-tion, hurled the ball at the plate.

"Well, I was sittin' in the bleachers behind home plate, 'cause I like to see what kind of stuff the pitcher be throwin'. I tell you, that ball came straight down the cen-ter of the plate. I ain't never seen nothin' like it. That nig-guh throwed that ball so hard, by the time it got to the catcher's mitt, it looked like a aspirin."

Jamie chuckled softly.

"Well, the chil' that was battin' fell to the ground jus' fo' the ball got there. That ball whizzed by his head and went straight in Billy Ray's mitt. And ain't nobody heard nothin' but the umpire hollering, 'Strike one!'

"Now that brought Coach Hobby out that dugout in a hurry. He ran out to that mound and commenced to talkin' to J.T. Now, I don't know what he said 'cause I wasn't out there. But I figure he said somethin' like, 'T., I don't want you to kill nobody tonight. Its 'bout a inch of the right-hand corner of that plate stickin' out. That oughta be enough fo' you to hit the strike zone without hittin' the batter.'

"Knowin' T. like I do, I reckon he said somethin' like, 'Mo 'n 'nough.'

"Boy, what I witnessed then I ain't never witnessed since in no ball park. I'm talkin' 'bout high school, college, minor league, or the majors. J.T. didn't throw nothin' but strikes. Seem like his pitches got faster 'stead of slower as the game went on. Boy, that negro threw that ball so hard, fo' so long, that fo' the game was over, I swear that if you was sittin' close to home plate, you could smell the air burnin'.'"

Both Jamie and Mr. Shorty laughed.

"That J.T. was some kinda ball player," Mr. Shorty continued, shaking his head in disbelief. "He didn't 'mount to much later on in life, though. He went to some junior college up yonder in Arkansas and threw his arm out. Then he got some high-yellow gal in a family way. Hear tell they married and J.T. been piddlin' 'round on one odd job after 'nother, tryin' to make ends meet."

Mr. Shorty took another long swig from the bottle and leaned back against the large oak tree. Again both were silent. Jamie Ray's eyes were fixed on the old dirt heap that used to be the pitcher's mound. In his mind, he conjured up images of J. T. Pickman, pawing the mound and throwing pitches that traveled so fast they burned the air. Without warning, the corners of Mr. Shorty's mouth began to turn up. Within seconds, a huge smile had spread across his face. He looked out across the old field and began to talk again.

"There was another fellow played at the colored school. He went by the name Mookie. I swear that boy was the greatest hitter I ever seen. There ain't been a ball park made that could hol' a ball when he hit it square. I remember one game up at the school twix Pinesboro and Bakersville. Now Bakersville had a woman coach, you see. I believe her name was Fannie Mae Jones. Yeah, that's it. Fannie Mae Jones. Boy, she was a sassy little devil if ever I seed one."

Mr. Shorty looked at Jamie with raised eyebrows and spoke in a hoarse whisper: "I figure most of the menfolk came to they games jus' to see Fannie parade back and forth in front of that dugout, in 'em tight little dresses she liked to wear."

"She was fine, hunh, Mr. Shorty?"

"As frog hair," Mr. Shorty exclaimed wildly.

Jamie laughed loudly.

"Well befo' the game started, Fannie Mae walked over to Coach Hobby and said: 'Hobby, I got somethin' fo' yo' boy Mookie. He can't hit my Sampson.'

"Now, Sampson was they pitcher. He was good too. One of the best in the state. He was big fo' a high school kid and strong as a ox. That's why folks called him Sampson on the count of he was so strong and could throw some hard." Mr. Shorty's eyes widened as though he'd had a revelation. "Come to thank of it, he kinda put you in the mind of J.T. Course, he didn't have T.'s accuracy."

Mr. Shorty raised his closed hand to his mouth and cleared his throat.

"Well, Sampson struck out Pinesboro first two batters with six pitches and he looked mighty good doin' it. Now, Mookie batted cleanup. When that boy sat his mind to it, he was a fierce hittin' machine. But that day, he didn't look like he could hit that ball if it was the size of a watermelon and he was swingin' at it with a telephone pole."

Jamie chuckled.

"Mookie walked up to the plate and that Sampson put a grin on his face that went from one ear to the other one.

Boy, you could feel the 'lectricity in that little ole country ball park. Folks didn't rightly know what they was fixin' to see. But they had a feelin' they was fixin' to see somethin' they wasn't gon' soon fo'git."

Jamie sat spellbound listening.

"Well, Sampson went into his windup and delivered a fastball, low and outside. Mookie swung like the ball was 'bout waist high. The catcher dug the pitch out of the dirt. The umpire hollered, 'Strike one!' Mookie had missed the ball by a country mile. That ole catcher stood up, threw the ball back to Sampson, and hollered, 'Two mo' like that un. This fool don't see good nohow.'"

Jamie watched intently as Mr. Shorty reached down, snapped off a blade of grass, and put it in his mouth.

"Well, ole Sampson took his time. When he was on that mound, he didn't never git in no hurry. Man, that big negro 'justed his hat, whopped the sweat off his fo'head, put the ball behind his back, and leaned forward. I swear that boy shook off the next five or six signs. When he finally got the one he wanted, he spit on the ground, went into his windup, and hurled the ball toward the plate. It was a off-speed blooper that got away from 'im—it was high and outside, but Mookie swung anyhow. Jus' like befo', he missed it by a country mile. The umpire hollered, 'Strike two.'"

Mr. Shorty turned his head and spit the grass out of his mouth. He uncapped the bottle and took another long drink.

"The third pitch that Sampson threw was jus' like the second, a off-speed blooper. 'Fo the ball had even reached the plate, Mookie'd done awready swung the bat. Well, the ball hit the catcher's mitt and that ole umpire straighten up, pointed to the bench, and hollered, 'Strike three, you're outta here.' Mookie jus' slung the bat over his shoulder and walked back to the dugout."

"Then what happened?" Jamie asked anxiously.

"Well, when Mookie got to the bench, Coach Hobby was waitin' fo' 'im—and he was some kinda mad. Mookie went to sit down and Hobby kicked the bench out from under 'im. Mookie got up real slow and unconcerned like. He went fo' cool, so he didn't never hardly let nothin' bother 'im. When he got up, Hobby lit into 'im. I mean, you could hear 'im clean 'cross the field. He was hollerin': 'I'm tryin' to win a ball game and you out there swingin' at pitches in the dirt and over yo' head. I oughta take my uniform off yo' back right out here in front of everybody!'

"Mookie tried to say somethin', but Hobby wouldn't let 'im talk. He jus' kept on hollerin': 'You out there embarrassin' everybody. Look at everybody laughin' at you. Sit down, while I find somebody who wanna play.'

"Then Mookie started beggin' Hobby not to pull 'im out the lineup. Well, Hobby turned his back to the boy, and tol' 'im real mean like, 'Go'n back out there, but if you even thank about makin' another mistake, you'll ride the pine fo' the rest of the year.'

"Well, three innings later Mookie got another chance to bat. Hadn't nobody come close to hittin' Sampson all night long. Yet and still, when Mookie took the bat and started toward the plate, Hobby hollered, 'You strike out this time you can turn in yo' uniform.'

"Son, I'm tellin' you, that Mookie stood in the box with water in his eyes, mumblin' to hisself."

Mr. Shorty paused and looked out across the field.

"How far you say that tree is from home plate?" he asked, pointing to an old oak tree that was well off the diamond.

Jamie put his hand under his chin, looked at home plate, then at the tree and back at home plate again.

"'Bout five hundred feet."

"Five hundred feet!" Mr. Shorty exclaimed. "Shucks, boy! That tree eight hundred feet if it's a inch."

Jamie laughed.

"'Bout how tall would you say it is?" Mr. Shorty asked.

Jamie studied the tree for a few minutes.

"Oh, it's 'bout sixty feet tall."

"Sixty feet the bottom of my foot," Shorty shot back. "That tree over ninety feet tall sho' as I'm sittin' here lookin' at it."

Again Jamie burst into laughter.

"The first pitch Sampson threw ole Mookie was a fastball straight down the middle," Mr. Shorty said, resuming the story. "And that was the only one—leastwise to Mookie. That negro caught it square with the meat part of the bat. Look to me like he put ever bit of anger and frustration he had in that swang. Boy, that ball cleared the top of that tree yonder by a hundred feet and it was still risin' when it went out of sight."

Mr. Shorty paused and fell back, shaking his head in disbelief as the both of them sat watching the imaginary ball climb high above the tree and disappear into the heavens. Then, he chuckled softly.

"While ole Mookie was runnin' the bases, guess what Hobby did?"

"What's that?" Jamie asked on cue.

"He walked over to ole Fannie Mae and said, 'Sugar, why don't you send somebody to find that ball?'"

Mr. Shorty laughed and slapped his knee with his hand.

"I tell you, them negroes back then was a mess." Suddenly, he became serious. "Life ain't treated Mookie no better than J.T. He stayed 'round here a little while and worked fo' the town. Ridin' on the back of that ole garbage truck. Wasn't long fo' he left and went up yonder 'round Chicago. Hear he got up there and fell in with the wrong crowd and got in trouble with the law. Last I heard, he was in the pen."

There was silence.

"Son, I guess we always had some pretty good ball players 'round here. But ain't none of 'em never 'mounted to nothin'. Leastwise, not 'cause of they ball playin' skills. Yo' mama's a good woman. She always tried to do right by everybody. She jus' tryin' to teach you how to make it in this world 'thout bein' beholdin' to nobody. I reckon she jus' tryin' to git you to see that this here is the white man's world and us colored folks is jus' livin' in it."

There was silence.

"Who knows?" Mr. Shorty continued. "You might go on to be the next Jimmy Brown. But if you do, you can bet it's 'cause some white man seed a need fo' you and give you a chance 'cause he figured you could help 'im. But Lawd have mercy on yo' soul if they decide they don't need you."

Mr. Shorty stood up to leave. He put the top on the half-empty wine bottle and pulled the brown paper bag up around it. Then he put the bottle in his back pocket, bent, picked up his walking cane, and surveyed the old field one last time.

"Sho' is a pretty day," he said.

As he started walking away, he turned to Jamie and said, "When a fruit's green it grow, but when it's ripe it falls off the vine and die. You study on that and see if you can't make some sense from an ole man's jabberin'."

Jamie watched Mr. Shorty move slowly across the field until he was out of sight. He looked at the large oak tree again and mumbled softly, "Ain't been a man born can hit a ball that far. Besides, it didn't matter if J.T. could throw that hard or if Mookie could hit a ball that far. Times were different then. Now there are more opportunities."

A faint voice singing in the distance jarred Jamie back

to the present. As he looked out across the grassy field in the direction of the tune, he could see a figure moving toward him, but he couldn't make out the face. Jamie cupped his right hand over his squinted eyes, leaned forward and listened.

> Give me that old time religion
> Give me that old time religion
> Give me that old time religion
> It's good enough for me
> It was enough for my mother . . .

As the voice grew stronger and the figure moved closer, Jamie saw that it was Reverend McCall. Overcome by feelings of dread, his first impulse was to turn and run, but he couldn't. Reverend McCall had already seen him. He sat very still with his eyes lowered, trying to think of an excuse to leave.

"Good evenin', Brother Griffin."

"Hi, Reverend."

"The Lawd sho' don blessed us with another beautiful day."

"Yessuh," Jamie mumbled, looking about.

"Well, I'm jus' out here tryin' to walk off yo' mama's good cookin'," he said, rubbing his fat stomach with his hand.

"Oh, I see," Jamie said, knowing different.

"Mind if I sat here with you a while?"

Jamie hesitated for a moment.

"Actually, Reverend, I was jus' about to go'n back to the house," he said, rising and brushing the dust from his pants.

Jamie watched Reverend McCall remove a handkerchief from his shirt pocket and gently dab the sweat from his moist brow.

"Well, I reckon I oughta be gittin' back myself. It's still a mite warm out here. You don't mind if I walk back with you, do you?"

"Nosuh, help yo'self, Reverend," he said, suppressing his anger.

Jamie walked beside Reverend McCall, wading across the grassy field at a much slower pace than he would have liked and anticipating the lecture he knew he was about to receive. For a few minutes, niether one of them said a word. Then suddenly, Reverend McCall's lips parted and he spoke in that sermon-like tone that Jamie had come to despise.

"The Lawd'll make a way outta nothin' if you jus' serve 'im and wait on 'im."

Jamie sighed softly, dropped his eyes, and averted his face.

"You can't git in no hurry, 'cause he got his own schedule fo' doin' thangs. Yessuh, he may not come when you want him, but he's always right on time. The Lawd sho' is good. Yessuh, he may not give you everthang you want, but he'll take care of all of your needs."

Reverend McCall paused.

"You know the problem with you young colored folks today?"

"Nosuh, Reverend," Jamie answered nonchalantly. "I can't say that I do."

"Y'all wants too much!" Reverend McCall said emphatically.

Involuntarily, Jamie turned and stared at Reverend McCall. Want too much? he thought, feeling his face flush hot with anger. What a hypocrite. Here he is, living in a nice house, driving a fancy car, wearing expensive suits, and telling me I want too much. Jamie wondered how often he had repeated those words and how many people had accepted them as the gospel. Jamie looked away and mumbled softly underneath his breath: "All of black folks' troubles ain't white."

Reverend McCall continued with his opinion.

"Y'all ain't satisfied 'less you got everythang somebody else got. But son, acquirin' a bunch of money and a lotta material thangs ain't important. You know why?"

Jamie didn't answer.

"'Cause thangs in this world only last a little while, heaven last fo'ever. All 'em worldly thangs you thankin' 'bout ain't important. You jus' need to keep yo' mind on Jesus. Let the rich folks have this world. We gon' have heaven."

Jamie began to gently pound the outside of his thigh with his clenched hand. He hadn't liked Reverend McCall's analysis when he had heard it in church; he liked it even less now that it had been customized for him. A surge of rage engulfed him and he choked back the angry words that had collected in his throat.

"Boy, it's hard fo' folks to learn to be patient in the Lawd. I know good strong Christian folks to git mad 'cause thangs in this world don't go exactly the way they want 'em to. You take yo' Grandma Griffin, God bless her soul. Been a good Christian woman all her life. I 'member one time ole Satan almost caused her to lose her religion. But the Lawd showed her that ole Satan is mighty, but Gawd is almighty. You see, my Jesus got the power over heaven and hell in his hand."

Reverend McCall paused, breaking off into a deep bass laugh. Jamie looked around. He hoped to see a friend or something that would serve as an excuse to part company with the Reverend.

"Well, it was durin' the Depression," Reverend McCall began, his lips pursed in the exact same manner as when he was preparing to launch into a sermon. "Times was real hard fo' everybody, but they was 'specially hard fo' colored folks. Money and food was scarce. People was jus' barely gittin' by. Well, it was Sunday evenin' and yo' granmama and granddaddy was out at the church. All the money they had in the world was the ole crumpled-up dollar bill in yo' granddaddy's pocket. And that dollar wasn't really theirs. You see, yo' daddy was still a baby at that time and that dollar was fo' milk to feed 'im."

Reverend McCall paused and looked at Jamie.

"Son, you ever heard the ole folks talk 'bout the Depression?"

"Nosuh, not much."

"Son, them was some terrible times. Now, grown folks could do without food fo' a while, but the chilluns had to eat."

Reverend McCall cleared his throat.

"Well that preacher got to preachin' so good that yo' granddaddy got happy. The spirit got in 'im like nothin' you ever seen. Yo' granddaddy got so full of the Holy Ghost that when they took up the collection he dropped the dollar on the table. Needless to say, yo' grandmama was fit to be tied. As much as she trusted in the Lawd, she couldn't see how the Lawd was gon' provide milk fo' that baby without money to pay fo' it. She jus' sat there and held her peace till they got home. But soon as they got in the house and outta earshot of the neighbors, yo' Grandma Griffin sat her religion aside and lit into yo' granddaddy. Way I hear it, she cut up fo' a while."

Reverend McCall's voice began high pitched.

"'You ole fool! What you go and give 'way our last dollar fo'? You knowed that was the baby's milk money. How that child gon' eat? If you don't care nothin' 'bout yo' own stomach, I figured you'd least care 'bout that child's. Hard as times is 'round here, you done went and put the last dollar on the table like you ain't got a worry in the world. Stupidest thang I ever seen. Reckon with all the fools in the church like you Reverend don't even know that it's a Depression. That dollar probably help pay fo' them steaks he'll be eatin' tonight.'"

Jamie watched as Reverend McCall stopped and doubled over with laughter. Was he laughing because her accusation was ludicrous or did he find it humorous the way some preachers preyed on the poor and the ignorant? He waited patiently for Reverend McCall to continue. They were close to home now.

"Well, now, yo' granddaddy didn't git mad 'cause he knowed that the Lawd would provide. He also knowed that wasn't his wife talkin', that was ole Satan. No he wasn't 'bout to give Satan the victory by arguin' with her. He jus' said, 'Glory be to Jesus fo' helpin' me make it through another day,' and he went to bed.

"Well, early the next mornin' 'fo sunup, yo' granddaddy got up, got dress, and tol' yo' grandmama he was goin' to town to make groceries. That sent yo' grandmama into another frenzy."

Reverend McCall changed the pitch of his voice again, imitating that of a woman. "She said, 'Ole man, I do believe you done taken temporary leave of yo' senses. What you gon' walk all the way to town fo' knowin' you ain't got no money? Hard as times is 'round here, ain't nobody gon' give you no credit. I do believe you done gone stone crazy.'"

Reverend switched to his normal voice.

"Well, yo' granddaddy didn't say a word. He jus' went on 'bout his business. He knowed that there was gon' be a raffle in town that mornin'—grand prize two bags of groceries. And he also knowed he had the winnin' raffle ticket in his pocket. Not 'cause the raffle was fixed, but 'cause he was trustin' in the Lawd. You see, yo' granddaddy was a prayin' man. And he'd done talked to Gawd 'bout them groceries."

Suddenly an elderly black woman spoke from one of the porches. "Hey, Reverend. How you doin' this evenin'?"

Both of them stopped and looked in the direction of the voice. Reverend McCall recognized her.

"I'm fine, Sister Phillips," Reverend McCall answered. "How you makin' it this evenin'?"

"Well, this ole rheumatism got me a little stove up. But other than that I'm makin' it awright."

"Well, thank Gawd fo' that," Reverend McCall told her.

"Who that with you, Reverend?"

"Sister Griffin's boy."

"How you feelin', Mrs. Phillips?" Jamie spoke.

"Aw baby, I'm doin' fairly. Tell Henrietta I got a mess of fresh catfish down here if she want some."

"Yes ma'am. I'll tell her."

"Sister Phillips, you gon' make it out to the church tonight?" Reverend McCall asked.

"Lawd willin'," she answered.

"Well, I'll see you then. Me and young Brother Griffin gon' be on our way. God bless you, now."

"OK, Reverend. I'll be seein' you."

As they walked again, Reverend McCall was silent for a moment, then he resumed the story where he left off.

"Town was 'bout five miles from yo' grandparents' house and yo' granddaddy had to be there befo' eight o'clock if he wanted to claim them groceries. Well, they say he walked along that ole country road into town at a pretty good gait. Folks that seed him walkin' that day say he was standin' tall and proud, even had a smile on his face. He didn't put nobody in the mind of a man that didn't know where his next meal was comin' from. I hear tell that when he made it to town folks was awready standin' 'round the platform where a ole white man was callin' out the winnin' number. Well, yo' granddaddy jus' walked through that crowd, climbed the steps to the platform where the man was standin', took the ticket out of his pocket, and without lookin' at it, handed it to 'im and said, 'Suh, I reckon them's my groceries.'"

Reverend McCall paused and gave a low chuckle.

"Well, that ole white man looked at that ticket, then at yo' granddaddy and back at that ticket again. Then he mumbled, 'I reckon they is at that.'

"Needless to say, when yo' granddaddy walked in the house with his arms full of groceries, yo' grandmama was taken aback. First thang she wanted to know was where he got 'em from. You know what he tol' her?"

Jamie didn't answer.

"He tol' her that he got 'em from Jesus."

When they arrived at the house, they walked across the yard, and stopped in front of the porch. Reverend McCall looked Jamie in the eyes and gently placed his hand about his shoulder.

"Son, do you understand what I'm tryin' to tell you?"

"Not really," Jamie mumbled.

"The Lawd done brung us colored folks a mighty long ways and I spect he's gon' carry us on. Don't git all worried 'bout what you ain't got. Jus' learn to trust in the Lawd."

C H A P T E R **5**

"JAMIE Ray! Jamie Ray! Come out that house. I got somethin' to tell you."

Jamie walked outside, stood on the porch, and looked at Eight Ball with sleepy eyes.

"Nigguh, is you crazy? Rooster ain't even got his drawers on yet, mo' less crowed, and you out here yellin' and screamin'. Don't you know it's befo' seven o'clock in the mornin' and Saturday on top of that?"

Eight Ball ran up the steps, threw his arms around Jamie,

and rocked him from side to side. "I don't care what time of the mornin' it is, or what day it is," he said enthusiastically.

Jamie pushed away and looked at him strangely.

"What in the world done got into you?" Jamie asked. "You act like you jus' won a million dollars."

"Cuz, I ain't won no million dollars, but it was jus' as good," Eight Ball answered, tossing his head back and laughing at the top of his lungs.

"C'mon man, spit it out," Jamie pleaded impatiently.

"Awright," Eight Ball consented. "Cuz, I ain't never gon' talk to no mo' sisters."

"What?"

"Last night, I had myself a white girl."

"A white girl!" Jamie shouted. His mouth hung open.

"Yeah man, a white girl."

Jamie took a step backward and stared at Eight Ball with wide, fearful eyes.

"Where?"

"In my car, back on one of them ole dirt roads."

"Man, you crazy?"

"Like a fox," Eight Ball boasted.

Jamie stood stupefied as Eight Ball doubled over with laughter.

"Know what, cuz?" Eight Ball asked, collecting himself.

"Naw, what?"

"That nappy hair them sisters got down there'll scratch you to death. But them white girls got somethin' soft! J.R., I mean it. I ain't never gon' talk to no mo' sisters."

Jamie stared, then they both burst into loud laughter.

"Eight, right now you pickin' in tall cotton. But if you ain't careful, you gon' mess 'round here and git a Chinese name."

"A Chinese name?"

"Yeah," Jamie warned. "He Hung Hi."

"Please," Eight Ball responded, chuckling lightly.

"All jokes aside," Jamie said seriously. "White folks 'round here'll put up with a lotta thangs, but that ain't one of 'em."

"J.R., you always worryin' 'bout nothin'. Ain't nobody gon' bother me. Not durin' this day and time. Besides, if you born to drown, you ain't gotta worry 'bout hangin'."

He paused for a moment and studied Jamie's face.

"Say, J.R., she got a friend that's dyin' to meet you."

"I don't want no part of yo' foolishness," Jamie replied immediately. "It's too many black girls 'round here fo' me to risk my neck fo' one of 'em white ones."

"That might be true. But after last night, I know that if a man die and go to hell without lovin' a white girl, he done missed heaven twice."

Again laughter ripped from deep within Jamie's stomach, passing from his mouth with such force that his entire body shook.

"Nigguh, it ain't gon' hurt you to meet that girl," he continued. "Ain't nobody gotta know but me and you."

There was silence.

"Where you s'posed to meet 'em?" Jamie asked.

"'Bout five miles down the Ole Binghamton Road, there's a abandoned barn out in ole man McDaniel's field. You can park yo' car in the barn and won't nobody in the world know you out there. It's perfect cause ain't no houses or nothin' out there."

"I don't know," Jamie said.

"What's there to know?" Eight Ball asked, throwing both his hands up. "I been meetin' that girl out there fo' mo' than two weeks now."

"Fo' real?"

"Yeah, man. And I ain't had no problems."

There was silence.

"Why you keep callin' her 'that girl'? Ain't she got a name?"

"Yeah. Cindy Anderson."

"Cindy Anderson! Ole man Bill Anderson's daughter? Cindy Anderson the cheerleader?"

"Yep, that Cindy Anderson."

"Man, everybody 'round here know her daddy is the most racist white man in the state of Louisiana. Nigguh, you oughta know that better than anybody. You work fo' 'im."

"That's my angle," Eight Ball said defiantly. "Bill Anderson ain't no different than none of the rest of the crackers 'round here. And I understand 'em all. 'Long as you play the nigguh, and 'yessuh' and 'nosuh' 'em and act like they scare you mo' than death itself, you can git anythang you want from 'em including they daughter."

Eight Ball smiled, showing his pearly white teeth.

"You see, J.R.," he began again. "Much as Bill Anderson hates nigguhs, he done convinced hisself that he likes me. Not only am I the perfect nigguh in his estimation, but I'm his nigguh to boot. The way I cut up 'round here and play the role, sometimes I thank I oughta move to Hollywood."

"You got it all figured out, hunh?"

"You better believe it," Eight Ball answered. "Bill Anderson's jus' another one of them ign'ant, racist white folks that can't see what's right under his nose. He worried 'bout all the rest of the nigguhs out there. Meanwhile he done built up enough trust in me to leave me guardin' the henhouse."

Eight Ball paused and smiled aloofly.

"J.R., I ain't thankin' 'bout Imperial Wizard Anderson. I got 'im jus' where I want 'im, under my thumb."

Jamie shook his head slowly.

"Boy, you playin' a dangerous game."

"Ain't that dangerous," Eight Ball responded.

"If the girl you seein' is Cindy Anderson, then I'm almost scared to ask who her friend is."

"Lori," Eight Ball told him. "Lori Crowe."

Jamie shrugged.

"I don't know no Lori Crowe."

"Her ole man's Vincent Crowe."

"Who?"

"Vincent Crowe. You know 'im. He works fo' the 'lectric company."

"Naw, man. I don't know 'im."

"Yeah you do," Eight Ball insisted. "He got a face look like it been run over by somethin'. He drives one of them white boy Cadillacs—ole red truck with them big wheels that got the cab jacked way up off the frame."

Jamie squinted as he tried to pull a picture of him from his memory bank.

"The only Crowe I know of 'round here is a guy in my class named Steven Crowe."

"Fool, that's her brother. Git me a yearbook and I'll show you her picture."

"Awright. Come in, but you better be quiet. Mama ain't got up yet; she worked real late last night. Ole lady Thompson had a dinner party and Mama had to do all the cookin'."

Eight Ball and Jamie quietly passed through the living room and went into his bedroom. Jamie crossed to his closet and dug out the yearbook.

"Here," he whispered, presenting the book to Eight Ball.

They sank on the bed and Eight Ball promptly turned to the correct page.

"That's Lori Crowe."

For a moment Jamie studied the picture. She had curly blond hair, dark blue eyes, and rosy red cheeks. What was it like to date a white girl? He was curious.

"Pretty, hunh?" Eight Ball asked.

"Yeah," Jamie responded, not looking up.

"You wanna meet her or not?"

"When?"

"Tonight."

"I don't know."

"Aw man, come on," Eight Ball begged.

Jamie hesitated and looked at the picture again. He could meet her once just to see what it was like. That wouldn't hurt anything as long as no one found out.

"What time tonight?"

"Well," Eight Ball sighed, looking up at the ceiling. "I gotta be home by ten o'clock and the later we meet them the better. What you thank 'bout eight o'clock?"

"I guess that's jus' as good a time to die as any," Jamie moaned.

"Aw, ain't nobody gon' die. It'll be fun. You'll see."

Jamie inhaled, inflated his jaws, and blew all the air out of his lungs. He mumbled uneasily:

"I can't believe I'm goin' 'long with this."

"Jus' be outside when I come."

"Awright."

That night, Eight Ball arrived outside Jamie's house at five minutes till eight. By eight, the two of them were headed out of town en route to the old abandoned barn in Mr. McDaniel's fields.

"You sho' this ain't dangerous?" Jamie asked softly.

"I tol' you ain't nothin' to worry 'bout."

Jamie glanced around nervously. As they traveled down the dark, unpaved road, there was no sound except the crunching of gravel underneath the car tires. Jamie could feel danger in the warm, humid air as they moved farther away from town and deeper into isolation.

"It's black dark out there. I can't see a thang. White folks catch us back here this time of night, God hisself won't be able to help us."

"Relax, cuz, I've done this a million times."

"Relax!" Jamie exclaimed. "Nigguh, how I'm s'posed to relax?"

"I don't know, but I wish you would, 'cause you gittin' on my last nerve."

They were silent.

"Eight, you must really trust that girl. How you know she won't set you up? How you know somebody won't follow her out here? How you know yo' little hideout ain't been discovered?"

"I don't know none of them thangs," Eight Ball snapped. "But I ain't crazy. I ain't gon' kill the engine 'til I know everythang's cool." He paused, rubbed his hand across his mouth, and sighed softly. "Why you lookin' fo' trouble? Everythang'll be fine if you jus' relax."

Eight Ball turned off the road onto Mr. McDaniel's land. Slowly they advanced over the bumpy stretch of plowed ground and followed the vehicle tracks that had been worn through the grassy field. Now and then the wheels sank into a rut or passed over a clod of earth causing their rear ends to fly off the seat. Suddenly the car lights fell on an old, ragged barn partially hidden by weeds and wild shrubbery. Eight Ball pulled up to it and stopped.

"This is it, cuz," he announced gleefully, "vanilla heaven."

"Man, this place looks abandoned," Jamie whispered. "Ain't nobody in there. Let's git outta here."

"They in there awright," Eight Ball assured him. "Everythang's cool, jus' like I tol' you it'd be."

"How you know that?"

"I tol' you this was a good place," Eight Ball laughed. "You lookin' straight at 'em and can't see 'em."

Jamie leaned forward and squinted.

"Where they at?" he asked.

"In the barn."

"How you know they in there? I don't see nothin'."

"See that green rag over there?"

Jamie leaned forward and looked.

"Yeah, I see it."

"That mean everythang's cool. If somethin' was wrong, it'd be red."

Slowly, Eight Ball pulled his car around behind the building, backed inside next to Cindy's car, killed the engine, and turned off his lights. As they sat letting their eyes adjust to the moonlit room, Cindy got out and walked around to the driver's side of Eight Ball's car.

"Y'all right on time," she drawled, leaning on the car window.

Astonished, Jamie watched Eight Ball poke his head through the window and kiss her for a long time.

"Jesus Christ," Jamie whispered softly. He turned and looked over his shoulder to make sure that they were alone.

"Say, man," Eight Ball said, turning to Jamie, "why don't you go let Cindy introduce you to Lori. Y'all can rap in her ride. And me and Cindy can stay in mine."

"You don't need to be introduced," Cindy said, rolling her eyes up toward the sky. "It's not like she ain't expectin' you." Jamie looked at Eight Ball with doubtful eyes.

"Well, cuz, what you waitin' on? Go'n over there. She ain't gon' bite you."

Jamie didn't like the idea of him and Eight Ball separating. What if someone came? Would they have enough time to switch cars and get away? Reluctantly, Jamie stepped outside, crossed over to Cindy's car, bent, and peeped through the window.

Lori, clad in faded blue jeans and a blouse, looked up at him.

"Hi, Jamie," she introduced herself. "I'm Lori."

"I'm Jamie," he responded nervously.

"I know." The corners of Lori's mouth turned up until her face was covered with a huge smile.

"Oh, I guess so," Jamie said, feeling somewhat foolish.

"Aren't you gonna get in?" she asked.

He opened the door and slid under the wheel. Feeling cramped, he let the seat back and extended his legs. Though he sat stiff and looked straight ahead, out of the corner of his eye he could see that she was looking at him. What was he doing here? He felt anxious. His heart accelerated as a nervous charge passed through his body.

"I d-didn't know white folks listened to that station," he stammered, feeling the need to say something, but feeling stupid as soon as the words had passed from his lips.

"What did you think we listened to?"

"Oh, I don't know—country and western or rock and roll. But I sho' didn't thank y'all lissened to soul music."

She smiled and hesitated before answering.

"Well, I like soul music. But to be perfectly honest, I can't listen to it at home."

"Why not?" Jamie wanted to know.

"My parents won't allow it. They say it's jungle bunny music."

Her answer had piqued Jamie's curiosity. She was offering insight into whites that he never had before. Sure, he had interacted with white males when the issue of race had come up, but those discussions were always guarded. She seemed willing to talk with an openness that he found intriguing. He turned and looked directly at her. Suddenly he no longer felt as he had when they first met.

"So, yo' parents don't like black people?"

"If you're asking me if my parents are prejudiced, I don't think so. My mother doesn't interact with a lot of black people, but a lot of my father's friends at work are black."

"He ever had one of his black friends over fo' dinner?" Jamie asked sarcastically.

"No, but it's not because he minds. He just don't think they'd come. He says it would probably be too uncomfortable for them."

"He ever asked one of 'em?"

"No, he hasn't; at least, not that I know of."

"So, how he know how they feel?"

"I don't know. Maybe he can tell just from talking to them."

"Maybe he jus' don't want 'em in his house."

There was silence.

"I could have a black friend come by the house if I wanted to," she said defensively. "My parents wouldn't mind."

"A girlfriend, but not a boyfriend," Jamie quickly added.

"That doesn't mean that he's prejudiced. It just means he doesn't think that white folks and black folks ought to mix. He just don't think God intended for people of different races to marry."

Jamie said nothing. He thought her explanation was peculiar. He wondered how her daddy knew what God intended.

"Jamie, I don't think my father's right when he says all those things. If I did, I wouldn't be out here with you now. But right or wrong, he believes them."

"Do yo' mama feel the same way?"

"Well," she sighed, "I don't think Mother would really mind personally. But she would be concerned about what the neighbors think."

"Oh, I see," Jamie said.

"Anyway, what she thinks really doesn't matter. My father decides what goes on in our house. And Mother is not going to go against him."

"What would yo' daddy do if he knew you were seein' me?" Jamie asked.

"He'd tell me to quit it."

"And if you didn't?"

She hesitated.

"He'd probably disown me," she said softly. "He might even put me out of the house."

Jamie knew that, but hearing her say it caused a flash of anger to pass over him. He blurted out, "If that's the case, why in the world you so interested in meetin' me?"

"Oh, a lot of reasons."

"Such as?"

Before she could answer, they heard something scampering through the weeds outside. Startled, both of them looked in the direction of the noise. It was an old grayish brown opossum, moving toward the door at such an angle that the light of the moon fell into his eyes, causing them to cast off an ominous yellow glow. Relieved, they watched the opposum scurry inside and disappear into the darkness of the far corner. Then he heard Lori ask softly, "Jamie, why are you asking so many questions about my parents?"

"No particular reason," he mumbled. "Jus' curious I guess."

He watched her turn in her seat, pull her legs under her Indian style, and stare directly at him.

"Well, what about your parents?" she asked. "What would they say?"

"Hunh?" Jamie asked, squinting.

"How would they feel about you talking to a white girl?"

Jamie swallowed and thought about the question. If his mother knew he was out there she would have a fit. Yet it was different. She would react out of fear and concern, not hatred.

"Oh, Mama wouldn't care if she didn't thank it was dangerous."

Lori looked at him surprised.

"What about your daddy?" she asked. "What would he say?"

Jamie dropped his eyes and lowered the tone of his voice.

"I don't know," he told her. "My daddy's dead."

"Oh, I'm sorry," she said, her voice becoming soft and compassionate. "It must be hard growing up without a father."

"Not really. In a lotta ways, it's jus' like I got a daddy. He jus' don't live in the same house with me."

"What you mean?" she asked.

"My uncle Rob act mo' like my daddy than my uncle. He don't live but 'round the corner from us and we do lots of stuff together. We go fishin', play ball, and he gives me advice." Jamie paused and smiled. "He use to even give me whuppins 'fo I got too big fo' 'em."

"Really?"

"Yeah. So, in a way, the only thang I miss is havin' another brother or sister. But then I got Booger and Eight Ball. So really and truly, I ain't no worse off than nobody else."

Lori placed her hand on top of his.

"And now you have my friendship," she said, smiling. "So you're better off today than you were yesterday."

Feeling the soft touch of her warm, moist hand upon his own, Jamie glanced down. Suddenly he could feel the blood pulsating through his veins.

"Thanks," he mumbled. "I don't guess you can ever have too many friends."

For a moment they were silent.

"You know, I was kind of worried that you wouldn't come tonight. Cindy told me that Eight Ball said you weren't too fond of white girls."

Jamie shifted uneasily and avoided her eyes. Why had Eight Ball told them that?

"It's not that I have anythang against white girls. I jus' don't thank it's a good idea. I'm jus' afraid of . . ." Jamie paused. "Well, nothin'." Why was he having this conversation with a white person?

"What are you afraid of?" Lori urged him to continue.

Jamie pulled his fist to his mouth and cleared his throat. What was he afraid of? How in the world could she sit there and ask such a silly question? He decided to change the subject.

"You never tol' me why you're so interested in meetin' me," he reminded her. He waited for her response.

"Oh, a lot of reasons," she said, squeezing his hand tightly. She tilted her head, smiled warmly, and began speaking in a flirtatious tone. "I think you're very attractive. I love the way you play ball. And Eight Ball is always telling me how nice you are. So I guess I just wanted to see for myself."

She didn't say anything about his being black. He wondered if that had anything to do with her interest in him. He stared at her blankly.

"You ever dated a black guy befo'?"

"Yeah," she answered without hestitation. "Not around here though. A year ago I spent summer vacation at my aunt's house in California. While I was out there, I met this black guy on the beach. We hung out for most of the summer. It wasn't that big a deal out there."

For a few seconds Jamie didn't speak. Her answer had surprised him. She had dated a black guy before. She knew her parents and her race didn't like it, but she did it anyway. Why? Maybe she was just being rebellious.

"Yo' parents don't like you datin' black guys, right?"

"Right."

"But you do it anyway."

"Uh-huh."

"Why?"

"Haven't you heard, once a girl goes black she can never go back?" she joked.

Jamie didn't answer. He couldn't believe she had said that.

"I'm just kidding, Jamie," she said gently. Then she paused and said seriously, "I guess I'm just an adventurous person."

"That's it?"

"Yeah. At first anyway. But after I started hanging out with that guy I told you about in California, and some of his friends, I started liking a lot of things about black guys."

"Such as?"

"They know how to laugh and have a good time. And they're so nice to me, it's unbelievable. That's one of the reasons I wanted to meet you—Eight Ball said you were a nice guy."

"Well, now that you've met me, what do you think?" he asked.

"I agree with him. You're real nice, real attractive, and just a all-around classy guy." She paused. "And what do you think of me?"

Jamie smiled.

"I thank you're all those thangs and mo'. So far, I've really enjoyed talkin' to you."

"I'm glad." She moved closer to him and laid her head on his chest. "I was afraid you wouldn't like me."

Jamie slipped his arm about her shoulder and began gently rubbing his hand up and down her right arm.

"It's strange, and I can't explain it, but it jus' don't seem like this is our first time together. I wouldn't of thought that I could be this relaxed with you."

Lori rose from his arms, reached up with her hand, and tenderly caressed the side of his face. "Neither would I, but I'm sure glad you are."

As Lori spoke, Jamie studied her face, looking directly at her for the first time that night. She looked exactly like the picture he had seen. Her blue eyes sparkled in the night light whenever she held her head in a certain position. She had red rouge on her cheeks and a light coat of red lipstick on her surprisingly full lips. He looked at her with inquisitive eyes.

Did white girls kiss like black girls? What would it be like to run his fingers through her long, fluffy hair? His curiosity fueled a mounting desire to sample that which he had always been warned against. Now he no longer saw Lori. But reaching back in the far recesses of his memory, he conjured up images of some of the most provocative and seductive white female personalities he knew of—actresses, models, athletes, playmates. . . . He looked at the dashboard, leaned forward, and then asked softly, "Is that yo' kissin' stick?"

She turned and looked.

"Yeah. Why do you ask?"

"Maybe we oughta try it out and see if it works," he suggested eagerly.

Smiling, she moved closer to him, placed her arms about his neck, and slowly moved her face toward his. When her lips were only inches away, she hesitated, then whispered, "I already have some on."

"Good."

Slowly, he moved forward, his lips gently touching hers. All his anxiety, fear, and tension left him as he reveled in the forbidden delicacy. As they kissed, eyes closed and heads slowly moving from side to side, Jamie felt the tips of her soft white fingers gently caressing the nape of his neck. His arms reached around her as his hands began exploring her body, gently moving down her back until he was passionately caressing her buttocks. A long time passed and she pulled away and let her head rest on his chest. He held her tightly in his arms. For several moments, neither one of them spoke. They just let their minds wander off to the soft sound of the car radio.

"Do you like to skate?" she asked, breaking the silence.

"Hunh?" He thought the question odd.

"Roller skating. Do you like it?"

"I don't know. I've never tried it. Why do you ask?"

"I know this place in Shreveport where we can go and skate. I was wondering if you might like to go sometime?"

"Shreveport, hunh?"

"Yeah. Cindy and I go there all the time." She paused, then explained further. "No one would think twice about us being together there. It's a bigger city and people over there mix all the time."

"Really?"

"Yeah. And it's only about a two-hour drive, so we could go over there early in the morning and be back before our curfew."

"It sounds like fun."

"Well, think about it."

"OK, I will."

Jamie looked over at Eight Ball's car.

"Lori, do you have the time?"

She switched on the inside light momentarily to look at her watch.

"Wow, it's getting late. It's ten thirty-five."

"Ten thirty-five!" Jamie exclaimed. "We shoulda been home thirty-five minutes ago."

Frantically, he hurried over to Eight Ball's car, gently tapped on the window, and paused. When no one answered, he called in a low, hoarse voice, "Eight Ball. It's me." He paused again. "Man, we better go. It's gittin' late."

The door creaked open and Eight Ball tumbled out. His shirt was completely unbuttoned and red lipstick was smudged all over his face and neck.

"Nigguh, what's wrong with you?" he asked angrily.

"It's ten-thirty, that's what's wrong."

"Man, she almost ready," he said with a look of disgust on his face. "I jus' need a few mo' minutes. We awready late. A few mo' minutes ain't gon' hurt nothin'."

"I swear, our folks gon' kill us," Jamie wailed, hoping to frighten Eight Ball into leaving.

"Aw, man, we ain't gon' be that late."

Jamie watched Eight Ball duck inside the car and shut the door. Disgusted, he went back to the other car and waited with Lori. It was another hour before he and Eight Ball left the old barn and headed home. Twenty minutes later, the two of them arrived at Eight Ball's house. The porch light was burning and the silhouettes of numerous people were visible on the window shades.

"Nigguh, you in trouble," Jamie said. "What you brangin' me to yo' house fo'?"

"'Cause thangs won't be so bad if you come in the house with me," Eight replied. "Mama'll take it easy if she see you."

"I ain't goin' in there. I'm goin' home and try to slip in the house without Mama hearin' me. She said she was goin' to bed early to catch up on her sleep. If Aunt Martha ain't called her, she probably don't even know I ain't home yet."

"Don't leave me hangin', cuz," Eight Ball pleaded.

"You done awready hung yo'self. Ain't nothin' I can do 'bout it."

"Nigguh, you ain't right."

"You might as well go'n inside. She can't kill you but once," Jamie said, laughing at the funny expression on Eight Ball's face.

"C'mon in with me and if she actin' too crazy, I'll come back out and give you a ride home."

There was silence.

"Awright, nigguh. Don't say I ain't never done nothin' fo' you," Jamie Ray said. "I don't really wanna walk home this time of night no way."

They climbed the steps and strolled into the living room. Eight Ball's mother sat in her favorite chair with tear-stained eyes, clutching one of his school portraits.

"Thank Gawd almighty!" Eight Ball's brother-in-law exclaimed. "Boy, where you been?"

"In my skin," Eight Ball smarted without hesitation. "When I jump out, you can't jump in."

Eight Ball's mother didn't speak. She sat very still, staring blankly ahead. The fresh tears that welled up in the corner of her eyes and slowly rolled down her face were the only sign she gave acknowledging their presence in the room. Jamie followed Eight Ball through the quiet, tension-filled room and into the kitchen. They sat at the small table crammed next to the wall. Immediately, the door swung open and Eight Ball's mother walked in.

"What you waitin' 'round here fo'?" she snapped.

Sheepishly, Jamie looked around, regretting that he had let Eight Ball talk him into coming in the house.

"Eight Ball say he gon' take me home."

"Mr. Eight Ball ain't steppin' foot outside this house no mo' tonight," she said angrily. "You best hit it. I 'spect you'll make home 'fo sunup."

Stunned, Jamie rose and left the house. He quickly descended the steps and was headed out of the yard, when he heard someone calling his name. He turned and looked back over his shoulder. It was Eight Ball's brother-in-law.

"Hey, hol' up."

Jamie stopped and waited.

"Don't take what happen back there personal," he said. "Martha jus' been scared half to death."

"Yeah, I know."

"Man, she was sho' them white folks had caught y'all with them white gals and strung y'all up somewhere."

Jamie listened. He knew that he was trying to trick him into telling where they had been, but he resolved to say nothing.

"She called me on the phone cryin' and talkin' crazy. She keep sayin' they done got my baby. When I got here, she was still cryin'. Man, we looked all over Pinesboro fo' y'all. And when we couldn't find you, we figured she must've been right."

They were silent.

"Say, you want a ride home?"

"Yeah. I sho' would appreciate it."

They walked over to his car.

"Did Aunt Martha call Mama?" Jamie asked.

"Naw, I don't thank so. She didn't call nobody but me."

When the car pulled to a stop in front of his house, Jamie climbed out, gingerly walked across the porch, put the key in the lock, and slowly opened the door. Inside, all was quiet except the heavy breathing sound his mama made when she was in a deep sleep.

Cautiously, he tiptoed to his room. Stepping out of his clothes, he crawled into bed and pulled the covers up about his neck. For a brief moment, he lay on his back staring at the ceiling wide-eyed. No. He didn't regret meeting Lori, but he shuddered as he thought of what could have happened. He brought his hands together, palm against palm, fingertips against fingertips. "God, thank you fo' watchin' over us," he whispered. Then he rolled over and went to sleep.

C H A P T E R 6

JAMIE walked through the two large double doors that led into the dressing room. He made his way to his locker, removed his jacket, and walked back up front to the laundry bin to get his workout gear.

"Say, man, coach looking for you," the manager said as Jamie approached the laundry bin.

"Awright."

"You might as well go'n now. Your stuff won't be dry for at least ten minutes."

"What he want?"

"How you think I know?"

"Well what he say?"

"He didn't say nothing. He came in here, looked around, then asked if I had seen you. I told 'im you weren't here. Then he told me to tell you he wanted to see you when you got here. Now that's all I know."

"Awright, thanks."

Jamie cut through the equipment room and entered the office through the rear entrance. Coach Terril was sitting with his back to him when he walked in.

"You wanna see me, Coach?"

Startled, Coach Terril turned quickly.

"Yeah, big-un. C'mon around and have a seat."

Jamie sat down in the chair and leaned back.

"Well Jamie, we're really pleased with the leadership you're showing on the field. Son, your attitude is just super."

Jamie smiled.

"Thanks, Coach."

"You're one of the hardest-working kids I've ever coached."

"I'm jus' tryin' to git a little better every day, Coach," Jamie said, feeling the need to say something but not knowing exactly what to say.

"Well, I guess you're wondering why I wanted to see you."

"Yessuh."

Coach Terril took a stack of letters from his desk drawer.

"I've received inquiries about you from some of the most powerful college programs in the country."

"Really?"

"Really." He smiled, warmly. "This is what I have received so far."

He handed the letters to Jamie. Stunned, Jamie silently

read the return address on each one of them: Alabama, LSU, Oklahoma, USC, Nebraska, ULNO, UCLA, Penn State, and Notre Dame.

"Now, they can't officially talk to you yet because you're only a junior. But they can send you these questionnaires. Take them home, fill them out, and send them back as soon as you can."

"I'll fill 'em out tonight," Jamie said enthusiastically.

Terril folded his arms and leaned back in his chair.

"Son, you know we've never had a kid from our program play major college ball before."

"Nosuh. I didn't know that."

"Well, it's true. This is quite an honor for you, this school, and for the community of Pinesboro."

"Yessuh."

"Now, I wanna talk to you before all the madness starts."

"Yessuh."

"Since no representatives can talk to you until next year, I suggest you start thinking about the school that you would like to attend before recruiters start putting pressure on you."

"Yessuh."

"Now, we'd like to see you stay close to home. That way we could support you and we would get to watch you play. I know it's early, but do you have any idea where you would like to go?"

Jamie hesitated.

"Well, I've always dreamed of goin' to UCLA."

There was silence.

"Well, they have a very strong program out there all right, but they also have a lot of competition. Maybe you should think about a program where you would be able to play immediately. Besides, they're really tough academically. What's your grade point average right now?"

Embarrassed, Jamie dropped his eyes and lowered his voice to a dull whisper.

"I don't know exactly. It probably work out to 'bout a strong C."

"Hmm. I suggest you speak to the guidance counselor about the academic requirement for admission to the various schools. That would probably narrow your choices some."

Jamie Ray fought back tears as he sat listening to Coach Terril tell him that he wasn't smart enough to go to certain schools.

"I wish I could have gone to a school like that when I was coming up. But I just wasn't smart enough. I'm not ashamed of it. Now there are a lot of state schools where you could handle the academic burden and play major college football at the same time."

"Yessuh," Jamie mumbled.

"Boy, we'd be tickled to death to see you down at LSU."

He paused, but Jamie didn't respond.

"Well, think about it. We're here if you need us."

"Yessuh."

"Make sure you get those in the mail as soon as you can."

"Yessuh."

"All right, big-un. I'll see you on the field."

The next day, Jamie and Booger sat with their backs against the aluminum math building, trying to stay warm during the noon recess period. The reflection of the November sun off the building made it one of the warmest spots on campus.

"What's botherin' you, J.R.?" Booger asked.

"Nothin'."

"Look here, man. You and me both know that I can jive most of my friends and you can jive most of yo's, but we can't jive each other. So if you don't wanna tell me what's wrong, don't. But don't sit here and tell me ain't nothin' botherin' you, 'cause we both know it is."

Jamie sat quitely for a moment, staring off in the distance.

"You right, Booger. Somethin' is botherin' me."

"What is it?"

"Man, yesterday Terril gave me a stack of letters from colleges that want me to play ball fo' 'em."

"No lie," Booger interrupted enthusiastically.

"Yeah. No lie."

"Hey, man, that's awright," he said, affectionately slapping him on the shoulder. "That oughta make you happy 'stead of sad. Nigguh, yo' dream comin' true."

"Booger, he practically called me a dummy to my face."

"So what?" Booger asked, angrily. "All of 'em thank we a bunch of dumb coons. You know that good as me."

"Yeah, its one thang to know it, but it's somethin' else fo' 'em to tell you to yo' face." Jamie paused. "I don't know. Maybe I jus' misunderstood 'im. Maybe I'm jus' feelin' weird 'cause I know what he said is true. I ain't exactly the smartest person in the world."

"If that's the way you feel, why you lettin' what he say bother you?"

"I guess 'cause I never really thought that other folks thought I was dumb. I guess 'cause I know I really can't go to the schools I wanna go to 'cause I ain't smart enough."

"Nigguh, them college coaches gon' take care of you jus' like these coaches 'round here doin'. 'Long as you keep playin' ball like you is, you can go to school wherever you wanna."

"I guess you right."

"You know I'm right. Have yo' grades stopped 'em from writin' you?"

"Nope."

"And they ain't gonna," Booger said. "Long as you got

somethin' they need, they'll make a way. Boy, white folks somethin' else. If you don't mind bein' used, they sho' don't mind usin' you."

He snapped a blade of grass from the ground and put it in his mouth.

"Booger, what you actin' like you mad at me fo'?"

"It ain't you, man. I'm jus' tired of playin' the game."

"What you talkin' 'bout, Booger?"

"School, man. Ever since we integrated, school ain't been nothin' but a game. You remember at the black school how the teachers at least acted like they cared?"

"Yeah. They were sho' different."

"Here either you do what they want you to or you're out. And if they don't like you, they gon' git rid of you somehow. They gon' call you a troublemaker when you won't follow them stupid rules they made up that ain't got nothin' to do with us nohow. And if they don't expel you, they gon' flunk you. Man, ain't none of these ole white folks interested in teachin' us nothin'. Homeboy, I can't stand this place."

"Booger, I don't like it either. But ain't nothin' we can do 'bout it."

"There's lots of thangs we can do."

"Yeah, like what?"

"Like not take it."

"Man, what choice we got? This whole school system run by white folks. All the teachers white. The principal white and all the school board members white. Booger, it's they school."

"Yeah, that's the problem awright. It's they school, and they don't want us here. And you know what?"

"Naw what?"

"I don't wanna be here."

"Man, you jus' need to cool out and do what it takes."

"Jamie Ray, I'm proud of you fo' comin' over here and

doin' as good as you is. Ain't no doubt about it, you gon' be somebody. But you know good as I do that you and me's different. I can't jus' do it, man. The longer I stay here, the madder I git."

"Man, you jus' gon' have to hang fo' a little while longer."

"Naw, home. I jus' can't stand it no mo'. I done made up my mind. I'm gon' git a job at the sawmill."

"Booger, you talkin' 'bout quittin' school? Man, that's crazy."

"I'm tired. And if I stay here any longer, I'm gon' git in trouble. Besides, I need to help out at home some. I'm ole enough to git a job at the sawmill. I can work there a little while and make enough money to git myself a little ole car."

"You ain't gon' make enough money at that mill to git a decent car no time soon."

"I can't git no new car. But I can git myself a little ole runabout."

"Runabout is right. Runabout a week and quit."

"Well, that beats nothin'. At least then Mama won't have to walk all over the place."

"Mrs. Irene ain't gon' let you quit school."

"I ain't gon' tell her till I got that job and been workin' fo' a while. Then it'll be easier to convince her. Besides, I don't see what the problem is noway. Finish school or not, I'm still gon' work at that mill. So what's the big deal?"

Suddenly Eight Ball walked up.

"What y'all sittin' here hoggin' the heater fo'?"

"Jus' tryin' to stay warm."

"Scoot over, nigguh, and let me squeeze in here." After he sat between them, he opened his civics book and took out a folded piece of paper.

"Say, cuz, yo' girl tol' me to give you this. I thank she wanna hear from you 'fo school's out."

"Awright."

Jamie reached into his coat pocket and took out a piece of paper similar to the one Eight Ball had handed him.

"This's fo' you."

"My girl!"

Booger sat quietly watching as the two of them unfolded the letters and silently read the contents. Jamie's eyes shifted back and forth across the paper.

Hey,

   The more time I spend with you, the more time I want to spend with you. I love you like I have never loved anyone before. I thought about you all night long. Sometime I hate that it's so difficult for us to get together. I don't want to wait until this weekend to see you. You guys talk it over and maybe we can get together tonight. Try to let me know before fifth period.

   Oh, do you know that in two days we will have been liking each other for six months? I'm so excited. You better be too. (smile) I hope we can get together soon. Always remember that there is a very special lady who loves you with all her heart.

Love Ya

Jamie finished reading the letter and put it in his jacket pocket.

"J.R., you gon' mess 'round here and blow yo' chance to be somebody," Booger said.

"What you talkin' 'bout, Booger?"

"You know good and well what I'm talkin' 'bout."

"Naw I don't. Man, we tight, but we ain't so tight that I can read yo' mind."

"Them white girls," Booger said, angrily. "That's what I'm talkin' 'bout. Homeboy, soon as one of yo' coaches find out what you doin', they gon' drop some change on you. And then it ain't gon' be long 'fo all them big-time schools gon' be talkin' 'bout you got a attitude problem or some crap like that. Then, ain't none of 'em gon' touch you with a ten-foot pole."

Eight Ball interrupted.

"What make you thank he foolin' 'round with white girls?"

"He hangin' 'round with you, ain't he?"

"What make you thank I'm messin' 'round with 'em?"

"Nigguh, don't play me fo' no fool. I don't know why you thank you gotta have massa's daughter when there's plenty sisters 'round here. But that ain't none of my business. Sooner or later somebody gon' git hurt and it's probably gon' be you, yo' mama, and everybody else that care 'bout you."

Jamie intentionally changed the subject.

"Say, cuz, I got my first recruit letters yesterday."

"Fo' real?"

"Yeah, man."

"What schools?"

"ULNO, LSU, Alabama, USC, UCLA, Penn State, Oklahoma, Nebraska, and Notre Dame."

"Man, that's awright. You on yo' way. You tol' Lori yet?"

"Naw, man. I jus' found out 'bout 'em yesterday."

"Hey, you oughta tell her. She'll be happy fo' you. Ain't no tellin' what she might give you next time you see her."

"Lori who?" Booger asked.

Jamie hesitated.

"Booger, you ain't gon' tell nobody, is you?"

"Man, you know you ain't gotta ask me that."

"Lori Crowe," Jamie confessed.

In the distance the bell sounded.

"Jamie Ray, jus' remember what I tol' you," Booger said, rising to his feet. "Don't mess yo' life up foolin' 'round with Eight Ball. Them white folks is all over you now, but if you mess 'round and git on they list, they gon' go 'round you like a bad spot in the road."

CHAPTER 7

E A R L Y one Friday night, during the summer before his senior year, Jamie received a frantic call from Lori. She said she had something important to tell him, but she couldn't go into it over the phone. Worried, Jamie borrowed Booger's old car and drove out to meet her. Everything was going so well between them, he thought as he drove. What could she possibly want?

When he entered the barn, Lori was standing in the corner. Both her eyes and nose were red. She had been crying.

Jamie hurried to her side and took her in his arms.

"Lori, what's wrong?"

She pulled away, walked to the door and peeped out.

"Didn't anybody see you, did they?"

"No. What's wrong?"

She looked at him with fear in her eyes.

"Jamie, we can't see each other anymore." Her words caught him by surprise.

"Why?"

"It's not safe anymore."

"What happened? Did somebody find out about us?"

"Not about us," she explained. "But I think some people know about Eight Ball and Cindy."

"What people? Lori, what's goin' on?"

"I don't know who all knows. But last night I heard my father talking about Thursday night's Klan meeting. He said they talked about killing some colored boy this coming Saturday to make an example out of him."

Jamie wrinkled his forehead.

"What boy?"

"He didn't say."

"Well, how you know they was talkin' 'bout Eight Ball?"

"Because the black boy they were talking about was fooling around with his boss's daughter."

"Lori, that could be anybody."

"Jamie, how many people do you know around here that description applies to? They were talking about Eight Ball and Cindy."

"You don't know that fo' sho'."

"I can't prove that's who they were talking about. But I'm pretty sure."

"How sho'?"

"Sure enough not to take any more chances." Suddenly her face became serious. "Jamie, those people don't play."

"You act like you know 'em personally," he snapped.

"I do," she acknowledged. "And so do you."

"What you mean?"

"Just that you'd be surprised at who-all's in the Klan."

"Who?" Jamie asked. "Name some names."

"I can't. But take my word for it, you know a lot of them. What you don't know is how dangerous they are. Jamie, please talk to Eight Ball and tell him to stay out of sight for a while. Maybe he could even leave town for a few days."

"I'll talk to 'im."

"Jamie, I better go now." She walked to the barn door and peeked out. All was clear. "Wait about five minutes before you leave," she whispered, "just in case we're being watched."

"Okay," Jamie said walking over and taking her hand. "Be careful."

"Jamie, I'm really gonna miss you," she moaned softly. "Could you just hold me for a minute?"

As Jamie embraced her, she laid her head against his chest and for a few minutes the two of them held each other in silence.

"I wish things could be different," she whispered, pushing arm's length away from him. "But they can't. And I couldn't live with myself if something bad happened to you because of me." Lori paused and turned away. "I better go."

"Lori," Jamie mumbled softly, as she pushed the door open. "I'll be thankin' about you."

Lori hurried through the barn door, climbed into her car, and drove away. Jamie watched the red taillights become more and more dim until they disappeared into the night. He paced back and forth across the barn floor until he thought it was safe to leave. Then he got in, drove through the bumpy field, and turned on to the dark desolate road back to town. Through the rearview mirror, he saw two headlights approaching at a high rate of speed. Jamie pulled to the shoulder of the road, slowed slightly, and checked the mirror again.

"C'mon by, fool," he said half aloud.

To his dismay, the car behind him pulled close and slowed. The driver was a middle-aged white man that Jamie had never seen before. What was he doing? Jamie felt his heart leap from his chest to the center of his throat. He wasn't sure what to do. Should he speed up or continue along at a slow pace? He tightened his grip on the steering wheel and gently pressed his foot against the accelerator. As the car picked up speed, his mind began to wander. Maybe the man had seen Lori leave the barn ahead of him? If he had, then maybe he knew what was going on. Jamie checked the mirror again. The man was still behind him. Maybe he was following him. Jamie's mind spun with frightening thoughts. He pressed the pedal even more. Dust from the unpaved road filled the air and he could no longer see behind him. Jamie was certain that he was being chased. Suddenly his car tires hit a pothole. The collision jerked the steering wheel from his hand and the vehicle began to skid out of control. Frantically, Jamie wrestled the vehicle to a screeching stop just as the front right wheel rolled off the road and slid into the drainage ditch.

Behind him, the dust cleared. The other car was no longer in sight. He must have turned off somewhere, Jamie thought. Somewhat relieved, he chuckled nervously, slowly backed the car into the road, and headed home. He drove, looking at the dark road unfolding in front of him one minute and at the rearview mirror the next. "Aw, I'm jus' bein' paranoid," he said out loud, desperately trying to reassure himself. "I'm Jamie Ray Griffin. Ain't nobody gon' bother me."

It was three o'clock the next day before Jamie had a chance to talk to Eight Ball. They sat on an abandoned car in Eight Ball's backyard.

"Mama said you been callin' me all day. What's wrong?"

"Maybe a lot. Maybe nothin'."

"Awright, cuz, what's up?"

"Man, I met Lori out at the barn last night."

Eight Ball smiled.

"How'd you git out there?"

"I drove Booger's ole car."

"If you drove that old jalopy out there, you must've really wanted to see her."

"Hey, she called me at the house and tol' me she had somethin' to tell me that couldn't wait."

"So what she want?"

"She said we shouldn't see each other no mo'. Man, she thank the Klan gon' try to kill you."

Eight Ball threw his head back and laughed.

"Nigguh, I ain't thankin' 'bout no Klan."

"Maybe we should cool it with these girls fo' a little while. You know, lay low—jus' in case there's somethin' to what she say."

"Cuz, you do whatever you thank's right fo' you and I'll do what's right fo' me. But I can tell you now, it ain't never gon' be right fo' me to let nobody besides my mama tell me what to do. And most of the time I don't even let her tell me."

"So you gon' jus' keep on seein' Cindy like ain't nothin' happened?"

"Nothin' ain't happened as far as I'm concerned. I'll stop seein' her when she don't wanna see me no mo'; but not until."

"What about Aunt Martha?" Jamie pleaded. "What she gon' do if somethin' happen to you?"

"Ain't nothin' gon' happen to me. And I ain't 'bout to let nobody scare me outta doin' what I wanna do."

"Eight, you talkin' crazy."

"Naw, cuz. You jus' don't understand. It's awready too many folks 'round here playin' it safe and stayin' in they place 'cause they scared of white folks. But the way I got it figured, if a man's scared to live, he might as well die."

"I guess ain't nothin' I can say to talk some sense in yo' head," Jamie sighed.

"Nope. It ain't, 'cause I figure I'm makin' sense."

"Man, jus' be careful," Jamie warned.

"You ever knowed me to be anythang but careful?"

"When you plannin' on seein' Cindy again?"

"We gon' hook up later on tonight."

Their conversation was interrupted. Eight Ball's mother yelled to him from inside the house.

"Eight Ball! Mr. Anderson jus' called here fo' you."

"What he want?" Eight Ball asked, disgusted.

"He wantin' you to work a couple hours tonight."

"Tonight! It's Saturday."

"He said he'd pay you time and a half fo' a few hours' work. He apologized, but said it was jus' some thangs he had to have done tonight."

"What kinda thangs?"

"Boy, I done tol' you all I know now."

"Man, I don't like this," Jamie said, his face marred with concern.

"J.R. I swear, you too young to worry much as you do."

"I jus' got a bad feelin', that's all."

"Bad feelin' or not, I'm fixin' to go up yonder and git that time and a half." Eight Ball smiled.

Eight Ball's mother stuck her head out of the back door.

"Eight Ball, you better c'mon in here and git ready to go. You don't wanna keep them folks waitin'."

Five minutes after Eight Ball left, Jamie became extremely restless. He couldn't shake the feeling that something was wrong. He decided to ride his bike by the Andersons' house just to make sure everything was fine.

Bill Anderson lived more than a mile away, on an isolated dirt road. As Jamie pedaled along the street, the muscles in his stomach began to tighten. He thought about Eight Ball being alone with Bill Anderson. He turned down the old dirt road that ran in front of the Andersons' house and began trying to formulate a plan just in case Eight Ball was in trouble.

When he was close enough to walk, Jamie stepped off his bike and laid it down in the drainage ditch that ran beside the road. From where he stood, he could see the house clearly. All was quiet. In fact, no one seemed to be home. All of the lights were out and the only vehicle in the yard was Eight Ball's two-tone car. He decided to walk closer and try to get a glimpse of what was going on or maybe even speak to Eight Ball.

Jamie reached the house and his feelings of fear mounted. He tiptoed into the yard and walked to the side. Quietly he crept to the back and peeped around the corner. Surprised to see people, he quickly drew his head back, collected himself, and peeped again. He saw a small group of white men sitting in a semicircle. Eight Ball was sitting on a tree stump next to Bill Anderson. Jamie could see them, but he couldn't hear what they were saying.

Cautiously, he dropped to his knees and slid under the house. With forearms on the ground and head held low, Jamie crawled to the opposite side and positioned himself behind one of the cement blocks that the house sat on. Now he was no more than fifteen feet away from them. He could hear them clearly, but his view from underneath the house was fringed by the slowly deepening dusk. Jamie shifted his weight, relaxed, and listened intently.

"We need to git that critter problem solved before Monday," he heard Mr. Anderson say.

Critters? Jamie thought. What in the world were they talking about? Something bothering Mr. Anderson's livestock? He closed his eyes tightly, concentrating on their words.

"Problem seems worse around here than anywhere else," Mr. Anderson continued. "A few of the neighbors say they spotted a critter or two around here the other night, but I ain't had no luck in finding hide nor hair of 'em. I don't know what to do."

Don't know what to do? Jamie thought. Ain't but one thing to do, and that's to set some traps. But they know that as good as anybody.

Bill Anderson looked at Eight Ball with quizzical eyes.

"What do you think, Eight Ball?"

"Well, Mr. Anderson, if it only hits at night, look to me like you need to set some traps," Eight Ball said nonchalantly.

"What kind of traps you figure we gon' need?"

"Well, suh, you got any idea what you tryin' to catch?" Anderson hesitated slightly.

"Yeah, I got a pretty good idea."

"What's that, suh?" Eight Ball asked.

Mr. Anderson straightened up and said angrily, "The nigger that's trying to hump my daughter." He stared at Eight Ball. "And look to me like we done already caught him."

Startled, Jamie's body stiffened. His heart pounded and his breath became short. The tightness in his stomach began to burn. He lay very still, watching as Eight Ball leaped from the stump and sprinted toward his car. Cautiously, Jamie eased to the edge of the house and peeped out. He saw Eight Ball turn the corner. Three white men were standing in the front yard, waiting. Jamie's eyes followed Eight Ball as he turned quickly and ran toward the nearby woods.

He saw Eight Ball race forward ten yards, then turn and look. The men following him weren't running; they were walking at a very brisk pace. Jamie watched intently, as Eight Ball slowed as he approached the woods. He froze completely as a mob of white men emerged from the trees armed with guns, knives, and clubs. Now Eight Ball was surrounded. He was trapped between them and they were slowly closing in on him. For a few seconds, Eight Ball stood spinning, looking, trying to figure out which way to go.

"We got you, nigger."

"It's all over, boy."

Suddenly Eight Ball dashed west toward the road in front of the house. But before he had run ten yards, two other men on horseback appeared, positioning themselves between himself and his escape. Seeming to realize that there was no place to run or hide, Eight Ball stopped and awaited his fate. The men, yelling and cheering, walked slowly toward him until they had him completely enclosed within arm's reach. Jamie looked on, terrified. He was afraid to move or speak.

"We got him now!"

"Grab him!"

A man carrying a rifle stepped forward.

"Uppity nigger."

He swung, striking Eight Ball in the face with the butt of his rifle. Eight Ball's head jerked back, his knees buckled, and blood began trickling from high on his cheekbone.

"Gawddammit, don't mark up his face."

The men holding him yanked him up straight.

"Let's take him to Bill."

"C'mon, boy, move."

They dragged Eight Ball to Bill Anderson, who still sat poised in the spot he had occupied before Eight Ball had fled.

"Take him over to that tree," he ordered dryly.

Four of them lifted him from the ground. Eight Ball was struggling, squirming, twisting. But he fought in vain. They had him stretched horizontally between them with a man on each limb of his body.

A fifth man approached carrying a short piece of wood.

"Be still, nigger, or we gon' have to get rough with you."

Suddenly he raised the wood high above his head and brought it down across Eight Ball's chest. Eight Ball screamed. The force of the blow shattered his rib cage. Several small bones tore through the skin on the right side of his body.

Jamie cringed. His heart began to pound rapidly. His whole body began to shake. He thought of going to get help, but he was too scared to move. There were too many of them. If he left his hiding place they would catch him for sure. In spite of his fear, he continued to watch. He saw them push Eight Ball against the tree, pull his arms and legs around behind the trunk, and tie them tightly. Then, while one held Eight Ball's head steady, another one took a piece of rope and wrapped it twice, tying his head back.

"That's got him.

"Get the cane, boys."

Jamie watched them walk to a small shed, arm themselves with dried sugarcane stalks, and walk back. Bill Anderson moved a stool in front of Eight Ball's bound body and sat down. He held a sharpening stone in his left hand and a large bowie knife in his right.

"Boy, what you got to say for yourself?"

Eight Ball swallowed, but didn't answer.

141

"Well, it wouldn't make no difference nohow."

He spit on the stone and began sharpening the knife. Wide-eyed, Eight Ball watched him slowly move the knife from the left side of the stone to the right, flip it, place the opposite side of the blade on the stone, and bring it from the right side to the left. After what seemed an eternity, Bill Anderson laid the stone aside and turned to one of the men.

"Go in the house and get Cindy."

Jamie surveyed the group as best he could from his position under the house. Events had happened so quickly that at first he could not identify any of the mob. But now he was surprised by the number of faces he recognized.

"Is this the nigger you been shaming the family with?" Bill Anderson growled as Cindy stood watching the blood ooze from Eight Ball's body.

"Daddy, we're just friends," she shouted hysterically. "Please don't do this. Oh God! Don't do this."

"Just friends!" Bill Anderson repeated bitterly. He reached into his pocket and slowly removed a folded piece of white paper.

"A letter," Jamie whispered.

"You recognize this?" Bill Anderson snapped.

Tears began streaming down Cindy's face.

"Daddy, we're just friends," she insisted.

"Your mother found this in your drawer. Do you know the shame she felt when the neighbors told her that you been running around with one of our niggers? One of their daughters said you been carrying on like some kind of fool—leaving notes in that boy's locker almost every day."

"No, daddy. That ain't true."

"Yeah it is. And this here proves it."

"Daddy, that note is from another friend of mine."

Bill Anderson frowned angrily.

"Don't you stand there and bring more shame on yourself and this family, lying to protect this stinking nigger. Don't you think I know this boy's scribbling as many times as I've seen it around here? Don't you dare lie to me." He crumpled the paper and threw it down. "I shouldn't've never trusted no nigger. They're all the same."

"Daddy, I swear before God almighty I'm telling the truth."

Bill Anderson turned to Eight Ball.

"Boy! We gon' teach you what happens when you forget the difference between white folks and niggers."

"No!" Cindy rushed forward.

Bill Anderson grabbed her and pushed her away.

"Have at him, boys."

As the men rushed forward with the sugarcane stalks, Eight Ball's eyes widened and his body stiffened. He tried to struggle against the ropes, but he couldn't. He could only move his eyes and mouth.

Jamie swallowed hard and began praying.

"Please Gawd, help us."

The first man reached him, drew back the cane, and brought it forward. There was a high-pitched whistling sound as the stalk cut through the air. Eight Ball's body flinched. The cane struck his already broken rib cage. A second blow. Eight Ball grunted, his trembling body arched, and his eyes became fiery red.

Again Cindy lunged forward, screaming.

"Stop it! Stop it!"

Two men grabbed her. She fought desperately, but they threw her to the ground, restraining her.

Now the vicious blows came faster, one on top of the other. Suddenly Eight Ball's arms and legs were twitching, jerking. He began spitting up large quantities of blood. His eyes rolled back in his head. He began passing in and out of consciousness, his mind instinctively trying to escape the unending torture.

Bill Anderson rose to his feet.

"That's enough!"

He moved next to Eight Ball and held the razor-sharp knife up to his face. Then he touched the edge of the blade with his thumb, mumbling, "Nigger, you got any last words as a man before I make you a woman?"

Cindy grabbed her father's legs.

"No, Daddy!" she begged. "Please don't!"

He looked down, infuriated.

"Somebody get her back."

Eight Ball's lower lip trembled as he struggled to gain control over the muscles in his mouth. Slowly, his bottom lip met his top. His jaws inflated. His eyes blinked and his eyebrows arched. Then, just as it appeared he was going to speak, he spat a mixture of blood and saliva into Bill Anderson's face. Instantly, the corners of his mouth turned up, forming a deviant smile.

Enraged, Bill Anderson wiped the spittle from his face. Then, using the back of his right hand, he leveled a vicious blow to the right side of Eight Ball's head. He pulled Eight Ball's pants down to his ankles, grabbed his testicles with his left hand, and squeezed them until his scrotum appeared ready to pop. Then, with one quick motion, he slid his razor-sharp knife down the right side of Eight Ball's scrotum. There was a faint popping sound as the right testicle fell from the sac. Eight Ball winced, as the pain raced from his loin to his head.

"Daddy!" Cindy wailed.

Behind her, the mob began to cheer.

Quickly, Bill Anderson sliced open the left side of the scrotum. Now both of Eight Ball's testicles hung, dangling. Bill Anderson grabbed both of them with one hand, pulled them tight, and then he slowly pulled the knife through the thin layer of flesh that held them in place. Both testicles came off in his hand.

The men cheered louder.

Cindy's screams became shriller.

Moving like a man possessed, Bill Anderson grabbed Eight Ball's uncircumcised penis by the loose foreskin and stretched it tight. He then raised the bloody knife above his head, and brought it down across Eight Ball's penis. Blood spewed out as it was sliced off at the base.

Cindy rose to her knees.

"No! No! No!" she screamed uncontrollably.

Suddenly her whole body was trembling. She covered her eyes with her hands. Her face turned pale white and her stomach's contents poured from her mouth.

Bill Anderson drove the bloody knife into the tree.

"Cut him down."

Several men rushed forward. While they worked, Bill Anderson went to his truck, got his rifle, and returned.

"Is the nigger dead?"

A man pressed his head against Eight Ball's chest.

"Not yet! Nigger still got a heartbeat."

"Pull his pants up."

Bill Anderson stood over Eight Ball's bloody body. He raised the gun to eye level, aimed, and fired. Eight Ball grunted. His body jerked. The bullet lodged in his chest. Anderson fired again. Eight Ball's legs twitched. The bullet ripped through his castrated groin. His body lay still, motionless.

Bill Anderson lowered the gun to his side.

"Ain't nothing I like better than the sound of a high-powered rifle and the groaning of a dying nigger." He barked out his final instructions. "Men, take the body in the house and lay it in the front corridor. I gotta call the police and report the accidental shooting of a burglar."

145

ERNEST HILL

The men carried Eight Ball's body into the house and they all left. Minutes later, Sheriff Dearborn arrived and went inside. Still lying under the house, paralyzed with fear, Jamie could hear them walking on the floor above him. He didn't know if he should try to sneak away while they were all in the house or wait until they had left. Before he had made a decision, Sheriff Dearborn and Bill Anderson came outside and walked to the tree where the murder had taken place. Jamie tensed up again as the fear of discovery gripped his consciousness.

The sheriff looked at the blood-soaked ground.

"Gawddammit, Bill. You really made it hard on me this time. Clean this blood up, before anybody sees it. And burn anything that could raise suspicion. Chances are won't nobody snoop around back here. But if they do, they sure as hell better not find anything."

Bill Anderson slapped him on the back.

"Don't worry about it, Glen. I'll get that old water hose from under the edge of the house and wash it down back here. Everything'll be fine. My story's airtight. As long as you don't panic, there won't be no trouble."

Jamie could feel his heart pounding in his chest as Bill Anderson walked toward him. Instinctively, he curled up into a tight ball and lay very still. Wide-eyed, Jamie watched Bill Anderson bend down on his knees, reach under the edge of the house, and grope for the hose. Petrified, Jamie placed his fist in his mouth, bit down on his knuckles, and held his breath. He watched Bill Anderson's hairy, pale white hand pass within twelve inches of his body.

"Gawddammit, Bill, hurry up," Sheriff Dearborn called angrily. "This whole thing's making me nervous."

Standing quickly, Bill Anderson marched over to the faucet, turned it on, and began washing away all the signs of the crime. Soon the ground was saturated and Jamie watched the bloody water run under the house and seep underneath his tightly curled body. He had a keen desire to move to a drier spot, but he was afraid to move. Bill Anderson might hear him.

When he had finished, he doubled the end of the hose in his hand, momentarily cutting off the water. He surveyed the area, smiled, and mumbled:

"Clean as a whistle."

He dropped the hose, turned off the water, and hurried inside. There was a sudden quiet. Jamie crawled slowly back to the opposite side of the house. There was nobody in sight. Again he had an urge to get up and run, but as before, fear gripped his legs and they refused to move. He waited. Minutes passed. He listened intently, then decided to leave. He poked his head out and looked around. Through the moonlit night he surveyed the path he would take. He braced himself ready, then lunged from his hiding place into the open. He stood. His knees were stiff and his feet were numb.

Slowly, he scuffled along the side of the house. He stopped at the front corner. Suppose someone was looking out of the window? What would happen if they saw him? He had to chance it; he couldn't stay here any longer. Fearfully, he fixed his eyes on the ditch. Between him and it stood open space. Jamie realized that he would have only the cover of darkness to shield himself from the eyes of the enemy. He tried to swallow, but he couldn't. His throat was dry.

Inside the house he heard feet moving. He crouched, sunk his teeth into his lower lip, lowered his head, and ran toward the drainage ditch. Now he measured each step with short, quick breaths. When he thought he was close, he leaped forward, landing facedown on the hard, sun-dried ditch bottom. He pulled himself along on his belly and kept his eyes straight ahead. Slowly he made his way to the bicycle he had hidden earlier.

Suddenly a thought pierced his consciousness. What if someone saw him riding along the old road? He stopped. His muscles flexed taut. There would be no way he could explain his presence. His brain groped for alternatives. He could go the long route through the woods to the main road. His mind drifted back to Eight Ball and he remembered the mob that had been hiding in the woods. The thought jarred him back to a sharp sense of danger. He moved forward. He was close now. He could see the light from the moon reflecting off his bicycle. Once on the bike, everything would be okay. In a little while he would be safe. He would be at home, away from this terrible nightmare. His thoughts shifted to Eight Ball again. If only he had listened. If only he had stayed home tonight like he told him.

Nervously, he lifted the bike out of the ditch, leaped into the seat, and headed home, pedaling frantically until he came to the paved highway. Then he went slower. Home was close now. He could see the railroad tracks. He crossed them and within seconds he was traveling downhill. He sped by Papa's and stood as he turned the bike into the large open field behind his house. Then within seconds, he passed through his backyard, rode around front, and leaped off the bike onto the porch. Panting and his eyes stinging with perspiration, he pushed through the door.

It was ten o'clock. His mother was sitting in her favorite rocker, mending a pair of his pants and watching the news.

"Boy what's the matter with you? Why you slammin' that do' like you crazy?"

She looked up at him and her face hardened. She stared at his soiled clothes.

"What you been doin' got yo' clothes lookin' like that? Lawd knows I ain't able to keep cleanin' and patchin' yo' thangs."

Jamie said nothing. He sat on the floor and buried his head in his hands.

"Jamie Ray, don't you hear me talkin' to you?"

There was silence. He raised his head and rubbed his long black fingers through his hair. Tears began to fall from his eyes.

"Mama, they killed Eight Ball."

Her eyes grew wide.

"Killed?"

"Yes ma'am."

"Somebody killed Eight Ball!"

"Yes ma'am."

Her eyes narrowed to thin slits of disbelief.

"You talkin' 'bout my sister's boy?"

"Yes ma'am."

"Who killed 'im?"

"White folks."

"What white folk?"

"Bill Anderson and a heap of other white folks."

"Who tol' you that?"

"Mama, I seen it with my own eyes. I was under the house when it happened."

"What house?"

"Bill Anderson's house."

"My Lawd, boy, what was y'all doin' up to that man's house?"

"He called over to Aunt Martha's fo' Eight Ball to come work tonight. That didn't sound right to me so I went up yonder to make sho' everything was awright. When I got there, they was sittin' 'round talkin'. So I slipped under the house so I could hear. That's when Bill Anderson accused Eight Ball of foolin' 'round with his daughter."

"Good Gawd almighty! That boy oughta had mo' sense than git hisself tangled up with a white gal."

"Mama, they beat 'im and cut his thang off. Then Bill Anderson shot 'im twice."

"Then what happened?"

"They took 'im in the house and the police came."

"The police?"

"Yes ma'am."

"Lawd Gawd in heaven have mercy on us, this is mo' trouble than I know what to do with."

She got up, went to the window, and peeped out. She checked all the doors and windows to make sure they were secure. Moving frantically, she turned off all the lights inside the house. Then she switched on a small night-light that cast off a dull orange glow.

"Jamie Ray, how long ago all this happen?"

"'Bout two hours ago, I guess."

"Did any of 'em see you?"

"No ma'am. I waited under the house till they all left."

"You sho' didn't nobody see you?"

"Yes ma'am, I'm sho'."

She sat down and began nervously wringing her hands. Her eyes, cloudy and frightened, stared into the dimly lit room.

"Jamie Ray, you ain't foolin' 'round with no white gal, is you?"

"No ma'am," Jamie lied.

"Jus' 'cause you go to school with 'em don't mean you can fool with 'em."

"Mama, I know that."

"Son, I pray to Gawd you do."

There was silence. Jamie searched her face for answers.

"Mama, what we gon' do 'bout Eight Ball?"

She sighed.

"Let it be. Ain't nothin' nobody can do 'bout it now."

Jamie looked at her strangely.

"But, Mama, I seen 'em. I seen all of 'em."

Suddenly, his mother sat up straight and her eyes became icy cold. "Jamie Ray, fo' Gawd's sake, don't you tell a livin' soul 'bout this. White folks come into knowledge you seed what they did, they'll kill you fo' sho'."

"Mama, I gotta tell Aunt Martha what happened."

"What good gon' come from tellin' her? Ain't nothin' she or nobody else 'round here can do. You can't brang that child back now and ain't no sense you gittin' yo'self strung up fo' nothin'. You understand me?"

"Yes ma'am."

"Nobody but the good Lawd can help Martha now."

Jamie let out a deep sigh.

"It jus' don't seem right to let 'em git away with this."

"I didn't say it was right," his mother said, looking deeply into his eyes and folding his hands in hers. "Baby, you learned somethin' today that you was bound to learn sooner or later. Colored folks and white folks is got a different station in this here world. You got to always respect that. 'Cause if you don't, ain't nothin' but bad thangs gon' happen."

She paused and tightened her grip on Jamie's hand.

"Lawd, it's times like this that I wish yo' daddy was still livin'. Best thang fo' you to do is go'n 'bout yo' business like you ain't seed a thang."

Jamie thought over her words.

"I'm supposed to go'n back to that school and play fo' that murderer?"

"What murderer?"

"Coach Terril. That murderer. He was one of the men up to Mr. Anderson's house."

"Good Gawd almighty."

She went to the window a second time and peeped out. Coach Terril's name rekindled her sense of danger. "Lawd, I knowed somethin' like this was gon' happen sooner or later. That boy jus' got too much beside hisself," she said, pacing back and forth across the small living room floor. "You jus' can't go 'round makin' no fool outta white folks and 'spect to git away with it." Turning her attention back to Jamie she said, "Son, jus' bear down and make out as best you can. Maybe one day thangs'll be different. But that day ain't come yet."

Jamie was angered and ashamed of their cowardice. He understood his mother and shared her fears, but there was still some element in him that wanted to act, that wanted to avenge Eight Ball's death. There was a sinking feeling in his stomach and he had a deep desire to be alone.

"Mama, I'm tired, I'm goin' to bed."

"Awright, baby. May the Lawd give us strength to face tomorrow." Her voice faded into a whisper.

Jamie went into his bedroom, undressed, and climbed into the softness of the bed. For nearly an hour, he tossed in the dark room, trying to purge himself of the haunting images thronging his mind. Then he fell asleep, only to have a dream that he would continue to dream for the next several months. He was back in Bill Anderson's backyard, but Bill Anderson, not Eight Ball, was tied to the tree. All the white people that were there during Eight Ball's murder were still there. But instead of them being the murderers, they were the victims. They lay on the ground in one huge bloody heap. Some dead, others dying and moaning their last sounds of life. Jamie stood in front of a battered, dying Bill Anderson, holding a knife in his hand. Just as Bill Anderson began to beg and plead for mercy, he whacked off his penis. Then Jamie beat him with a club until he died. Sometime the person in Jamie's dream tied to the tree was not Bill Anderson but a faceless white man. But the dream always ended the same.

The next morning Jamie was awakened by a knock on the door. Tired and restless, he sat in bed listening. He could hear his mother talking.

"Who is it?"

"It's me, Henrietta. Irene Mitchel."

Mrs. Griffin opened the door.

"How you feelin' this mornin', Irene?"

"I'm doin' fairly," she said absently. "And yo'self?"

"Aw, I'm makin' out," she replied. "Come on in and sat down."

Jamie heard the door open and feet walking across the floor. Suddenly all of his attention was focused on the voices in the other room. Irene lived next to Aunt Martha and he knew the reason for her early morning visit.

"Irene, what got you out so early this mornin'?" his mother asked. "Anythang wrong?"

Mrs. Mitchel was silent a moment, then said softly, "Well, Henrietta, I'm afraid so." She paused and sighed deeply. "Yo' sister's oldest boy got killed last night."

Jamie heard his mother groan.

"My Gawd no! What happened?"

"Well, the way it was tol' to me, old man Bill Anderson seed the boy in the house and took 'im fo' a burglar. Say he shot 'im two times. They tell me he actin' real to' up over killin' the boy."

"Wonder what that child doin' in that man's house?"

"Don't rightly know. But you know a lotta the colored folks say he was slippin' 'round up yonder tryin' to court that gal of Bill Anderson's."

"What the law say 'bout it?"

"Martha say the sheriff tol' her that the whole thang was a accident and they wasn't gon' take out no charges against old man Anderson."

There was silence.

"Well, how Martha holdin' out?"

"She ain't takin' it too good. You know how crazy she was 'bout that boy."

"Lawd, I better try to git some clothes on and go be what comfort I can to her."

"I'm goin' back over yonder myself. You want me to wait fo' you?"

"Naw, you go'n. I'll be over there directly."

"Awright. If I can be any help to you or yo' family jus' let me know."

"I sho' will. Thank you fo' comin' by."

After she left, Jamie entered the room frowning deeply.

"Lying white folks always stick together. It jus' don't seem right to sit by and let 'em git away with this."

His mother gazed at him. Her face looked tired and drained.

"Son, what can you do?" she snapped. "It'll be yo' word 'gainst ole man Anderson. Who you thank they gon' believe?"

He didn't answer. He went to the window and stared out into the street. After a moment, she moved beside him and began to gently caress his hand.

"Jamie Ray, like I tol' you last night, it's best you jus' fo'git the whole thang."

They were both silent. He knew she was waiting for him to speak. The sinking feeling in his stomach returned and he felt as though his whole world had been torn apart. But he realized that there was no point in arguing further.

"I guess you right," he said softly.

She looked at him sternly.

"Jamie Ray, ain't no guess to it. I'm right and you gon' do what I say."

"Yes ma'am."

"Now, I'm gon' go tend to Martha. Lawd knows that chil' gon' need all the strength she can git."

On the day of the funeral, Jamie sat next to Booger in the front of the church, staring aimlessly at Eight Ball's coffin as Reverend McCall began his sermon.

"To the family of the deceased. I know that right now the road seems a little rocky. I know this is hard to understand. But be not dismayed. My God got it all worked out. You got to trust 'im. He's too wise to question. Too perfect to doubt. Too merciful to be cruel. He ain't never made a mistake. And you got to trust he ain't made one now. Young Harris is in God's hands.

"In these difficult times jus' take comfort in the fact that while young Harris lived, Jesus was with him. And now that he done passed on, he's with Jesus. My heavenly father got it all worked out."

"Amen, Reverend."

Reverend McCall turned way from the family and now addressed the entire church.

"Sometimes death may be hard to understand, but it ain't never complicated. Death ain't nothin' but a passport to life. Fo' any of us can git to heaven, we's all got to pass death's way."

"Amen."

"I don't feel no need to preach no funeral fo' young Harris now. He done awready lived his funeral. I don't know 'bout you, church, but I can't be sad right now. Of course, like everybody who knowed 'im, I'm gon' miss his company. His kind words and his friendly smile. But once I git past my own selfish feelin', I can't help but be happy."

"He in heaven now. He won't cry no mo'."

A big smile spread across Reverend McCall's face.

"Church, knowin' there ain't no tears in heaven jus' makes me happy. Can you imagine a land where you never cry, where you never grow ole? Where you never git tired. Where there ain't no mo' misery and ain't no mo' pain. Oh what a place!"

"Amen, Reverend!"

"Hallelujah!"

Reverend McCall stepped away from the pulpit, paused, and placed his hands together.

"Church, how I'm gon' be sad 'bout bein' in a place where it's always howdy, howdy, and never good-bye? Soon as I see Jesus, I'm gon' thank 'im fo' lettin' me git over. I'm gon' walk me some streets of gold, I'm gon' take a seat in the New Jerusalem, I'm gon' sing and shout. Oh! Glory hallelujah. I'm so glad I got religion."

For the next forty-five minutes, Reverend McCall talked about heaven and urged all those present who didn't know the Lord to get right. Then after he sat down, Jamie watched the undertaker remove the flowers from the coffin, open the lid, and slowly elevate Eight Ball's head.

Jamie heard his aunt wail.

"My baby!"

Suddenly tears began streaming down his face. He sat motionless as scores of people filed by the coffin. Then it was his turn. Rising slowly, he walked up to the coffin and stood paralyzed, staring at Eight Ball. His face was slightly darker than normal, but otherwise he looked as though he was in a deep sleep.

"Why didn't you be careful like I tol' you?" he whispered to the corpse. He reached into the coffin and, taking Eight Ball's cold, hard hand, he softly whispered, "I'm sorry, cuz, I'm so sorry. What I'm supposed to do without you, man?" he asked as warm, salty tears flowed into his mouth. "I'm gon' miss you."

Booger walked up and placed his arms around Jamie's shoulders. "C'mon, J.R., you gotta let 'im go."

Jamie laid Eight Ball's hand back in place, kissed him on the cheek, mumbling softly: "Rest in peace, cuz."

Jamie's entire body shook as he tried to balance himself on his unstable legs. He laid his head on Booger's shoulder and the two of them made their way back to their seats.

They both sat silently watching as people continued to file by the coffin. Jamie's emotions were confused. He felt angry, sad, and guilty all at the same time.

After everyone else had viewed the body, Eight Ball's mother made her way to the coffin. "What I'm gon' do now, Jesus?" she kept asking as though she expected an answer.

"I want my baby, I want my baby," she said gently lifting Eight Ball's head and burying it in her bosom.

Jamie laid his face in the palms of his hands and sobbed heavily. The sight of Eight Ball's mother lifting her dead son's body and embracing it for the last time was too much. He wanted to rush to her and tell her everything, but fear and shame held him firmly in his seat.

"I done my best fo' you, son," she said as she walked from the coffin. Her eyes were closed and tears streamed down her face.

"Don't worry 'bout 'im, Sister Harris," Reverend McCall yelled from the pulpit. "He's in Jesus' care now."

Jamie's body stiffened as Bill Anderson approached Eight Ball's mother at the front of the church. His beet red face held an expression of deep sorrow and pain as large tears rolled down his cheeks. Outraged, Jamie watched him place his arms around the mournful woman, pull her close, and hold her in a tight embrace. Then, as he whispered something in her ear, she compassionately patted his back, nodding her head up and down. After a brief moment, he moved his arms from around her and walked out of the church with his head bowed down.

On the way to the cemetery, Jamie sat quietly in Booger's car staring out the window, thinking about the night of the murder, his watching and not being able to do anything about it, even after Eight Ball was dead.

"I hate 'em, Booger," he shouted angrily. "I hate all of 'em."

"Who you talkin' 'bout, Jamie Ray?"

"Bill Anderson and all the white folks like 'im. I can't believe he had nerve enough to show up here, mo' less do what he did. Bad 'nough he got away with murder, but showin' up at the funeral and carryin' on the way he did is mo' than I can stand."

"Yeah," Booger said sympathetically.

"And I could have kicked Aunt Martha's butt fo' allowin' that murderin' bastard to hug her like that. She jus' cryin' and noddin' like she forgive 'im." Jamie clenched his teeth. "Can you believe that lie Bill Anderson tol'?" He was tempted to tell Booger all he had seen that night.

"Hey," Booger began, "I learned a long time ago that white folks won't tell the truth when a lie will do."

"Yeah, but his lie jus' don't hol' up."

"Who says it has to?" Booger responded. "White folks say it was an accident, it was an accident. Who gon' question a decent, law 'bidin' white man fo' killin' a nigguh?"

Booger and Jamie Ray stepped out of the car and followed the long line of mourners to the grave site. Eight Ball's mother and her five other children sat in chairs that had been placed there for them.

Reverend J. D. McCall stood at the head of the grave. He gripped his Bible with both hands and held it tight against his chest. The pall bearers lowered the coffin into the grave and he began:

The Lawd is my shepherd; I shall not want.
He maketh me to lie down in green pastures:
he leadeth me beside still waters.

He restoreth my soul: he leadeth me in the paths of righteous-
ness for his name's sake.

Yea, though I walk through the valley of the shadow of death,
I will fear no evil: for thou art with me: thy rod and thy staff
they comfort me.

Thou preparest a table before me in the presence
of mine enemies: thou anointest my head with oil; my cup
runneth over.

Surely goodness and mercy shall follow me all the days of
my life; and I will dwell in the house of the Lawd for ever.

Ashes to ashes and dust to dust. The Lawd giveth and the
Lawd taketh away. Blesseth be the name of the Lawd.

After the funeral, everyone gathered at Aunt Martha's
house. Sister Jones, the head deaconess in the church, had
also come by to help out. She was an old godly woman,
who loved to minister to those in need. She was good-
hearted, but she tended to ramble on and on.

When Jamie walked into the room she was consoling
his aunt. "You jus' gotta stay prayed up and hol' on to
God's unchangin' hand," he heard her say. "Jus' take comfort in knowin' that folks down here was able to touch
that boy's body but couldn't nary-a-one of 'em touch his
soul."

After some twenty minutes of testifying, Sister Jones
started tapping her foot, clapping her hands, and thanking

and praising Jesus for calling Eight Ball on home away from this old sinful world.

"The Lawd ain't put none of us here to stay fo'ever. When he calls us on home, we gotta go. Only thang we can do is be ready."

Eight Ball's mother's sad heart opened up to Sister Jones's words. Before long, she was praying and rejoicing in the glory of the Lord for giving her a forgiving heart. Rocking back and forth, she explained, "I don't hol' no bad feelin's toward nobody. Father jus' let yo' will be done."

Jamie went out and sat under a tree in the backyard. He had an overwhelming desire to be alone. He sat staring at a spider sucking the life out of a fly that had gotten caught in its web. He wasn't out there long before Booger joined him.

"Booger, what you thank happens when you die?"

"I don't know. I guess yo' soul go to heaven or hell."

"You reckon Eight Ball in heaven?"

"I don't know, man. I hope he is."

"Booger, do you really believe that there is a heaven and a hell? I mean really believe it. Not jus' 'cause it's what folks expect you to believe. But because you know it's so."

"Yeah, man, I believe it."

"Mama don't thank I believe in God 'cause I don't agree with everythang Reverend McCall say. She go on 'bout how dedicated he is and how dedicated her churchgoin' friends is and how much they trust in the Lawd. But to me, they seem like a bunch of ignorant fools that's doin' mo' harm than good."

"Man, I know what you mean."

"I don't know, Booger. Maybe you do and maybe you don't."

"Go 'head and tell me what you sayin'."

"Sometimes I don't thank bein' dedicated is enough fo'

black folks. 'Specially when you dedicated to the wrong thang. Last Sunday everybody got mad 'cause that old man said folks need to send the preachers off to be educated at one of them Bible colleges. Everybody got to talkin' 'bout you can't teach nobody how to preach at no school. You got to be called to preach. That's the only teachin' you need."

"That's sho' what they say," Booger said, laughing.

"To me, that jus' don't make no sense at all. Common sense tell you if you been called to preach, you got to prepare yo'self to fulfill yo' callin'."

"I hear you."

"Mama and the rest of 'em don't understand that. The way I see it, right now it's two kind of folks in the church. Them like Reverend McCall who supposed to be dedicated, but sho' ain't educated. And them that's educated but ain't dedicated. Don't neither one of 'em 'mount to nothin'."

"Man, know what's funny 'bout what you sayin'?"

"Naw, what?"

"Them same folks who buckin' 'gainst education in the church would have a fit if they went to that schoolhouse and the teachers didn't have no degrees, but said they had done been called to teach."

The idea of a schoolhouse full of illiterate teachers was amusing to Jamie and Booger. Neither one of them could stop laughing. Just when one seemed to have himself under control, he would look at the other and the laughing would start all over again.

"Then you got people like Reverend McCall who ain't finished the third grade and gon' teach the gospel," Jamie said, clutching his stomach. "How a third grader gon' teach a twelfth grader somethin'? The man can't hardly even read the Bible, mo' less teach it."

Again they laughed.

"Man, you oughta be shame."

"Well, it's the truth," Jamie shouted. "I don't mean to sound uppity or nothin' like that. And I ain't sayin' you gotta be educated to be a Christian, but I do figure you gotta be educated to be a preacher. Shucks! Anybody can follow, but you gotta know mo' than a follower to be a leader."

"I heard that," Booger responded.

They were silent.

"Man, it's a shame how ole lady Jones in there convincin' Aunt Martha that Eight Ball's murder was the work of the Lawd. Both of 'em so ignorant, they thank it was jus' his time to die."

"Aw man, it ain't really they fault," Booger said. "They jus' done been brainwashed."

C H A P T E R **8**

WITH much trepidation, Jamie made his way across the campus. He spotted Coach Terril clad in shorts and a T-shirt, standing in front of the gymnasium. He dropped his hands to his side and stood erect as Coach Terril bound forward, a wide grin lighting up his face. All the wisdom he knew counseled him to follow his mother's advice and forget Eight Ball's murder. But Coach Terril's sudden appearance brought to the surface all the frustration, anger, and hatred that he had fought all summer. Jamie grew tense fighting against the rage building deep within him.

"Jamie!" he exclaimed, briefly embracing him. "It's good to see you."

"Hi, Coach," Jamie responded, trying not to let his anger show.

"How was your summer?"

"Fine," Jamie said lamely.

"You in shape?" he asked, playfully squeezing Jamie's biceps.

"Yessuh."

"That's good," Terril added, throwing his arm around Jamie's shoulder. "We only have three weeks before the season opener and I want to put in a new offense to take advantage of your catching ability."

"Oh," Jamie said, careful to keep his face averted from the coach's gaze.

"Son, I've been on the phone all summer," he said, as they walked through the dressing room door. "A lot of college scouts want to see you catch the ball more this season. That's why I'm upgrading our passing game."

Jamie was silent for a moment, considering whether or not he should respond. He wondered how this person, whom he had watched help brutally lynch his cousin, could act as if he was concerned about his well-being. He decided not to speak.

"You give any more thought to where you would like to go to school?"

"Nosuh."

"Well, you still have plenty of time. Son, I'm fired up. I have a feeling that this is going to be your year."

Dismayed, Jamie sat in front of his locker trying hard to reconcile his feelings. For him to act as he always had toward Coach Terril seemed to be forgiving him. But to act on the anger he felt for him would be taking a chance on alienating a person who, in many ways, controlled his future. He had planned on a professional football career as his ticket out of Pinesboro. He didn't want to jeopardize his future. Silently, Jamie vowed never to forget or forgive Coach Terril or anyone else who had a part in Eight Ball's murder. But he couldn't give up on his dream.

Four months later, Jamie walked slowly off the Pinesboro High School football field for the last time. Exhausted, he held his helmet in his left hand and the game ball in his right. Everyone in the capacity crowd stood cheering as he made his way toward the sidelines. His final game had been his best—five touchdowns and three hundred sixty-five yards on twenty carries. For a few moments as he stood watching the final seconds tick off the clock, the anxiety of the past few months was almost behind him. He had managed to play his last year for Coach Terril without any incident. Soon he would go off to college. Then Pinesboro and the nightmarish memories it held would be behind him.

Two weeks after his final game, Coach Jerry Wells from Michigan A&M came to visit him. He was the fifth recruiter in as many days. Wells's intent was the same as all the others', to secure Jamie's signature on scholarship papers. Jamie could tell from the gleam in his uncle Rob's eyes that Coach Wells was pushing all the right buttons. Jamie hated the way his uncle sat grinning and saying "yessuh" to everything that white man said. It angered him to see how scary and unnatural he looked, sitting all rigid and stiff like he was in that white man's house instead of the white man being in his.

After about forty-five minutes of selling the school and talking about what a wonderful education Jamie would receive at Michigan A&M, Coach Wells said what he really came to say.

"Listen, Mrs. Griffin and Mr. Taylor, I'm going to give it

to you cold and straight. Signing Jamie is our number one priority. Without a doubt, he's the best player in the country this year." Wells paused to let the full force of his words sink in. "Now, I realize that he has worked extremely hard to develop his talents and put himself in this kind of position."

"Yessuh, he's a real hard worker," Jamie's uncle agreed.

"I know you all have had to make a lot of sacrifices along the way, not only to keep him in school, but also to support his athletic goals."

"Yessuh, that's right." Jamie's uncle nodded his head in agreement. "Henrietta don't hardly put nothin' 'fo that boy."

"Well, we can appreciate that at Michigan A&M. We like to look at ourselves like one big happy family. We like to help out the families of our kids as much as possible." He lifted his black briefcase and laid it across his lap. "Believe it or not, the Griffin family has a lot of friends in Michigan, as well as those right here in Pinesboro, who have expressed a desire to assist with any financial responsibilities you may have."

"Folks 'round here always been good to us," Uncle Rob interjected. "That's one thang we been thankful fo'."

Jamie stared at his uncle, then sighed softly. Uncle Rob knows good and well ain't nobody 'round here never gave us nothin', he thought to himself.

"We would like to make sure that you all are able to enjoy your son's college days without having to worry about finances. The bottom line is this," he said, seeming to tire of his own rhetoric, "we feel that Jamie will guarantee us a national championship. If he's the only player we sign, we still would have had a successful recruiting year."

"That's mighty high praise, suh," his uncle said, smiling with pride.

"And I mean every word of it," Coach Wells added. "I

know that words alone don't really mean that much. That's why I'm prepared to show you how badly we want your son to attend our university. And how much we are willing to help out."

Wells took his glasses from his shirt pocket and put them on. Then he took a piece of paper from his briefcase and examined it. "We are prepared to build you a home in Michigan so that you can relocate up there if you want. We also are prepared to provide Jamie with a car and an unlimited account at various clothing shops in Michigan. Plus, we will give him and you a handsome monthly allowance as long as he attends the university. We also will guarantee him a career in whatever field he chooses once he graduates from the university."

"Suh, this sound real good, but it's hard to believe," Jamie's uncle said. "I don't mean to question yo' word," he quickly added, "but it's hard to believe."

Coach Wells handed Jamie's uncle a stack of letters.

"Mr. Taylor, these letters are from ten of the wealthiest businessmen in the state of Michigan. They have all pledged their financial support and are willing to make sure that everything I have promised you becomes a reality. Look them over, and if you like, I can set up a meeting with any or all of them any time you like."

"OK, suh," he said, obviously stunned.

A few minutes later, Coach Wells took the scholarship papers from his briefcase.

"Well, what do you say? Will the State of Michigan have a couple of new residents?" He asked, placing the papers on the table in front of him.

"It's up to my son," Mrs. Griffin said.

"Well, Jamie, can we count on you being in that blue and white next fall?"

"I need a little time to thank about it," Jamie said, not committing himself to anything.

"I understand that. This is one of the biggest decisions of your life. Is there anything that we can do at Michigan to help you make it?"

"Nosuh. It's jus' that I have offers from some pretty good schools, and I jus' need time to make the right decision."

"I understand that. But I hope you understand how badly we want you to play ball in Michigan. Take your time, just promise me that you won't make a decision without talking to us first."

"Yessuh, I can do that."

After Wells left, Jamie, his mother, and his uncle discussed what had been said.

"Boy, I don't see how you can turn 'em down," Uncle Rob began.

"Somethin' don't seem right 'bout this far as I'm concerned," his mother spoke up. "I ain't never hear tell of nobody doin' all that fo' no high school ball player."

"Henrietta, they do it all the time."

"I don't care if they do. I ain't never sold no chil' of mine and I never will. That man come in here like we's interested in all them worldly thangs he got to offer. Jamie Ray, what you thank 'bout all this?" she asked.

"Probably cause a lotta trouble, Mama. They can't do all that stuff without the NCAA findin' out 'bout it."

"Boy, don't you thank them folks know what they doin'?" his uncle asked.

"Uncle Rob, jus' 'cause they white don't mean they know everythang," Jamie said angrily.

"This ain't got nothin' to do with 'em bein' white. I jus' figure they know they business."

"Well, I ain't gon' do nothin' that could hurt my chances of playin' pro ball."

"How you know you gon' ever git a chance to play pro ball?" his uncle asked. "Anythang could happen. These folks is guaranteein' you a life. Son, a bird in the hand is worth two in the bush."

"Uncle Rob, I don't wanna talk 'bout this with you."

"Rob, I gotta 'gree with that boy on this," Mrs. Griffin said. "I don't trust them folks far as I can chunk 'em. Besides, we doin' jus' fine by ourselves. Ain't no sense in that boy gittin' mixed up in no lotta mess. And what them folks' talkin' 'bout ain't nothin' but a heap of wrongdoin'. I ain't gon' stand fo' that."

"Jamie Ray, don't be no fool," his uncle said, ignoring Mrs. Griffin's comments. "Ain't every day black folks find theyself in a position to bargain with white folks."

"Mama, I thank I'd like to go to a black school."

"A black school!" Uncle Rob shouted. "Ain't a black school in America can match what these folks offerin' you. What in the world you wanna do somethin' foolish like that fo'?"

"Uncle Rob, ain't nobody talkin' to you," Jamie snapped.

"Jamie Ray, I ain't gon' tolerate you talkin' to grown folks like that," his mother interrupted abruptly. "You been raised better than that." There was silence. "Now, I 'gree with Rob," she continued. "I jus' ain't got much confidence in them colored schools."

"But Mama, a place like Grambling got everythang I need," Jamie pleaded. "Coach Robinson done put mo' folks in the pros than anybody."

"Honey, all you thankin' 'bout is playin' ball. But what 'bout yo' education? Right now them colored schools jus' ain't good as the white ones."

Jamie frowned. "Education!" he mumbled underneath his breath. "I ain't goin' to college fo' no education noway."

"What you say?" his mother asked.

"Nothin', mama. I ain't gotta decide on a school right now noway."

The following week, Coach Leroy Hunt from the University of Louisiana at New Orleans sat in the Griffins' living room courting Jamie Ray. He was the first black recruiter Jamie had seen. His visit was different from all the rest. He didn't spend a lot of time selling his school.

"I'm not going to come in here with a big sales pitch. I'm sure you've probably heard more than enough of that by now," Hunt began. "We can just talk about what you're looking for and how that fits with what's at ULNO. I'll be as straight as I can with you. You can ask me anything."

"How many black coaches are there at ULNO?" Jamie asked.

"Well, unfortunately, I'm it. But that's probably going to be the case regardless of where you decide to play ball. There just aren't many blacks working in major colleges right now. But if you decide to come to ULNO, you'll probably get tired of looking at me since I'm the running back coach."

"What kind of backs y'all got over there?"

"Our starter is a graduating senior. And both of our second and third team players are sophomores. They're both pretty good backs, but neither one of them has your speed or quickness. The way it stands right now, you could see a lot of playing time your first year, depending of course on how quickly you adjust to college ball and learn our system. Believe me, regardless of where you go, you'll get plenty of playing time."

For the next half hour the two of them discussed the finer points of ULNO's program. The schedule, the offensive scheme, television time, their success in getting their players in the NFL, the advantages and the disadvantages of playing at ULNO. After they had finished talking, Coach Hunt turned his attention to Jamie's mother.

"Mrs. Griffin, are there any questions I can answer for you?"

"Well, suh. I really don't know much 'bout football. So if Jamie Ray satisfied with the ball playin' part, I'm satisfied. But I'm mo' interested in the education he gon' git at yo' school. He my only child and the first Griffin from 'round here to go off to college. I jus' wanna make sho' he pick a school gon' do right my 'im."

"Yes, ma'am, I can understand that. I was the first person in my family to go to college."

"Is that right?" she asked.

"Yes ma'am. ULNO is a good solid academic institution and it's widely respected as one of the best schools in the South. But I'll be frank with you. The type of education he'll receive there is going to depend on him. Like anything, he'll get out of it what he puts into it."

"Another thang I wanna know 'bout is his scholarship. We ain't the richest people in the world. I do awright, but I ain't got no lotta money to put toward his schoolin'. Or to git 'im back and forth from New Orleans. I'd hate to thank he was off somewhere 'thout enough money to live on."

"Finances won't be a problem for him. His scholarship will cover all of his school expenses—room and board, books, fees, etc. Plus the university will take care of any other needs he might have. You don't have to worry about a thing. If he decides to come to ULNO, I'll make sure to look after him."

"Can I ask you a personal question?"

"Yes ma'am."

"Where you from? I don't mean to be nosy, but you a lot different from all the other recruit folk been by here."

"Oh, I was born and raised about two hours from here. I'm from Port City," he said, smiling.

"My Jesus! You mean you from right over yonder in Shreveport!"

"Yes ma'am."

"So if I was to say I was fixin' some turnip greens, fried chicken, yams, and hot water corn bread fo' supper, you'd know what I was talkin' 'bout?"

"Yes ma'am, you talkin' 'bout some mighty good eatin'." Hunt grinned, rubbing his stomach.

"Well, Mr. Hunt, would you do us the honor of havin' supper with us this evenin'?"

"Yes ma'am, the honor is all mine if it's not any trouble."

"Ain't no trouble at all. Besides, it's my Christian duty to feed a man proper what ain't been eatin' nothin' but gumbo."

The chemistry between the three of them was evident. Four days after Coach Hunt's visit, Jamie signed the national letter of intent with the University of Louisiana, New Orleans.

A few weeks later, a brooding and despondent Jamie shuffled up the steps of Papa's. Draped over his arm was the matching jacket to a three-piece polyester suit he was wearing.

"J.R.!" he heard a familiar voice call as he pushed through the door.

He turned and looked. Booger was sitting at a corner table, drinking a can of beer.

Jamie walked over. "Hey, Booger," he mumbled, then sank into a chair across from him. He felt drained. Earlier that night at the football awards banquet, he had become so angry that he still felt agitated.

"Nigguh, you sharp as a tack," Booger said admiringly.

"Thanks," he responded, forcing a faint smile.

"Man, I know you picked up enough metal at that banquet to open up yo' own hardware sto'."

"Not hardly," Jamie said dejectedly. "Didn't none of the brothers do too good."

"What you mean?"

"I was the only one of us to win somethin'. And all I got was the best offensive back award; quarterback got the MVP."

Booger frowned deeply. "Man, I swear!" he said, bringing both fists down hard on the table. "Them white folks ain't right."

"You can say that again," Jamie responded.

"Man, if I was you, first thang in the mornin', I'd bust into Terril's office and tell 'im to lick me where the good Lawd split me."

Jamie threw his head back and laughed at the top of his voice. "Booger, you know that ain't me."

"Well, somebody up there would have to tell me somethin'," Booger said emphatically. "'Cause if you ain't the MVP, there ain't nairn."

"Can you believe I ain't never been the MVP?"

"That's a shame," Booger said, shaking his head from side to side.

"And I know at least one of the other black players shoulda got somethin'," Jamie said.

"What you gon' do, J.R.?"

"I don't know. But I'm gon' do somethin'."

The next morning while waiting for the bus, Jamie felt a gentle tug on his sleeve. He glanced around to see a couple of guys from the basketball team smiling at him.

"You ready?" one of them asked.

"Ready fo' what?"

"The game, fool. What else would we be talkin' 'bout?"

Jamie blinked. In all the excitement over the football banquet, he had forgotten that tonight was the first round of the district basketball tournament. That was the solution he had been looking for. It had been right under his nose and he hadn't seen it.

"Naw, man. I ain't gon' play," he heard himself say.

"No kiddin'?"

"No kiddin'," he replied bitterly.

"What's wrong?" one of them asked. "You hurt or some-thin'?"

"Naw."

"Then why ain't you gon' play?"

"I guess y'all ain't heard what happened at the banquet last night."

"Naw, what happened?" they sang out in unison.

"Them white boys got all the awards."

"So what?"

"It ain't right, that's what," Jamie said angrily.

"All them trophies you got at yo' house and you mad 'cause you didn't git one last night."

"Fo' yo' information, I got a trophy last night."

"Then, what you mad fo'?"

"'Cause it wasn't the only one I shoulda got and 'cause some of the other guys shoulda got one."

"Aw Jamie, you know white folks ain't never gon' do right. So you might as well go'n 'bout yo' business."

"That's right," the other one agreed.

Jamie looked at one then the other. "How y'all know they won't do right? Either one of y'all ever tried to make 'em?"

"Naw."

"Why not?"

They looked at each other uneasily.

"I don't know, man."

"That's a lie!" Jamie shouted. "Tell the truth."

"I tol' you I don't know."

"Sho' you do," Jamie said with a resentful tone. He paused. Neither one of them spoke. Then he fired back the answer to his own question. "'Cause you black, that's why. And black folks ain't nothin' but do' mats. They jus' let white folks walk all over 'em without doin' a thang about it."

"That how you see it, hunh?"

"Yeah, 'cause that's how it is."

"Jamie, what's done got into you?"

"I'm jus' sick and tired, that's all. And that's why I ain't gon' play. It might not be much, but at least it's somethin'."

Their conversation was ended by a shout in the distance. "The bus here." Silently they marched toward the bus, Jamie in front and the two boys directly behind him. Jamie took his place in line and waited as those in front of him climbed aboard. Suddenly the boy directly behind him leaned forward and whispered, "Jamie, if you ain't gon' play tonight, I ain't gon' play either." Within seconds, the other one echoed, "Me neither."

Twenty minutes into first period, Jamie was summoned to the principal's office. As he walked through the door, he noticed that Mr. Watkins, Coach Terril, Coach Stevens, and the school superintendent were all sitting and waiting for him.

"What's this I hear about you leading a boycott against the basketball team?" Mr. Watkins asked.

Stunned, Jamie cringed a bit. He could scarcely believe what he had been asked. How had they found out so soon? He quickly composed himself. "I don't know nothin' 'bout no boycott," he said, looking Mr. Watkins straight in the eye.

"You trying to tell me that you boys haven't gotten together and decided not to play in the tournament tonight?"

"I don't know what they've done," he said sternly.

Momentary silence hung in the room.

"Son, why don't you sit down and tell us what's going on?" Mr. Watkins asked.

Jamie sat down. He looked from the superintendent, to Coach Terril, to Coach Stevens, then to Mr. Watkins.

"All I know is that I said I wasn't gon' play another game of no kind fo' Pinesboro. What the other fellows decide to do ain't none of my business."

"Son, what's this all about?" Mr. Watkins asked.

Jamie cleared his throat.

"I don't thank it's right the way the awards were handed out at the football banquet last night," he said in a steady voice.

"Awards!" Coach Terril said, his eyes filled with disbelief. "Son, that's what's bothering you?"

Jamie looked at Coach Terril. For a brief moment his mind shifted back to Eight Ball. He could feel his rage rising.

"Yessuh, that's one of the things," he said angrily.

"Listen, Jamie, we're all friends here," Coach Terril said jovially. "Obviously this thing has you a little upset. But it appears to me that there is a simple misunderstanding. I'm sure we can get it straightened out in a little or no time."

Jamie listened with clamped teeth. He knew Terril was attempting to placate him with his mild manners and polite tone. But he had no desire or intent to be placated. For once, he wanted Terril and the rest of them to feel the full force of his anger. He could feel the white men's eyes searching his face, trying to read him—waiting for his reaction.

"I don't know how fast it can be straightened out," Jamie said. "But until it is, I ain't gon' play no mo' ball here."

"Is that a threat?" Mr. Watkins asked, his voice now cold and hostile.

Jamie parted his lips to speak, but before he could,

Coach Terril answered. "Of course not," he said forcing a smile and shaking his head disapprovingly at Mr. Watkins. "Jamie, just tell us what's on your mind."

"I'm jus' tired of bein' cheated and mistreated."

"Cheated and mistreated by who?" Mr. Watkins asked.

"This school in general and the coaches in particular."

"Look! I've been more than fair with you," Coach Terril yelled, becoming incensed by Jamie's personal indictment. "I won't stand by and have you question my honesty."

"I ain't questionin' nobody's honesty," Jamie said, refusing to be intimidated. "I jus' don't see what certain awards are based on 'round here. It sho' ain't stats. 'Cause if it was, a lot mo' awards would've gone home with black players last night. And ain't nobody on this team never had no better stats than me, but I ain't been the most valuable player since I been here."

"Son, we been doing things this way long before you got here and we're not going to change them now. Neither me nor my coaches have to answer to you or anybody else concerning how we select our awardees."

"Nosuh, you don't," Jamie said. "But then neither me or any other black person have to play here either."

"Jamie! I'm surprised at you," the superintendent interrupted. "Son, I could pick up that telephone right now, call over to ULNO and tell them about your bad attitude, and you won't play for them or nobody else around here."

"Go 'head," Jamie said pushing the phone over toward the superintendent. "If they take yo' word fo' it, I don't wanna play fo' 'em nohow."

The superintendent leaped to his feet, his face twitching.

"I'm not going to stay here and be a part of this crap," he shouted, storming from the room.

Jamie had become so angry that his eyes began to water.

"Y'all do what you wanna, I'm goin' home," he said, standin' up to leave.

"Sit down, son," Mr. Watkins said. "Let's see if we can't reach some understanding here."

"Ain't nothin' to understand," Jamie said, his nostrils flaring in and out. "Right is right and wrong is wrong. And ain't nothin' right 'bout this situation. I got some little cousins at home that's gon' wanna play here one of these days. And it don't make no sense fo' 'em to have to put up with this kinda stuff."

For several seconds, they were all silent. Then Coach Terril took a deep breath and collected himself. Jamie could tell from his beet red face that he was still angry.

"Starting with the next banquet, all awards will be based solely on statistics," he conceded, not looking at anything or anyone. He turned to Jamie. "Now, I don't want you leaving here thinking that we're doing this because you forced us to. We had already decided this before you came in here this morning."

Later that day, Coach Stevens asked Jamie Ray to help him pack the sandwiches and cold drinks that the players would eat after the game that night. For a long time they worked methodically. They didn't speak or look at each other.

"Jamie," Coach mumbled, wiping sweat from his face.

"Suh?"

"I want you to know that I think what you did was right. I'm sorry that I couldn't back you up. But Coach Terril calls all the shots around here. I hope we can just put this thing behind us and go out and win this tournament."

"Yeah, Coach," Jamie said absentmindedly as he walked away.

A week later, Jamie asked Booger and several of the black athletes to meet him at his house before school.

They arrived confused.

"What you call us over here so early fo'?"

"We gon' ride old man O'Riley's bus to school this mornin'."

"Nigguh, you know O'Riley don't allow no blacks on his bus."

"He gon' allow it this mornin'," Jamie snapped. "He drives the last bus to school every mornin', don't he?"

"You know he do."

"Well it don't make no sense fo' us to have to walk to school if we miss the early bus jus' 'cause that man prejudice, do it? Startin' today, we ain't gonna," Jamie said.

At seven-thirty they all walked to the bus stop and waited. The bus arrived and Booger moved toward the door. As O'Riley slammed the door, Booger lowered his shoulder and rammed the door open. They all climbed aboard.

O'Riley turned and yelled over his shoulder. "I'm not movin' this bus till y'all git off."

"We ain't goin' nowhere."

Angered, O'Riley climbed off the bus and walked away. A short time later he returned, accompanied by the superintendent.

"Men, what's going on here?" the superintendent asked. Jamie stepped forward.

"We jus' tryin' to make it to school, that's all."

"Why are you all on this bus?"

"'Cause we missed the early bus."

The superintendent paused and looked around.

"Jamie, could I see you fellows outside?"

They climbed off the bus.

"Look, this is not the way to handle this situation. Technically, you boys are right. But let's try not to create any more problems here than we have to. We can't solve this thing this morning, but I promise you I'll handle it."

"How we supposed to git to school?"

"Yeah, we all can't fit in yo' car."

"And I ain't 'bout to walk."

There was silence.

"I'll send somebody out to pick y'all up."

The superintendent left. The boys walked over to Jamie's house and waited.

"Man, you thank he really gon' do somethin' 'bout O'Riley?"

Jamie paused, pondering.

"We'll wait a week and see. If he don't, we'll do it all over again."

Outside, a horn honked. Booger walked to the window and peeped out.

"Man, guess what?"

"What?"

"Stevens out there in the team bus."

They all laughed.

"C'mon fellows, let's go."

They walked out to the bus and the doors swung open. Coach Stevens had a forced smile on his face.

"You fellows need a ride?"

"Yessuh."

Silently they boarded the bus and sat down. The engine roared and the bus lurched forward out of the yard and down the narrow, bumpy road. As the bus moved through the community, no one spoke. Jamie sat staring out of the window. He saw the puzzled stares of onlookers who he knew were trying to figure out what was going on. Far in the distance he heard the courthouse bells chime. It was eight o'clock. They were already late, but he didn't care. They had made a statement.

Minutes later, Coach Stevens pulled up to the front of the school building and stopped.

"Hustle up, men. The bell has already sounded."

"Awright, Coach."

They unloaded and paused briefly as the bus pulled away. Jamie spoke first.

"Thanks, fellows."

"No problem, Jamie."

"Remember, we gon' keep on till O'Riley lets black folks ride his bus."

"Awright, man. Jus' say the word and we'll be there."

After school, Jamie's mother was waiting on him at home.

"Jamie Ray, is that you?" she asked as he entered the house.

"Yes ma'am."

She hurried in from the kitchen.

"Is what I hear true?"

"Is what true, Mama?"

"You tryin' to ride ole man O'Riley's bus."

"Yes ma'am."

She stared at him strangely.

"Boy, what done got into you lately?"

"Nothin', Mama."

There was brief silence.

"Look to me like you jus' tryin' to ruin yo' life."

"Mama, I'm jus' standin' up fo' what's right. Now, what's wrong with that?"

"Everythang, baby."

"Ma'am?"

"Honey, you makin' the wrong people mad over thangs that ain't even important."

"But Mama, they important to me."

She turned to go back into the kitchen.

"Well, I jus' hope you know what you doin'."

"I do, Mama."

A few months later, Pinesboro's black community threw a farewell party for Jamie in the gymnasium of the old colored school. He received a lot of gifts, mostly things people thought he would need in college. His mother spent most of the evening smiling and listening to folks tell her what a good job she had done raising him.

Later that evening, Jamie went over to Papa's place and said good-bye to the rest of his friends. Then, feeling restless, he wandered out onto the campus of the old colored school. The day had been more than he had expected and he felt a deep need for solitude. An hour later, the peaceful silence was broken by Mr. Shorty's familiar voice.

"What you sittin' out here studyin' over?" Mr. Shorty asked.

"Nothin'," Jamie said, looking up to see the old white-haired man standing over him. "How you makin' it this evening, Mr. Shorty?"

"Oh, I'm doin' fairly well fo' an ole man," he said, slowly lowering himself to the ground next to Jamie. "I do believe I'd be doin' a whol' lot better if I could jus' git my speed up."

"I hear you, Mr. Shorty."

There was silence.

"You sho' you ain't got nothin' on yo' mind?" Mr. Shorty asked again.

"I guess there is somethin' I'm kinda worried about," Jamie said reluctantly.

"I'm all ears," he said, patiently waiting for Jamie to begin.

"Mr. Shorty, you ever wanted somethin' so bad that when it seem like you was gon' git it, it almost scared you half to death?"

"Can't say that I have. Somethin' scarin' you?"

"Yeah, kinda. You know I'm leavin' fo' New Orleans tomorrow?"

"Yeah, that's all folks 'round here been talkin' 'bout fo' the last week or so."

"Everybody 'round here makin' out like it's such a big deal."

"Ain't it a big deal?" Mr. Shorty asked.

"It's what I want. But fo' the first time in my life, I'm worried 'bout not makin' it. What if I go down yonder and I can't do the schoolwork? Or what if I can't cut it on the football field?"

"Boy, let me tell you somethin'," Mr. Shorty began. "Long time ago colored folks what had to make it in the white folks' world killed can't and whumped couldn't till he could, so ain't no such thang as can't and couldn't."

Jamie chuckled.

"Best thang fo' you to do is decide what you gon' do with yo' life. Way I see it, you got two choices. You can either stay 'round here and be a big ole fish in this here little ole stanky pond, or you can go out and test the waters."

"Yeah, that's 'bout the size of it," Jamie said, slowly nodding his head in agreement.

"Ever since you been big 'nough to talk and make sense, you been goin' on 'bout all the big thangs you wantin' to do. Now that they right in front of you, don't be scared to go git 'em. Comes a time in everybody's life when they gotta walk they talk. Shucks! To my knowledge, folks what's scared to make a step, usually don't never git nowhere."

"Mr. Shorty, that's jus' what I am right now," Jamie said, dropping his eyes to the ground. "I'm shame to admit it, but I'm near 'bout scared to death. All them folks today seem like they countin' on me to prove somethin' fo' 'em. They expectin' me to go down yonder and turn New Orleans out."

"Son, if I was you, I wouldn't be studyin' them folks. Half of 'em hopin' you don't make it. And the other half don't really care one way of the other long as ain't nothin' in it fo' them. It's sad to say, but that's how us colored folks is."

"I guess you right."

"Guess! Boy, you know I'm right. You go'n down to New Orleans and do the best you can. And if thangs don't work out exactly the way you figure they oughta, you c'mon back proud. The way I figure it, if you gon' git a F in life, you oughta git the best F you can git."

"Mr. Shorty, I know what you sayin' is right, but all I can thank about is how scared I am."

"Ain't nothin' wrong with bein' a little scared. What matters is how you act on it."

"What you mean?"

"Being scared is natural. I 'spect anybody what ever mounted to anythang in life was scared at first."

"You really thank so?"

"Yeah. You need that scared feelin' to make you do yo' best. You can either be so scared of failin' that you don't try, or you can be so scared that you do everythang in yo' power not to fail. I 'spect you gon' do the right thang and rise to the top."

Jamie began to smile. Mr. Shorty was saying everything that he needed to hear.

"Son, ever since I first started talkin' to you I been a little partial to you. You always been different. Most colored folks these days satisfied. They ain't got nothin' and don't want nothin'. The mo' you got, the mo' you gotta do. You ain't got nothin', you ain't gotta do nothin'. That's the way most us colored folk like it."

Jamie laughed at Mr. Shorty's summation of black people.

"You bein' a little hard on us, ain't you, Mr. Shorty?"

"Naw, son. I done seen too many of us waitin' on a blessin' and too sorry to git up and go 'round the corner to git it when it come. We too busy waitin' on the Lawd to do it all. It's jus' good to see a young man out here tryin' to make a blessin' fo' hisself." Mr. Shorty paused. "Might not mean nothin' to you comin' from a ole winehead like me, but I'm proud of you. You becomin' the man I always wanted to be, but the time I was livin' in wouldn't allow it. Lotta ole heads like me toted and piddled fo' the white man so young folks like you could have a chance to do better."

"Thanks Mr. Shorty," Jamie said. "I feel a lot better."

"Son, if you wanna thank me jus' don't be satisfied till this ole life give you what it owe you."

The next day Jamie sat at the station with his mother and Booger waiting for the New Orleans bus. His mother handed him a slightly smudged brown paper bag.

"Mama, what's this?"

"I made you some chicken to eat case you git hungry."

"Mama, I ain't gon' git hungry. Besides, I can't carry that on no bus. Folks'll thank I'm some kind of country bumpkin."

"Chil', what you care what folks thank? You best take that little somin' t'eat. Ain't no tellin' what might happen fo' you git where you goin'."

His bus pulled up. Jamie took the bag from his mother.

"Okay, Mama, thank you." He let out a deep sigh. "Well, look like that's my bus. So, I guess it's 'bout that time."

She wrapped her arms around him and pulled him close.

"Be good, son. And take care of yo'self, hear?"

"Yes ma'am. I will."

"Now, if you need anythang, you call me."

"Yes ma'am."

As he pulled away, his eyes met Booger's.

"Stay cool, man," Booger said softly.

"Yeah, Booger. You too."

Jamie climbed aboard and took a seat. He stared at the two of them as the bus slowly pulled away.

CHAPTER 9

A T exactly fifteen minutes after three, Jamie's bus arrived in New Orleans. Anxiously, he stepped off the bus, collected his luggage, and entered the terminal. For a moment he stood in the center of the crowded room staring about.

"Jamie," someone called his name.

It was Coach Hunt. He was approaching rapidly with a wide smile plastered on his face. He reached out, clasped Jamie's hand, and shook it firmly.

"How was your trip?"

"It wasn't bad."

"It's good to see you again."

"Yessuh, it's good to see you too."

"You ready to run that pigskin?"

Jamie smiled.

"I was ready yesterday."

"That's the kind of talk I like to hear," Coach said, looking about. "Is this all of your luggage?"

"Yessuh. This everythang."

"Good, we can get out of here, then," he said, taking a couple of the bags and leading Jamie through the door and out onto the street. "I'm going to take you to the dorm so you can check in and relax for a little while."

"OK, Coach."

"Your roommate's already here. He checked in yesterday. His name is Michael and he's a defensive back from New Orleans. Y'all should get along fine. He's a real good kid."

"I'm sho' we will, Coach."

"Now, make sure you're at the stadium by five o'clock for your physical and we have a team meeting at seven. Whatever you do, don't be late for the meeting. That's one thing Mills don't tolerate."

At ten minutes till five Jamie pushed through the stadium doors. Wandering aimlessly, he entered the training room and stared wide-eyed at the tables and medical equipment that strategically lined the walls. He was early. The only people there other than the trainers were two black veteran players. Jamie looked in their direction. One was lying on a table rubbing his knee with a cup of ice and the other had an electronic device attached to his right shoulder. Both of them had on workout shorts and T-shirts. Suddenly the one icing his knee shouted, "Hey boy, what yo' name?"

"You talkin' to me?" Jamie asked, pointing to himself.

"Yeah, pretty boy. Mr. Lloyd talkin' to you."

"I'm Jamie Ray Griffin."

"From now on, you Mr. Lloyd's boy."

"Man, you don't know nothin' 'bout me," Jamie said, becoming irritated.

"Hey, Moon," Lloyd yelled across the room. "Check out homeboy's feet. What kinda shoes he wearin'?"

Moon raised himself to his elbows and gazed at Jamie's feet. He rubbed his chin slowly, then mumbled, "Stacy Adams."

Lloyd leapt from the table, got down on his hands and knees, and studied Jamie's shoes.

"Yeah, Moon. I do believe you right. Stacy throwed 'em away and he went at 'em."

They both howled with laughter.

Still chuckling, Lloyd stood up and began circling Jamie. He was studying him. Suddenly he paused and stared at Jamie's hair.

"Moon, this boy some kin to you?" he said with a strange look on his face.

"Naw, he ain't no kin to me."

"Yeah he is."

"Why you say that?"

"Check out his head. He got that fo' E hair jus' like you."

"Fo' E?"

"Yeah. Nappy, knotty, kinky, and when you try to comb it you holler, OH LORDY."

As the two of them laughed hysterically, a thin, middle-aged white man emerged from the office in the corner of the room.

"Aw, leave him alone, fellows. Y'all done had your fun."

Jamie turned in the direction of the voice.

"Don't let them bother you. They're just clowning around."

Jamie frowned, but didn't speak.

"This ugly guy here is David Lloyd. He's probably the best wide receiver in the conference. And that big brute over there is Jerry Green. He's our starting fullback. Everybody around here calls him Moon."

Jamie's eyes followed the man's words. He looked at Lloyd, then at Jerry, and back at Lloyd.

"Now, Lloyd probably has the biggest mouth in the conference. But everybody around here knows his bark is worse than his bite."

The man turned and extended his right hand to Jamie.

"Oh, by the way, I'm Charley Parker, the head trainer. Most folks just call me Doc."

"Hi, Doc, I'm Jamie Ray Griffin."

"Pleased to meet you, Jamie. I've heard a lot of good things about you."

"That's good, I guess."

"You bet it is," he said, his gray eyes staring directly into Jamie's. "I guess you're here for your physical."

"Yessuh."

"Well, one of the doctors from the school infirmary will examine you. He should be here any minute."

"Okay."

"In the meantime, you can get started filling out one of the medical questionnaires."

"Awright, Doc."

"C'mon. You can sit in my office."

"See you around, crab," Lloyd teased.

Angrily, Jamie followed Doc Parker into his office, sat behind his huge desk, and busied himself filling out the forms. Soon the training room was swarming with players. Three doctors wearing white jackets pushed their way into the room. One of them stepped forward.

"Men, we're going to check your heart rate, your blood pressure, your immunization record, and a few other things. Any questions?" There was silence. "OK, then. Who's first?"

"I am," Jamie said stepping forward.

"Come this way."

"Yessuh."

Jamie followed him to an examination table, handed him his completed form, and took a seat.

"I see you had all of your shots."

"Yessuh."

"Are you sure?"

"Yessuh."

"Well, that's great. Most of our black kids' immunization cards usually aren't up to date when they come in here."

"Is that a fact," Jamie mumbled sarcastically.

The doctor stared at the form.

"So, you haven't had any major injuries, illnesses, or surgery?"

"Nosuh. I haven't."

"OK," he said, laying the form aside. "That's good."

He took Jamie's blood pressure, listened to his heart, and examined his ears, eyes, and mouth. Then he put on a pair of clear plastic gloves.

"OK, Jamie, stand up and drop your pants," he commanded.

Jamie did as he was instructed. The doctor wheeled his chair close and strategically situated his hand.

"Turn your head and cough."

Jamie obeyed.

"Again."

Jamie coughed a second time.

"That's good."

The doctor pushed away and removed his gloves.

"That's it, hoss," he said, rising to rinse his hands. "You can pull your pants up. You're as fit as a fiddle."

Relieved, Jamie slid off the table, fastened his pants, and walked out into the hallway. When it was time, he went inside the meeting room and took a seat with the other first-year players. He glanced around fascinated. It was a huge double room, furnished with rows of plush theater chairs, carpeted floors and divided down the center by a retractable partition. The entire front wall was a huge chalkboard. In the middle of the board was a large white film screen.

At exactly seven o'clock Coach Mills, flanked by his assistants, entered the room and positioned himself front and center.

"Good evening, men." His voice was cold and stern.

Suddenly the door crept open. Coach Mills spun around on his heels. His angry eyes followed the player up the steps to a seat in the last row. For half a minute Coach Mills stood staring right at the offender. Slowly he turned to one of the assistant coaches.

"Get that young man up early tomorrow morning and run him until he understands that when I say a meeting starts at seven, I don't mean one second after seven."

A tense, awkward silence hung over the room.

"There're a few things you'd better get straight right now," Mills growled, his teeth clenched tight and his face one huge frown. "At ULNO we do things two ways. My way or Trailways."

Jamie cringed and his body became stiff. He quickly forgot the kind words spoken to him during his recruitment trip.

"The second thing you need to understand is that around here we on Gene Mills time. It ain't six o'clock till I say it's six o'clock." His voice became low and threatening. "And by God, if any of you don't like the way I run things, I got an apple and a road map for you."

Everyone in the room sat straight and rigid in their seats,

staring at Coach Mills. Fear and anxiety gripped them. Mills moved his head slowly from side to side as he looked from one player to the next. Jamie listened to his every word. He hated the feeling of powerlessness that he sensed creeping over the room.

"Is that clear?" Mills snapped.

Jamie slumped in his chair and remained defiantly silent as the chorus of young voices sang out, "Yes sir."

Coach Mills lips twisted into a wry smile.

"Now that we understand each other, let's get down to business. These men sitting to my left are offensive coaches and those to my right are defensive coaches. Now, I want all defensive players to move to the right side of the room and all offensive players to move to the left."

He paused. Everyone clung to their seats.

"Hurry up! Hurry up!" he yelled. "Jump! Jump! Jump!"

Jamie watched everyone frantically scramble to the proper side of the room. Suddenly his eyes fell on the coaches seated against the wall. True to his word, Coach Hunt was the only black person on the coaching staff.

Coach Mills took a step backward, leaned against the chalkboard, and folded his arms.

"Now, starting on the last row and moving from left to right, I want each one of you to stand and introduce yourself to the group."

Jamie turned in his seat and watched as the players behind him introduced themselves. Then it was his turn. Slowly he rose, cleared his throat, and spoke in short, deliberate sentences:

"Jamie Ray Griffin. Tailback. Pinesboro, Louisiana."

He could feel their curious eyes piercing his back as he took his seat. He had received extensive media coverage since signing with ULNO and he knew that his new teammates were sizing him up.

"Franchise," someone taunted from behind him.

Reverberating laughter filled the room. Jamie sat staring ahead as though unaware of them. When the introductions were completed, Coach Mills removed the huge white screen covering the chalkboard. Sprawled across it in several neat columns was a long list of professors.

"These are your friends," he said in a monotone voice. "Look through the schedule and find the classes they're teaching and enroll in them. Now, you need twelve units a semester to be eligible to play ball. Our meetings start at one-fifteen and practice starts at three-thirty. So don't schedule any classes in the afternoon." He paused, crossed to the door and stuck his head out. "Dr. J., we're ready for you now."

An elderly white man walked into the room and sat behind the large wooden table the coaches had dragged up front. Jamie studied him. He was tall and slender with a small, round-shaped head that was covered with slick white hair. His skin had a pale sickly tint and, as he sat puffing on a cigarette, Jamie noticed that his hands shook uncontrollably.

"Men, this is Dr. Jerry Jenkins. He's the athletic department's academic adviser. Right now I want all of you to take some time and fill out your schedules. If you need help, come down front and see Dr. J. Men, let's get it done."

Jamie looked around the room. He didn't know how to make out a schedule. Confused, he got out of his seat, walked down the steps, and stood in the line that had formed in front of the table. When his time came, he sat in the empty chair and stared at the stack of blank schedules.

"And you are?" Dr. J. asked.

"Jamie Ray Griffin."

"Hello, Jamie.

"Hi."

"Have you decided on a major?"

"Nosuh. Not yet."

"Ok. We'll fill out a general studies schedule for you. You should go light during the fall semester because of practice. Let's see, you'll have to take introductory English."

"OK."

"You like music?"

"I guess so." Jamie found the question strange.

"Good. Then you'll enjoy music appreciation. Can you bowl?"

"Nosuh. I can't."

"Well, now is as good a time to learn as any. We'll sign you up for bowling. Three, six, nine," Dr. J. counted the units. "You need one more class."

"Don't I need a math class?"

"No. We'll take care of that during the off-season. Let's get you another elective. How about athletic injuries, taught by Doc Parker?"

"OK."

"Awright then, Jamie. You're set. Just sign at the bottom and leave it on the table."

Jamie signed the paper, moved back to his seat, and waited for the others. When everyone was finished and back in their seats, Coach Mills stepped out front again.

"Men, tomorrow at seven we'll have a continental breakfast in the dorm. At eight, I want you dressed and in the weight room to stretch and max out. At nine-thirty, I want you on the field for gut check. You'll run a quarter, rest four minutes, then run another one. You'll have a ten-second split between them. If your second quarter time is ten point zero one seconds slower than your first, your ass is grass and I'm the lawn mower." He paused, then growled: "Now get out of here."

Jamie stood and watched as the players down front filed out of the room grim and silent. As he neared the door, he saw one of the assistant coaches place his arm around one of the players and murmur, "You been working out, big-un?"

"Yes sir, Coach. I'm in good shape."

"Son, for your sake I hope so, because if you're not, to-morrow morning you gon' wish like hell you were."

That night Jamie didn't sleep at all. He closed his eyes a thousand times, hoping to get some rest before the morning workout. But every few minutes they would fly open. All he could think about was the two quarters he had to run the next day and what would happen if he failed to make his time. He wanted to get off on the right foot. Everybody back home was counting on him. At six o'clock in the morning, a loud bell rang, followed closely by the muffled sounds of a coach's voice echoing through the hallway:

"Let's go, men. Get up. Time to hit it."

Jamie lifted himself on his elbows and looked toward his roommate, who hadn't budged.

"Say Mike, it's 'bout that time."

"Yeah," he mumbled, his voice hoarse with sleep. "I'll catch you over there."

Jamie scrambled out of bed, slipped on a pair of cutoffs, pulled a T-shirt on over his head, and stepped into a pair of thongs. Down the hall, he crowded into the small communal bathroom. He quickly brushed his teeth, splashed a little water on his face, and dashed downstairs to the lobby. One of the assistant trainers was standing behind a foldout table loaded down with honey buns and orange juice, yelling, "Continental breakfast. Come and get it. Eat now and hope you don't see it later."

Jamie grabbed a bun and a cup of juice and slowly walked out of the dorm, turned on to the wide sidewalk and started toward the stadium. The morning air was crisp and damp. Overhead the sky was a dark shade of gray. To his eyes, it could just as easily have been night instead of the early hours of the morning. As he neared the stadium, he became tense. He wondered what the day held in store for him. He opened the stadium door, walked down the hall, and turned in to the dressing room. It looked different than when he had seen it on his recruit trip. Now all the gear was in place and people were hustling in and out. He walked to his locker, paused, and took the shiny gold helmet off the hook.

"Nice, ain't it, Franchise?" the player at the adjacent locker asked.

"Yeah," Jamie answered, slipping the helmet over his head. It was a perfect fit.

"Say, I'm Jeffrey."

"What's up, man?" Jamie said, slipping the helmet off and placing it back on the hook.

"You nervous?"

"A little bit, I guess. You?"

"Yeah. I ain't gon' lie. I didn't work out like I should've this summer."

"Aw, it ought not to make that much difference," Jamie told him. "It's jus' two quarters."

"Yeah, I hear you."

Jamie sat staring at his locker.

"Man, how you git this thang open?"

"You gotta git the combination from the equipment man."

"Fo' real?"

"Yeah, man. No joke. You gotta go ask 'im fo' it."

Jamie hurried up front, pausing in front of the gaping window-like opening that separated the dressing room from the equipment room. He leaned on the eave and looked inside; no one was in sight.

"Say, anybody back there?"

A chubby white man in his mid-fifties appeared.

"What you need?"

"The combination to my locker."

"What's your name?"

"Jamie Ray Griffin."

The man stared at him.

"So, you're Jamie Ray Griffin?"

"Yessuh."

"You good as they say you are?"

"Well, I guess time'll tell."

"You right about that," he said, smiling. "Hold on, let me look up your combination."

As he disappeared inside a small room, Jamie was startled by a voice behind him.

"Listen up."

Jamie whirled. It was one of the coaches.

"Men, when you get dressed come to the turf room and get stretched out. We don't want no pulled muscles out there today."

Filled with nervous anticipation, Jamie returned to his locker, dressed, and moved to the turf room across the hall. Soon he was sitting on the floor stretching with the rest of his anxious teammates. The painful tightness in his legs gradually subsided as his muscles began to loosen. He knew the high expectations everyone held for him and he felt the pressure not simply to perform admirably but to be outstanding. Within an hour they had completed their weight test. Then Jamie, along with his teammates, slowly walked out toward the track. Outside he could feel the ominous heat from the hot morning sun sapping the energy from his slightly aching muscles. As they walked past the stands, several veteran players who had come out to watch began taunting them.

"Hey, crab," Jamie heard them clearly, "watch out fo' that bear hidin' in that curve."

Their words caused Jamie to survey the large open track

and he thought of all the miles he had logged preparing
for this moment. Why was he putting so much pressure
on himself? He was prepared. He tilted his head back,
blew all the air out of his lungs, and tried to relax. When
he became aware of himself again, he and his teammates
were huddled around Coach Mills in the middle of the infield.

"Men, some of you turned in some very fast times. Now,
I don't expect you to run those times today; by God, I demand it." He paused. A tinge of anxiety flashed through
Jamie's already tense body. "If you don't make your
times," he growled, "I promise you that you'll be out here
every day, before and after practice, running until we're
satisfied that you're in the kind of shape you gon' have to
be in order to help this ball club win. Now let's get after it.
Give me that first group on the track."

Jamie sat watching and keeping his legs loose as the
first group ran, rested four minutes while the second
group ran, and then ran again. As the second group approached the straightaway for the final time, Jamie stood;
his group was next. He watched an overweight player
stumble across the finish line, stagger off the track, bend
at the knees, and throw up loudly. The players in the
stands howled with laughter.

"Hey, boy, who you callin'?"

"Sound like he sayin' E-Earl. E-Earl?"

"Fool, Earl can't help you now."

Again they laughed.

"Next group," Coach Mills shouted.

Jamie nervously stepped out onto the track with the
others.

"OK, Griffin," Coach said loudly. "Show them old-
timers sitting up there what a forty-eight-second quarter
looks like."

"Forty-eight!" he heard someone yell from the stands.

"Who?"

"I got to see this."

Anxiously, Jamie looked around. He noticed that everyone had moved to the edge of the track. Suddenly his legs felt rubbery. He lowered his head, leaned forward, and retreated inside himself.

"Ready." He paused. "Go."

Jamie exploded off the line and raced toward the curve. He glided through the first turn and sped down the back stretch. Now no one was close to him; he was racing against the clock. Everyone stood marveling and screaming as his long, fluent strides led him into the final curve.

"Watch out for that bear," someone joked.

"Push."

"Stay relaxed."

"Drive. Drive."

The track straightened out before him and he accelerated. His legs were heavy and his breath was short, but he held his form and raced through the finish line. Panting heavily, he coasted to a stop, bent over, and rested his hands on his knees.

Coach Mills stood gaping at the watch. Everyone was quiet, anticipating. He smiled wryly and bellowed, "Forty-six point nine."

Jamie's head jerked up and a smile spread across his face. Screams of disbelief filled the air.

"Way to run, Franchise."

"Stay loose."

Fatigued, Jamie stepped off the track onto the infield and cupped his hands behind his head. Slowly he walked back and forth, taking slow, deep breaths in an attempt to suck air into his depleted lungs. The hot, humid air had dried his mouth. He wished he could get a drink of cool water. He pushed that thought from his mind and began speculating on how much time was left in his rest period.

He thought of the quarter he had just run. Why had he run so fast? Now the pressure was on him to run the second one much faster than if he had run the first one slower. In the distance he heard Coach Mills call for his group.

"Awready," Jamie mumbled softly.

He felt more exhausted now than when he had first completed the run. Wearily, he walked back out onto the track and prepared himself.

"Let's go, Jamie," he heard someone shout.

"Another one just like the other one."

"Ready." He paused. "Go."

Jamie exploded off the line again, his body leaning slightly forward and his long, graceful strides gobbling up the track. He was tired; his jaws inflated and deflated as he sucked air into his bursting lungs. Halfway down the backstretch, he stole a look at the approaching curve. He ran faster, fighting against the tightness pulling against his legs. Again he became aware of everyone.

"Looking good, Jamie."

"Git down, homeboy."

Jamie burst through the final curve, flew down the straightaway, and sailed past Coach Mills. He slowed to a walk, clasped his hands behind his head, and slowly walked back toward Coach Mills.

"Hey, hey, hey," Mills yelled excitedly. "Forty-seven flat."

"Good job, Franchise."

"Way to get after it, son."

Exhausted, Jamie stepped off the track, kneeled on the ground, and tried to block out everything around him. His breath came in quick, short spurts, his thigh muscles ached, and he felt a sharp, excruciating pain throbbing in the center of his head. In spite of it all, he was elated.

CHAPTER 10

IT was the second week of a two-a-day practice. Carl Bodkins, the second team fullback, had just sustained a leg injury in a three-on-three drill. Momentary silence filled the air as concerned teammates awaited the approaching trainer. Suddenly Coach Mills pushed next to Carl.

"Get up from there," he shouted angrily.

"I can't," Carl moaned, painfully.

Stunned, Jamie watched Mills draw back his leg and kick Carl in the seat of his pants.

"I said get up."

Slowly, Carl struggled to his feet. Obviously in intense pain, he stood with most of his weight on his healthy leg. Mills moved forward until only inches separated the two of them. His face was red and his teeth were clenched.

"Son, you better suck it up and get after it."

Carl stared at him but he didn't answer. His lips were trembling slightly, his eyes filled with pain and hatred.

"Son, if you looking for sympathy you can find it in the dictionary between shit and syphilis. But by God, you ain't gon' find none out here. Do you understand me?"

"Yessuh," Carl answered, his voice shaking.

"Now get back in there."

Carl gingerly walked back to his position.

"Hurry up! Hurry up!" Mills yelled, shoving him violently in the back.

Carl joined Jamie on the field.

"You awright, man?" Jamie asked.

"I guess I have to be," Carl said, snapping his chin strap.

"They probably ain't gon' give you the ball noway."

"I wouldn't bet on that."

Coach Green, the defensive coordinator, walked behind the three defensive linemen. Jamie watched dumbfounded as Green pointed to Carl, then to the right side of the line, yelling, "This back! This hole!"

The ball was snapped. Carl, limping badly, lunged forward and plowed into the right side of the line. There was a thunderous collision. Carl grunted, his head jerked backward, and his body toppled awkwardly to the ground, pinning his injured leg beneath the pile.

"Goddammit, Ken Blackett!" Coach Green yelled, running forward and hitting Ken over the head with his cap. "Don't let that running back fall forward!"

"Same backs," Mills yelled quickly.

Grimacing, Carl got up and moved back into position—his limp was noticeably worse. Jamie looked over at Carl. He stood crouched over with his exposed stomach rising and falling rapidly. His eyes were watery but his face held the look of a person determined not to be broken. Out of the corner of his eye, Jamie could see Mills poised on the sidelines, watching. Why was he doing this? Why was he being so cruel?

Mills stepped onto the field, cupped his hand around his mouth, and yelled, "Get mad, Carl! Get mad at me, you big bastard!"

Again Coach Green pointed at Carl.

"This back! This hole!"

The players on the sideline stood quietly staring in disbelief. The ball was snapped. Carl hobbled to the line. Again he was pounded to the ground. But this time he didn't get up; he lay moaning and clutching his injured leg.

"Get up! Get up!" Mills's voice rang through the air.

Suddenly Jamie felt a strange, strong feeling coming from the depths of his stomach. His legs started trembling and his body became tense. It was that same feeling he had while crouched underneath the Anderson house the night Eight Ball was killed. He was watching another white man mistreating a black man and he was still powerless. He couldn't do anything to stop it now or prevent it from happening again in the future. He had a wild desire to grab Mills by the throat and strangle the life out of him. But Mills controlled his destiny; he could revoke his scholarship at any time.

Coach Mills moved forward.

"Get up!" he yelled again.

Carl avoided Mills's eyes and made no attempt to stand. Disgusted, Mills turned to one of his assistant coaches.

"Move the drill over," he ordered coldly.

"Let's go, men. Hustle up."

"Give me two new backs."

As they shifted the drill over a few yards, Doc Parker hurried to Carl's side, kneeled next to him, and began examining his injured leg. After Jamie made it off the field, he turned and looked. Carl had risen and, with Doc's assistance, was slowly limping toward the sidelines.

Later, as Carl stood watching the conclusion of practice, Jamie approached him.

"How's yo' leg?"

"It's probably broke."

"That's too bad, man."

Carl looked at him coldly.

"Let me give you a little free advice, Franchise."

"Yeah, what's that?"

"Don't git hurt. 'Cause if you do you gon' find out how much they love you 'round here."

Jamie stood listening and avoiding Carl's eyes.

"Around here the motto they live by is kill a mule, buy another one. Kill a nigguh, hire another one. The work gon' git done one way or the other."

Across the field the horn sounded. Practice was over. Exhausted, the players gathered around Mills, removed their helmets, and dropped down to one knee. Mills, standing front and center, stared directly at Carl.

"Men, there's a difference between being hurt and being injured. When you hurt, you can play. But when you're injured, you wish like hell you could play. And by God, if a bone ain't sticking through the skin, you ain't injured. Is that clear?"

"Yessuh," they responded collectively.

Jamie didn't answer. Instead he looked up at Mills, then at Coach Hunt. Why had Hunt stood by and allowed Mills to mistreat Carl? Why hadn't he said anything?

"As a team, we got better today. Let's make sure we do the same thing tomorrow. Take it in."

Yelling and screaming, they leaped to their feet and hurried toward the locker room. Inside, Jamie quickly showered and dressed. He started to leave but didn't. Instead, he walked to Coach Hunt's office, knocked on the door, and entered. Smiling warmly, Coach Hunt rose and placed his arm around his shoulders.

"Son, you did a good job out there today. Boy, you hell when you well."

"Yeah, but what happens when I'm sick?" Jamie asked bitterly.

"What you mean?" Hunt responded, releasing Jamie from his embrace.

"I mean, what happens when I can't go no mo'? Do I git a white man's shoes up my butt till I git better? You know, like Carl got out there today?"

Hunt looked at Jamie angrily.

"Son, that's just football."

"Naw, Coach, that ain't football. That's a white man puttin' his foot up a black man's butt 'cause he know he can."

Hunt pointed his finger at Jamie.

"Don't go trying to make something out of this that it ain't. I don't know what's eating you. But whatever it is, you better let it go and do what you came here for."

Jamie sighed, shaking his head slowly.

"I can see it was a mistake comin' in here. I'm talkin' to the wrong man."

"Son, what do you want me to do?" Hunt asked angrily. "I'm just an employee. Mills calls all the shots around here, including who gets hired and who gets fired. I got a family to feed and this job is how I feed them."

"Yeah, right," Jamie mumbled.

"Look," Hunt continued, "my advice to you is go out there and do the best that you can. The things that I can help you with I will. Son, you're a helluva running back, but I'd advise you not to cause too many waves. Good running backs are a dime a dozen. And ULNO got plenty of money."

"Awright, Coach," Jamie said sarcastically, "I'll try to remember that."

Two weeks later at the season opener, Jamie stood watching from the sidelines as ULNO pushed the ball across the fifty-yard line. He glanced at the clock—there were five minutes remaining in the first quarter.

"All right, Griffin, get in there."

Jamie nervously snapped his chin strap and trotted out onto the turf. Suddenly there was a deafening roar as the capacity crowd acknowledged him. Jamie reached the huddle, placed his hand on his bent knees, and sighed deeply. Though he had yet to run a play, he felt exhausted. His mouth hung open, his eyes were wide, and his breath came in short, quick spurts. The quarterback knelt and looked up at him.

"Here we go, Franchise. Get your name in the paper."

Jamie leaned forward and listened intently.

"Strong right, twenty-eight toss, on two. Ready break."

Jamie took a deep breath. He was going to carry the ball around the right side of the line of scrimmage. He took his position behind the fullback, put his mouthpiece in place, and carefully checked the defensive formation. Again the crowd cheered loudly, but Jamie didn't hear them. He was in that quiet zone, anticipating the play and visualizing its outcome in his mind.

The center snapped the ball. Immediately Jamie took a counterstep to his left, then sprinted right, receiving the toss from the quarterback. The left cornerback read the play perfectly. He sailed across the line of scrimmage and rammed his helmet into Jamie's thighs just as he was receiving the pitch. There was a thunderous crash, but somehow Jamie maintained his balance and spun out of the tackle. He spotted an opening, accelerated through it, and cut back across the defense. He picked up a block, sprinted outside, and high-stepped down the far sideline. He crossed the goal line and the crowd exploded. Elated, Jamie made his way to the chaotic sidelines.

"Way to run tough."

"Helluva job, son."

When the game ended, Jamie hustled off the field and into the dressing room. He had rushed for one hundred twenty-five yards and scored three touchdowns. For a long time, he sat in front of his locker answering reporters' questions and having his picture taken.

At seven-thirty the following Monday morning, he rushed through the cafeteria door. It was the first day of classes and he was running late. He hesitated in front of the check-in table.

"Hey, Coach, you got me?"

"Yeah, stud. I got you."

As the coach checked his name off the list, Jamie moved to the back of the breakfast line. Amused, he stood watching one of his teammates teasing one of the workers.

"Baby, what's yo' problem this mornin'?"

"What?" she responded sheepishly.

"You ain't got but two flapjacks on that plate."

"So?"

"So!" he mocked her. "What's a big ole nigguh like me

gon' do with two little ole flapjacks? Girl, you better put a little mo' height on that stack."

Laughing, she complied, piling several more pancakes on his plate.

"Right on, baby," he said, moving on through the line.

Jamie got his food and moved to a table in front of the large bay window where several other players were already sitting.

"Say, fellows, can I sit here?"

"Hey, you the man. You can cop a squat anywhere you wanna."

"C'mon man, cut me some slack," Jamie said, taking a seat.

Jamie silently organized his utensils, blessed his food, and began eating. There was the sound of approaching footsteps behind him. A deep, burly voice filled the air.

"What's happenin', fellows?"

Jamie turned and looked back over his shoulder. It was a guy they called Money.

"You ain't, that's fo' sho'," one of the guys teased him.

"Man, you look like somebody whupped you with a ugly stick."

"Nigguh, that's cold-blooded." He sat down next to Jamie.

"Might be, but it's right on time."

"I don't know what we gotta git up and eat breakfast fo'."

"'Cause Gene Mills say so."

"Mills ain't my daddy."

"You got yo' rusty butt in here, don't you?"

They all laughed.

"Aw, nigguh, that ain't funny."

"So you say."

Jamie watched him open the small container of jelly and stir it into his scrambled eggs.

"Man, I swear," he mumbled angrily, "this is the stupidest rule I ever heard of. I can understand curfew. I can understand not bein' late fo' a meetin'. But no matter how I look at it, I can't understand makin' a man git up befo' seven-thirty every mornin' to eat breakfast."

"Maybe Mills figure if you git yo' big butt out the bed, you'll go'n to class."

"Aw, nigguh, Mills don't care if he go to class or not. He jus' wanna make sho' y'all eat and git big and strong. Why you thank we got our own trainin' table?"

"You reckon that's it?"

"You seen 'im run cats fo' skippin' breakfast, right?"

"Yeah."

"You ever seen 'im run a cat fo' cuttin' class?"

"Naw."

"Well then."

At seven-thirty, big Benny Norman, the right defensive tackle, walked over to their table, rubbed the sleep out of his eyes, and sat down.

"Say, Money."

Immediately Money plugged his ears with his fingers.

"Don't say it, Ben."

Ben opened his mouth as if to speak.

"I'm tellin' you, Benny, don't say it."

Benny chuckled.

"Money, if I was you, I wouldn't go to class today. It's jus' too nice outside."

Dumbfounded, Jamie watched Money drop his fork and rub his chin with his hand.

"By Gawd, Benny, you talked me into it."

The two doubled over with laughter.

"Hey, let's go to the union and shoot some pool."

"That'll work."

"Good. I oughta be able to take all yo' little BEOG money befo' we have to go to practice."

Jamie listened, stupefied.

"You cats really gon' cut class?" he heard himself ask.

"Like a knife cut butter."

"No foolin'?"

"Man, let me rap to you," Money began. "Ain't but two thangs you need to know 'round here."

"Yeah, what's that?"

"Always let Dr. J. fix yo' schedule."

"What else?"

"Always give yo' extra tickets to yo' professor."

"You serious, man?"

"As a heart attack."

"What about study hall?"

They looked at each other.

"What about it?"

"We have to go, right?"

"Naw, man."

Jamie looked confused.

"Mills said that all freshmen and players with less than a two point zero have to go to study hall every Tuesday and Thursday from seven to eight-thirty."

"Somebody clue this crab in?"

Again the older guys laughed.

"Look here. The athletic department hires a professor, right? Now, he suppose to go over yo' homework and stuff like that. Man, fo'git that. A week befo' the exam, he gon' brang a ole test."

"Man, you lyin'."

"Please. Most times what he brang gon' be the real thang. All you gotta do is memorize the answers."

"You gotta be jokin'."

"Homeboy, Mills got the whole thang rigged. You jus'

gotta play the game; he gon' make sho' you git over."

"He ain't lyin', man. Mills got plants everywhere at this school to look out fo' athletes."

"Fo' real?"

"Right on."

"Look here, man. They done hipped you to the professors and study hall and that kind of stuff, but check this out. If you play the game right, you won't never flunk no class, even if you don't never study."

"I know what you fixin' to tell 'im."

"Most of the time professor don't grade yo' test nohow."

"Ain't that a trip?"

"Who grade 'em?"

"Readers, man. Jus' regular ole students."

"Yeah, and a lot of 'em is hooked up with the athletic department. They'll take care of you."

"Take care of you?"

"Yeah. Say you don't know some of the answers. All you gotta do is leave 'em blank. The grader'll fill in enough of 'em fo' you to pass. But you gotta make sure that they know you a ball player."

"So you can waste yo' time goin' to class if you wanna. But you don't have to."

"Yeah, don't nobody go to class but crabs."

"Hey look."

One of them leaped up and tapped on the large bay window trying to get the attention of an attractive girl passing by outside.

"Man, that's gotta be the baddest honey I seen on the yard since I been here."

"That high yellar heifer?"

"Yeah, man. That's the way I like 'em."

"Me too."

"That's what I don't like 'bout you south Louisiana nigguhs. All of y'all color struck."

211

"And proud of it."

"I guess you like 'em black."

"Yep. The blacker the berry the sweeter the juice."

"Yeah, but if that berry too black it ain't no use."

The table erupted with laughter.

"Man, I ain't gon' lie. I done had 'em both, but it's jus' somethin' about a high yellar babe."

"Nigguh, what you sound like? Black as Kunta Kinte and got nerve enough to be color struck."

Again they laughed.

"Hey, fellows. Talkin' 'bout high yellar women—guess who came by my crib the other night?"

"Who?"

"Pam."

"Pam who?

"The cheerleader, fool."

"Nigguh lyin'."

"Fo' real, fellows."

"Boy, that girl won't give you the time of day."

"Keep on thankin' that."

"Did you do her?"

"Did I! Man, she's a freak."

"Please."

"Nigguh. I ain't gotta lie."

"When?"

"I tol' you, the other day."

"The other day when?"

"Friday night."

"What time Friday night?"

"Midnight, nigguh. Why you askin' me all them stupid questions?"

"Cause you lyin'."

"What I gotta lie fo'?"

"If you ain't lyin', tell us how you did it?"

"Easy," he boasted. "I sweet-talked her outta it."

"Aw, man, git outta here. You can do better than that."

"Aw, man, nothin'. Ya'll know my rap deadly. Boy, I'll sweet-talk the sugar outta syrup."

Everyone cried with laughter.

Before Jamie realized what he was doing, he had entered the conversation.

"Ain't no female visitation during the week."

They all laughed.

Jamie stared blankly.

"Man, what's so funny?"

"Franchise, I don't care how good you play ball, you still a crab."

"That's fo' sho'."

"What?" Jamie asked, confused.

"Fool, them rules ain't got nothin' to do with us. Mills makes the rule fo' our dorm and the university ain't got no pull with him. Besides, all our RAs is coaches and ex-jocks. They don't care what we do."

There was brief silence. Then the conversation switched back to the original debate.

"Man, I still say you lyin'."

"If I'm lyin', why she comin' back tonight?"

"Aw, you done stepped in it now."

"Fo' real! She'll be by after bed check."

"Uh-huh. Right."

"I'll prove it."

"Prove it then."

"You nigguhs come by my window 'bout a quarter till midnight. I'm gon' leave a crack in the curtain so y'all can see me work."

"Boy, you wild."

"Jus' be there."

"Awright, big mouth. We'll be there."

Jamie looked at his watch. It was five minutes until eight.

"I'm outta here," he said, rising quickly.

"Where you goin', Franchise?"

"Class."

"Aw, you gon' be a L-seven."

"What?" Jamie asked, confused.

"A square, fool."

"Hey, call it what you wanna. I'm goin' to class till I can git the lowdown fo' myself."

CHAPTER 11

BATTERED and worn, Jamie limped to the sidelines and solemnly glanced at the scoreboard. It was fourth down, with four seconds left to play, and they were down by two points to crosstown rival LSU. The game had been so bitterly contested by both teams that it seemed only fitting that the final outcome should be determined in the waning seconds. As the field goal unit hustled out, Jamie stared at the ball. It would be a forty-two-yarder. If the field goal was good, they were conference champs; if not, they would be haunted all year by thoughts of what might have been. Suddenly, a voice rang from the stands and fluttered down to the field.

"Let's go, baby. Kick it through."

Methodically, the kicker advanced toward the ball, drew his leg back, and snapped it forward. Breathlessly, Jamie watched the ball rise from the tee, sail through the uprights, and crash against the scoreboard. A violent roar went up and hundreds of exuberant fans leaped from the stands and stormed the field. Somewhat fearful, Jamie darted from the sidelines, raced through the tunnel, and headed for the safety of the locker room. Inside the building, Jamie sprinted into the dressing room, slammed his helmet into his locker, and screamed, "SEC champs!"

For the next half hour, frenzied mirth filled the locker room; screaming players pounded on lockers and danced in the aisles; coaches hugged and congratulated each other; and reporters, seeking interviews, jostled for position in front of key players' lockers. When things finally simmered down, Jamie took a long, soothing shower, got dressed, and started the short, solitary walk back to the dorm. Unlike many of his teammates who were rushing out to paint the town red, Jamie sought a quiet place to contemplate his very successful first year of college football.

Outside, he walked to the edge of the stadium, stopped, and looked around. The streets were full and noisy. Celebratory automobile operators departing the parking lot gleefully honked their horns as they patiently navigated through the cheering pedestrians milling about. Seeking anonymity and protection against the cold night wind, Jamie pulled the hood of his coat over his head. Then with much of his face covered, he surreptitiously moved through the crowd. It was too cold to sit outside, but he didn't want to go back to the dorm, which he imagined was probably swarming with people. Besides, he was hungry. He stopped, took his wallet from his back pocket, and looked inside. There was a five-dollar bill and several ones. He went off campus to the least crowded fast food place he could find, got something to eat, killed a few hours, and then headed back to the dorm.

When he made it to the parking lot, everything seemed to be relatively calm. He entered through the back door, climbed the stairs to his room, and went inside. He clicked the light on and, as he expected, his roommate still wasn't there. He quickly undressed, pulled the covers back, and eased beneath them, sighing pleasurably as his skin made contact with the cool sheets. No sooner had his body sunk into the softness of his bed than the door cracked open and the light from the hallway pierced through his pitch dark room.

"Hey, man, you 'sleep?"

Jamie rolled over and looked at his clock; it was five minutes past two.

"Naw. What you want?"

"Come down to the first floor."

"Fo' what?"

"Jus' come or you gon' miss it."

"Awright."

His curiosity was piqued. He would go downstairs, see what was going on, and then go back to bed. He tumbled out of bed, got dressed, and still clumsy with sleep, descended the stairs to the first floor. Though it was the early hours of morning, a large group of guys were milling around the hallway outside one of the rooms.

"Man, what's goin' on?" Jamie asked the first person he saw.

"They got a girl in there."

"A girl?"

"Yeah. They picked her up at a bar."

"Man, y'all trippin'."

Jamie pushed to the door and looked inside. A slender, well-built white girl, wearing nothing but a football jersey and cowboy boots, was sitting on the bed smoking a cigarette. Standing around the room were mostly white boys—some of them drinking beer, but all of them acting rowdy. Jamie was suddenly wide awake. He stood wondering whether he should stay and watch or go back upstairs. It made him uneasy looking at her. He was about to leave when she spoke.

"I wanna do the whole football team starting with the linebackers."

The room erupted with shouts and catcalls. Dazed, Jamie stood perfectly still, watching as one of his wild-eyed, half-drunk, white teammates walked over to the bed and began unbuttoning his pants.

"You ain't no linebacker," she drawled, taking a long drag on her cigarette.

"Yeah I am," he slurred.

She ground the cigarette in an ashtray, pulled the jersey over her head, and lay back on the bed. Transfixed, Jamie stared hypnotically at her large white breasts and curvaceous body as she moaned sensually; "Bring it on, big daddy, and show me what you got."

"All right, baby, let's get it on."

Again the room erupted into a wild frenzy—fists drummed against the walls, feet pounded the floor, and screams filled the air.

"Work on her, Slim."

"Do it to her."

"Ride her, cowboy."

Jamie stood watching but not believing what he was seeing as the two closely pressed bodies swayed rhythmically upon the bed, slowly at first, then more rapidly, keeping time to the musical taunts of their hysterical audience. Then, with a violent shudder of his hips, and a single, deep-throated grunt, it was over. Satisfied, he rose from the bed and began pulling up his pants.

"That's it?" she wailed.

"Hey, baby, that's all I got," he answered her.

Disgusted, she sat up and lit another cigarette.

"Hell, I want a real man," she mumbled. "I'm in the jock dorm and can't get a good roll."

Everyone in the crowded room howled with laughter.

"Aw, Slim, she dogging you out, man."

Simultaneously repulsed and fascinated, Jamie watched as one guy after another took his turn amid thunderous yelling. Suddenly the room grew quiet. David Freeman, a black defensive back from Houston, stepped forward.

"We fixing to see something now."

"Wear her out, Dave."

As David approached the bed, she arched her back and slowly ran her tongue across her lips.

"Now you're talking," she crooned. "C'mon, big boy, let's show 'em how a real man makes love."

Instinctively, Jamie stepped forward, grabbed Dave by the hand, and led him away from the bed.

"Aw, leave him alone, Franchise."

"Yeah, let him have his fun."

Suddenly they began to chant.

"Party, party, party . . ."

Jamie led David out into the hall.

"Man, don't git involved in this thang," he advised sternly. "Tomorrow when everybody sobers up, they might see this situation differently."

"Yeah, man, you right."

"C'mon. Let's go."

The two of them walked slowly up the stairs together. Neither spoke. Jamie could see that David was a little upset with him, but he didn't really care. He reached the door, said good night, and went inside. He climbed into bed and pulled the covers up tight under his chin. As he lay staring into the darkness of the room, he thought of what he had seen downstairs. Though he had heard his black teammates brag about their exploits with women, he had never known any of them to publicly humiliate a woman like that.

When the season had ended, with them as conference champs, Jamie eagerly anticipated long periods of idleness and relaxation. But to his dismay, the off-season workouts, which began almost immediately, were just as grueling, if not more so, than those during the season. NCAA rules prohibited teams from practicing during the off season, except for the twenty days allotted for spring drills. But at ULNO, the coaches circumvented the rules by requiring each of the players to enroll in a "P.E." course taught by the strength coach that, in reality, was nothing short of a football conditioning program. For Jamie, each day was just like the other—eat, sometimes go to class, but most times not, work out, sleep, and then start the whole routine again.

All afternoon he lay across his bed dreading the day's workout. His tired, aching muscles hadn't recovered from the day before. From across the room Michael's weary voice called out, "'Bout that time, roomy."

Jamie raised to his elbows, glanced at the clock, and pulled a pillow over his head.

"Man, I swear, they work us harder now than they did durin' the season." The pillow muffled his voice.

"Yeah, they gittin' their money worth outta us, awright."

"It don't make sense. What all this gotta do with next season?"

"I don't know, but I'm lookin' forward to spring practice. At least then we'll git some relief."

"Yeah."

"Well, roomy, I'm gon' head on over. You goin' now?"

"Naw, man. I ain't goin' till I have to," Jamie said defiantly.

"Awright then. Later."

"Yeah, man, later."

Jamie laid his head down and dreadingly watched the minute hand on the clock climb slowly toward the twelve. If he could have willed time still he would have. When he couldn't put it off any longer, he reluctantly got up, stretched his arms high above his head, and yawned loudly. He moved to the mirror, quickly ran a comb through his hair, and headed out the door. As he stepped outside, he noticed the other students enjoying the afternoon sunshine and smiling and laughing as though they didn't have a care in the world. He stared enviously at them. What would it be like to be a regular student, having control over his time, instead of being obligated to spend most of it at the football stadium?

"Hey, Griffin." One of them recognized him.

"Yeah."

"Congratulations on y'all's season."

"Thanks, man."

"Boy, what I wouldn't give to be you."

Jamie smiled.

"I'd probably give jus' as much to be you right now."

Slightly amused at the puzzled looked on their faces, Jamie slowly walked past them, envying their freedom even more and trying to envision what sort of torture awaited him at the stadium. Though he had slept all afternoon, he didn't feel at all rested—either mentally or physically. As his sore, muscular legs brought him to the stadium door, he sighed deeply, pulled the door open, and mumbled softly, "Please give me the strength to make it through this one."

Inside the locker room, all was quiet except for the monotonous tune blaring over the radio. Jamie put on his shorts, T-shirt, and sneakers, and then walked out into the hall, joining the other players scheduled for the next workout. The hour drawing near, they all stood silently listening to the torturous-sounding screams and shouts seeping underneath the closed doors of the turf room.

"Man, Wheeler know how to whup a body."

"You ain't never lied."

Suddenly the door flew open and a small group of players, drenched with sweat and visibly exhausted, staggered out, followed closely by David Wheeler, the strength coach. In one hand he carried a clipboard and in the other a whistle. As the stern, muscular man approached, his angry eyes roving back and forth, Jamie could see that his mood was even worse than usual.

"I hope y'all came to work," he barked. "That last group sure as hell didn't."

Wheeler flung the door open and they all followed him inside. It was a huge room with a forty-yard artificial surface. During the season it was used for practice when the weather prevented the team from going outside.

Coach Wheeler had placed a portable weight machine in the center of the right half of the room and he had positioned free weights in various other places.

"Men, we have twenty-one stations. I want you to divide into groups of twos. Each group will spend ten working minutes at each station. You'll lift for one minute, rest ten seconds, lift for another minute, rest ten more seconds, and lift for another minute. Then you'll switch with your partner. If anybody quits, or hesitates on a set, we start the whole thing over. If anybody throws up on my floor he's gon' do five hundred yards of Russian hops. We got some trash cans in corners. If you need them use them.

But if I see you standing over a can you better be calling Earl."

Jamie felt a slight lessening of tension as he looked at the setup. This was going to be a piece of cake, he thought. For the past month they had been in the regular weight room, which had more equipment and heavier weight. At least this would be light and quick.

Halfway through the workout, Rabbit, a small walk-on running back from the area, began having trouble with his set. He was on the squat rack and his legs were exhausted. He strained but couldn't get the weight up.

"Don't you quit on me, Rabbit," Coach Wheeler yelled.

Rabbit hesitated under the strain of the weights.

"Men, that set don't count," Wheeler yelled.

A chorus of moans filled the air.

"What you gon' do, Rabbit?" Wheeler challenged. "You gon' feel sorry for yourself because you a little tired? You gon' let your teammates down? Or you gon' suck it up and get after it?"

Rabbit gritted his teeth and attempted to complete the set. Halfway through he paused.

"That set don't count," Wheeler yelled again. "Rabbit's dogging it." He walked closer to Rabbit. "C'mon, son, it's the fourth quarter, we counting on you to score. Let's go. It's fourth and goal. What you gon' do?"

Rabbit crouched underneath the bar. His face was sweating and legs were trembling. He struggled against the weight, but couldn't lift it any higher.

"If I could lift it, I would," Rabbit yelled out.

"If! If!" Coach Wheeler yelled, the veins in his head popping up. "Son, 'if' is the biggest little word in the English language," he growled. "Only quitters make excuses. Only quitters talk about what they could've done or would've done if this would have happened or if that

223

would have happened. How I'm gon' defend a championship with a loser like you? You make my butt crawl."

For the next couple weeks, David Wheeler's workouts got progressively harder. After one of the most grueling conditioning workouts he had ever been through, Jamie Ray sat in front of his locker, unable to move. He had managed to dress, but felt too weak to begin the trek back to the dorm. His swarming head told him that any minute now he was going to throw up.

A teammate approached his locker.

"Say, Franchise, you all right?"

"Yeah, man." He forced a smile.

"You want a ride back to the dorm?"

Jamie's pride prevented him from revealing how much the workout had taken out of him.

"Naw, man. I'm gon' walk."

"All right. Check you later."

Twenty minutes later, Jamie shuffled into the parking lot in front of the dorm. An ambulance had backed to the entrance and the doors were flung open. When he came to it, he stopped and stared curiously inside. It was empty. Someone inside must be sick. He squeezed past the ambulance and hurried inside the building. Some of his teammates had congregated at the foot of the stairs.

"Hey, what's goin' on?"

"They takin' Rabbit to the hospital."

"What's wrong with 'im?"

"Don't know, man."

"Well, what happened?"

"One minute he was walkin' up the stairs and the next minute he was lyin' on the floor shakin'. That's all I know."

Concerned, Jamie's eyes followed the paramedics as they wheeled Rabbit toward the door.

"Say, mister, what's wrong with 'im?"

"He's suffering from exhaustion. We gon' take him in. He ought to be all right in a couple of days."

Jamie watched them lift the stretcher into the back of the ambulance and speed away.

"One of these days Wheeler gon' mess 'round here and kill somebody," he mumbled angrily.

"You ain't lyin'."

Jamie climbed the stairs to his room, went inside, and stretched out on the bed. He lay very still. He felt that if he tried to move anytime soon, his body would rebel against him. He buried his head into the softness of his pillow, closed his eyes, and fought against thoughts of tomorrow until his weary body gradually succumbed to sleep.

Slowly, days and then weeks passed until the team was no longer reporting to Wheeler, but now was going through their regular twenty days of spring football practice. During the second week of contact drills, Jamie suffered a slight shoulder injury. After practice, he spent an hour in the training room receiving treatment. That night when he got back to his room, Michael was lying in bed smoking a joint and listening to the radio.

"What's goin' on, roomy?" Michael asked as Jamie entered the room.

"Not much, man."

"I hear you," Michael said, giggling. "Where you been?"

"Trainin' room."

"What's wrong?"

"Sore shoulders," Jamie said, slowly rotating his arm. "Man, I can barely lift my arms above my head."

"You wanna hit this 'erb?" Michael asked, handing him the joint.

"Man, you know I don't mess 'round with that stuff."

"Hey bro, this ain't messin' 'round, it's stayin' around."

"Man, you losin' yo' mind."

"Look, you gon' have to play with that pain or you ain't gon' play at all, right?"

"Yeah." Jamie nodded.

"Well, this is the best medicine in the world," Michael said, putting the joint to his lips and taking a long drag.

Jamie shook his head slowly as he watched the end of the joint glow and the small circles of smoke rise up toward the ceiling.

"Roomy, if I gotta git it that way I jus' as soon not have it."

"Hey, suit yourself," Michael said, hunching his shoulders and throwing his hands up. "Now me, I choose to follow Malcolm's philosophy: 'By any means necessary.' That's what I'm talkin' bout."

"Man, you crack me up."

"Hey, I'm jus' tryin' to make it."

"Say, bro, whatever works fo' you."

Jamie took off his shirt and his shoes and then stepped out of his pants.

"You want this light on?"

"Naw."

Jamie turned the light out and laid across the bed trying to ignore the heavy scent of marijuana lingering in the air.

"Say, Mike."

"Yeah, roomy."

"You know you smoke too much weed, don't you? I mean you on that stuff twenty-four-seven."

Michael laughed loudly.

"Yeah, me and jus' about everybody else 'round here."

Jamie knew he was telling the truth. All but a few of his teammates were doing some kind of drugs.

"But why?"

"Hey, it's easy to git caught up in it. First time I took a hit was when I came here on a recruit trip last year. You know, to show cats I was cool. Then after I got here I started hittin' it befo' practice so I could play hurt. Then after practice to relax. Now, I take a hit justa git off. But hey, I don't smoke nothin' but weed. I don't mess 'round with that hard stuff."

Jamie chuckled.

"Yo' folks know you a dopehead?"

"Please. My ole man'd kill me if he knew."

"Ain't you scared that Coach or somebody gon' bust you?"

"Man, them coaches don't care 'bout us smokin' weed. I heard Coach tell a cat the other day that he didn't care how much weed he smoked jus' 'long as he burned some incense or opened a window."

"Is that right?"

"Yeah, man. Long as the cat don't git careless and git caught by folks outside the athletic department, he awright. But if he git hung up outside he on his own. That's why I smoke my stuff in the dorm."

"Well, I probably won't ever understand it."

"I'm tellin' you, man. A lot of cats smokin' 'erb justa deal with college ball."

"If you say so."

"Ask 'em. Half of 'em'll tell you they can't play unless they high."

Almost five months later, the joy that followed the championship season had all but dissipated and in its place were the angry frustrations of a talented team that found itself one game under a five hundred season with two games left on the schedule. For Jamie, his sophomore season was nothing short of spectacular. But graduation, untimely injuries, and the complacency of having won a championship the year before had all but decimated the competitiveness of the team.

Late Sunday afternoon, the first team meeting since the

team's most recent blowout, a despondent Jamie ambled into the large meeting room and took a seat.

"I ain't lookin' forward to this."

"Me neither."

"I'm sho' Mills gon' go off."

Suddenly the door flew open and Coach Mills entered the room.

"Speak of the devil."

Coach Mills moved to the right side of the room, stopped, and surveyed the group.

"Wonder who he lookin' fo'?" he whispered, cautiously.

"I don't know."

"Reggie?" Coach Mills bellowed.

"Up here, Coach," Reggie, a senior defensive back from Arkansas answered.

"Son, did somebody make you the defensive captain and not tell me about it?"

"Nosuh."

"Well, you keep your mouth shut in the huddle, you understand?"

"Certain people out there oughta do they job," Reggie mumbled.

Suddenly Coach Mills raced up the stairs, pulled Reggie out of his seat, and pushed him into the wall.

"Get out of here!" he screamed. "Clean out your locker and get out."

Stunned, Reggie stood watching as Mills leaped down the stairs, grabbed him, and pushed him toward the door.

"Get. We don't need you around here. You find somewhere else to eat and sleep."

Jamie felt a lump of anger rise from his stomach and lodge in his throat. What's Mills trying to prove? He watched Reggie collect himself and slowly leave the room. Mills quickly turned and faced the team.

"If anybody else got a problem, you can get out too."

A tense quiet fell over the room.

"This afternoon we're gonna look over the film from that pitiful performance you gave last night—tomorrow night we're gonna go over the scout report—then over the next couple of weeks we're gonna play out the schedule. After that, the coaches and I will evaluate each and every one of you. And if we feel that you're not a winner, we're gonna get you out of here and bring in somebody who is. Is that clear?"

On cue the chorus sang out, "Yes sir."

That night, Jamie and several of his black teammates went to the Soul Shack for a late evening snack. As they sat at a back table near the wall eating barbecue, someone broached the subject of what had occurred in the meeting room a few hours earlier.

"Man, what Mills did wasn't right."

"Homeboy jus' frustrated 'bout the season."

"So. That don't make it right."

"Hey, I didn't say it did."

"Don't make no excuses for 'im."

"Chill out, man."

"Yeah, ain't no sense us fightin' each other."

There was silence.

"Y'all noticed it's always a black guy Mills go off on."

"Yeah," Jamie said quickly. "I noticed that when I first got here."

"As long as he needed 'im, Reggie couldn't do nothin' wrong. But now that Reggie's a senior and we ain't got but two games left, he kick 'im out."

"Yeah, man, homeboy can't sleep in the dorm or eat on the trainin' table."

"Ain't that a trip?"

"Wonder what he gon' do?"

"Him? What we gon' do?"

"What you mean?"

"Ain't nothin' we can do."

"Yeah it is."

"What's that?"

"We can go by Mills' office and tell 'im that if Reggie don't play ain't none of us brothers gon' play."

"Man, that ain't gon' work. He'll kick us all outta here."

"Naw he won't."

"I don't know, man, he might."

"Even if he don't, you ain't never gon' git all the brothers to go 'long with that. They ain't gon' take no chance on losin' they scholarship fo' Reggie. Man, that cat on his own."

"Yeah, a lot of 'em thank he had it comin'."

"Boy, I swear. My people, my people."

Jamie took a bite out of his chicken. As he chewed, he looked out in front of him. It was obvious his mind was no longer focused on them. The conversation brought back memories of the talk he had with his mother the night Eight Ball was murdered. She had felt that there was nothing they could do about that. Now these guys felt there was nothing they could do about this. When were black people going to find the courage to stand up against white folks when they were wronged by them?

"You brothers go to ULNO?"

They were interrupted by the guy sitting at the next table. The sound of his voice broke the trance Jamie had slipped into.

"Yeah."

"Y'all football players?"

"Uh-huh."

"Hey, I don't mean to be gettin' in y'all's conversation, but seems like you brothers would be interested in some of the thangs we gon' be discussin' at the meetin' tomorrow night."

"What meetin'?"

"The Black Caucus meetin'."

A couple of them stared, confused.

"You brothers familiar with the Black Caucus, ain't you?"

"Yeah, man. We heard of it," Jamie said, speaking for the group.

"Good. Y'all ought to come check us out tomorrow night. We meet at eight-thirty above the student union."

The following night, Jamie attended his first black caucus meeting. He needed some answers and he figured that this was as good a place to start as any. Shortly after he got there, a tall, slender, dark-skinned guy walked up front and stood behind the podium. He was the president of the association.

"Black folks of ULNO, you're bein' lynched," he began. "Not physically, but mentally. Everyone from our black faculty members, our black student body, our black athletes, to our black Greeks has felt the sting of this white, racist educational system. No one or nothin' has been spared. The hour has come fo' us black folks to band together and git about our people's business. Together we stand. Divided we fall."

Jamie settled into his seat and focused his attention on the skinny man. Then the corners of his mouth turned up, forming a faint approving smile.

CHAPTER 12

FRIDAY evening during the spring semester. Responding to a soft knock, Michael pulled the door open and a young brown-skinned woman stepped inside.

"Stacey! Girl, what you doin' over here?"

"Hello to you too, Mikey," she said, embracing him.

"Oh, I'm sorry. How you doin'?"

"I'm fine."

"Jamie, this is my cousin Stacey Lefere."

"Hi, Stacey," Jamie called from the other side of the room.

"It's a pleasure to meet you, Jamie."

Jamie's eyes were wide taking in Stacey. She was tall with a voluptuous build. Her soft brown eyes were accentuated by long black eyelashes. She had long, lustrous hair and full, oval-shaped lips.

"Now," Michael asked again, "what you doin' over here?"

"I'm spendin' the weekend with one of my sorors. Do you know Linda Jones?"

"She kinda short and skinny and goes out with Marvin?"

"Yeah, that's her. She brought me over here to meet him. And since I was in the building, I decided to drop in on you for a minute."

"How long you gon' be on campus?" Mike wanted to know.

"Oh, until tomorrow."

"Good. Maybe we can hook up befo' you leave."

"Sure. Call me at Linda's so we can set up something. Look, I better go. I don't want to keep her waiting."

"OK. Let me walk you out."

She looked across the room and smiled.

"Good-bye, Jamie."

" 'Bye, Stacey."

Jamie went to the door and watched the two of them walk down the hallway and disappear into Marvin's room. He paced back and forth pondering whether he should go and talk to her before she left or before some of the other guys saw her. He brushed aside the idea of going to the room. He didn't want to appear too eager. As he sat thinking, Michael returned.

Jamie leaped from the bed and looked at Michael with wide, shining eyes.

"Man, yo' cousin bad."

"You ain't lyin'."

"Roomy, I'm in love."

"Nigguh, you mean in lust."

"She got a boyfriend?"

"I don't know, home team. She used to date some light-weight guy from back east. But I don't know 'bout now."

"Is she still down the hall?"

"Naw, man, she went by Linda's crib."

"Alone?"

"Yeah."

Jamie hesitated a moment.

"You know the phone number over there?"

Michael smiled wryly.

"Matter of fact I do. She gave it to me right after she tol' me how cute you are."

Jamie looked stunned.

"Man, you lyin'."

"If I'm lyin', I'm flyin'."

Michael took a slip of crumpled paper from his shirt pocket and handed it to Jamie.

"You thank I should call her?"

"If you don't somebody else will."

Jamie called her. To his delight, she agreed to see him.

"Say, man, you got any advice befo' I go over there?"

"Yeah, play it cool. Jus' be nice and sincere. That's what she goes fo'."

"I hear you."

"I'm serious. Don't try no jive stuff like: 'Aw, baby, I'd rather be blind than have to watch you walk away from me.'"

They both exploded into thunderous laughter.

"I'll try to remember that."

"You better. 'Cause if you don't, she gon' send you packin'."

Jamie exited the dorm, walked across the footbridge,

and followed the winding sidewalk to Linda's door. He took a deep breath, cleared his throat, and knocked loudly. Inside he heard a chair scraping the floor and then the sound of faint footsteps. Stacey opened the door and the anxious tension he felt subsided.

"Hi, Jamie," she said with a warm smile. "Please come in and have a seat."

Jamie hesitated.

"Stacey, would you like to sit on the bayou fo' a while? It's kinda nice out tonight."

She smiled.

"Sure, but first I have to put on some sleeves."

"OK."

"Please come in."

Jamie entered the small living room and took a seat next to the window while she disappeared into the bedroom. Sitting alone, his eyes began to wander around the room. Unlike the single dormitory room that he shared with Michael, this one was more like a two-bedroom apartment.

"So Jamie, how are you and my crazy cousin getting along?" Stacey called from the other room.

"Fine. Michael's a good roommate."

"Yeah, he's good people. Are you from the area?"

"No. I'm from Pinesboro."

"Pinesboro! I never heard of it."

"It's a little farm town up 'round Shreveport."

She walked into the room, crossed over to the table, and scribbled something on a sheet of paper. She attached the note to the door and donned a sorority cap.

"Ready?" she asked politely.

"Yeah," he responded.

Outside, they walked behind the building and made their way to the bayou. On the edge of the bank, there were several small wooden benches, each strategically placed. As they slowly strolled along, Jamie patiently searched for the perfect spot.

"Stacey, what school you go to?"

"South Louisiana State College. It's in Baton Rouge."

"An all-black school?"

"That's right."

"How long you been there?"

"Oh, this is my junior year."

"You like it?"

"Yeah, it's sound academically and the people are friendly."

"Well, that's good."

"Maybe you can come over sometimes and I can show you around."

Then before he realized what he was saying, he blurted out, "You seein' anybody over there?"

As soon as the words passed from his lips, Jamie wished he could recall them. He didn't want to give the impression that he was trying to come on to her.

"I wouldn't wanna cause you no trouble," he said, clarifying the meaning of his words.

Her lips parted as a warm smile spread across her face. "That's very kind of you. But if I was seeing someone I wouldn't have invited you over." She put her hand on her hip and added playfully, "Besides, I'm just not that kind of girl."

The soft tone of her voice and her jovial sense of humor put him at ease and he began to slowly relax. For a moment they walked in silence.

"What about you?" she asked.

"Hunh?"

"Are you seeing anybody?"

"No. Nobody at all."

They reached a secluded spot along the bank of the

bayou and sat on one of the small wooden benches. It was a beautiful clear night and the light of the moon shimmered off the water. A small flock of ducks glided across the bayou so effortlessly that it appeared that they were being pushed along by the cool spring breeze. On the opposite bank, the light from the dormitory buildings cut through the darkness, giving them the illusion that they were on a deserted island far away from the rest of civilization.

"Jamie, you were right. This is a beautiful night."

Jamie nodded his head in agreement. For a moment, both of them sat taking in the night.

Jamie broke the silence.

"You from a big family?"

"No, I'm an only child."

"Is that right?" he asked excitedly. "So am I. What do your parents do?"

"Well, Mother doesn't work," she explained. "But she's really smart. She graduated from a women's college back east. Father doesn't want her to work, so she doesn't. Since I went off to college, she spends most of her time doing charity work. I'm really proud of her. She's been a great role model."

"What does yo' father do fo' a livin'?"

"He runs a catering service."

"Lefere's!" Jamie exclaimed. "You're that Lefere."

His reaction startled her momentarily.

"I guess you've heard of him."

"I sho' have," Jamie said. "Lefere's is one of the biggest caterers in south Louisiana. And they got the best food too."

She smiled casually.

"Oh, have you been to an event Lefere's served?"

"Yeah. Last year they catered our awards banquet."

"That doesn't surprise me. Father's quite a sports fan."

"Is that right?"

"Yes, it's a fact."

"Yo' folks seem interestin'."

There was silence.

"What about your parents, Jamie? What do they do?"

Jamie shifted slightly in his seat. He didn't want to tell Stacey that his mother did domestic work.

"Are you a big sports fan like yo' father?" he asked, abruptly reverting back to her previous comment.

"Big enough to know who you are," she said with a faint smile.

Jamie's face brightened.

"Oh, really?"

"Sure, I know you're the BMOC," she explained. "But I didn't want to relate to you like some kind of groupie. I'm sure you get enough of that."

Now Jamie relaxed even more. She was a sports fan and she knew who he was. For the next few hours, the two of them were lost in conversation. Never before had he enjoyed time spent with anyone more than with her. He felt a tinge of sadness when she got ready to leave.

"Jamie, I better be getting back. Linda's probably beginning to worry."

As he walked her back to the dorm, he knew that he wanted to see her again, but was unsure of how to ask. He felt that she liked him, but part of him wondered if she was just being polite. They reached the door and he decided to approach the subject cautiously.

"Stacey, I had a really nice time," he said awkwardly.

"So did I," she said, searching her bag for her keys.

"Can I see you again?"

"Sure. I'd love to spend more time with you."

"How 'bout tomorrow?"

"I don't see why not."

"What time's good fo' you?"

"Let's have breakfast," she suggested. "I know this great place in the French Quarter called Café Du Monde. Have you ever eaten there?"

"No I haven't."

"Would you like to?"

"Yeah, it sounds like fun."

"Well, it's nothing fancy, but I think you'll like it."

"OK."

"How does ten o'clock sound?"

"That's fine with me," he said. "Maybe we could even make a day of it."

"OK. Let's plan on it." She smiled.

There was an awkward silence, "Stacey, there may be a slight problem. I don't have a car," he said, looking past her. "But I can borrow one. So I'll have to call you to let you know exactly when we can leave."

"Don't bother," she responded matter-of-factly. "I'll pick you up tomorrow."

The next morning, at exactly ten o'clock, Stacey rolled in front of the dorm.

"Hello, Jamie, how are you this morning?" she asked, sliding out of the car.

"I'm fine, and you?"

"Fine."

"That's good."

"Would you like to drive, Jamie? I could use a break."

"Yeah."

Jamie climbed under the wheel and buckled his seat belt. His attention fell on Stacey as she walked to the passenger side of the car. She wore a beautifully crocheted cotton sweater that matched the designer shorts hugging her tiny waist. In her ears were tiny gold earrings which complemented the golden luster of her light brown skin. Her small, perfectly shaped hands were adorned by a gold class ring and a small opal bracelet on her right wrist that matched the heart-shaped necklace draped about her neck. As she slid into the car, Jamie took in every detail, even noticing her carefully painted toenails and her soft Italian sandals. She looked even more beautiful than when he had first seen her. Already, she loved her dazzling smile, her soft brown eyes, the tilt of her head, and the pride and air of sophistication she exuded each time she moved or spoke. Never before had he been so impressed with a woman as he was with her.

"Do you know where the park on St. Charles Avenue is located?" she asked.

"The one across from Tulane?"

"Yes, that's it."

"You wanna go there?"

"Yes, we can park the car there and ride the trolley to the French Quarter."

They rolled swiftly through campus and entered the tree-shaded streets running alongside the park. They got out and walked over to the trolley stop. By the time they boarded the trolley, there was standing room only. The car moved forward, passing the big beautiful houses lining both side of St. Charles Avenue. Many of them had large balconies and stained-glass windows that faced the well-swept streets. But Jamie paid little attention to their picturesque journey. All of his senses were tuned to Stacey. He stood so close to her that he found himself intoxicated by the smell of her perfume. It was a smell that would bring him great joy each time he received one of her scented letters.

They departed the trolley downtown and walked one block to the French Quarter, then over to the waterfront where the restaurant was located. Inside they took a seat on the terrace overlooking the river. As they waited to be served, they could smell the soothing scent of fresh Mississippi mud emanating from the river, mixing delightfully with the stimulating fragrance of fresh coffee brewing inside the café.

"Have you eaten beignets before?" Stacey asked lightly.

"No, I can't say that I have."

"Well, you can't live in New Orleans and not eat beignets."

"Is that right?"

"Yep, it would be sacrilegious."

"Whatever that means."

Stacey playfully batted her eyes.

"How hungry are you?"

"Not very."

"Well, they come in baskets of three, six, or twelve and they're quite filling. So, which should we order?"

"Let's try six."

"OK, six it is."

Jamie listened intently as Stacey ordered.

"We will have two orders of beignets and two cups of café au lait." She spoke so clearly and precisely that just listening to her was a treat.

The waiter left and quickly returned with the order. He carefully placed the baskets of beignets and the cups of coffee on their table and departed. Jamie removed one of the sugar-covered morsels, bit into it, and chewed slowly. Both his lips were covered with powdered sugar.

"Aren't they delicious?" she asked, smiling.

"Yeah," he said, wiping the powdered residue from the corners of his mouth. "Tastes like a homemade doughnut with a fancy name."

"That's what they are," she agreed. "Square-shaped doughnuts without a hole in the center. Try your café au lait," she suggested.

Jamie lifted the cup to his lips and carefully sipped the hot liquid.

"It's good," he said, setting the cup back on the table.

She smiled.

"I'm glad you like it."

There was silence.

"I spoke to my father last night on the phone, and I told him that I met you."

"Really?"

"Does that surprise you?"

"A little," he responded. "What did he say?"

"Well, first of all, he already knows who you are. So you know that he asked a million questions. Then he asked me to invite you over for dinner. Are you interested?"

"When?"

"Later on tonight."

Jamie hesitated.

"I ain't exactly dressed fo' dinner, Stacey."

"Oh, you look fine. He just wants to meet you. It'll be really casual."

There was silence.

"Is yo' house near here?"

"It's about a twenty-minute drive."

"OK, I'll go if you want me to."

"Good," she said, smiling. "I thought that we could spend a few hours in the French Quarter and go out there around four. Is that OK?"

"Yeah. That's fine."

Stacey was more assertive than the girls Jamie knew back home—a quality he found surprisingly appealing.

Stacey pushed away from the table.

"Would you excuse me for a minute, Jamie? I should call home and let them know that we're definitely coming."

"Awright."

Jamie smiled as he turned and saw the other men staring at Stacey as she walked to the phone booth.

When she returned, Jamie paid for their breakfast and

they left. Outside the sun was climbing to the center of the sky and the narrow cobblestone streets were beginning to fill with people. They paused and looked around. Both sides of the street were lined with shops. On one side T-shirts, fine art, and leather shops stared out. On the other side there were crystal, quilt, and even witchcraft and voodoo stores. After hours of exploring Stacey turned to Jamie.

"You want to ride the riverboat for a while?"

"Yeah, but first I wanna buy somethin' fo' yo' mother."

"Jamie, you don't have to do that."

"I know I don't, but I want to."

Earlier, Stacey had mentioned that her mother loved pralines. Jamie purchased a box, had them gift-wrapped, and the two of them made their way toward the dock.

"Oh, it's so beautiful down here now," she said, leading the way to the riverfront.

"It sho' is."

"It used to be such a wreck."

"Really?"

"Yeah, and dangerous too. The whole city seems to be changing for the better."

They purchased some tickets, climbed aboard the boat, and moved to an isolated corner close to the first deck railing. The riverboat moved slowly away from the pier. As it pushed through the water, Stacey's hair blew in the cool afternoon breeze. Agitated, she pulled it back from her face and wrapped it in a scarf. She then put on a pair of sunglasses. Jamie was struck by her aloof beauty.

"Aren't those old plantation houses the most beautiful things you've ever seen?" she gasped, now leaning over the railing.

"Personally, I can't git past what they represent," Jamie answered.

"What do you mean?"

"Plantations, masters, slaves, oppression, bigotry— those kinda thangs."

"Well that was a long time ago," she said, naively. "Things have changed."

Jamie thought of Eight Ball and a surge of anger passed over him.

"They haven't change that much," he mumbled. Irritation was in his voice.

"Why do you say that?" she asked.

He stared at her with a puzzled look on his face. Could she really be that gullible? He was attracted to her in part because she seemed so sophisticated. But maybe she had been so sheltered that she was not aware of how most black folks really lived, or what many white people were capable of doing.

"Stacey, you ever been discriminated against?"

She didn't answer immediately. Instead, she stood gently rubbing the corners of her mouth with her thumb and forefinger. Jamie could see that she was searching her memory for an unkind word or an unfair act.

"No. I can't really say that I have."

Jamie's lips parted in surprise.

"Well, all of us haven't been so lucky in our dealings with white folks," he snapped.

"Maybe some of us just choose not to see the world in strictly black and white terms," she responded defensively.

"If I see the world in black and white terms," he rallied, "it's only because white folks force me to see it that way."

"What do you mean?"

Jamie let out a deep sigh.

"Stacey, down here in New Orleans it seems like a lot of people, black and white, do what they wanna. But where I come from, the good jobs, a stroll in the park, sittin' in certain seats at the movies, and eatin' in restaurants is still fo' whites only."

"Jamie, do you hate white people?"

Her question caught him off guard and for a moment they were separated by an awkward silence.

"No. I don't hate 'em. But sometimes they sho' make it hard fo' me not to. As long as they got everythang and black people ain't got nothin', then they satisfied. But soon as we start doin' better or actin' in ways they don't like, they kill us!"

"Kill!" Stacey echoed.

"Yeah, kill," he growled. "And we ain't supposed to do nothin'. Jus' act like ain't nothin' happened and try to git along with 'em."

"Jamie, what are you talking about?"

He was silent. In his moment of anger, he had said too much. He looked over the edge of the boat and watched the calm water part as the boat surged forward. Again, painful images of Eight Ball danced before his eyes.

"Stacey, a few years ago I watched a bunch of upstandin' white folks kill my cousin."

Stacey stood speechless. Although her eyes were hidden behind dark glasses, Jamie could tell that they were opened wide with surprise and horror.

"What happened?" she asked sympathetically, removing her glasses and looking into his eyes.

"He was messin' 'round with a white girl. And her racist daddy and some of Pinesboro's finest found out. Then they killed him. . . . They beat 'im and they castrated 'im and then they shot 'im dead."

Jamie looked away. His jaws were clamped tight and deep furrows raced across his forehead. When he looked at her again, she was staring at him with cloudy eyes.

"What happened to them?"

"Nothin'. Nothin' at all."

"Why not?" she wanted to know. "I don't understand."

Her words caused Jamie again to recall the night of the murder. He thought of the shiny knife slicing through Eight Ball's genitals, remembered his own fear as he crouched underneath the house watching it all, heard again those nightmarish laughs and shouts of the white mob ringing in his ears. He felt anew the guilt of not acting and the shame of consummating the lie surrounding Eight Ball's death with his silence.

"Because I was the only black person that saw it and Mama convinced me that wasn't nothin' we could do," he offered dryly.

"Why didn't you turn them over to the police?"

"Stacey, the police were in on it."

This time her eyes held the cold distant look of disbelief.

"I can't believe that something like that can still happen in this day and time," she moaned.

"Well, it does," he mumbled painfully. "Now, you still wanna tell me how much thangs done changed?"

Her eyes dropped to the floor. Jamie saw from her reaction that his words hurt her and immediately he was sorry.

"Stacey, I didn't mean that the way it sounded."

"Were the two of you close?" she asked, seeming to accept his apology.

He smiled.

"As teeth and tongue."

They were silent for a long time. Stacey slipped her arm about Jamie's waist and pulled him close.

"I'm very sorry about your cousin," she whispered. "I can see how much he meant to you. If there is anything I can do, or if you ever need to talk, just know that I'm here for you."

For the first time since the murder, Jamie felt some relief. For years he had longed to tell someone other than his mother what actually had happened that night. He had needed to verbalize his guilt and pain much the way a devoted Catholic needs confession. There had been something strangely medicinal in Stacey's naive but compassionate words.

"Thanks, Stacey," he said softly. "I really appreciate you tryin' to understand."

Jamie remembered the vow of silence he had taken before his mother. He was glad he had told Stacey, but yet there was a request he felt obligated to make. He swallowed hard and tried to ignore the shame that he felt.

"Say, Stacey," he began, still speaking softly.

"Yes, Jamie."

"Please don't tell anybody what we talked about. It could still cause a lot of trouble if folks back home found out."

"I won't say a word," she promised.

At three-thirty the boat docked and the two of them stepped onto the pier.

"Well, Jamie, are you ready to meet my folks?"

"Ready and willin'."

They quickly made their way back through the French Quarter, took the trolley to the park on St. Charles Avenue, and walked back to her car. Stacey eased behind the steering wheel and when Jamie was safely inside, she pushed the gear into first, gently stepped off the clutch, and eased forward. She drove east, turned off the cobblestone street onto a side street, and then onto Interstate 10. As the car glided over the smooth asphalt and moved farther outside the city limits, Jamie leaned back into the soft plush seat and stared ahead. He felt his stomach muscles pull as the car climbed to the top of a very steep bridge. From there he could see the whole city. He had never been in this part of town before and his curiosity was piqued.

"Where are we?" he asked.

"This area is called New Orleans East," Stacey told him. "My parents live out here."

He sat up in his seat.

"You mean this is a black neighborhood?"

"No, not exactly." she answered. "But black people do live out here."

In Jamie's world, black neighborhoods were narrow unpaved streets lined with rows of poorly kept tin-roofed shacks. Although there was some variation, all of them were basically the same. Most were made from scrap lumber and rested on triangular-shaped cement blocks. Out front usually was an old wooden porch with steps pushed up next to it. More often than not, the yards were littered with old junk cars and usually there was a clothesline strung next to the house in plain view or hidden out back.

"Here we are," she announced. "Home sweet home."

His eyes widened as Stacey stopped in front of a large multilevel house. She quickly punched in the code and the gate opened up on an immaculately landscaped yard. She drove the car slowly around the long driveway, stopping outside their three-car garage.

"I wonder where everybody is?" she mumbled softly.

Jamie got out and looked around. Now, this is living, he thought to himself.

They entered the house through an unlocked door and went immediately into the family's game room, where they found her father shooting pool. Jamie quickly studied the man's appearance. Mr. Lefere was about five feet eight inches tall, well groomed and in his early forties. As he shot the last ball off the table, Jamie looked over his surroundings. The huge, dark, oak-paneled room was filled with several table and video games. To his immediate right was an indoor pool that opened onto an outside patio, through which Jamie could see a lighted tennis court in the distance. Above the pool table, a fancy ceiling fan whirled slowly. Framed pictures of famous black athletes lined one wall, a small trophy case stood proudly in one corner, and a large family portrait adorned another wall. Jamie continued to look on, his eyes moving swiftly as he took in the low sounds of jazz emanating from a nearby stereo. He glanced down at the polished wooden floors and large Navajo rug placed in its center just as Mr. Lefere looked up to greet them.

"Hi, Daddy," Stacey sang, falling into his arms and kissing him on the cheek. She was a daddy's girl.

"Daddy, this is Jamie Ray Griffin. Jamie, this is my father."

Jamie smiled, then extended an open palm toward him.

"How you doin', Mr. Lefere?" he asked cordially.

"Fine, thank you," he responded, shaking Jamie's hand firmly. "Have a seat, Jamie. Make yourself at home."

Mr. Lefere turned his attention to Stacey.

"Precious," he began, "would you please tell your mother that you-all are here? Ask her, if it's not too much trouble, to please bring some refreshments out to the deck."

Stacey disappeared inside the house and Jamie and Mr. Lefere took a seat out on the deck in the sunshine.

"Say, Jamie, what's this I hear about y'all having Alabama on the schedule?" Mr. Lefere asked.

"Yessuh," Jamie answered. "That's our season opener. Then we got Nebraska, Oklahoma the third week, and we end the season with LSU."

Mr. Lefere whistled, shaking his head from side to side.

"That's some schedule. But it should work in your favor."

"Sir?"

"The Heisman."

Jamie shifted his weight and smiled uncomfortably.

"It's like I was telling the fellows at the office," he began. "To win the Heisman you need four things—a talented player, a competitive schedule, national exposure, and a winning season. The only factor in doubt at this point is the last one."

Stacey returned, followed by her mother.

"Jamie, this is my mother," Stacey announced, while placing their iced tea on a table.

"Please to meet you, Mrs. Lefere," he said, standing "These are fo' you."

He handed her the tiny box.

"Oh, you didn't have to do that!" she exclaimed.

"It's not much," Jamie said.

She took a seat and opened the box.

"Pralines! Oh, thank you Jamie. These are my favorites."

"You're welcome," Jamie said, smiling.

Again Jamie's roving eyes looked over his surroundings.

"You got a beautiful home."

"Thank you." She smiled. "We've been very comfortable here. I have always believed that home should be a special place."

"Yes ma'am, this home is certainly special. Believe me."

They all shared a friendly chuckle.

"Son, you have another season like your last one and you'll be able to afford a block of homes like this one," Mr. Lefere joked.

"Thank you, suh," Jamie said, acknowledging what he felt was a compliment.

"Do you have any brothers or sisters?" Mrs. Lefere asked.

"No ma'am. I'm it."

"Well, I know your parents are proud of you." She hesitated for a moment. "You know, my husband is a pretty good athlete himself."

"Is that right?" Jamie asked.

"You better believe it," Mr. Lefere interrupted.

"I couldn't help but notice yo' tennis court," Jamie said.

"Oh, that's my game," Mr. Lefere announced boastfully.

"You don't say?" Jamie responded.

"Do you play?" Mr. Lefere's inquiry had a competitive tone.

"Every now and then," Jamie said modestly.

"What do you say we play a quick game before dinner? You know, to work up an appetite." Mr. Lefere smiled.

"Oh, I'm not dressed to play," Jamie hedged.

"We can do something about that," Mr. Lefere added quickly. "What size do you wear?"

"What size do I wear?" Jamie repeated the question loudly.

Mr. Lefere laughed and turned to Stacey.

"Baby girl, show Jamie where we keep our sportswear."

Jamie followed Stacey back into the house and down a long, narrow hall. A moment later they stood in a room unlike any he had seen in a private residence.

"This is where Daddy's business associates change or relax when they come over to play tennis," she explained. "You'll find everything you need in here."

Jamie spent a few minutes exploring the room. It was much like a dressing room at an expensive athletic club. There was a wet bar in the corner and a wide-screen television built into the center wall. In front of the television there was a large plush circular sofa. Across the back wall was a series of stylish oak lockers. Around the corner was a spacious bathroom complete with several showers and a sauna.

"Stacey," he teased, "y'all livin' like white folks."

She laughed softly, but did not respond.

"You know, Jamie, Daddy's a pretty good tennis player."

"He better be," Jamie exclaimed. "He got his own personal court."

Again Stacey laughed.

"How's yo' game?"

"Oh, it's OK," she answered.

"And yo' mother's?"

"Mother plays well also."

"Good. Maybe we can play doubles. I wouldn't wanna beat yo' daddy on his own court."

"Or get beat," she said.

"You ain't lyin'."

The four of them played doubles for an hour and a half, then went inside to clean up and eat dinner. Afterward, Jamie and Stacey went outside on the deck to share a glass of lemonade in the cool night air.

"You have a nice family, Stacey."

"Thank you, Jamie. That's sweet of you to say."

"I really like 'em a lot."

"Well, they like you too."

"What time you goin' back to school tomorrow?"

"Early afternoon."

"When will you be comin' back?"

"Not for a couple of weekends."

There was silence.

"Can I call you?"

"You better."

She got a pencil and wrote her Baton Rouge number and address on a piece of paper and handed it to Jamie.

"You should think about coming to Baton Rouge."

"Really?"

"Yeah, take the bus over. I'll pick you up at the station."

"Don't be surprised if I do jus' that."

When Jamie returned to the dorm, that night, Michael

was lying in bed watching the small black-and-white television they had purchased together.

"You married yet?" he teased.

"I wish," Jamie said, taking a seat on his own bed. "Man, I ain't never seen no black people livin' like that—indoor swimmin' pool, tennis courts, the whole nine yards."

"Yeah, Stacey's used to the good life, that's fo' sho'. But she's not stuck up. Neither is her family."

"Man, what kinda guys do she usually go out with?"

Michael sighed.

"She used to date some Ivy League guy. But distance killed that relationship."

"Ivy League, hunh?" Jamie mumbled. "It figures."

"How you talkin'?" Michael shot back. "Jamie, you ain't exactly no everyday Joe Blow."

They laughed loudly.

A few weeks later Jamie traveled to Baton Rouge to spend the day with Stacey. She picked him up at the bus station and they spent much of the morning touring the campus. As he walked with her, he could feel a pride and confidence that were absent among the black students at ULNO.

At the end of the day, they went back to her apartment to be alone before he had to catch the bus to New Orleans.

"Stacey, I have something I wanna give you."

"OK," she said. "I love surprises."

"Its not much," he said handing her a tiny box that was neatly wrapped in multicolored paper. "But I want you to have it."

"Jamie, what is it?"

"Open it and see."

On a gold chain was his Conference Championship ring.

"I know it's probably not worth much, but it's the most prized possession that I have."

"Jamie, I can't accept this."

"Stacey, I love you and I want you to wear it," he told her.

"What did you say?" she asked, startled.

"I want you to wear it."

"No," she said. "What did you say before that?"

"I said I love you."

She turned her face to him and whispered, "I love you too."

He bent down, took her in his arms, and kissed her.

CHAPTER 13

FOUR weeks later a nervous, jittery Jamie stood outside
Dr. Bumguard's office. He adjusted his shirt collar, took a
deep breath, and knocked on the door.

"Come in!" a voice called from the other side.

He pushed the door open and stepped inside.

"Good mornin', Dr. Bumguard. You wanna see me?"

"Yes I do. Have a seat. I'll be with you in a minute."

Jamie sat eyeing Dr. Bumguard. He was a huge, dark-
complected man, six feet five inches tall. He possessed a

massive chest, bulging biceps, thick forearms, and a shiny bald head.

"Well, Jamie, I was going over my grades for this semester and I see that your midterm average is a borderline D."

"Yessuh?" Jamie answered, obviously unconcerned.

"Son, I have watched you closely over the last several weeks. You have a good mind, but it doesn't seem to me that you are applying yourself."

Dr. Bumguard rubbed his chin, rose from his seat behind the large oak desk, walked to his bookshelf, and removed a manila folder. He returned to his seat, sat down, crossed his legs, and began mindlessly thumbing through the papers. When he located the proper paper, he removed it and placed it on the desk in front of Jamie.

"Now, let's take your last essay for example. It shows some potential but it is full of inexcusable oversights— misspelled words, grammatical errors, sloppy presentation, and there is no conclusion. . . . I don't think you took this assignment very seriously."

Jamie shifted his weight in his chair and studied the paper slightly. On the last page, written in red ink, was the grade D+. He sat back relieved. He had passed and that was all that mattered to him.

"You know, there are special tutors here that can help you straighten out your writing problems," Dr. Bumguard began again.

"Yessuh," Jamie said, unconcerned.

"Also, Jamie, I've noticed that you haven't been to class lately. Is there a problem that I can help you with?"

"Nosuh. Not really."

Jamie looked into Dr. Bumguard's eyes and saw that he wanted an explanation.

"Right now the football team is goin' through spring drills."

"Yes, I'm aware of that," Dr. Bumguard told him.

"Well, the last few weeks I've been reportin' to the trainin' room befo' practice fo' treatment," he offered.

"So you are injured."

"Yessuh."

"What type of injury do you have?"

"Ankle," Jamie mumbled. "I hurt it a few weeks ago."

Dr. Bumguard leaned back in his chair and rubbed his chin with his right hand. "Jamie, I'm going to be frank with you, OK?"

"OK, Professor," he said.

"It seems to me that your priorities are all wrong."

Jamie sat up, stung by Dr. Bumguard's words. His emotions quickly slid to the verge of anger.

"Well, Professor Bumguard," he began, "I know education is a priority to some people, but not to me."

Professor Bumguard looked at him disbelievingly, his mouth drawn into a straight expressionless line.

"And why is that?" he wanted to know.

"I wanna be a professional football player. It's what I've wanted to be every since high school. And I got a good chance to make it. It's not that I don't care 'bout my future. I jus' thank that the best thang fo' me to do is spend most of my time makin' sho' that I'm the best football player that I can be. In the meantime, I'm jus' tryin' to git by the best I can in the classroom."

"But what if you don't make it to the pros?" Dr. Bumguard asked the obvious question.

"I will. There ain't no doubt about that." Jamie chuckled assuredly.

"Well, I hope your athletic abilities carry you as far in life as you want to go," Dr. Bumguard responded blankly. "But perhaps you should consider an alternate plan in case they don't. If by some slight possibility you don't make it in football, you should realize that you can still 'make it' by utilizing your mind."

Jamie sighed deeply and began fiddling with the papers on Dr. Bumguard's desk. He could feel the hair on the back of his neck tingle with anger. He sat very still while his mind raced on, trying hard not to let his anger show. He desperately wanted to leap out of his chair and shout, You educated fool! Yo don't understand nothin'! White folks don't care 'bout no strong black mind. All they interested in is what you can do fo' 'em.

Dr. Bumguard continued, seemingly unaware of Jamie's inner turmoil.

"Son, not only do I want you to see the urgency of using your mind, but I also want you to understand your responsibility." Now hesitating slightly, he added, "Your obligation to your parents and the black community at large. They deserve a better effort than you are giving here."

Jamie turned his head and looked at the clock. Maybe he could tell Dr. Bumguard that he had a class to go to or that he was late for a meeting. Almost automatically, his mind shut off, refusing to accept anything his professor was saying.

"Jamie, how many young black men would you say there are on the football team?"

"About ninety, I guess."

"How many would you say are on full scholarship?"

"About eighty," he said, after thinking for a few moments.

"Son, do you realize the opportunity that's being wasted?"

Jamie didn't answer. He sat staring blankly ahead, wishing he was somewhere else.

"To put it bluntly," Dr. Bumguard began, "I feel that to survive in this world, you have to take what you have and make what you want. What we have here is a large group of black men on one of the most prestigious college campuses in America. Many have full athletic scholarships. Now, what we need in the black community is more educated people. The opportunity is there. We must take advantage of it. From those black athletes we need to produce x numbers of doctors, lawyers, engineers, teachers, scientists, et cetera. We must take what we have—a large number of black athletes with four years of school paid for—and make what we need—an educated, vibrant black community." He paused. "Do you understand what I'm saying?"

"Yessuh," Jamie said halfheartedly.

"Jamie, it's obvious from your tone that you have a problem with my perspective. I would be very interested in hearing why."

Jamie sat up straight in his seat and began nervously biting his fingernails. He wanted to ask how black athletes were going to accomplish all those things when white people, who had no interest in helping them achieve anything off the playing field, were in control of their lives from the time they entered college until they left. Coaches told them what classes to take, what time of the day to take them, and what professors to sign up with. Dr. Bumguard had to know how it was for them. Jamie decided that it would be in his best interest to keep quiet.

"Feel free to say what's on your mind," Dr. Bumguard encouraged. "Forget that I'm your professor and let's talk like two black men."

"Well, suh, it seem to me that what you talkin' 'bout ain't very likely to happen," Jamie began.

"Oh, so you don't think black athletes are capable of becoming doctors, lawyers, et cetera?" Dr. Bumguard retorted.

"It's not that we ain't capable. It's jus' that the system is holdin' us back."

"Could you explain what you mean by 'the system'?"

"The whole school system! From the classroom to the football field, it's designed to keep us back," Jamie said excitedly.

Dr. Bumguard leaned back in his chair, clamped his hands behind his head, and looked up at the ceiling.

"Jamie, you're being very vague," he said after a short silence. "Could you go into more detail as to how 'the system' prevents you from taking advantage of the opportunities I've described? Your education is paid for, all you have to do is be a student."

"Dr. Bumguard, like I said a while ago, I jus' don't know if all of them opportunities you talkin' about really exist."

He paused to try to gauge Dr. Bumguard's reaction. He wanted to be careful not to say the wrong thing.

"Please continue. I'm listening."

"Even fo' the black folks who do git into this school, they don't really have no opportunity. Leastwise not no real one."

"Why would you say that?" Dr. Bumguard asked.

"Because the system is racist," Jamie said, deciding to throw caution to the wind.

"The way I see it, most of the professors are white. And a lot of 'em have a thang against black folks. So when a black person walks in they classroom, nine times out of ten, he don' awready flunk. And don't let the professor find out that he's a athlete," Jamie added. "Then they gon' make it double hard on him. 'Cause they thank the only reason he in the school in the first place is 'cause he can play ball."

"Jamie, can't you see that you're using racism as an excuse to fail and a rationale for not trying?" Dr. Bumguard asked. "Regardless of whether that professor likes you or dislikes you, he can't just arbitrarily fail you. The only way that you will fail is if you don't apply yourself. Now, racism might cause you to get a B instead of an A when you are on the borderline. But racism won't get you an F. You have to earn an F."

He paused and cleared his throat.

"Racism can slow you down but it can't stop you. As a black person, you must realize that until racism is completely moved from your path, you have to figure out a way to get around it. The ultimate factor in whether you fail or not is you, and not some other people. See, when you start seeing other people as being omnipotent, you're also seeing yourself as being inferior."

"Dr. Bumguard, I understand what you're sayin'. But I thank it's mo' than a attitude we talkin' 'bout. Black students usually have to work a job or two jus' to be at the university. Jus' like me. Playing football is my job. I do it well, but it takes almost all of my time and energy to stay the best. That cuts out a lot of study time and causes me a great deal of stress. But if I didn't have my job, I wouldn't be in school. My mama couldn't afford to send me to no college 'less I had a scholarship. Most white kids don't have to worry 'bout money." Jamie paused briefly. "And a lotta black kids ain't as prepared fo' college work 'cause of where we come from. Our background makes it hard fo' us to compete at these big universities."

"Jamie, the main deficiency as I see it is not a lack of financial support or academic preparation, it's the fact that we are getting outworked."

"Suh, are you sayin' that blacks fail 'cause we're lazy?"

"No I'm not. What I'm saying is that we are getting outworked."

Jamie looked at him, obviously confused.

"There is a huge difference between being lazy and getting outworked. Jamie, permit me to tell you a short story to illustrate my point. When I was an undergraduate at Yale, I had many of the same attitudes about racism that you now possess. I felt that black students were doomed to fail because of our cultural background, which is quite different from those who created such an institution. We spoke differently from white Yale students. We were poorer. We had to work at night. And we didn't have blacks in certain academic positions to help solve our problems. But, during my second semester, my attitude changed. Not because I wanted it to, but because I met David Wu."

"David was from Taiwan. New Haven was the first American city that he had lived in. He was in a foreign land, he could barely speak English, and he was at one of the most demanding universities in the world."

"Well, when I first met him I didn't think there was any way in the world he could compete at Yale. Not only did he have to overcome a tremendous language deficiency, but he also had to deal with his cultural differences. Plus, he had to work in order to supplement his income.

"But you know what?"

"What's that, suh?"

"At the end of the first semester his grades were better than those of many of the black students I knew on campus and the reason was evident. He outworked us. David would step out of bed at seven o'clock and study until noon. He would eat and then go to work from one o'clock to five o'clock. At five, he ate dinner but at six, he was back in his room studying, this time until two o'clock in the morning. He only slept a few hours every night. David followed that routine seven days a week. The only adjustment he made was the time he spent in class."

"I thought he was crazy until I took the time to talk to him. In the course of our conversation, he used words like

'discipline,' 'motivation,' 'self-determination,' and 'obligation.' But Jamie, it wasn't so much the words he used
that impressed me as the ones he didn't—'racism,' 'dis-
crimination,' and 'inequality.'

"After I talked to David, I realized that he was self-
directed while I was other-directed. And as I began to pay
more attention to other minorities on campus—Koreans,
West Indians, Chinese, Japanese, Africans—I realized that
all of them emphasized what they had to do and did it. Few
of them found time to sit around looking at the white man."

Jamie listened patiently. He sat on the edge of his seat
waiting for an opportunity to speak, but Dr. Bumguard
continued.

"It was at that time that I realized that black folks were
getting outworked. Son, if we're going to make it as a
people we must not only learn words like discipline, motivation, self-determination, and obligation; we must in-
corporate them into our lifestyles, we must act on them."

"Well, Dr. Bumguard, it seems to me like you're placin'
all the responsibility fo' changin' racism on black folks,"
Jamie sniped.

"That's not what I'm saying at all, Jamie. I know the system and I'm the first to agree that inequalities exist and
they must be eradicated. However, I'm also saying that
changing the system won't mean a thing if we don't take
advantage of the opportunities those changes bring about.
It took hard work to obtain the opportunities we have
right now. And it takes hard work to benefit from them.
That's all I'm saying. But let's talk about you specifically.
How much study time do you put in each day?"

"I don't know exactly," Jamie said.

"But you can tell me how much time you put into football practice, can't you?"

Jamie began repeating his schedule almost mechanically: "Meetings start at one forty-five and practice at about three-thirty." Jamie paused. "We probably average 'bout three hours a day."

"It's not just practice, it's intense practice, wouldn't you say?" Dr. Bumguard pressed.

"Yessuh."

"And it's that intensity that causes you to improve and excel, right?"

"Yessuh."

"So wouldn't you agree that it's not practice, but perfect practice, that makes an athlete perfect?"

"Yessuh, you have to pay attention to technique in sports. You can do somethin' wrong all day and you won't git any better."

"So what you're saying is that in athletics there's a formula for success, just as there is one for failure."

"Yessuh, you have to know how to do something as well as what to do."

"Don't you feel that if you applied those principles to the classroom, you would improve your circumstances?"

Jamie didn't answer.

"See, Jamie, you know exactly how much practice time you put in each day. But you don't have a clue as to how much time you spend studying. When you go to practice you've prepared yourself mentally to work hard and to concentrate. You have an established routine. That same discipline and dedication would make you and your teammates very successful in the classroom."

"I guess we do kill a lot of time jus' messin' 'round." Jamie admitted reluctantly.

"Son, I'll tell you what. If you haven't learned anything else today, remember that the best way to kill time is to work it to death."

Involuntarily, Jamie's lips twisted into a wry smile.

"Awright, Professor," Jamie said. "I'll remember that."

"Now, Jamie, don't leave my office thinking that I'm one of those black men foolish enough to deny the existence of racism. Don't think that I don't understand the need to attack the system; because I do. However, attacking the system does not absolve us from our responsibility. There are many things that blacks must do. All of us have a duty—parents, teachers, preachers, politicians, and students."

"Dr. Bumguard, are you familiar with Dr. Karen Russel's work?" Jamie asked, feeling the need to try a different approach. He felt that Dr. Bumguard would listen to what he was saying if he backed it up with evidence.

"Yes, Karen and I go back a long way," Dr. Bumguard responded. "Why do you ask?"

"Because I'm takin' her class this semester—Inequalities in the Educational System."

"Oh, I see."

"Well, she talks a lot about self-fulfilling prophecy. She assigned this book called *Pygmalion in the Classroom*."

"That would be Robert Rosenthal's work."

"Well, there's a couple of thangs in the book that made me see how powerful racism is."

"Really?"

"Yessuh."

"OK, Jamie, I'm listening."

"Well, the first one was a rat experiment where a professor gave two groups of students some rats and tol' 'em to teach 'em to run a maze. He tol' one group that they rats were bred to be smart so they wouldn't have no problem learnin' to run the maze. Then he tol' the other group that they rats couldn't learn, so they probably wouldn't be able to teach 'em to run the maze."

"OK." Dr. Bumguard nodded.

"Well, at the end of the teachin' period, the kids with the smart rats had taught most of 'em to run the maze.

And the kids with the dumb rats wasn't able to teach hardly none of theirs to run it. Then the professor tol' 'em that all the rats was exactly the same, there wasn't no difference between the smart rats and the dumb ones."

Jamie hesitated.

"I'm following you," Dr. Bumguard said, enjoying Jamie's enthusiasm. "Please continue."

"Well, the book also talked about some experimenters who gave a test to some elementary students who were goin' to attend a different junior high school the next year. I believe it was supposed to be able to predict when a student was gon' have a academic spurt. Well, after the results came in, the examiners gave the teachers a list of all the kids in they class who was gon' have this spurt. All of the kids on the list did good that year. But a lot of the others did bad.

"The funny thang 'bout it was that the experimenters didn't even record the test scores. They jus' made up a list of people that was gon' spurt. So there really wasn't no difference. The teachers jus' thought there was."

"So Jamie, how do you explain the students' performance?"

"Self-fulfillin' prophecy."

"Meaning?"

"The teachers expected 'em to do better, so they did."

"Why?"

"Because they treated 'em different. Jus' like the group with the smart rats who rewarded they good behavior. They was mo' patient with 'em. They patted 'em mo'. Because they expected 'em to learn. The group with the dumb rats jus' didn't try to teach 'em 'cause they didn't thank they could learn noway.

"The same thang was true with the students. The teachers paid mo' attention to the so-called smart students. They pointed out mistakes quicker 'cause they monitored

266

their work. They touched them mo'. They were nicer to 'em. They made 'em feel like they were smart. So they acted smart."

"So, how does this tie into what you and I are talking about?"

"Racism, suh. When white teachers go in the classroom thankin' black folks can't learn, then they don't try to teach 'em and the students don't try to learn, 'cause they don't thank they can.

"Dr. Bumguard, that's why I thank the system need to be changed. We need mo' black teachers to encourage the students."

"That's partially true," Dr. Bumguard agreed, "but we also need to share the knowledge you've just shared with me with parents, students, and also white teachers. All of them may not realize how their behavior affects the students. But even if they are racist, if black parents understood how self-fulfilling prophecy works, then they could still prevent black children from feeling inadequate and teach them how to succeed. The solution to the problem is not either/or, it's both."

Their conversation was interrupted by a soft knock on the door. Jamie watched Dr. Bumguard cross the room, then he heard him tell someone that he would be with them in a minute.

"Well, I have another appointment," Dr. Bumguard told him.

"OK," Jamie said, rising.

"Please think about our conversation, Jamie. Don't make the mistake of limiting yourself to football while you're here. Also seek knowledge and wisdom, but, above all else, seek an understanding."

Jamie, limping slightly, walked out of the building and down the stairs and came to a halt on the sidewalk.

"I awready understand," he moaned.

In the distance, he could hear the university bell tolling, signaling twelve o'clock. Pushing Dr. Bumguard's words behind him, he headed down the sidewalk. He advanced toward the cafeteria, feeling a sense of urgency. He had to eat, receive treatment, and be dressed for practice before one o'clock.

I T was the opening play of the annual ULNO spring intrasquad game. Jamie lay sprawled on the thirty-yard line clutching his right leg. An eerie silence fell over the capacity crowd. It seemed to him that everything was moving in slow motion—his teammates yelling for the trainer and the bodies advancing toward him from the sidelines. Soon Doc Parker was kneeling over him.

"Son, where are you hurt?" he asked.

The throbbing pain was almost unbearable. Jamie didn't speak but pointed to his right knee.

"Is the pain inside or outside?" Jamie heard Doc's second question.

It was a simple question, but he didn't know the answer. The pain was acute, but yet he could not identify its exact location. He closed his eyes and fought back the tears pushing against his eyelids. Doc Parker gently lifted Jamie's injured leg to an upright position. Carefully, he moved Jamie's knee from side to side. Suddenly a sharp pain raced down his leg and exploded in his right knee. Jamie grabbed his head, screaming, "Inside! Inside!"

Coach Mills was now standing next to Jamie.

"Hold it, Doc," he ordered. His fiery eyes held the dull glow of concern. He knelt down beside Jamie and placed his hand on his shoulders.

"Son, where did you take the hit?" he asked.

Jamie searched his mind, but the whole thing was a blur. One minute he was turning the corner running to daylight, the next minute he was lying on the turf with a throbbing knee.

"I don't know," Jamie moaned.

"Doc, how bad is it?" Jamie heard Coach Mills ask.

"Well," Doc sighed. "It doesn't look good."

Now, what did that mean? It doesn't look good. Did he mean he would be out for a few days, a couple of weeks, what?

An ambulance rolled onto the field. Two paramedics got out, lifted Jamie onto a stretcher, slid him into the back of the ambulance, and proceeded to the hospital. As they rolled off the field, Jamie could hear the faint sound of applause rising over the dull roar of the engine, penetrating the thin walls and closed windows of the ambulance. Outside the stadium, the driver switched on the flashing lights, but not the siren, and sped toward the hospital.

"Suh, could you please turn on the game?" Jamie asked the paramedic sitting next to him.

"Sure," he said, picking up the transmitter and sending the request to the driver.

Lying flat on his back, his eyes staring blankly up at the ceiling, Jamie lost awareness of his leg as he focused on the broadcast. He heard the raspy voice emanating from the radio speaker say: *". . . but preliminary indications are that Griffin has suffered both cartilage and ligament damage and is probably lost for the upcoming season."*

Stunned, he closed his eyes, replaying the whole scene over in his mind, trying to visualize a different outcome. He should not have been running so straight up. He was hurt because he got careless and didn't protect himself.

"Don't pay them any attention," the paramedic advised. "They're just speculatin'."

Suddenly the tires of the ambulance leaped over a bulge in the asphalt, reigniting the fire in Jamie's knee.

"Hey, take it easy," the paramedic yelled to the driver.

"Sorry," the driver mumbled over the radio. "The city ought to do somethin' about these roads."

As the ambulance rolled on, a new, more terrifying thought occupied Jamie's mind. He was injured; there was nothing he could do about that now, but what about the future? Could he make it back during the season in spite of the bleak prognosis he had heard relayed over the radio? Would he be the same?

The driver pulled to a stop in front of the emergency entrance of the hospital.

"Made it," he said, turning in his seat. "That knee feelin' any better?"

"Little bit."

"Good," he said. "ULNO ain't much without you."

Jamie heard him open the door, start toward the back of the vehicle, and stop. Then he heard a different voice, more authoritative sounding.

"Is this Griffin?"

"Yes sir," he heard the driver say.

"Take 'im to exam room B."

The door opened and the bright afternoon sun fell in Jamie's eyes. Jamie squinted and braced himself as the two men pulled him out of the ambulance and moved forward through large double doors.

A few moments later, Jamie was sitting on an examination table with his legs dangling over the edge. He was more relaxed now; the pain in his knee had begun to subside.

A tall silver-haired white man advanced toward him.

"Hi, Jamie, I'm Dr. Davenport."

"Hi, Doc." Jamie nodded. He recognized the voice as the one he had heard outside the ambulance.

"Let's see what we have here."

Jamie watched the doctor fold his pants leg back over his knee. Then, just as Doc Parker had done, he lifted Jamie's leg and moved it in several different directions. The pain was not as sharp as before, but it was still quite intense.

"We need to get him admitted," he heard Dr. Davenport say. Admitted, Jamie thought. He was anxious, jumpy. No one had told him anything definite, but he was beginning to assume the worst.

Dr. Davenport turned his attention to Jamie.

"After you've checked in, I'll come to your room and explain what's goin' on."

Outside in the corridor, Jamie heard the muffled sound of a familiar voice. He looked around and saw Stan, one of the assistant trainers, standing in the door.

"Hey stud, the maroon squad could use you right about now."

Jamie smiled but did not answer.

"We're gon' to have to keep him," Dr. Davenport told Stan. "Would you roll him down to intake and get him checked in?"

"You bet, doctor."

Gingerly, Jamie slid off the bench, hobbled across to the wheelchair, and sat down. Soon he was being wheeled down a long hall, past an information counter, and finally into a small room marked INTAKE.

"Wait here while I get the forms," Stan spoke nonchalantly.

"Where else would I go?" Jamie asked dejectedly.

The small room was filled with people and reeked of sickness. As Jamie sat brooding, he saw a frail white boy huddle up next to a short, robust lady. They both were staring at him. That must be his mother, Jamie told himself. But why were they staring at him? Confused, he watched them rise and walk toward him.

"Ain't you Jamie Ray Griffin?" she asked.

"Yes ma'am."

Jamie watched the boy glance at him, look down, and begin to fidget.

"I'm Mrs. Davis and this is my son, Troy."

"Hi," Jamie spoke.

There was silence.

"Is there somethin' I can do fo' y'all?"

Mrs. Davis pushed her son forward.

"Go 'head, Troy. Ask 'im."

Troy held a plain white envelope in one hand and a pen in the other.

"Mr. Griffin," he mumbled, softly, "could I have yo' autograph?"

Jamie signed the envelope and gave it back to him. He

watched Troy run to his mother, smiling and waving the paper over his head. The boy's enthusiastic reaction caused Jamie to forget his own anxiety momentarily. He had to be positive. He would wait for some definite word of his condition and prognosis for recovery.

After all his forms had been completed, Jamie changed into a hospital gown, and climbed into bed. A few minutes later, Dr. Davenport walked into his room carrying a replica of a knee.

"Well, Dr. Parker was right. You have some cartilage and ligament damage."

Jamie swallowed and stared blankly as Dr. Davenport demonstrated on the replica what damage had been done.

"Doc, when will I be able to play again?"

"Well, we've called your mother and she has agreed to the surgery. So, we're gon' to operate tomorrow morning. After that, you'll be in a cast six to eight weeks. The rest is up to you. That's as specific as I can be."

"Yessuh."

"Well, I'll see you in the morning."

"Okay, Doc."

As Dr. Davenport was leaving, a middle-aged black woman entered pushing a small tray.

"Hi, I'm the lab technician," she introduced herself.

"Hi," Jamie spoke to her.

"They tell me you givin' away blood in here."

Jamie chuckled. She reminded him of the women he knew back in Pinesboro.

"Yes ma'am I guess I am."

"Well, that's good 'cause that's jus' what I'm lookin' fo'."

She took a narrow strip of rubber from the tray and tied it tightly around his right arm.

"Sugar, you that ball player, ain't you?"

"Yes ma'am."

She handed Jamie a small rubber ball.

"Squeeze this till I tell you to stop."

"Yes ma'am."

"Honey, how ole are you?"

"Twenty-one."

"Twenty-one!"

"Yes ma'am."

"My Lawd," she exclaimed. "You jus' a baby. And out there gittin' all broke up over nothin'."

Jamie laughed.

"Well, I wouldn't exactly call it nothin'."

She ran her finger across the inside of his arm.

"That's the one I'm lookin' fo'."

Gently, she rubbed the vein with a cotton swab and took a hypodermic syringe from the tray.

"Now, I'm gon' stick you but it shouldn't hurt much."

"Awright," Jamie said, grimacing.

Skillfully, she pushed the needle into the vein. When the syringe had filled with blood, she quickly removed it and placed a Band-Aid over the small puncture in his arm.

"Jus' what exactly they gon' do to you tomorrow?"

"Knee surgery."

She screwed up her face and shook her head.

"Lawd, I hate that ole football."

That night a white nurse, about the same age as the lab technician, took him to a small room with a large metal tub in it. He watched her pour a yellowish solution into the water.

"OK," she instructed, testing the temperature of the water with her hand. "You need to bathe thoroughly in this."

"What is it?" Jamie wanted to know.

"PhisoHex," she told him, leaving the room.

Cautiously, Jamie stepped into the tub and began washing himself. A few minutes later, he heard the eerie sound of hinges creaking. Out of the corner of his eye, he saw the nurse peeping through the door. Her presence both angered and amused him as he decided to disclose her curiosity. Without warning, he leaped to his feet, exposing himself.

"Is this what you tryin' so hard to see?"

Jamie stood watching as the woman turned fiery red and raced from the doorway. His knee pained him slightly when he jumped up but it was worth it just to see the look on her face. As soon as she had raced away, Jamie slumped back into the tub and burst into loud laughter.

At seven o'clock the next morning, an orderly came, started an IV in Jamie's arm, and helped him onto a gurney. Moments later he was lying in the operating room, surrounded by nurses clad in surgical clothing.

"Mr. Griffin, are you ready?" one of them asked.

"Like Freddy," he answered, trying to keep a sense of humor.

His answer was her signal. She placed a syringe in Jamie's IV and injected a clear solution. Immediately he was asleep.

A few hours later, Jamie woke up in the drab, stuffy hospital room, hearing dull, breathless chatter and feeling excruciating pain assaulting his injured leg. As he tried to lift his leg, he slowly became aware of the heavy, uncomfortable cast stretching from just below his hip down to his ankle.

"Jamie Ray," came his mother's familiar whisper. "How you feelin'?"

Still groggy from the anesthetic, Jamie lifted his head and looked about. Through hazy, unfocused eyes he made out the image of his mother leaning over him, and Booger and his uncle Rob standing next to the door. He opened and closed his eyes, trying to focus them. He tried to speak, but his thick tongue only allowed him to mumble a series of unclear words.

"Boy, why you actin' so crazy?" his mother wanted to know.

"I need a shot. I need a shot," he moaned.

Mrs. Griffin pushed the call button next to Jamie's bed and a nurse came in and gave him a painkiller that put him back to sleep. When he awakened again, it was the next day and the only evidence of his mother's visit was a note saying that she had to be back to work and that she had talked to the Lord and everything was going to be fine.

That evening, Jamie was transported from the hospital to the ULNO infirmary. Shortly after he had settled into his room, Coach Hunt came in, still wearing his coaching gear.

"How you doin', big-un?"

"Awright."

"Dr. Davenport tells me that the operation went well."

"That's good to hear."

Coach Hunt sat next to the bed.

"Well, the coaches made a decision about you earlier."

Jamie raised himself to a sitting position and pushed back against the headboard.

"What kinda decision?"

"Are you familiar with the NCAA rule that gives a player five years of eligibility to git four?"

"Yessuh."

"Well, since you were injured befo' the start of yo' senior season, we can invoke that rule and give you an extra year of eligibility."

Jamie looked at him with suspicious eyes.

"It's up to you, of course," Coach Hunt added. "Dr. Davenport feels that you could possibly make it back at some point durin' the season. But we don't advise it."

"I have to thank about it," Jamie said in a noncommittal voice. "I'll wait and see how thangs look this summer."

Coach Hunt looked at Jamie strangely, then rose to his feet.

"Well, I'm sure everything'll work out for the best."

"I guess time'll tell," Jamie responded.

"Yeah." Coach Hunt agreed. "You need anything?"

"Nosuh."

"Well, just let us know if you do."

"Awright, Coach. I'll do that."

"Take care now," Coach Hunt said and left.

In May, the school year ended. Jamie went to Pinesboro, stayed three weeks, and then returned to New Orleans where Dr. Davenport removed his cast and gave him permission to start his rehabilitation regimen. Jamie decided to try to make it back by the sixth game of the season. He had a feeling that if he stayed out the entire year something bad would happen.

One day, after completing his workout, Jamie went to the practice field. He stood watching as Dwayne Hicks, the sophomore who had replaced him, broke a long run.

Suddenly, Coach Hunt rushed past but didn't speak.

"That's a helluva run, son," Coach Hunt shouted.

Jamie's heart sank. He had seen coaches snub players before, but he never believed it would happen to him. But what was the point of getting down on himself? He resolved to work harder.

During the next few weeks, Jamie stopped going to class. Instead, he devoted all of his time to getting back on the field. Each morning he would go to the track and run. Then he would go to the training room where someone would see that he got treatment. During the afternoon, while the team was on the field, he worked out in the weight room. In the evening, after all the players had left, he returned to the track.

For Jamie, the most difficult part of his rehabilitation was the isolation. Except for a couple of his closest teammates, everyone seemed to ignore him. But over time, he learned to cope by finding solace in the advice Mr. Shorty had once given him.

"Don't spend yo' life worry 'bout nobody's friendship. A friend ain't nothin' but a bum and critic. If they ain't got their hand out beggin' fo' somethin', they talkin' 'bout you behind yo' back. If you ever gon' be anythang in this world, you gon' have to be it all by yo'self."

When Jamie finally made it back to the team—with only three weeks left in the season—his less than enthusiastic coaches played him sparingly. Week after week, he stood on the sidelines waiting for an opportunity to play. He was desperate to prove himself. But since his return, he was averaging only two carries a game.

Numerous pro scouts interested in his comeback flocked to the stadium, but Jamie soon realized that game day was not going to be the time for him to prove that he was healthy enough to play professional ball. Desperate to prove himself, he tried to impress the few scouts who came out to watch practice. But to his dismay Mills highlighted the quarterback, who was also a senior. Again, Jamie found himself standing on the sidelines watching. By season's end, he was hoping that his past accomplishments were enough for someone to take a chance on him.

Two days before the draft, the local sportswriters began making predictions about his chances. They all had him going between the sixth and ninth round. Their projections were based on false rumors of his having reinjured his knee and on the fact that he had lost some of his speed and quickness.

At exactly eleven-fifteen on the second day of the draft, Jamie's phone rang.

"This is the New Orleans Gators calling," said the voice on the other end of the receiver. "How are you?"

"I'm fine."

"Jamie, the draft officially ended seventeen minutes ago," the voice informed him.

Stunned, Jamie didn't speak. He had a strange, uncomfortable feeling in the pit of his stomach. Never in his wildest imagination had he envisioned not being selected at all. He was on the verge of panic when he heard the voice say, "We would like to bring you into camp as a free agent. Are you interested?"

"Yessuh," Jamie answered quickly. "I jus' want a chance to show everybody I can play professional ball."

"That's the right attitude, son. But no one in the League is questioning your abilities," he said. "The only reason you weren't drafted is the rumor that your knee is still weak."

"That's not true," Jamie responded defensively. "My knee's fine."

"Good," the voice boomed through the phone. "If your knee holds up, you shouldn't have any problems making this ball club."

"I'm sho' my knee will be fine," Jamie reiterated.

"Well, son, we look forward to having you in a Gators uniform and I'm sure that the local fans are happy to keep you here in New Orleans."

Jamie gently placed the receiver back on the hook, closed his eyes, and softly mumbled, "Thank you, Jesus." He looked at the clock. It was too late to call his mother, but he needed to talk to someone. He wasn't exactly happy, but he was relieved that it was over and that his dream of playing professional ball was still alive. Call Stacey . . . the thought came to him suddenly. He lifted the phone, waited for a tone, then dialed her number. They talked for a long time and she made him see the advantages of what had happened; most important, he would still be in New Orleans.

Some weeks later, on a sunny Friday afternoon, Jamie and Stacey stepped out of her car and walked toward her backyard. It was the Fourth of July, and her parents were having a family cookout. As they walked they smelled the appetizing scent of fresh barbecue lingering in the air.

"Look at all the people," Jamie said, stopping in his tracks.

"Yeah, a lot of them are out-of-town relatives," Stacey explained. "This is kind of an unofficial family reunion.

Jamie spotted Mr. Lefere fast approaching. He wore a big smile on his face, had a white apron around his waist, and held a large pronged fork in his right hand.

"Y'all just in time," he shouted as he neared the two of them. "I just took the last ribs off the grill."

"It smells good, Daddy."

"Only the best for my baby girl," he said, embracing Stacey. He released her and gave Jamie's hand a firm shake. "I'm glad you could make it, Jamie."

"I wouldn't miss it fo' the world."

"Daddy, I'm going to go say hello to Mother."

"OK, baby. She's around here somewhere."

They watched Stacey walk to the door, then disappear inside the house.

"Jamie, come this way," Mr. Lefere instructed. "Let me introduce you to some of my relatives from Mississippi."

Jamie accompanied Mr. Lefere to a table where several middle-aged men were playing cards.

"Fellows, this is Jamie Ray Griffin," Mr. Lefere introduced him. Suddenly, all eyes turned toward him.

"How y'all doin'?" Jamie spoke awkwardly.

His words were greeted with a mixture of nods and waves.

"You ain't quite as big as you look on television," one of them observed.

"It's the pads," another explained.

"How's that knee?" someone else wanted to know.

"It's awright," Jamie answered quickly.

"So exactly when do you have to report to camp?" Mr. Lefere asked.

"In three days."

"That soon?"

"Yessuh."

"Football is in the air," one of them said. "And I can't wait for the season to start."

"You!" Mr. Lefere, shouted. "I already have my season tickets."

"Yeah, this just might be the Gators' year."

"Aw, it will be," Mr. Lefere said, affectionately squeezing Jamie's shoulder. "They got Jamie Ray Griffin now."

Stacey approached the table, followed closely by her mother. Mrs. Lefere greeted Jamie, while Stacey spoke to her relatives. Relieved to see her, Jamie excused himself and led Stacey to an empty table under a large pecan tree.

"What's wrong, Jamie?" Stacey asked.

"All this football talk is beginnin' to git to me."

"They don't mean any harm."

"I know they don't," he said. "But I'm not so certain that everythang's gon' work out. After all, I'm goin' in as a undrafted free agent."

"You know what you need?" Stacey whispered.

"What's that?"

"To get out of town for a few days. You need to relax before camp starts."

"Stacey, I can't leave town. It's jus' three days befo' camp and a long trip is the last thang I need."

"What about a short trip?"

"Hunh?"

"Baton Rouge is not that far. Why don't you come back with me tonight? You could relax and we could have some quiet time together before you have to go to camp."

"Hey, maybe that's just what the doctor ordered."

"May be."

That night, Stacey drove Jamie back to his dorm to pick up a few pieces of clothing. An hour and a half later, he was stretched across her bed. Stacey dimmed the lights, switched on some soft music, then gingerly sat on the bed in front of him. Slowly he unfastened first the top button, then the next, until both sides of her blouse separated, revealing a black satin lace bra. Gently, Jamie took Stacey in his arms and kissed her softly. Then, reaching behind her, he released both of the tiny metal hooks holding her bra in place. Stacey, looking deep into his eyes and breathing slightly heavier than normal, removed his shirt and gently ran her hands over his smooth, muscular chest. He pulled close to her, sliding his arms around her, letting them rest in the small of her back. Feeling the warmth of his bare flesh next to hers, Stacey moved her full, oval lips close to his ear and whispered, "Jamie, I love you so much."

That night they shared each other's company as they never had before.

A few days later, Jamie was sitting in the meeting room preparing for his first workout as a member of the New Orleans Gators. His emotions were mixed. On one hand, he was excited about an opportunity to play pro ball. His mother and friends had all been so happy and proud when he called and told them that he was going to the Gators. Yet he was terrified by the possibility of not making the team. He was worried about his knee. He just wasn't sure how it would hold up.

At six o'clock the head coach walked in and moved to the center of the room.

"Look around, men." The tone of his voice was very

businesslike. "Don't loan nobody any money. They probably won't be around long enough to pay you back."

Jamie broke out into a cold sweat. Somehow he felt as though he was talking about him. Subconsciously, he began to massage his bad knee with his hand.

"Please hol' up long enough fo' me to make this ball club," he whispered to himself.

"Men, the situation is simple," the coach continued. "We have forty-five jobs and right now every one of 'em is taken. For you rookies and free agents, that means to get a job, you have to take it. We coaches don't have any favorites. We're going with the best players out here."

That day Jamie performed well in both the morning and evening practice sessions. That night all was quiet in his room. Although he had three roommates, the first night they didn't talk to each other. Concerned with their tenuous situation, they all sat up studying their playbooks.

The next morning at exactly five o'clock, the phone rang. Startled, Jamie leaped to his feet, listening intently as one of his roommates answered.

"Yeah. Yeah. OK," Jamie heard him mumble.

Wide-eyed, Jamie watched him slam the phone down, clear his stuff out of the closet, take his playbook, and leave. Relieved, Jamie sighed and laid his head on his pillow. He was there for at least one more day. He closed his eyes and rested for the morning practice.

An hour and a half later, fully aware of his sore, aching muscles, Jamie entered the meeting room and slumped into his seat. Astonished, he surveyed the room, marveling at the number of guys who had been cut after the first day. Like death, they had been hustled out in early hours of the morning while everyone else was sleeping. Soon no one would mention them; it would be as though they had never been there.

Each day witnessed the same routine, practice in the

morning, meetings in the afternoon, practice in the evenings. Never before had Jamie experienced such grueling physical and mental pressure. After the second week, only one of his three roommates was still on the team. He was much older than Jamie and had been in several other professional camps. He had a wife and two children and, like Jamie, no college degree. He had decided that if he didn't make it this time he would have to find another way of taking care of his family.

It was five-thirty in the morning, the third week of camp, and Jamie was stretched on top of his bed, finding it difficult to sleep. To his dismay the phone rang.

"Hey man, it's for you," his roommate told him.

Nervously, Jamie took the phone.

"Hello," he spoke into the receiver, prepared to hear the worst.

"Jamie Ray, how you makin' out?" It was his mother.

He closed his eyes and sighed deeply.

"Awright, Mama," he answered. "Is anythang wrong?"

"Naw baby, everythang here's jus' fine," she answered. "I'm jus' callin' to tell you yo' picture was in the town paper."

"Yes ma'am."

"Everybody 'round here is so proud of you."

"Yes ma'am."

"You need anythang?"

"No ma'am. I'm jus' kinda tired. But I don't need nothin'."

"OK, baby, I'm gon' let you git yo' rest."

"Mama, tell everybody I said hi."

"OK. I will. And we'll be prayin' fo' you, hear."

"OK, Mama. Bye-bye."

By the fourth week, Jamie's last roommate and two others were cut, leaving him as the sole free agent in camp. He felt sorry for them, but now he felt that his chances of making the team were extremely good. He had performed well in the preseason game the previous week and he was having a good week of practice. Only two weeks stood between him and the final roster. He knew that they were going to keep five running backs. And there were only seven of them left in camp.

After practice, the day before the second preseason game, a reporter hustled after him as he made his way off the field.

"Griffin. May I have a word with you?" he asked.

"Yeah," he said.

"How does it feel to be the only free agent left in camp?"

"I came here to make this team," Jamie began. "The fact that I'm still here today don't mean that much to me. Ask me that question two weeks from now after the final cut."

"Can I quote you as sayin' you're sure you're gonna make this ball club?" the reporter asked, scribbling on a note pad.

"You can quote me as sayin' that I plan on bein' here two weeks from now," Jamie said confidently.

"How did you feel when you weren't taken in the main draft after such a distinguished career at ULNO?"

"I was disappointed. But I know that my knee scared a lot of people. I understand that this is a business. And I'm sho' my knee makes me a business risk."

"Had you not been injured, how high do you think you would have gone in the draft?"

"I don't know. But I tell you what. When they signed me with the rest of the free agents, they got a diamond fo' the price of costume jewelry and I don't thank it'll take 'em much longer to figure that out, if they haven't awready."

The next day during the morning practice, Jamie was hit squarely on the knee and had to be taken to the training room.

"You've slightly damaged the ligaments in that bad

knee again," the trainer told him. "You should stay off it for at least a week."

Jamie sat aimlessly fighting back tears.

"Say, could I make it with a good tape job if you'd shoot me up?" he said, looking for another alternative.

The trainer paused, took a deep breath, and sighed deeply.

"Yeah, I could do that. But I don't recommend it." He paused again. Then he ran his hands through his short reddish brown hair. "I suggest you have orthoscopic surgery. Your recoup time would be brief."

"How brief?" Jamie wanted to know.

"Oh, you could be back at full speed in a week."

Jamie sat in the training room staring blankly into space, pondering. Should he have the surgery? If he did, there was the real possibility that he would be released while recuperating. But if he went to practice limping badly or did more damage to the knee, they would surely release him.

He had the surgery, rehabilitated the knee, and made it back just in time to play in the final preseason game. After the game, he felt good about his performance. His knee was stiff but it didn't hamper his performance. By the following Tuesday, the team had to be down to the final roster.

Early Monday morning his optimism quickly faded. The phone rang, he answered, and the coach told him to meet him in his office with his playbook. Filled with sadness, he hung up the phone and sat staring out of the window. He knew that they were going to waive one more running back, but when he wasn't released after his injury he figured he had made it. Jamie packed his bags, took his playbook, and stepped onto the elevator. Plagued by a sense of dread, he stood combating numb, nauseating feelings. In a matter of minutes his whole life had been al-tered. What was he going to do now? For the first time in his adult life, he had no direction.

The bell sounded and the doors sprang open. Jamie stepped off the elevator, walked down the corridor, and stopped in front of the head coach's office.

He pause to collect himself, knocked, and then entered. Inside, the air was filled with an uncomfortable tenseness. He handed over his playbook and with eyes lowered, sat painfully listening.

"It was a tough decision," the coach explained. "But we had a choice between keeping a player with a bad knee or a healthy player. It was simply a business decision."

"I understand," Jamie replied.

"We shopped you around but we couldn't get any takers. Everybody's concerned about that knee."

He paused to take a phone call. Jamie saw him push the hold button.

"Well, Jamie, running backs go down every day," he said, extending his right hand. "The only advice I can give you is to keep working out and stay in shape. If somebody goes down, we'll give you a call."

"I appreciate that, Coach," Jamie said, fighting to maintain control of his voice. "I jus' wanna thank you and the Gators organization fo' givin' me a chance."

Dejected and disoriented, he walked out of the building and checked into a hotel across the street and called his agent. Jamie listened most intently as his agent explained the situation. He said that he would shop his name around the league and get back to him as soon as possible, but he shouldn't be too hopeful—hundreds of agents would be doing the same thing. In the meanwhile all he could do was wait. Jamie hung up the phone. He decided to keep a low profile and not talk to anyone until he knew something definite.

Early the next morning, Jamie hurried downstairs to the hotel lobby and purchased a newspaper. Returning quickly to his room, he opened the paper to the sports page. The headline jumped out at him—ULNO STANDOUT RELEASED BY GATORS. Before the day was over everyone would know what had happened. What would the folks back home think? Jamie forced himself to think more positively. If only another team would give him a chance, everything could still work out. For three days he sat in his room waiting. When no one called, he tried to come up with a plan. He sure couldn't go back to school, because he wasn't on scholarship anymore and he hadn't save enough money for tuition. But he couldn't get a decent job because he didn't have a college degree. As his ideas all fizzled away before him, Jamie faced the inevitable decision. He had to go home. He also had to tell Stacey.

The thought of facing Stacey, or even talking to her on the phone, depressed him even more than thoughts about his future. But he knew he had to call her before he left New Orleans. For a while, he sat at his desk with his face buried in his hands. Then slowly, he lifted the phone receiver. Again he hesitated. What was he going to say to her? By now she had heard what had happened. What was she thinking? What would she say? He dreaded the thought of hearing the concern and anxiousness in her voice. He'd keep the conversation as short as possible—just tell her he'd call back when he figured out what he was going to do.

Jamie dialed her number. The phone rang.

"Hello," Stacey answered in a clear voice.

"Hi, Stacey."

"Jamie, I've been worried about you," Stacey responded quickly. "Are you OK?"

"Yeah, I guess so."

"I've been trying to call you for three days. Where are you?"

"I'm still in New Orleans."

"Where in New Orleans?"

"In a hotel across from camp."

"I'll come over right now," she suggested eagerly.

"No, I jus' wanna be alone."

"Jamie, please don't shut me out like this," she pleaded. "I love you. Let me help you."

"There ain't nothin' you can do, Stacey."

"But I can be with you and we can talk things out. Things might seem bad now but we can work it out."

"There ain't nothin' to talk about or to work out. They released me and that's that. It's over, at least fo' the time bein'."

"Jamie, what happened? Everything seemed to be going fine."

"Stacey, I really don't wanna git into it right now."

"But maybe you would feel better if you talked about it."

"I don't thank so."

"It can't hurt to talk."

"Stacey, what you want me to say?" Jamie snapped. "Everythin' gon' be find and we'll live happily every after? Well, right now I don't feel like that. I feel like my whole world jus' fell apart and I don't know if I can put it back together. I feel like I lost everythang."

"But Jamie, that's just not true."

"Fo'git it," he muttered. "You don't understand."

"I understand that you have more going for yourself than football," she continued.

"Fo'git it!" he snapped.

For a moment neither one of them spoke.

"Don't be mad at me, Jamie."

"I ain't mad at you." The tone of her voice had calmed him a bit. "It's the situation I'm mad at."

"Baby, I know you're disappointed and things look bleak right now," she said. "But believe me, we can work it out. I'm going to law school and eventually you can go back to college and finish your degree. Then everything'll be fine. You'll see. It'll all work out for us."

"Stacey, I ain't nowhere close to gittin' no degree and you know it. And even if I was, I ain't got no money to go back to school with."

"I can talk to my father. He'll help you get a job in New Orleans. You could work for a year or two, then go back to school. You know how much he cares about you. Just let 'im help you. He'd do anything for you and I would too."

"Stacey, I can't go beggin' yo' daddy fo' no job," Jamie answered bitterly. "What kinda man do you thank I am?"

"But who's talking about begging anybody?" she asked, obviously offended.

"What else would you call it?"

"I'd call it utilizing your options," she said softly. "Or just letting the people who care about you help you."

For a moment, Jamie sat silently listening to the static in the phone line. Was it him that her father cared about or the idea that he was a star football player? Stacey was certain, but he wasn't. He stared deeply into the dimly lit room and tried to think of things working out the way Stacey described them. She loved him and for her love conquered all. But her proud, successful father would only see him as a failure, a man who couldn't give his daughter the life that she deserved. He couldn't see it any other way, Jamie concluded to himself. It was the truth.

"Stacey," he whispered. "Right now I thank the best thang fo' me to do is go'n back home. I'll call you when I've worked some thangs out fo' myself."

The idea was so unexpected to Stacey that it took her a minute to respond.

"Go home? For what? And for how long?" she asked, the hurt apparent in her tone.

"I don't know."

"But what about us?"

"I don't know."

"But what does that mean, you don't know? Don't you still love me? Don't you still want us to be together?"

"Stacey, maybe the best thang fo' us right now is to be apart. At least till I'm back on my feet, anyway."

"Jamie, you can't be serious?" she asked, her voice trembling.

"Baby, I mean it. The last three days have changed everythang."

"Let me come see you," she pleaded. "We can work it out."

"No, Stacey. My bus is leavin' in a couple of hours."

She began to whimper. Then, in a voice that was almost a whisper she cried, "Jamie, please don't do this to us. I love you so much. At least give us a chance. We could have a wonderful life together. Please don't throw everything away like this."

Jamie closed his eyes and tried to ignore the impact of her words, but he could feel himself weakening. Any minute she would talk him out of the decision that he knew was right. Softly, he spoke into the receiver. "I gotta go, Stacey. Take care of yo'self, OK."

"But when am I going to see you?"

"I don't know. I'll call you when I git to Pinesboro."

"But, Jamie . . ."

"Stacey, I gotta go. 'Bye."

No longer able to stand the pain in her voice, he gently set the receiver back on the hook. Lifting the hem of his shirt to his face, he wiped his misty eyes and stretched out on the bed. The frustration and anxiety of the past few days had depleted him. He felt tired. He closed his eyes and stared at the inside of his eyelids.

An hour later, Jamie sat on a bus headed for Pinesboro. Too anxious to sleep, he spent much of the trip counting mile markers and dreading the time that he would be forced to face everybody.

That night when the bus arrived, his mother and Uncle Rob were there waiting at the station. Still dejected, he stepped off the bus and stood face to face with his mother.

"Boy, what you got yo' head hangin' fo'?" his mother asked forcefully.

"Mama, I got cut. That ain't exactly nothin' to cheer 'bout."

"Did you do the best you could do?" she wanted to know.

Jamie thought about the question for a little while before answering.

"Yes ma'am, I did everything I could to make that team."

"Well, ain't no sense hangin' yo' head. It jus' wasn't fo' you. Gawd got somethin' else he 'tendin' on you doin'. You can be sho' of that."

"Mama, now I won't be able to do the thangs I wanted to do fo' you," Jamie moaned apologetically. "I wanted to buy you a new house and do a lot of thangs fo' you."

"Boy, I got everythang I need. I got my health and my strength and, most of all, I got you and Jesus. Honey, that's mo' than enough."

Jamie hugged his mother tightly. He was coming home under less than ideal circumstances, it was true. But at least his mother was making it easier for him to do. The rest of Pinesboro was less gentle in their approach. For the next few days, Jamie found himself bombarded with the same questions. Everyone he met asked relentlessly:

"What happened, man?" "How come you didn't make it?" "You gon' try it again?"

The first couple of days, he spent much of his time actually trying to explain what had happened. He gave long explanations about his knee problems and the difficulty of trying to make it at the professional level as a free agent. Despite his efforts to make them understand, he could see that most of Pinesboro thought he was just making excuses. Most seemed to believe and that the pure and simple truth was he just wasn't as good as he thought he was. After that realization, Jamie began to say what he knew they were thinking—he just got cut and that was all.

A few days after his return to Pinesboro, he decided to get back on a recovery program. He would get a temporary job, get his knee back in shape, go back to New Orleans, and try again. He wanted a job that he wouldn't be tied to and could quit whenever he was ready. After giving it some thought, he swallowed what was left of his pride and decided to do what the majority of black people from the parish did—field work.

On his first day of work, Booger gave Jamie a ride to Charles Smith's cotton field. He pulled to a stop and asked softly:

"J.R., want me to pick you up after work?"

"Naw, man," Jamie answered quickly. "I'll jus' catch the truck back."

"Man, I don't know why you wanna be slavin' out here in this hot sun when you could c'mon down to the mill."

"Mill seem too permanent. I'm jus' gon' do this fo' a little while. Then I'm outta here."

"Awright, man. Suit yo'self. I'll check you later!"

"Awright, Booger. Later."

Jamie tumbled out of the car and walked to the toolshed, where an older black man was filing the hoes. As he stood waiting, he noticed some of the others staring at him.

"Ain't that Henrietta's boy?" he heard a woman ask.

"Yeah, I heard he was back home."

"Wonder what he doing out here."

A familiar voice grabbed Jamie's attention.

"Hey college boy," Stanky teased. "You didn't have to go to college to git no job choppin' cotton."

They all laughed and Jamie joined them.

"Stanky, you better enjoy my company while you can," Jamie said loud enough for them all to hear. "I won't be out here long."

"Me neither," Stanky joked. "Soon as I finish workin' out the details on my big south Louisiana oil deal, I'm outta here."

Again, everyone laughed.

"Right," Jamie snapped sarcastically.

For the next year, Jamie worked on the plantation—driving tractors, hauling hay, and even hoeing and picking cotton. But he didn't give up the idea of returning to the Gators. Each day after work, he would get the weight room key from his high school coach and lift weights for an hour. Then he would go to the track and run.

One evening, after returning home from the gym, Jamie noticed a letter that his mother had left for him on his bed. It was from the front office of the New Orleans Gators. Frantically, he ripped open the envelope. He stood motionless as his eyes quickly scanned the page. Suddenly, a smile raced across his face and he began shouting at the top of his voice. The Gators were holding a mini camp in June to determine which free agents they were going to bring to the regular camp in July. And he had been invited to participate. Excited, he raced from the room.

"Mama!"

"What is it baby?"

"They invited me to mini camp."

His mother smiled warmly.

"That's good, honey. I'm sho' happy fo' you."

"I got another chance."

"Thangs usually work out fo' the best."

"Sometimes I guess they do."

"You gon' call Stacey? I'm sho' she'll be glad to hear it."

"No ma'am. Not yet. I'm gon' wait till after the mini camp. Then I'm gon' surprise her."

Rejuvenated by the news, Jamie intensified his workouts. With only three days before the reporting date, he stood at the bottom of the high school bleachers. He took a deep breath and lunged forward, racing up the steps toward the top. Halfway up his knee buckled, he stumbled, and then toppled forward.

For an hour he sat in the bleachers crying. He realized that his knee had been damaged to the point where he would never be able to play ball again. The dream was dead.

C H A P T E R 15

T H E alarm clock rang. Jamie rolled over in bed, reached to the night stand, and turned it off. It was five o'clock. Mr. Smith's field truck would roll through at exactly six. He had to be dressed and at the corner in an hour. For a few minutes, he sat on the side of the bed with his elbows resting firmly on his thighs and his face buried in the palms of his hands. He stood, stretched his arms above his head and yawned loudly. He was still drowsy—it had been a long, difficult week and he was exhausted. He glanced at the calendar hanging on a nail above his bed and mumbled softly to himself, "Thank God it's Friday."

He had been back in Pinesboro a little less than two years, but it had seemed much longer. In a lot of ways, he was now living the life that he had wanted so desperately to avoid. He was no longer a talented youth with a promising future but an adult, trapped in Pinesboro's poverty-stricken black world. It was each morning, when he went to work or when circumstances forced him to cope with all the anguish and hopeless uncertainty that filled each passing day, that he still longed for the opportunities that had eluded him.

Jamie walked across the floor, turned on the lights, and stepped into his pants. Then, moving quickly, he took his shirt and socks and hurried into the bathroom. He washed up, finished dressing, and sat down to a breakfast of cold cereal and toast. After he finished eating, he began his dreaded journey to the corner to catch the truck.

As he walked, his thoughts were consumed with the strange feeling that had plagued him all morning. He felt that his every move was being watched; not by a stranger, but by himself. Not by the Jamie Ray he was; but by the Jamie Ray that he knew he could have been. It was as if the person that he could have been was taunting him for what he had become. Earlier, he had ridiculed him when he stepped into his old, worn work clothes. He had laughed at him while he ate his cold cereal and toast. And now, he shook his head in pity as he watched him leave the house en route to Mr. Smith's cotton field.

Five minutes after he arrived at the corner, the truck came and the workers were transported to the field. For the next five hours, Jamie toiled alongside the other workers, as the hot July sun beat down on his back. At precisely twelve o'clock the workday ended. Friday was always a short day for Mr. Smith's field workers.

Exhausted and covered with dirt, Jamie positioned himself at the rear of the line. He glimpsed Sam Butler, Mr. Smith's foreman, sitting behind the pay table. In front of him was the old battered cash box. He watched Sam lift the lid. Then he saw his right hand dart inside and remove a handful of bills and lay them on the table. Immediately the workers began jostling and shoving in the pay line. Jamie stared. His somber, sullen mood quickly turned to anger. He felt ashamed. Were these disgraceful and indifferent beings his people? Suddenly he saw them as he thought white people saw them and he felt contempt. He needed desperately to believe that he was different. But with each passing day, that difference became more difficult for him to see.

Now his eyes were glued to Sam. Only two years in age separated them. They had never been friends in the truest sense of the word, but they had been teammates. Although Sam had never liked him in high school, he knew that he had secretly admired him. Now he felt uneasy standing in line waiting on him to count out his meager pay. He hated the satisfaction he saw in Sam's eyes each Friday when he approached the pay table. It was as though Sam was thinking, When you left here you thought you was so much. But now you done learned that you ain't nothing but a nigger.

"Settle down," Sam yelled, spitting out a long stream of brown tobacco juice. "There's enough to go 'round fo' everybody. Charles Smith always takes care of his niggers."

There it was, Jamie thought. He had said it. There was no distinction between any of them. They were all alike. They were all niggers. Jamie watched Sam take some bills from the stack, count a few out, and hand them to Mr. Bobby Sledge.

"Thank you, Mr. Butler suh," he heard elderly Mr. Sledge say.

"Now, Bobby, don't you spend all that money in one place," Sam smirked paternalistically.

One by one Jamie watched the men file by until it was his turn. Awkwardly, he moved forward, trying to avoid Sam's eyes. When he reached the table, Sam reared back in his chair, a wide smile etched across his face. Then he slowly counted out a sum and handed it to Jamie, blurting out, "Here you go, superstar. One hundred and thirty-five dollars. Keep up the good work."

Jamie felt the sting of Sam's taunting words. He wanted to snatch the money from his hands and throw it back in his face. But he knew he could never do that. Forcing a faint smile, he took the money and walked away. How had he fallen so far in such a short period of time?

Fighting against shame, he climbed aboard the transport truck with the others. As the truck lugged along the dusty road home, many of the men cheered and sang. Jamie sat quietly holding the wad of worn bills in his hand. His emotions were mixed—he felt anger toward the men riding in the truck; remorse for having to work for such exploitive wages; and a deep sense of depression because of the hopelessness of his present condition.

When he reached home, he went inside, undressed, and took a hot bath. Then, spurning his mother's pleas to sit down and eat dinner, he stretched out on the living room floor and stared up at the ceiling. Emotionally, he was exhausted. He had lost all sense of self. He wasn't a twenty-seven-dollars-a-day field hand. But who was he? He needed desperately to know.

He went into his bedroom. Then, lying flat on his stomach, he groped underneath the bed. Within seconds he pulled out an old dust-covered box. Rising slowly, he crossed to the chair, sat, and opened it. Inside were years of old pictures, newspaper clippings, and recruit letters.

Jamie sat methodically thumbing through his memorabilia. He removed one of the clippings and read the headline GRIFFIN SUFFERS SEASON-ENDING INJURY. He paused, frowning; he clasped the paper in his hands and stared. It all seemed so long ago. How different things might have been had that never happened. For a moment he pondered the thought. Then he resumed his search. A thin envelope lying in the bottom of the box caught his attention. It was from Dr. Bumguard. Jamie picked it up and removed a faded slip of paper from inside. He stared at the words summoning him to the professor's office. Dr. Bumguard had been so vehement with him that day; now he understood why he had pleaded with him to seek an education above all else.

Jamie set the letter aside. A snapshot of a smiling Stacey looking up at him. He took the picture from the box, held it about eye level, and sighed deeply. As his eyes probed the photograph, his mind drifted back to the happier times when the two of them were discovering each other. She had taught him so much about life, about love and about romance. She was everything that he had ever wanted in a woman. But the day that circumstance forced him to call her from his hotel room had ended it all. He still regretted letting her go, but what choice did he have? He had nothing to offer her. Gently, he rubbed the picture with the tip of his fingers. She's much better off without me, he thought.

He laid the picture aside and took a clipping from the box that had been folded over. Opening it slowly, he saw a large photo of himself in a New Orleans Gators uniform. Atop the picture read the headline: GATORS RELEASE FORMER ULNO STANDOUT. He sat looking at the words on the page as though he was seeing them for the first time. As his eyes moved over them, he felt the same pain that he had felt the day he was released. He had been so close. If only his knee had held up. Why was it always like this?

Despondently, Jamie put the clippings back in the box; he couldn't stand to read any more. He could feel the walls closing in on him; he needed to get outside. He pushed the box under the bed and hurried out of the house. As he walked, there was a space of time in which he neither saw nor heard anything. When he became aware of himself again, he was walking up the front steps of Papa's. Although it was still early, Papa's had already begun to fill. Jamie entered the juke joint and sat at the counter, waiting for Papa to come close enough to hear him.

"Papa, can I git a cold one?"

"Awright, baby boy. What you drankin'?"

"Beer."

"What kind?"

"I don't care, 'long as it's cold."

"Awright," Papa said moving away to get Jamie's drink.

Jamie sat looking around the room. Everything was in place. The jukebox in the corner was playing at full blast. Hangman was controlling the pool table. Stanky, Big Jack, Booger, and Pepper were playing dominoes. And a small group of guys were shooting craps in the corner.

Jamie took his drink and moved to an empty table in the back next to the window. At the table next to him, two field workers, Slop Jar and Full Bosom, were engaged in the type of heated conversation for which Papa's was famous.

Full Bosom, whose nickname was derived from his thick, muscular chest, had worked as a field hand most of his adult life. Slop Jar, a former janitor in the local hospital, turned to field work only after he had been laid off.

"See, Full Bosom, you jus' don't want nothin'," Jamie

heard Slop Jar say. "You don't want none of the finer thangs in life."

"Man don't need no mo' than he can eat," Full Bosom replied. "Long as he got three hots and a cot, he ought to be satisfied. Naw, I don't want no million dollars."

"What? That ain't enough fo' you?" Slop Jar asked sarcastically.

"Naw. That's too much," Full Bosom shot back.

"Why don't you tell the truth, Bosom?" Slop Jar asked, swinging around to face him. "See how you talkin' now. You'd talk a little different if you had a million dollars."

"What I'm gon' do with it?" Full Bosom asked. "A man can't live in but one house at a time. He can't drive but one car at a time. He can't wear but one suit of clothes at a time. And he can't take none of that with 'im when he die. So what I'm gon' kill myself tryin' to git all 'em thangs fo'? Besides, money ain't everythang. It's a heap of thangs lot mo' important than money. Personally, I don't need nothin' but a couch and TV."

"You talk like a fool or a man scared he gon' have to do a little work," Slop Jar replied.

"Ain't a little work I'm scared of," Full Bosom said. "I'll do a little work, but when you start talkin' 'bout hard work, I don't want no part of that. Nosuh. I jus' as soon go home than work myself to death fo' nothin'. Beside, I done worked hard long enough. Leave all that hard work fo' them young folks. Ole Bosom done made all the meat he gon' make. I'm workin' fo' a little gravy now." He paused and chuckled. "Naw, I ain't gon' try to break no speed record fo' nobody. When you gittin' paid by the day, you work by the day. Ain't no sense rippin' an' runnin'. You jus' need to git yo'self a gait you can hol'.'"

"That's what wrong with black folks," Slop Jar responded. "We always schemin' and dodgin' and tryin' to git over, instead of doin' what we s'pose to do."

"What you thank we s'pose to do?" Full Bosom asked. "Work ourselves half to death fo' the white man? Where that gon' git us? We do all the work. He git all the pay."

"Everybody always talkin' 'bout the white man," Slop Jar said angrily. "Let me tell you somethin' 'bout the white man. He awready got his. We tryin' to git ours. Now, when you tryin' to git what somebody else awready got, common sense tell you that you gotta work harder. I know you thank you hurtin' the white man by draggin' 'round on a job. But, the truth of the matter is, the only person you hurtin' is yo'self. You do yo' best, the best'll return. I don't care who you workin' fo' or under what conditions."

Full Bosom shook his head in disagreement.

"What's the purpose of doin' yo' best? Look to me like the harder the black man works, the less he got to show fo' it."

"There you go talkin' like a fool again," Slop Jar said, obviously frustrated.

"Nigguh, I ain't talkin' like no fool. If you jus' listen to what I'm sayin' you'll see that it makes a lot of sense," he said, scooting up closer to the table. His voice was getting louder and louder.

"If the black man work hard enough to make three dollars, the white man gon' take two of 'em. If the black man work hard enough to make five dollars, white man gon' take fo' of 'em. So no matter how hard he works, his condition don't git no better. Matter of fact it git worse."

"Hey wait a minute, Bosom," Slop Jar said, placing his hand on Full Bosom's shoulder. "Now you sho' nuff talkin' crazy. How you gon' sat there and tell me that a man's condition gon' git worse 'cause he works hard?"

"Easy," Full Bosom said, sighing deeply. "You see, if the black man follow yo' advice and go out and work harder, his hard work make mo' money fo' the white man. Meanwhile, he git the same money he always been gittin'. Since the white man got mo' money, prices on everythang go up. Food cost mo', gas cost mo', jus' livin' cost mo'. Now, the white man ain't hurt none. But the black man can't hardly make it, where he could befo' 'cause he makin' the same money he always been makin'."

"Seem to me like the solution is fo' the black man to stop dependin' on the white man's wages and start learnin' how to work fo' hisself. Then if he make three dollars, he can keep three dollars," Slop Jar said.

"White man ain't gon' stand fo' that," Full Bosom replied, with a grimace on his face.

"Full Bosom, I do believe white folks scare you half to death."

"Naw! They don't scare me. I jus' understand 'em. White folks own and operate this country. They livin' in the White House, makin' laws to protect white folks. And sho' as yo' mama's black, you can bet they done rigged it so they gon' always be on top."

"Let me explain somethin' to you, Slop Jar," Full Bosom said, in a serious tone. "The white man understand that fo' him to git rich, he need po' folks. He gotta have somebody that's so bad off, they'll work all day fo' next to nothin'. To make 'em do that, he gotta have some mo' folks worse off than the ones he workin' fo' nothin'. So when them that's workin' start complainin', he can tell 'em that them that's a little worse off will be happy to take they jobs. He know he gotta have slums and high unemployment 'mong po' folks fo' 'im to make money."

"Sounds like slavery to me," Slop Jar said.

"There you go!" Full Bosom said. "You keep on talkin' to ole Bosom, you gon' mess 'round and understand white folks."

"Sometimes I thank I'm the only man in the world that understand the white man," Bo Willie butted into the conversation.

ERNEST HILL

"What make you thank you're an authority on white folks?" Full Bosom shouted across Slop Jar.

"Experience," Bo Willie exclaimed. "You see, I done wined and dined with kings and queens. And I done slept in alleys and ate poke and beans. So I guess I done dealt with 'em all."

"You might of ate plenty poke and beans, but I know you ain't never seen no kings and queens," Full Bosom challenged. "Tell me where you seen a queen. You ain't been far enough 'round a tea cup to know if it got a handle on it, mo' less far enough outside the city limits to see a queen," Full Bosom said with a loud laugh.

"If I tell you a mosquito can pull a plow, don't ask how, jus' hook 'im up," Bo Willie shot back. "If I tell you it's so, it's so."

"Full Bosom, let the man talk," Slop Jar commanded.

Bo Willie paused to collect his thoughts.

"Preach the gospel or git out the pulpit," Full Bosom said impatiently. "You got somethin' to say, say it. Ain't no sense bitin' yo' tongue."

"Certain way you gotta act to git 'long with the white man," Bo Willie began. "You speak up too soon, you a hot-head. You hol' yo' peace too long, you a coward. Either way you lose."

"Man ain't never lost nothin' fo' standin' up," Full Bosom interrupted. "Some thangs in this world worth standin' up fo', no matter what the cost."

"Ain't nobody disagreein' with that," Bo Willie said. "But you gotta learn how to stand up. And learnin' how comes with understandin'."

"And I guess you understand."

"Yeah. I understand that we too concerned with tryin' to git white folks to like us. White man don't work like that. Ain't too many things he do like. But it's a heap of thangs he respect. The main one is money and power ain't

306

too far behind. He'll git rid of his own mama if it's a dollar in it. The love of money is what makes the white man different from all the other people in the world."

"Nigguh, what point you tryin' to make?" Full Bosom asked impatiently.

"We gotta quit worryin' 'bout gainin' the white man's affection and start concentratin' on makin' 'im respect us."

"Makin' 'im respect us!" Full Bosom laughed. "Bo Willie, you can lead a horse to water, but you can't make 'im drank."

"You hol' his head under long enough, he gon' drank or drown," Bo Willie countered. "And I'm willin' to bet cash money he'll drank."

They all laughed.

"Black folks got a serious problem," he continued. "White folks gittin' rich off our ignorance and we ain't gittin' nothin' in return."

"Bo Willie, that's what I been tryin' to tell Slop Jar," Full Bosom said. "Black man gotta take what he want, jus' like the white man did."

"You gon' end up in jail, you start takin' stuff from white folks," Slop Jar said defensively. "Jailhouse full of nigguhs crazy 'nough to try to take somethin' from the white man. Crime jus' don't pay," Slop Jar mumbled under his breath.

"You always hear folks talkin' 'bout crime don't pay. Well, that's the biggest lie ever been tol'," Bo Willie said, shaking his head from side to side. "It might not pay fo' black folks, but it pay 'bout ten dollars a hour fo' white folks."

"How you figured that?" Slop Jar asked.

"Well," Bo Willie began. "Black folks foolish enough to thank white folks is losin' sleep tryin' to figure out how to stop 'em from committin' them little ole petty crimes.

Truth of the matter is the white man don't wanna stop 'em. In fact, he happy to see 'em committin' 'em. Black man go to jail, them white folks make money. Police, lawyers, judges, all of 'em. Wasn't 'fo the black man, the jail house'd close down, then all of them white folks be outta business."

"Black folks you talkin' 'bout don't even count," said Slop Jar. "I ain't worried 'bout them. Folks that can do better need to do better. Thems the folks that gon' make a difference. If they quit schemin' and dodgin' and do what they s'posed to."

"Guess you talkin' 'bout folks like me?" Full Bosom asked.

"If the shoe fits, wear it," Slop Jar responded.

"Long as I'm black, I don't reckon I'll ever understand how folks can care mo' 'bout a soda water can, than a black man that done made a mistake or two in life," Bo Willie said. "I mean folk'll dig in the bottom of a ole nasty trash bin fo' a empty soda water can 'cause they see the value in it. But them same folks, black and white, wanna lock a black man up forever 'cause he made a mistake. Folks can't see the value in 'im. World gittin' to be a sad place when folks put mo' value in recyclin' a can than recyclin' a man."

"Bo Willie, some folks is jus' rotten to the bone and ain't worth worryin' about."

"Well, Slop Jar, I do worry 'bout 'em. See, I claim all my people 'cause I know it's so much good in the worst of us and so much bad in the best of us till it don't behoove none of us to talk 'bout the rest of us. When we start claimin' and lovin' one another again, we gon' find out that the white man ain't that big of a problem."

"You thank so, Bo Willie?"

"I know so and the white man do too. See, he countin' on us to stop carin' 'bout one another. He know a house divided gon' soon fall. Boy, you gotta git up real early when you foolin' 'round with white folks. You stay in the bed too long, the white man gon' have you thankin', talkin', and actin' the way he want you to."

Jamie lifted the can to his lips and tilted his head back. A loud sound came from deep within his throat each time he swallowed. Then slowly, he pushed away from the table and walked over to the bar and ordered another can of beer. Taking care not to stir the contents, he pulled the top back and drank again. As he sat savoring the taste, his mind began to drift. Papa's was just as noisy as when he first walked in, but now he heard nothing. Into his consciousness crept images of the young Jamie Ray Griffin— high school superstar who dreamed of one day rewriting NFL record books. The young Jamie Ray who had scorned education and everything else for the sake of what he thought would be his glorious destiny. Again he returned to the question that had been haunting him all day: how could his life have turned out this way?

His mind told him that he was responsible. But seeking solace, he shrank from this reality and sought someone else to blame. White folks had a hand in the way his life turned out. Yeah! They used him and when they got all they could out of him, they threw him out the same way they would throw out an old shoe. Next his mind told him that he had not applied himself in high school. But he also fought against that idea with every fiber of his body. The school had failed him; he had not failed the school. His thoughts shifted to the adults he had known while growing up. He thought about when he failed those two courses in high school and was supposed to be kicked off the football team, but Coach talked his teachers into giving him passing grades. He remembered how special he felt then. That was when he began to think that school wasn't important. As long as he was a star, everything would be OK. He just had to keep running touchdowns, keep scoring baskets, and keep winning races. White folks had encouraged him to fail by rewarding him for not trying. They didn't expect much from his mind, so he hadn't given much.

His thoughts quickly shifted to his mother. When he had brought home bad grades, she had always dismissed them by saying that book smarts just didn't run in the family. As he sat staring at the wall, he began to resent her too. He felt that she had let him down. She had allowed him to play into their hands. Why didn't she make him buckle down and do his work? Why didn't she encourage him, instead of giving him her permission to fail?

He began fumbling with the beer can sitting in front of him. As he sat thinking, he knew in his heart that his mother was not fully to blame. She had done all she knew how to do. But he had to blame someone. He couldn't convince himself that he was solely responsible. He had been so full of life and so full of dreams back then. All he had lacked was guidance, and there was no one there to give it to him.

For a moment that thought occupied the full force of his mind. He wondered if things would have been different if there had been a black coach or more black teachers at the white school he had attended. Maybe they would have made him work harder in the classroom. What if someone had leveled with him about the hardships of being a black kid in a white world? What would have happened had someone tried, during those critical years, to teach him that he didn't have to make a choice between academics and athletics? Why didn't someone tell him he could do both? Why didn't anyone tell him when he was at the age when he would listen—before folks started bragging on how good a ball player he was?

His thoughts shifted to the few black teachers who were working in the desegregated schools in town. He thought about how invisible they were. They could have pushed the black kids more. They could have been more involved with the parents. He couldn't understand why they sat back and watched kids like him fail.

Still protecting himself from his mind, his thoughts shifted to the local black church. Now he was beginning to get angry. Reverend McCall and his followers always talking about don't dream, don't want. Always encouraging black people to do nothing. They talk like it's a sin to work hard and to dream. Why did he teach us that we have to wait until the next world to be happy? White folks supposed to be Christians just like us, but they got everything right here in this world.

Jamie felt as though his mind was going a mile a minute. But maybe it wasn't too late, he heard himself say. Maybe he could get a job in New Orleans like Stacey had suggested. Maybe he could go back to school. It was like Dr. Bumguard had told him, if he applied the same drive to school that he had applied to football, he could succeed. Why hadn't he listened to them? Things might be so different now. As he sat at the counter thinking about his life, his pitfalls, and where he went wrong, he found himself getting more and more anxious. Not fully aware of what he was doing, he picked up a can of beer and drank from it. No sooner had he set the can back on the counter than Clyde Duncan grabbed him under the collar.

"Nigguh, you got paid today jus' like me. What you drankin' my beer fo'? You ain't no woman of mine and you ain't no friend of mine. Now, if you don't slap some money on that counter real fast, ole Clyde gon' do somethin' bad to you."

Jamie pushed Clyde's hand away from his collar.

"Man, it was a simple mistake. Ain't no sense in you actin' no fool over a can of beer."

Jamie stood, reached into his pocket, and pulled out a five-dollar bill. He crumpled it and forcefully threw it on the counter. It skidded across the counter and fell to the floor.

"Take that five dollars and go drank yo'self to death if you wanna. That's 'bout all you good fo' anyhow. That's what wrong with black folks, too many fools like you."

Clyde pushed the money away with his foot, took one step forward, pointed his finger in Jamie's face, and shouted: "Nigguh, who you callin' a fool and tryin' to talk down to? You ain't nobody. You jus' a regular ole field nigguh."

"Man, why don't you go somewhere and leave me alone," Jamie said, sitting down and gripping the corner of the counter with his hands.

Clyde was semidrunk. His eyes were glassy and he was beginning to lose his equilibrium. Slowly he lowered his hands to his side and looked directly at Jamie.

"Use to read 'bout you in the paper," he began, his speech slurred and the pitch of his voice slightly higher than normal. "Folks 'round here was talkin' 'bout you gon' be a star. You a star awright, out there pickin' mo' cotton than anybody in north Louisiana."

Everybody in the juke joint laughed. Jamie turned his head and slowly surveyed the room. Almost everyone had stopped what they were doing and had focused their attention on him and Clyde. He felt that Clyde had put into words what most of them were thinking. He felt compelled to say something to defend himself. But at the same time, he wanted to avoid a bad situation. Jamie slowly took his can of beer from the counter, drank it, and gently set it back in place. Then speaking without looking directly at Clyde, he said, "You ain't even worth it." He stood and started walking toward the door.

Clyde started to follow him, but his intoxicated state prevented him. He placed his right hand on the counter and used it as a guide rail. Then speaking to Jamie's back he yelled, "You uppity bastard. Sometimes I feel like brangin' you down a peg or two."

"Take it easy, Clyde," Papa ordered from behind the counter. "He done paid you fo' yo' drank, so jus' leave 'im alone."

"Don't tell 'im nothin', Papa," Jamie said, turning around to face Clyde. "What you call me that name fo'?"

"'Cause that's what you is, college boy. A uppity bastard."

Jamie didn't respond to Clyde. He just stood there staring into his cold, drunken eyes. He felt a strong desire to do something to him, but exactly what he didn't know. He had an almost uncontrollable urge to lash out at something or somebody. Deep in the pit of his stomach he felt that doing something to Clyde would release all of his anxiety. Nobody would be able to blame him. Clyde had asked for it.

"Jus' go'n 'bout yo' business," Papa advised Jamie. "Don't pay 'im no mind. He half drunk."

"Ain't nobody drunk," Clyde yelled, looking like he would collapse any second.

The tense muscles in Jamie's neck relaxed. His face softened and the corners of his mouth turned up. Suddenly he began laughing—softly at first, then almost uncontrollably.

"Nigguh, what's so funny?" Clyde asked.

"You," Jamie responded.

A puzzled look spread across Clyde's face. Jamie, doubled over with laughter, staggered over to one of the tables and sat down.

"I was jus' thankin' 'bout yo' mama, Clyde. She musta been a desperate woman to lay down with the kinda low-life it took to produce a ignorant fool like you."

The room erupted in laughter. Clyde stood upright as though he had been pierced with a dagger. His face was marred with anger and his chest rose and fell rapidly.

"Ain't nobody never talked to me like that and live to tell it," Clyde shouted. "Take it back! Take it back!"

The louder he screamed, the louder everyone laughed.

"So help me Gawd, I'll kill you if you don't take it back," he yelled, clumsily fumbling with his back pocket. Before anyone knew what happened, Clyde pulled a gun and aimed it at Jamie.

Jamie leaped from his seat. As he stood staring into Clyde's eyes, silence fell over the room.

"Put that thang up befo' somebody git hurt," Papa commanded from behind the counter.

"I don't hear you laughin' now," Clyde said, the gun shaking in his unsteady hand. "You git down on yo' knees and take back what you said."

Jamie looked around the room. His eyes met Booger's. Booger nodded as if telling him to do as Clyde instructed. Everyone else sat still, staring at the gun Clyde held in his hand.

"Nigguh, ain't nobody playin' with you," Clyde yelled, pulling the cock back with his thumb.

Jamie stood smiling and refusing to bow to Clyde. He didn't move a muscle. It was as if he was daring Clyde to carry out his threat.

Suddenly, Clyde fired twice in Jamie's direction and staggered from the café as Jamie fell to the floor clutching his stomach. Booger hurried to his aid and ripped his shirt open, exposing the wound. Jamie could feel the warm blood running down both sides of his stomach.

"Call an ambulance! Call an ambulance!"

Booger lifted Jamie's head and placed it in his lap. Jamie was very still and quiet, but he was conscious. He didn't seem to be suffering much. The alcohol he had consumed that evening had numbed him. He couldn't feel anything. Booger began to gently rock him back and forth. With tears streaming down his face, he began to talk to him.

"Hol' on, man. Help is comin'. You gon' be awright. You the best friend a nigguh ever had. You gon' be awright. You got too much to live fo'. Too much to do yet. You a fighter. Been a fighter all yo' life. You jus' twenty-five years old. Still a baby. You gon' be awright. Do you hear me? You still got them dreams to catch up with."

Jamie lay there with his eyes closed. He was breathing easily. He felt numb and better than he had felt in a long time. All of the previous thoughts about his past life were far from him now. He felt at peace.

He could hear Booger talking to him, but the words were bouncing off his head. There was nothing in them to which he could cling. He wondered why Booger was telling him to fight something both of them knew he couldn't beat. Why was he encouraging him to open his eyes and look at dreams he could no longer see?

A cold chill passed through his entire body. He began to tremble. Booger removed his shirt and spread it over Jamie. Booger nuzzled him up against his chest and squeezed him tightly. It was as if he thought he could keep death from taking Jamie's soul from his body. Jamie began to think about death. How wonderful it was going to be not to have to worry about things anymore. He was tired. He longed for the peace and tranquility that he had always heard came with death.

Booger was still pleading with him to hold on to life. Jamie wanted to tell him to shut up. He wanted to tell him that when it really mattered, no one had ever encouraged him. No one had ever given him hope. No one had been there.

A single teardrop formed in the corner of Jamie's closed right eye and hung from his eyelash. His body had become very still, but his mind was extremely active.

Booger continued to beg him, but to Jamie the words meant nothing. He began to think about his short life—about all of the people who told him to be realistic about life and what it had to offer him; about all of the people who had told him he wanted too much; that he had to learn how to stay in his place and not be so uppity.

Slowly his body began to relax. He felt Booger's hand behind his neck steadying his head. He did not move. His body had gone almost completely limp. A sense of freedom overcame him.

"Don't quit, Jamie! Don't you give up!" Booger yelled desperately. "Help'll be here any minute. Only weak people give up."

Jamie smiled as he pictured himself lying in the dingy little juke joint, the angel of death hovering overhead and his best friend begging him to fight to hold on to a life that he despised. He could hear Booger clearly. His voice seemed to be amplified a thousand times. As the words "Everythang gon' be fine" rolled off Booger's tongue, Jamie opened his eyes, looked up at Booger, and with his last breath said, "NIGGUH, PLEASE."